M000196733

PORTAL SLAYER

PATH OF DECEIT

S.L. DOOLEY

This is a work of fiction. Names, characters, places, and incidents are products of the author's imagination or are used fictitiously and are not to be construed as real. Any resemblance to actual events, locales, organizations, or persons, living or dead, is entirely coincidental.

Cover design by Rob Williams, I Love My Cover

Map artwork by Matthew Robinson

Hardback ISBN: 978-1-956418-00-2

Paperback ISBN: 978-1-956418-01-9

Dedicated to
The Dooley Huddle
My safe place

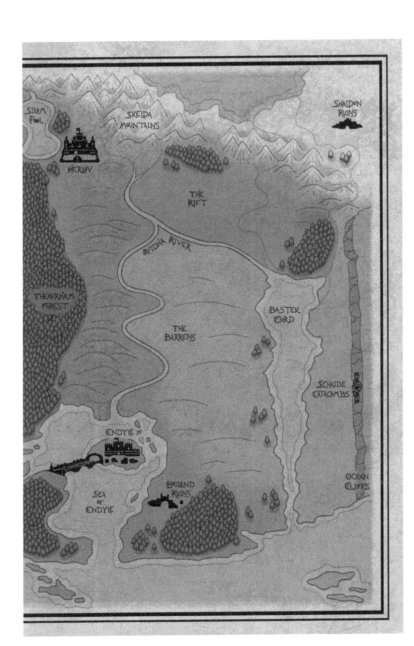

PROLOGUE

Everything we call real is made of things that cannot be regarded as real. -Neils Bohr

For we are not fighting against flesh-and-blood enemies, but against evil rulers and authorities of the unseen world, against mighty powers in this dark world, and against evil spirits in the heavenly places. -The Apostle Paul to the Ephesians

An explosion broke a large stone loose just outside Durnoth's Castle's great hall. It crashed to the ground in a plume of dust.

They are close.

Kade waited for the tremor to pass before pulling the hood of his cloak over his head and, dodging the stone, continued down a wide passageway. His resolve to defeat their enemy could not overtake his long understanding: The reign of all six temporal kingdoms would end with the siege of Durnoth. But hope kindled with the prophecy . . .

He came to what was once the gilded banquet hall, splintered tables and chairs scattered among the rubble. Lanterns hanging around the room cast frantic flickers of light. A long, fractured mirror still clung to the closest wall. It reflected Kade's golden light radiating from his face sending a whorl of prismatic light across the high walls. Kade caught a glimpse of the white dust coating his black hair and beard, creating the illusion of great age. Though, as a guardian, he did not grow old, it felt as though age had finally found him.

He reached the top of the stairwell leading to the Main Guard and out onto the lawn. Distant shouts came from outside the castle walls. The enemy had yet to enter the stronghold, but that would soon change and he would fight side-by-side with the brave soldiers of Durnoth.

"Kade!" A woman's desperate scream came from the far side of the hall. Kade stopped and spun around and strode to a woman cowering just inside the arched doorway of the robing room, her likely hiding place. Wisps of black hair, spilling from a matted bun, were tangled in a glittering comb. Her sheer blue stola was torn and stained. Kade glanced at the small girl clinging to the woman's skirt.

Nahor.

The mother scooped her up and placed her on her hip and wrapped her other arm around the thin shoulders of a young boy, ushering him from the shadows.

Moses.

Kade spared a quick glance at the stairs. He could hear nothing of the guards. They had either abandoned their post or were dead. He turned back and searched her frantic blue eyes.

"Durnoth is lost," she whispered. Nahor's dirty fingers gripped her shoulder as she watched Kade with wide, brown eyes. Her lip quivered, but she did not cry. Kade looked down at Moses. His jaw was set in a show of bravery, but fear shined in his pale, blue eyes. At seven he had seen more death than most seasoned soldiers.

"What of Moses' mother and father?" Kade asked the mother as he met the boy's measured stare. She shook her head almost imperceptibly.

The mother took a step closer to Kade. "This was Nahor's last refuge when Shaldon was destroyed."

Kade nodded but duty tugged at him from the stairwell. For over two hundred years he had faithfully defended every temporal city established in the Periferie. In less than two years he had failed all but one.

Shouts and screams echoed through a narrow window followed by the frantic clop of horses as soldiers raced across stone street. A thunderous blow shook the castle, sending small rocks and grit from the ceiling and walls and filling the room with dust. Kade clenched his jaw. He could answer his calling by fighting for Durnoth and fail. Or he could fulfill his oath by rescuing these children only to lose them.

The woman reached out and gripped Kade's arm. "Take the children to the prescail," she begged. "The portal will send them to safety in Earth Apparent." She shot a look to the window. Swords clashed and the roar of the enemy swelled, drawing closer.

Was Cosyn among them?

The sudden thought brought a wave of a bitter anger. A wrath, born of faltering hope and absolute betrayal. Kade grit his teeth and forced Cosyn from his mind. He could do nothing for his brother.

Kade covered her hand with his. "What of your son?" She dropped her gaze and pulled her hand away, tears filling her eyes.

"You are our guardian." Her voice was surprisingly steady. "Should the children not have the chance to make a way in Earth Apparent?"

Guardian. Yes. But the children's chances in Earth would be uncertain at best. It was too late for the mother. Her body would never adjust. But the children . . .

Kade swept his cloak to one side and knelt in front of Moses. He pushed the boy's dark hair out of his face. "Will you be brave, Moses?" Moses nodded silently.

Kade straightened and stroked Nahor's soft cheek. "Be strong, little one. You will be the mother of the descendants of the Periferie." Nahor gazed at Kade solemnly.

The mother set Nahor down and thrust both of the children's hands out to him. "Kade, please."

"Come." Kade took their delicate hands, but addressed the fearful woman. "May the valor of Arkonai be with you."

She did not respond. Her eyes darted from him to the window where another shout carried from directly below. He released the children's hands and cradled the woman's face in his palms. Heat entered his chest and passed through his arms into his hands. The effect was instant. Her shoulders relaxed and she smiled thinly.

"Yes, for the valor of Arkonai," she whispered.

Kade planted a kiss on her forehead and took hold of the children's hands. He rushed around her into the robing room. At the back wall he pushed aside a torn tapestry on which an embroidered white horse trotted between folds, exposing a wooden door, ajar on its iron hinges. Kade steered the children into a dark narrow tunnel. The door creaked shut behind them and the noise of battle was abruptly silenced. Their soft footfalls and swishing cloaks whispered down the hall to another set of stairs. He gripped their hands to keep them from stumbling as they circled down, down in the darkness.

The prophets had warned the temporals of the encroaching evil. The leaders of the temporal kingdoms, made complacent by centuries of peace and provision, humored the prophets, building thick walls and training able soldiers. But the walls were hollow. As were their intentions. The soldiers, arrogant and apathetic, mirrored the motivations of the leaders. Even Kade had believed the inhabitants of the six cities to be prepared, girded. Cosyn, the enemy of creation and Arkonai himself, destroyed them all. Moses and Nahor would be the temporal remnant, driven from Alnok.

Kade slowed then stopped at the base of the stairs and stood before a door he could not see but felt. He pushed it open and a golden brilliance pierced his eyes. Kade squinted against the light and coaxed the children into an empty circular room. The walls were a smooth stone, like crystal, while the floor shone like pearl. A glowing arched ceiling, the source of the light, soared above them. At the center of the room, the air swayed with a mild distortion. Kade's skin prickled and his inner ear hummed in rhythm with the undulating air. The children gazed around the room, oblivious to the portal in front of them. Very good, Kade thought. Without the sensitivity to the gateways these two might have a chance in Earth Apparent. He knelt and ushered them around to face him.

"Moses and Nahor, I cannot follow. You must find your way. When you cross over, there will be no return."

"Kade, where are we going? Who will be with us?" Moses trembled, letting some of his bravado slip. Kade laid a hand on each of their heads.

"The valor of Arkonai will be with you and will guide you." Kade spoke rhythmically, chanting. "Be strong. Be courageous. Wisdom and success will be yours." Kade closed his eyes and continued his prayer at a whisper. A warmth filled his chest and ran down his arms to his palms. Golden light radiated from his face and hands. He remained kneeling in front of them, his voice echoing and reverberating against the walls in a deep soulful song.

When the blessing was complete Kade opened his eyes and smiled softly. The children seemed to relax, and each offered a small smile in return. Kade took a hand from each child and kissed their palms.

"Moses, take this," Kade said as he reached into his robes and retrieved a flat, circular, copper amulet. It gleamed in the light as

Moses took it in both hands. He brought it close to his face and traced the three concentric circles carved into the surface. At the center, a tree with willowy branches shimmered as if made of precious jewels.

"The Durinial will direct your steps," Kade said, pointing to the amulet. "You will feel its promptings and you must pay close attention to its guidance. It is for you, your children and your children's children. Keep it safe, Moses." Kade straightened and gently turned them to the center of the room and coaxed them forward. Neither child looked back. They took two steps forward and disappeared.

CHAPTER ONE

Raelyn perched on the bus-stop bench and tugged the leg of her jeans over her ankle monitor. She leaned forward, peering around the elderly woman sitting next to her. Bryant Avenue, its busy Friday traffic and crowded sidewalk, faded to the background. A cold breeze stole the warm Texas sunshine from Raelyn's face. She squeezed her eyes shut then opened them wide, trying to make sense of what she was seeing.

A pack of wild dogs? Downtown?

Half a dozen of them, gray and semi-starved, hunched in a tight circle, teeth bared. Not dogs exactly. More like, hyenas, or . . .

Chupacabra.

A panicked giggle escaped her lips. She broke into a cough when the woman next to her gave her a sidelong glance. Raelyn held her breath as two construction workers in yellow vests passed by the pack. But the men didn't react, and the dogs didn't attack. A group of chattering girls strolled by, oblivious to the threat just a few feet from them. Raelyn stood and took a breath, ready to shout a warning. But at that moment a droning engine announced the bus's approach and the waiting passengers gathered on the curb, blocking her view. Brakes squealed as the bus belched bitter, black smoke and pulled to a stop. Raelyn hoisted her backpack onto one shoulder, trying to keep the dogs in view. She offered her elbow to the elderly woman.

"Thank you, dear." The woman grasped Raelyn's arm to heft herself up, giving Raelyn a pat before she tottered off.

Raelyn caught another glimpse of the dogs. No one reacted. No one else saw them. Everyone would think she was crazy. She shook her head and pulled her phone from her back pocket as she boarded the bus. She was hit by the smell of strong coffee and dirty socks particularly pungent in the August heat. She showed the driver the bar code on her phone.

He glanced at it with a short nod, not making eye contact. "Hey, Raelyn."

"Hi, Paul." Raelyn gave a quick smile, but he wasn't looking anyway. The bus lurched as she tucked her phone away and found an empty seat next to a tall, skinny man in an ill-fitted ivory suit.

She grasped the upper handhold and looked over the man through the smudged window as they drove away. A gangly boy with a skateboard slung over his shoulder slouched where the dogs had been. They passed a brick building and her reflection came into view. Raelyn flinched, ran a hand over her long, tangled hair, and pulled at her rumpled T-shirt, fresh from the pile on her apartment floor. She sure looked crazy.

She slumped into the seat, eased out of her backpack, and rested it on her knees. Someone would have reacted if they'd seen the dogs. What would her therapist say to dog illusions? *An overactive imagination.* Her mind interpreting what was probably scattered trash bags, creating a weird metaphor for the anger and frustration she held about her life. There, already in the analytical mindset for her class in contemporary British Lit.

Raelyn closed her eyes as the bus swung onto Boston Avenue and she let the familiar stops and acceleration lull her until she knew her stop was close. The coffee-and-sock smell was tolerable. Even the inconvenience. But the daily reminder of why she couldn't drive, that was the slow wear on her already tired mind.

This could all be over on Wednesday.

Out of instinct, she opened one eye. Several backpack-toting students had got to their feet, most holding paper coffee cups. Raelyn squeezed into line and shuffled forward as the bus jerked to a stop. Her cell phone buzzed in her back pocket. She dug it out and looked at the screen as she tramped down the steps. Peter.

"Hey, big brother." She tried for her brightest voice.

"Rae." Peter's slow way of saying her name was like a warm blanket on a cold night.

"What's up?"

"Raelyn," Peter sighed, "you know what's up."

"I know, I know." Her shoulders sagged as she dodged the other students and switched the phone to her other ear. "Look, I just took an extra shift at the coffee shop and I'm grading essays for Professor Bartlett this weekend. It's been a busy week . . ." All true. All excuses.

"Dad asked if you were coming."

Raelyn's breath caught and she slowed to a stop. Not a word from her father in nearly a year. Wait. He wanted to know if she would be at his birthday party? "Are you sure, Peter?" She blinked back biting tears.

"Yeah. It's about time, don't you think?"

Someone bumped into Raelyn's shoulder, prompting her to resume walking. She touched the raised scar running temple to jawline before raking her fingers through her hair. "Maybe. I don't know Peter, what if —"

"He says something rude? Ignores you? Changes his mind — " Peter broke into a cough.

"Yeah, all of the above." Raelyn stopped outside Blackston Hall. "You okay?"

Peter cleared his throat, but the wheezing rattle remained. "Yeah. Don't worry. I'll be there and I won't leave your side. Sunday, ten o'clock."

"Right." Raelyn blew out a long breath. "Okay, I'll be there."

"Thanks, Rae. He might not act like it, but he does miss you."

A multitude of angry responses backed up against her gritted teeth.

You don't consistently ignore someone you miss.

You don't leave bitter accusations hanging for a year.

"Yeah, okay, sure. See you Sunday," Raelyn grumbled and punched the screen with her thumb. Peter, ever the peacemaker.

Three hours later Raelyn climbed back onto the hot but mostly empty bus. She glanced at the unfamiliar driver as he scanned her phone. A few rows back she dropped her backpack, heavy with books and frantically scribbled papers from the English comp students, into a seat and slumped next to it. She usually enjoyed it when the professor let her teach a class or two, but today all she could do was watch the clock. She glanced at her phone. One missed call. Her probation officer, Patricia, no-nonsense but not unkind, had already called this month. With Raelyn's final hearing next week, hopefully the call didn't portend complications. Raelyn took a deep breath and let it out slowly, trying to force the knot forming in her stomach to unwind. Every month for a year she'd had the same bubbles of dread rising in her gut, like thick stew on a low heat. Raelyn sat up straighter. This would be different. The final page in this nightmare chapter of her life could be over on Wednesday. She had obeyed every instruction and her attorney was optimistic.

She leaned forward and pressed her palms into her eyes. She had to get through Sunday's party first. She didn't know which made her more nervous. If it weren't for Peter . . .

The bus let her off at her stop and she navigated the block's irregular sidewalk, where massive trees had shoved their roots beneath the concrete. In no rush to get to her apartment, she inhaled the smell of sycamore and warm soil. The scent of childhood bike rides and hide-and-seek. But there was no comfort in that nameless memory. Just an empty wistfulness and a hollow longing for something she had lost. Maybe something she never really had.

Early evening brought muggy shadows as Raelyn opened the apartment's outer door. She had just enough time to call Patricia and have a quick shower before the AA meeting. She could start grading papers tomorrow after work —

Raelyn stopped on the threshold. Movement, a few paces down the sidewalk. One of the dogs from the bus stop. She held her breath, her heart thumping.

Go Raelyn. Get inside.

But she froze, staring at the dog until it sunk back into the shadows, becoming nothing more than the neighboring apartment's trashcan. She hurried through the doorway as a sharp chill ran down her back.

Once inside her studio apartment, she cracked a window, releasing some of the pent-up heat. She left the lights off, allowing the late sunlight to linger across the walls and illuminate the room. Catching glimpses of shadows or movement wasn't a new occurrence. Not for Peter either. They used to tease each other about it. But never had she seen something so clearly. And twice in one day. She pulled up Patricia's phone number and crooked the phone between her shoulder and ear as she paced.

"Raelyn."

Raelyn let out a breath she didn't realize she was holding. Patricia didn't sound upset. "Hey there! Everything okay? I'm all ready for the hearing." An upbeat attitude might head off bad news.

"Everything's good. Just thought I'd check in before the weekend. Tell you I'm rooting for you."

A surge of gratitude filled Raelyn's heart. "Thanks. I'm ready to get it all over with."

"I bet." It was a simple statement, but it contained deep compassion. "I'm sending up a prayer for Wednesday," Patricia continued.

"Appreciate that. Really. You'll be there?"

"I have my report ready. Yeah, I'll be there."

Raelyn smiled as she disconnected the call. It really would be over soon. She showered and, wrapped in a towel, made a PB&J, swigging the last of the milk from the container.

With wet hair braided and a clean pink blouse replacing her dirty T-shirt, Raelyn returned to the sidewalk. The sun had given up the day but the meeting was within walking distance. No reason to bother with the bus. Actually, there were plenty of reasons, a whole pack of them. Raelyn locked the door behind her. It would be dumb to give in to baseless fear. But a block from her apartment, she wished she had. The sickly street lamps gave off anemic halos and Raelyn rushed between each one as gusts of warm wind caused the leaves above her to whisper. Every shadow seemed to have fangs. A dog barked from behind a chain-link fence and Raelyn nearly fell when she jumped away. She grumbled a few choice names for the dog and picked up her pace.

Ten minutes later, her blouse sticking to her sweaty back, she ducked through the doorway of what used to be a donut shop. Humming fluorescent lights illuminated three rows of white folding chairs facing a center aisle. Two dozen men and women mingled in groups of three and four, sipping coffee and chatting in quiet, reverent murmurs.

"Howdy Raelyn!" Bonnie waved Raelyn over to a chair next to her. "You doin' alright?" Bonnie, who was around the age Raelyn's mom would have been, frowned and looked Raelyn up and down. Unlike Raelyn's mom Bonnie had lived a hard life which showed in her heavily lined face, bloodshot eyes and thinning hair. A sweet woman, just rough around the edges.

"Sure. Yeah." Raelyn sat down and wiped her forehead with the back of her hand. "Just warm."

"No kiddin' sweetheart. Hotter'n a toad's fart." Bonnie cackled. Raelyn forced a smile and tugged at her jeans.

The meeting went as expected: quick, impersonal, predictable. Required.

Bonnie gave Raelyn a ride home in her "vintage" Ford F-150, for which Raelyn was grateful, even if it did smell of greasy fried chicken and stale cigarettes.

"You getcha some rest!" Bonnie called and Raelyn gave her a wave as she hurried into her apartment.

It was time to be done with this day of canine illusions and difficult conversations. Raelyn changed into shorts and a T-shirt. She plugged in her ankle monitor, sprawled out on her futon under a droning fan, and passed out.

Morning came too soon. Late for work, Raelyn dressed, yanked her hair into a ponytail, and grabbed her apron on the way out the door. A knot in her stomach twisted as the Saturday regulars rushed the day away. Sweeping the floor, she watched the last customer walk out into the dusky heat with their iced mocha. Sunday was sprinting straight for her.

Just call Peter. Tell him a shift came up at work. They need me on campus. I broke my leg.

But each time she pulled up his contact, she hesitated. She had promised.

Raelyn returned to her apartment and pulled the English papers from her backpack. She settled on the futon, shifting so her ankle would reach the charger, and propped her bare feet on the coffee table. After an hour of staring at the first page, red pen poised as she read the same paragraph over and over she tossed the pile onto the table.

On Sunday she could Uber over, pop in, eat some birthday cake, and duck out whenever she was ready. Peter hadn't said who else would be at the party, but what did it matter? No one had spoken to her since the accident. *Why should they?*

Raelyn pushed the papers off the TV remote. There had to be some mindless movie to distract her. The station was set to the local news.

" . . . wonder what role the DOD will play in the dimensional research?" Standing in front of a glass building, a pretty red-headed reporter held out a microphone to a nervous-looking man in a short-sleeved button-up and a plaid tie.

"I, uh, the government has some oversight, but ultimately we are a privately-run research company."

"Can you speak to the recent leak of, what some are calling, a major breakthrough in multi-dimensional science?"

He blinked and shifted on his feet. "I —" He coughed. "No comment."

Poor guy. He looked like he would rather be in front of a firing squad. Raelyn curled her legs under her and flipped to the next channel, halfway through *Star Trek Into Darkness*.

Good enough.

A few minutes in she tucked her pillow beneath her head. She closed her eyes and saw Peter, smiling at her in that gentle way of his. Then her dad, the last time she had seen him, at the funeral, eyes red, shouting something she couldn't make out. Raelyn drifted off to sleep and dreamed of wild dogs prowling the sidewalk outside her apartment.

CHAPTER TWO

Raelyn jerked her head off the pillow and groped for her phone, blinking her eyes open. She swiped the black screen. Nothing.

"Crap!" She yanked the cord from her ankle monitor and stumbled to her feet, squinting at the microwave clock: 09:15. "Crap!"

She plugged in her phone and rushed to the bathroom. As she brushed her teeth, she surveyed her closet, where a few T-shirts accompanied several empty wire hangers. Pushing them aside she found the only suitable blouse: simple, blue, clean.

Within fifteen minutes she was dressed, wiggling her feet into her shoes as she powered up her phone.

Five missed calls. Two texts. All from her father. A wave of nausea washed over Raelyn as she sank into the kitchen chair and pulled up the first text.

6:07 a.m. - Peter taken to ER.

Bile hit the back of Raelyn's throat. Her hands trembled as she went to the next text.

8:02 a.m. - Waiting on Dr.

Peter's cough, the wheezing. She had known something was wrong. It could be anything, something minor that a dose of fluids and antibiotics would cure. Or a car wreck, head injury . . .

Raelyn requested an Uber, yanked the phone charger from the outlet, and started for the door. Cursing, she dashed back for the ankle monitor's charger and shoved both chargers into her purse. As she stepped outside on rubber legs she tried to take a deep breath of thick, humid air, but her lungs wouldn't fill.

The driver pulled up in a blue SUV and she climbed into the back seat.

"St. James Memorial?" he asked and glanced back, his gaze dropping to her leg and the bulging monitor on her ankle. Raelyn nodded, not bothering to adjust her jeans.

The ride took no longer than twenty minutes. She whispered "thank you," her throat too dry to allow anything more.

The glass doors whooshed open and she stepped into a hushed waiting room. Too quiet to be a place for emergencies. She gripped her phone as she scanned the area for her father's tall form, broad shoulders, dark hair. Raelyn spotted him, his back to her, but only because she recognized the striped golf shirt, which hung loose from his thin shoulders. His hair was longer, peppered with gray. She cleared her throat and forced her legs to carry her closer until she was right behind him. He was talking to a short, round woman in blue scrubs and a white lab coat. She peered around her father and raised her eyebrows.

Raelyn's face flushed. "Um . . . I . . . I'm —"

Her father turned halfway and looked down. She pulled at her jeans and brushed a hand through her hair, pressing it over her scar.

Her father turned back to the doctor. "This is Peter's sister."

"Ah, Miss Witt?" The doctor offered her hand. "I'm Dr. Holland." Raelyn eased around her dad and shook Dr. Holland's hand.

Dr. Holland tucked her hands into the pockets of her lab coat. "As I was telling your father Peter's O2 levels are dangerously low. He's dehydrated. The fever is under control and we've started antibiotics while we wait for radiology so we can take a look at his lungs." She sighed. "But right now I would say pneumonia."

"So, it can be treated," Raelyn's father said.

Dr. Holland nodded. "But the infection is advanced. There's the chance of any number of complications. I'll know more when we get his blood work back."

"Can we see him?" Raelyn asked.

"He's unconscious," her dad said, still looking at the doctor.

Dr. Holland gave her a compassionate smile. "Until we have more answers I'll ask that you just hang tight. I, or someone on my team, will keep you updated. In the meantime, there's coffee"—she pointed to a countertop with a large dispenser—"and the cafeteria is down that hall."

Raelyn glanced where Dr. Holland gestured. A teenager scanned his phone near the hall next to a huddled family who may have been waiting for news. A man, maybe a little older than her father, leaned against a wall nearby and held her in a steady gaze. Jet black hair fell to his shoulders and framed brilliant blue eyes. He wore a long, tailored, indigo coat. *In August?* She met his stare for a moment before turning back to the doctor.

"You can trust he's getting the best care." Dr. Holland finished with a short nod then left, swiping a key card next to a set of double doors.

Raelyn's father finally looked down at her. His cheeks were hollow and his eyes sunken. Raelyn opened her mouth, her mind working frantically on what her first words should be.

"Fulton!" a woman called as she swept into the room, wearing a brightly colored floral dress, complete with hat, heels, and a pink handbag hanging from the crook of her arm. Aunt Betty, taking up all the space in the room as usual. She was as tall as Raelyn's dad, thirty pounds heavier and only knew one volume. Loud.

She brushed past the huddled family, reached Raelyn's dad, and wrapped her arms around him. She cut her eyes to Raelyn before patting Fulton's arm. "Is Peter okay? I came as soon as . . ."

Raelyn slunk away to the coffee bar, shutting out Betty's rambling. She pulled the lever and watched black coffee drain into a Styrofoam cup. Raelyn found a seat where the man in the indigo coat, now gone, had been standing and sank into it. She sniffed and with the next exhale the dam broke. She drew her knees to her chest, wrapped her arms around her legs, and buried her face. Peter would be okay. He had to be. There was no one left.

"Rae?" Her dad's deep voice, quiet but firm.

Raelyn lifted her head and wiped her nose with the back of her sleeve, nearly tipping the coffee down her shirt. She didn't take her eyes off him as she unfolded her tingling legs and set her feet on the floor. She hadn't heard him say her name since the funeral.

Fulton frowned as he bit the inside of his cheek and crossed his arms. "Doc says the lab work's back. She wants to talk to us."

Raelyn nodded and stood. She tossed the full coffee cup in the trash as she followed her dad to Dr. Holland. Aunt Betty stood to one side, wringing her hands.

Dr. Holland gave the three of them a quick sweep with her eyes. "We're still waiting for more tests." She paused and frowned, looking from Fulton to Raelyn. "We've narrowed it down to a fungal infection. Not uncommon, but it's rare to have such an extreme and advanced reaction in a young, healthy individual. We've started treatment and we're moving him to ICU where a few family members can visit. What questions can I answer?"

"Is he awake?" Fulton asked.

"Not yet. But give the treatment time to do its work. We should see him turn the corner in twenty-four hours."

Fulton nodded. "Thank you, doctor."

"Of course. I'll have the nurse come get you once he's settled." Dr. Holland gave another nod and left.

"Oh, Fulton!" Aunt Betty cried and gripped his arm. "It's just horrible."

Fulton patted his sister's shoulder. "The doctor said twenty-four hours. That's promising. Get off your feet for a bit." He nodded to a grouping of empty chairs. Betty released his arm, wiped the mascara from under her eyes, and wandered away.

Fulton spun his wedding ring around his finger and stared at the ground. Raelyn waited. He should say something. Her heart pounded at the thought. He might tell her to get lost. That she had already caused one tragedy, no need to stick around for another. He could tell her how much he missed her. That this had been the longest year of his life. Finally, he looked up and met her eyes. His hair, always trimmed short, hung across his forehead and gray stubble covered his slack cheeks. He looked eighty, not sixty. Raelyn forced herself to hold his gaze.

He cleared his throat. "Have you eaten?"

Raelyn blinked. *Eaten? As in food?* She shook her head.

"Come on. Let's grab something." He steered her toward the hallway, his hand gentle on her arm.

"Betty," he called over his shoulder, "we're going to get a bite. Want anything?" Betty shook her head and sniffed.

Raelyn walked next to her dad, neither of them speaking. They followed cafeteria signs down the hall, around a corner, and through another corridor. In a wide dining hall, hospital staff pushed food trays through a line and a refrigerated case held pre-made sandwiches and salads. Raelyn went to a counter labeled "soup." She dished creamy potato soup from a deep, metal container as her dad grabbed a sandwich. He paid and they found a booth under a wall of windows, sliding in across from each other.

Raelyn took a sip from the steaming bowl and glanced at her dad. He took his time studiously unwrapping the cellophane from his sandwich.

"Peter will be fine." Fulton unwound the last of the plastic and wadded it into a ball.

"I know." Raelyn's shoulders relaxed under his quiet tone. "I'll be glad to see him awake." Seemed an obvious statement, but neutral. Safe.

"Yeah," he murmured and fell silent again. As Raelyn brought the spoon to her lips, Fulton lifted his head, his body suddenly tense. "Raelyn." He leaned forward and paused, his mouth working. Raelyn lowered the spoon. This was it.

"How's . . ." His shoulders slumped. "How's school?"

"Um, fine. Busy."

"The book? How's it coming?"

"On hold."

"Yeah." Fulton nodded his head, though he didn't seem to be listening. There was so much more to say. Food, school, the book, all avoiding the real issues.

"Dad, I—"

"Fulton!" Aunt Betty rushed to the table, her chest heaving and her cheeks bright pink. "The nurse is looking for you. We can see Peter."

Fulton bumped the table as he stood. "Did they say he was awake?"

"No. Just that we could go into the ICU."

The three hurried to the ER and met a tall, thin brunette in blue scrubs. She led them to a nearby area with a set of five windows lining one wall, each allowing a view into its own room. One with closed curtains, one contained an empty hospital bed, two were occupied. In the last room was Peter.

Raelyn's throat closed with a painful ache. Machines surrounded him; a bag of clear liquid hung above his head. Fulton reached for the door.

"I'm sorry, Mr. Witt." The nurse touched his arm. "Until we can determine the source of the infection, we're not allowing anyone in."

"The source?" Fulton dropped his arm. "I thought you had."

"Dr. Holland will join you in a moment to explain more. Don't worry Mr. Witt, he's getting the very best care." She gave Raelyn and Betty a quick smile and strode away.

Raelyn stood at the window. White blankets were pulled up to Peter's shoulders, a clear mouthpiece covered his nose and mouth. The last time they'd spoken she had snapped at him about the party.

Dr. Holland stepped out of the room with the closed curtain and swung a stethoscope around her neck as she walked up. She glanced through Peter's window before ushering them to a set of chairs in one corner. Aunt Betty sat down. Raelyn and her father remained standing.

"We're bringing in a specialist. The tests came back . . . inconclusive. We are still treating it as a fungal infection. But we can't identify the type of fungus." She held up her hand when Fulton opened his mouth to speak. "He's stable. We'll take him in for a CT scan in a few hours. At this point, I suggest you go home. Until we can determine more, Peter will benefit most from a rested family."

"What if he wakes up while we're gone?" Fulton asked.

Dr. Holland nodded. "We have a care-staff who will keep you apprised of any changes. Keep your phone close. We'll call or text you with updates."

Fulton frowned and glanced at the window, spinning his ring.

Raelyn took a breath. "I'll stay. You've been here since early morning." When her dad gave her an uncertain look she glanced at Dr. Holland. "It'd be okay for us to trade-off wouldn't it?"

Dr. Holland smiled, an understanding expression that showed she was accustomed to this response. "Of course. I'll ask that you stay in this area only." Raelyn nodded vigorously.

Fulton sighed and ran a hand through his lank hair. "Okay, but just a few hours." He turned to Raelyn. "Call me if his eyelids so much as flutter." He looked down at Betty. "Com'on. I think Rae has this."

They left, and Raelyn's chest swelled as she wandered back to the window. Her dad trusted her. Was relying on her. She stood at the window for a moment, watching the machine check off Peter's heartbeat.

She settled into one of the chairs and scrolled through her phone. But each time a nurse entered Peter's room Raelyn stood and watched through the window. When they rolled him away for his CT scan Raelyn paced the hall until they returned. The nurse replaced his IV fluid and wrote some notes on a chart at the end of his bed. It was another hour before Dr. Holland rushed back into the room followed by the same nurse. Something about their exchange made Raelyn uneasy.

Finally, Dr. Holland came out. She motioned to the chairs. "Have a seat."

"What's wrong?" Raelyn sat without taking her eyes off the doctor, who eased into the seat next to her.

"The scan revealed a more advanced infection. Something I've only known to affect people with chronic lung conditions, emphysema, tuberculosis. He should also be responding to the steroid and anti-fungal meds and be alert."

"What does that mean? Should I call my dad?"

A small frown creased Dr. Holland's forehead for a split second. "We will continue treatment and we've called in a specialist who will be able to tell us more. He can assess Peter for possible surgery to remove the fungal mass."

Raelyn nodded, her head spinning. "Okay, I'll call my dad to come back," she said, her lips numb.

"Good." Dr. Holland stood and took a breath. "We'll get this figured out."

Raelyn waited for the doctor to leave then resumed her post at the window, her phone poised to dial her dad.

"I have deep respect for healers." A man's quiet, resonant voice spoke close to Raelyn's ear. She jumped and turned around. The man from the waiting room. His eyes, impossibly blue, sparkling. They crinkled with a kind smile, full of calm compassion.

"I'm sure they're doing everything they can." Raelyn glanced up and down the corridor. The area had nearly cleared out.

"But they do not always hold the answers." He pressed his palms together.

Raelyn narrowed her eyes. The long hair, the coat, everything about him seemed out of place.

"Yeah, well, they know best." She took a small step toward the exit.

"Sometimes." He looked past her through the window to Peter. "If you find they cannot help . . ." he turned back to Raelyn and held out a folded note on yellowed paper, ". . . I may have an answer."

"Oh, no, really that's okay." Raelyn took another step away, but he kept the note extended, holding her in his gaze.

Raelyn looked down at the note. Maybe he'd go away if she took it. "Well, okay. Sure. Thanks." She plucked it from his hand.

The man nodded. "You might find the answers lay outside your understanding. But well within your abilities." He smiled again, warm, caring, fatherly. And then he was walking away. Raelyn looked at the note. A gold wax seal held the tri-folded paper together. She peeled it apart and read the flowing script:

Some answers you can trust though not understand. Some explanations you believe to be true are meant to deceive. Your world only perceives a glimmer of what really is. Reach beyond what you seek, and you will find. When all seems hopeless, I offer a way to heal Peter but it will depend on you. I request your presence at 118 West Highway 182 in the town of Silo, Texas on the eighteenth of August at eight o'clock in the evening.

For the Glory of Arkonai,

Kade

Raelyn meandered back to the row of chairs rereading the note and sat down. She punched her dad's contact, put the phone to her ear, and leaned her head against the wall.

Great, a nutcase.

CHAPTER THREE

Over the next two days, Peter's health declined. The specialist, Dr. Brand, a tall man with sharp features and thinning hair, determined surgery would have little effect as the infection was spreading rapidly. On Tuesday afternoon Peter slipped into a coma.

Fulton and Raelyn were allowed in Peter's room and Dr. Brand stood at the end of his bed flipping through the chart. He sighed and shook his head. "I've consulted with some colleagues. We can try a few more treatments, but I've never seen such an extreme case and I've never heard of one resulting in a coma."

"What does that mean?" Fulton held the side-rail to Peter's bed as though to hold himself up.

"If this persists, and his lungs stop doing their work, we may need to move him to life-support."

A strangled sob escaped Fulton. Raelyn's legs gave way and she slumped into the seat next to Peter's bed.

"That will give us extra time to find the right treatment," Dr. Brand said.

Raelyn knew he meant the statement to be encouraging, but hope seemed elusive, distant. And how was she going to tell her dad she couldn't be at the hospital tomorrow? She briefly considered asking if her hearing could be rescheduled. But there was no way she could risk a delay affecting the judge's ruling.

In the end, she told her dad she had to make some arrangements. He didn't need details. She had already called the dean to request leave and asked her boss at the cafe. In the wee hours of Wednesday morning, she went home to sleep a few hours before the hearing. As she sat outside the courtroom she pulled the note from her back pocket, where she'd carried it since Sunday, rereading it a few times each day. She ran her finger over the gold seal before unfolding it.

" . . . *offer a way to heal Peter . . . it will depend on you . . .* "

As the doctors tried one treatment after another and Friday the eighteenth had drawn nearer, Raelyn imagined driving the hour to Silo. What cure could be in that farm town?

Raelyn's attorney strode up and led her into the courtroom where the judge waited on her high bench. Patricia joined them and after a brief exchange, it was over. With a strike of the gavel, Raelyn was released. She waited for the sweeping relief, the lifting burden, but even after Patricia walked her to the police station and her ankle monitor was removed, she had only a vague sense of being untethered. And a realization that a trip to Silo was now possible.

When Raelyn returned to the hospital, evening was fast approaching. They had moved Peter to his own room. Fulton sat in a recliner next to the bed, his head propped on his fist and a halo of light from a table lamp shining over him. In the silence, the ventilator produced a steady, inhaling hiss. Raelyn crossed the room to stand beside Peter's bed, opposite her dad.

"Saved you some pasta," he said, gesturing to a tin container on the table. " Aunt Betty made it."

"Thanks." Raelyn tried to smile.

Fulton shrugged and stood. "You know how she gets when she's upset. My whole kitchen's been upside down for days."

"Yeah." Their eyes met over Peter's sleeping form. Tubes and wires surrounded him, keeping him alive.

"I don't understand what's happening." Fulton's eyes filled with tears and he looked at Peter.

Raelyn shook her head. She couldn't watch her dad cry. Not again.

"You know, I would've called . . ." Fulton said without looking up.

"I know, Dad. I just didn't know what —"

"But," he continued, as though he hadn't heard her, "the time passed so quickly. It's been a fog . . ." He took a deep breath and looked up. "When you . . . when your mom and Harlan died, I was looking for anything to understand what happened." Tears welled in his eyes and he shook his head. "I just don't think I can do this again —" His voice broke.

Raelyn circled the bed and leaned in close to him. He put his arm over her shoulders and she wrapped her arms around his waist burying her face in his thin chest, as though holding a life raft in a rushing tide. It didn't last long, but it was enough. When he released her, he patted her shoulder and wiped his face with his palm.

"Dad, we're not going to lose him. The doctors are doing everything . . ." *They don't even know what it is.* " . . . he'll get better . . ." *He's been unconscious for three days.* " . . . and we'll do anything, I'll do anything, to make sure he does."

. . . it will depend on you.

Fulton nodded and collapsed into the chair.

By Thursday afternoon, Raelyn had decided. She would go to Silo and find out what the note promised. She had sold her car to pay for the ankle monitor and, even though an Uber would cost the rest of her paycheck, her mind was made up. Whatever it took.

On Friday morning, Raelyn and Fulton sat talking, which was becoming easier. Dr. Brand came in, read over Peter's chart, and hung it back on the end of the bed.

"Mr. Witt, we still have a few more therapies to try, but I need to be frank. As Peter's condition continues to decline, I will ask that you consider alternatives. Only after every possibility has been explored. But I want you to be prepared."

Fulton gripped the arms of the recliner. He stared hard at the doctor, a muscle tensing in his jaw. But then he relaxed and sat back nodding.

"I appreciate all you're doing," he said in a dry whisper.

"Of course. We haven't given up."

Raelyn and Fulton said nothing long after the doctor left.

"Dad."

Fulton grunted, looking down at his hands.

"I, uh, I might know someone who can . . . help." *How much should she tell him?*

"Help? How?" He looked up at her with tired, red eyes.

"Something, experimental. Nothing guaranteed. But it might be worth looking into."

He studied her face, as though wondering if she was worth trusting. Considering if he believed she could actually find a way to save Peter or if she would just let him down. "Okay," he said slowly. "You need some money?" He reached for his back pocket.

"No, no. I don't know what to expect really." Raelyn stood. She would need to leave in the next two hours to make it by eight. "It might take a little while."

"Oh?"

"Just . . . whatever happens, promise me you won't . . . do anything. Make any decisions."

"How long?" He frowned as though already doubting her.

"I don't know. Maybe not long. But I have to go find out." She crouched in front of him and looked him in the eye. "Just promise you'll wait until I come back."

Fulton nodded and gave her a small, pained smile. "Okay. Be careful."

"I will." She stood and hurried from the room.

Raelyn watched the passing cornfields from the window of the Uber as they left Torst heading for Silo. Rows of tall, green stalks waited to be harvested a few yards from the two-lane highway. The field abruptly ended, replaced by rolling, closely-shaved hills with clusters of black cows and rolls of hay. It all seemed quiet and peaceful in the encroaching twilight. Amazing how quickly the city faded and the farms took over.

She hadn't been outside a twenty-mile radius from her apartment for a solid year. But the new freedom meant nothing more than an opportunity to cure Peter.

The driver, a thirty-something man who bobbed his head and tapped his fingers on the steering wheel to some imagined music, drove the hour to the small town of Silo in complete silence. As the ruby sun touched the horizon, sending warm rays through her window, he slowed and pulled over.

"One-eighteen, West Highway one-eighty-two." He looked at Raelyn through the rearview mirror.

Raelyn peered at the massive chain-link fence surrounding an expansive, empty parking lot and a shadowy, multi-storied concrete building. A large, white sign just outside the gate announced *B & K Electronics*.

"You meeting someone here?" The driver seemed to share Raelyn's misgivings.

"Um, yeah, should be."

"You want me to wait?"

Raelyn glanced at her phone. No service. "You know, that would be great. Just for a minute. Thanks." She opened the door and stepped onto the dusty shoulder, immediately enveloped in still, muggy air. As she took a few steps toward the fence the trill of cicada rose and fell.

"What in the heck?" she mumbled and strode through the open gate. No cars. No people. A single light shone from a low awning. This was where she would find answers?

Or get murdered.

Car lights came into view up the road. She stopped and eased a few steps back to the Uber car. A pick-up swung off the road and lumbered through the gate.

Yep, murdered.

The truck squealed to a stop, the engine chugging. The driver's door opened and a man emerged and stepped in front of the headlights. Maybe late-thirties, tall, muscular, dark-brown hair trimmed so short his ears stuck out.

"You here for the . . . uh, invitation?" Deep, with a south-Texan accent, his tone was uncertain enough to suggest he probably wasn't with Kade.

"Yeah, you?" It had never occurred to Raelyn there might be others.

"Yeah. This your ride?" He put one hand in the pocket of his cargo pants and cocked his head. As casual as if they were meeting for coffee. The light winked on a pair of dog tags hanging against his T-shirt. "I can give you a ride on up." He gestured to the building.

"No, I'm fine." Raelyn waved her driver on. She wasn't alone and no immediate alarms were going off in her head.

"Name's Joshua Spurgin." He took two strides toward her, holding out his hand.

Raelyn stared for a moment before stretching forward and giving it a strong shake, hoping to prove she wasn't an easy target. "Raelyn."

Joshua gave a tight smile and a nod before returning to his truck, slamming the door and rolling forward. Raelyn followed on foot, and he drove slowly enough that she could keep up. Two cars were parked beneath a portico on the south side of the building and

Joshua pulled in behind them. Raelyn waited by the glass double doors beneath a single, yellow light bulb. The truck stopped grumbling and Joshua walked up to the building, swinging his key ring around one finger. Raelyn's heart thumped. Maybe letting the Uber driver leave was a bad idea. But every hesitation was met with a vision of her dad's sad eyes and Peter's pale face.

Joshua pulled open the door and swept his arm in front of him. "After you."

Raelyn took a deep breath and walked into a brightly lit, sparsely furnished waiting room. As the door closed behind them a young man, slightly shorter than Joshua and not more than twenty, scurried into the room. A mess of red hair fell across his glasses.

"Hello." He smiled nervously and shoved his hands into a pair of khakis. A wrinkled white shirt was tucked in tightly and the whole ensemble was mismatched by a pair of white tennis shoes. "Welcome to Beeghley and - um B & K Electronics. My name's Gabe, uh, McKaney. You're here at Kade's invitation?"

"Yeah, 'bout that." Joshua pulled a folded sheet of paper, similar to Raelyn's, from his pocket and glanced around the room. "Not sure I get the plan. Feels like some kind of timeshare presentation."

Gabe shook his head. "Oh, nothing like that. Kade couldn't be here this evening, but I can explain everything. If you'll follow me?"

Joshua cocked an eyebrow at Raelyn. She slipped her own note from her purse and unfolded it, scanning the words once more.

. . . *when all seems hopeless* . . .

Peter's condition was indeed, hopeless. Whatever snake oil Gabe was selling, she'd buy it.

"Yeah, okay." She breathed the words through a dry mouth.

Gabe punched in a code on a touchpad next to a set of steel doors. He pressed his thumb on the screen and the doors clicked. Gabe pulled at one and held it for Raelyn and Joshua to follow.

"It's funny," he said as they proceeded down an empty, sterile hallway, "we're the only ones from Texas."

"Only ones?" Raelyn asked. "There are others?" The cars under the portico.

"Well, not tonight. But yes," Gabe pulled open a glass door to the next room, "there are others."

Automatic lights winked on, sending a florescent glare down an echoing stairwell.

"Underground?" Joshua peered down the multitude of steps.

Gabe shifted on his feet. Maybe he was nervous about where he was taking them. Or what he had to tell them. Or intimidated by Joshua. But something told Raelyn that Gabe didn't get out much. Maybe he was just uncomfortable with talking to other people.

"Our company is very private. Most of our offices are below ground." He paused for a moment before hurrying down the steps.

Joshua shrugged but his shoulders tensed as he followed Gabe. Raelyn glanced back at the door. No one would hear her scream.

Why didn't I at least bring my taser?

But she followed anyway.

Four flights down Gabe led them through another doorway into a narrow, carpeted hall. They passed several doors on the left and right, but Gabe led them to another set of metal doors at the very end. With a similar keypad to the one above, he opened the doors and lights stuttered to life inside a narrow board room with concrete walls. A heavy center table ran the length of the room, which ended with a whiteboard affixed to the far wall scrawled with numbers and symbols.

"Have a seat." Gabe gestured to one of the black chairs as he walked to the head of the table and waited.

Both Raelyn and Joshua eased into chairs facing each other across the middle of the table. Gabe, seemingly more at ease, gave each of them a long, thoughtful stare.

"I'm sorry Kade couldn't be here. But I want you to keep an open mind. I can't say I exactly understand all this myself."

"Understand what?" Joshua leaned forward. "You said you had . . ."—he flitted his eyes to Raelyn— "answers."

Gabe pushed up his glasses. "Answers, yes." He nodded. "But not exact solutions." He held up a hand to stave off their protests. "At least not yet. Have you been watching the news, the press conferences, about the quantum physics discovery six months ago?"

"You mean the dimensions?" Raelyn raised her eyebrows. "How would that have anything to do with my brother?"

Joshua splayed his hands out on the table and said nothing. His mouth was drawn tight and his eyes were like flint.

"Okay, hear me out." Gabe turned to the whiteboard and erased a portion of the scribbled equations. "Okay," he said pulling off the top of a marker, "you know the basic equation for gravity." He wrote $E=mc_2$.

"Can we cut to the chase?" Joshua rose from his seat.

Gabe turned and fidgeted with his marker. "Just, just hear me out."

Joshua looked back at Raelyn, who shrugged. What could she lose? Peter's time was running out and she had no other answers. Joshua sighed and sat back down. Maybe he had nothing to lose either.

"Right." Gabe turned back to the whiteboard. "In the past, gravity gave scientists a great way to make sense of some forces in our universe. But not all. There were also electromagnetic forces." He wrote a series of equations with upside-down triangles and weird letters. "But QFT, uh . . ." Gabe paused and turned halfway around. "That's Quantum Field Theory," he explained before resuming marking up the whiteboard. "It didn't work well for gravity. So to explain the gravitational forces and unify the two theories, scientists developed string theory."

Gabe turned around, his face bright with excitement. But his smile fell when he looked at Joshua and Raelyn. "Okay, well, out of the six string theories was born M-theory. This gave rise to our understanding of the eleven dimensions of the universe."

The room seemed warm and Raelyn was keenly aware of the layers of concrete pressing in from above. She frowned at Gabe. "They've been talking about dimensions on the news. They discovered something. But, Gabe, I really just want to know what Kade meant." She pulled out the note and spread it on the table. "He said he had a way to heal Peter. Are you saying there's some cure you've found from one of these dimensions? Like a radiation therapy?"

Gabe shook his head, his blue eyes wide. "Not a cure, necessarily. An entire world. These dimensions are all part of what Kade calls the Periferie. Many layers of worlds."

Joshua snorted. "You sure you didn't read this in a comic?" He stood, pushing his chair back. "This is wasting my time."

"Wait." Raelyn scooted to the edge of her chair. "No cure?"

Gabe looked at Joshua and spoke in a rush. "B & K Electronics has a division. A department that began in the eighties. Back then, the U.S. government was looking to compete with the Swiss in their quantum research. Turned out to be a huge failure and they shut it down. That's when Beeghley and his partner Kanabel bought the property and continued the project."

Joshua narrowed his eyes. "You're saying, right here, you have a . . ."

Gabe nodded vigorously. "An LHC." He looked at Raelyn. "Large Hadron Collider. For almost thirty years they've worked continuously. I came on just a few months ago."

"A few months?" Raelyn shook her head. Whatever a Large Hallidrome whatchacallit was, this kid was clearly out of his depth. "I still haven't heard anything about a way to help my brother. And this company, do they know you've brought us here?"

Gabe's face turned bright red. "Not exactly, no."

Joshua interrupted. "The fifth dimension is hardly new information."

"Right." Gabe's enthusiasm returned. "The entire time they were using the LHC the company only managed to thin the dimensional layer. But apparently just before I started, B & K made a huge discovery. I was here, working late. They had just shut the machine down and everyone had left. And there he was."

"He?" Raelyn asked.

"Kade." Gabe replaced the cap on his marker. "From the fifth dimension. From Alnok."

Joshua folded his arms across his chest. "You're saying this is a real place. With real people living in it."

"Not people necessarily." Gabe looked uncertain and uncomfortable again. "I told you, I don't exactly understand it all."

"Anyone else know about him?"

"No, he was actually looking for me specifically."

"Lucky, you being here."

Gabe shrugged. "You can call it luck. But here's the thing, whatever Kade told you he had,"— he gestured to Raelyn's note —"it's in that dimension."

Raelyn looked at the words on the invitation. Did she think the answer would be simple? Easy? That they would hand her a bottle of pills and send her on her way? The words blurred with her tears. She had promised her dad she would find a cure. They were out of options and she had to follow where ever this path led. For Peter.

She looked up at Gabe as a single tear escaped and rolled down her cheek. "What do I need to do?"

Gabe nodded and looked at Joshua, who let out a long breath. "Yeah, sure. Why not?"

"How long will this take, Gabe? My brother, he doesn't have much time."

Gabe shook his head "I don't really know. But Kade understands why we're all here. And I've talked with him enough to trust that he wouldn't invite us there if he didn't think he could help. He pressed something to the right of the whiteboard. The wall rolled back and Gabe walked through without a word. Raelyn followed him onto a metal mezzanine surrounded by glass. Through a single glass door, the mezzanine continued between two house-sized machines made of colorful, concentric circles facing each other. One was open in the center, the other had a solid protruding center.

"Okay, wait here." Gabe strode into a dark adjacent room and sat down at a station of computers. As he furiously typed on one of the keyboards a motor began to hum and the two large machines lit up.

"Whoa," Joshua breathed.

"Right." Raelyn backed up a step as the metal platform vibrated. "Should we be out here?"

Gabe rushed back in. "I know." He grinned. "It's great huh?"

"Yeah, but this can't be safe." Joshua took a step closer to Raelyn and away from Gabe.

"That's been the general consensus." His eyes swept up and around the two machines, now blinking red and blue lights. The humming from an unseen motor grew. "But, like I said, there have been others. Also . . ." He shifted and cleared his throat. "Kade advised me that electronics don't work in that dimension and likely won't pass through the portal." Gabe gestured to Raelyn's phone and held out a large plastic bag.

"You want to keep my phone?" Raelyn put her hand to her purse. "How will I contact my family?"

Gabe shook his head. "You can't." He raised his voice above the sound of the motor and shrugged. "You have to decide if what you seek is worth the risk."

Raelyn didn't need to think about it. "What now?" She glanced at the machines, the lights now a blur as something like heat waves appeared at the center.

"There!" Gabe called and opened the glass door as the grinding motor reached a deafening pitch. "It won't last long, so enter quickly!"

"Enter! You mean walk through that thing?" Joshua shook his head.

But Raelyn didn't care. They'd discovered a fifth dimension. That's where Peter's cure was. That's where she was going. She gave a short nod and stepped past the doorway. A violent vibration took her breath away, but she moved closer. The motor screeched and she covered her ears, taking another step. The light penetrated her vision, then her mind.

All went black.

CHAPTER FOUR

Before Raelyn even opened her eyes, she knew she was no longer in the B & K warehouse. The stale air was replaced by the scent of damp stone after a rain shower. She was sprawled on her back in . . . *grass*?

Her heart pounded as bits of memory surfaced, distant and disjointed. She forced her eyes open but lay still.

A pale sun filtered through hazy clouds draped across a pallid sky. Raelyn shifted her head to the right, taking inventory of what was immediately visible. Dry, prickly grass pressed into her cheek. Crumbling, gray stone formed a low wall next to her and a gravel road was a few paces away. A crow cawed in the distance.

She sat up and pressed her palms against her eyes to ease a throbbing headache and ran her fingers through her wet, tangled hair. She looked down at her clothes. Her jeans were soaked, muddy, and grass-stained. Her blouse was also damp and filthy. A scientific lab, underground. She had agreed to journey to the fifth dimension, where a young man . . . Gabe, had said they would find Peter's cure.

The portal.

She scrambled to her feet, blinking away a head rush, and searched for the opening, the machines, any sign of Gabe or Joshua. Her hands shook as she pushed her hair from her face, tracing the slender scar. A vise of panic bound her lungs, making the air seem thin and each breath shallow as she surveyed her surroundings. Behind her and across the roadway, a forest of bare, charred trees stretched in both directions. Towering cliffs rose into the sky in the distance. Everything in her direct line of sight was clear, the trees in sharp focus. But in her peripheral vision, the trees were blurred, rippling, and swaying. The grass, the road, even the sky was obscured in a haze unless she looked directly at it. Her stomach rolled and she squeezed her eyes shut, willing her head to stop pounding.

A distant screech and guttural chortle drove all thought from her mind. Not human. Not like any animal she'd ever heard. She shivered and squinted into the woods. The crowded trees made it impossible to make out anything in between. She swallowed hard and took a deep breath. Blinking back tears and hugging her arms to her waist she took two steps back, away from the sound. A dry wind caused the dead limbs to scrape and the crow cawed again. But otherwise, silence.

Raelyn took a few tentative steps to the path. Multiple fragmented walls littered the land on both sides, a ruin of some sort. What might have once been stone barriers, buildings, houses, lay scattered around her. But intermingled were crumbling, dusty bricks of deep purple, ocean blue, and emerald green. Small, dusty pebbles of more multi-colored stones made up the path. She glanced left, then right. It all looked the same. She dropped her shoulders and sighed.

Left it is.

She crept forward, eyeing the forest on either side. The ruin soon became little more than scattered rocks in rich but muted colors. The haze at the corners of her eyes surged and blocked her vision. She stopped, leaned over, and put her hands on her knees as pain stabbed her temples. A sound, like a rush of wind, filled her ears.

Not wind.

Fast-moving traffic. A car horn blared directly behind her. She scrambled off the path, sliding on the gravel and landing hard on her hip. By the time she spun around on her knees, all had gone silent. There was nothing on the road. She sat back for several minutes trying to steady her breathing, then stood and brushed off her jeans, waiting for the noise to repeat. But there was only a dry wind and expectant hush.

She took an unsteady step forward, wincing at the pain in her hip. The path ahead may not be safe, but she couldn't stay here. She resumed her walk, away from the strange animal call. Her crunching footsteps sounded like gunshots in the silence. She squinted her eyes against her worsening vision.

The harsh terrain triggered a wave of deep loneliness. Tears stung Raelyn's eyes as she recognized how cut-off she was from everyone in her life, as few as those people were.

Even without an immediate threat, the portentous screech signaled danger was lingering just out of sight.

"How do I even know if this is the right way?" she mumbled. She considered turning around when she heard a rhythmic scraping behind her.

Not wind.

Not traffic.

Footsteps.

She spun around. In the distance, someone was following her.

"Hello?" Gabe called out, his voice cracking. Raelyn's vision rippled. She blinked quickly and the sensation passed. Gabe had to know where to go from here. Kade must've told him something.

"Hey." A different voice, right behind her.

Raelyn screamed and turned back. Joshua held out his hands in a gesture of peace. Her shoulders dropped and she let out a slow sigh.

"This everything you expected?" he said, making a wide gesture.

"Didn't really know what to expect." She looked over her shoulder. Gabe had closed half the distance.

"Now what?" Joshua called, striding past Raelyn.

"I'm not sure." Gabe removed his glasses as he approached, wiping them on his wet shirttail.

Raelyn's chest tightened. They were being too loud. She cast furtive glances at the trees and followed Joshua. "I thought you knew how this worked?" she said to Gabe with a pointed look.

"Yeah . . ." He settled his glasses back on his face. "I'm not sure this is right. Kade should have been here."

"Great." Joshua rubbed the back of his head. "Already off-plan."

"Do you have a Plan B?" Raelyn lowered her voice, hoping the two men would follow suit. "I'm not so sure staying here is a good idea."

Joshua put his hands on his waistband and stared at Gabe, who stammered

"I — no. No Plan B."

Joshua shook his head. "Right. Okay. Let's head south, follow the rising terrain. Maybe get our bearings from higher ground." He pointed in the direction Raelyn had already been traveling.

Anything was better than staying near the strange screech. "Let's see what we find there," she agreed. "We can decide what to do at that point." Gabe nodded, shaking his tousled red hair.

Raelyn felt a bit like they were about to start on the yellow brick road to the Land of Oz. After only a few steps, the same screech and wet gurgle came from the dark shadows of the trees, just behind them. They stopped and turned.

"What do you suppose that is?" Raelyn whispered, glancing at Gabe, who shook his head, his eyes darting around the forest.

"Nothing good," Joshua said in a low voice. "Keep moving." They resumed, moving faster.

"How do you know we're going south?" Gabe asked Joshua, keeping his tone hushed.

"Since I've been here, the sun has moved in that direction." He pointed to the sky, opposite the cliffs, and then took a quick look behind them.

Raelyn looked up at Joshua. "Wait, we left at the same time, from the same place."

Joshua shrugged. "I woke up in the middle of that scorched forest maybe an hour ago."

"I'd been walking for 15 minutes or so before I saw you," Gabe said.

Did any of them really understand how portals worked? The important thing was putting distance between themselves and whatever was out there. A dark tunnel was closing in on Raelyn's vision. She focused on the path just ahead. It could be some side-effect. Even though Gabe seemed to believe it was safe. The headache, blurred vision, traffic noise; something felt wrong.

When she glanced up she could make out the silhouette of a large, dark structure in the distance. As they drew closer, an archway came into focus, a formidable stone header balanced on two massive pillars.

Joshua cocked his head. "That structure outlasted all the other —"

The high-pitched screech sounded to their immediate left. Close. A second screech to their right. A call and then an answer? They slowed their pace to a complete stop. Raelyn stared hard between the trees swaying and dancing in her declining vision. A shadow? The sun had slipped to their right, casting hundreds of tree-shaped shadows. There was no way to tell.

No one spoke. Raelyn tried to steady her breathing. Her pulse pounded in her ears, making it hard to hear. Joshua took a step toward the noise but Gabe took a step back.

Two screeches echoed one after the other, the guttural sound trailing. Then the forest was filled with shrieks. Raelyn saw shadowed movement from the corner of her eye. Low to the ground, melding into the trees.

Joshua backed up. "We need to move."

"Agreed." Raelyn jogged two steps back before turning to run at full speed away from the threat. Gabe raced ahead of her, Joshua on her heels. She focused on the stone portico, everything else a blur. Her legs burned as her feet slammed into the rocky path.

As they neared the threshold Raelyn's foot slid on the pebbles. Flailing her arms in panic, she tried to regain her balance. She stumbled but managed to keep her feet beneath her and chanced a fleeting look back. Just behind Joshua, creatures surged from the forest. Hairless, wolf-like animals, the size of small horses. The dogs from the bus stop. Dozens of them. She saw a flash of fangs in a slender snout. Pushing her legs faster, she caught up to Gabe. As she passed him, she grabbed his shirt at the shoulder.

"Move it!" she yelled, pulling him along with her. The screeching of the wolf-horse-hounds drew closer.

Fifty feet.

Twenty.

Ten.

The animals were nearly on top of them when they raced through the gateway, passing a narrow, towering pyramid of black stones on their left. A man charged from behind the obelisk, directly toward the creatures. But Raelyn kept running until she heard him shout.

"Viltinen varga!"

She slowed to a jog, looking over her shoulder. The man had thrust his right hand toward the animals. His indigo cloak billowed around his feet and a golden light gleamed around his black hair, his shoulders, and hands.

Raelyn and Gabe skid to a stop as Joshua caught up to them.

The creatures halted as though a barrier had been slammed in front of them. With their pointed ears pulled back, they gnashed sharp teeth at the man but made no move forward.

"Kaider fylo," came his voice deep and commanding. Familiar.

If the creatures attacked there would be no out-running them and no protection except for the power the man seemed to hold over them. A few of the hounds directly in front of him slumped backward but their blotchy bodies remained hunched and taut, as though considering a strike as they watched him with pale-blue eyes. Their shrieks echoed, followed by the sickening thick gurgle. The man made no move.

Instead of an attack, the closest animals twisted around and streaked away. The others followed suit. The man kept his back to Raelyn, Joshua and Gabe until every beast had disappeared back into the trees. Raelyn took a great ragged breath and turned her attention to their defender. She watched closely, poised to run again should the man prove to be a foe. He finally turned.

His dark hair was streaked with gray and his olive skin contrasted with his blue eyes. Though older-looking and dressed differently, Raelyn knew exactly who he was. The man from the hospital. Kade.

CHAPTER FIVE

"What the heck was that?" Joshua shouted, adding a few angry curse words and advancing a step toward their savior.

Kade inclined his head, seeming to acknowledge Joshua's incredulity. "Please, there is much to explain." He gestured for them to follow. "Come." He strode back to the stone monument. His cloak, embroidered with red and gold thread, swept the ground as he walked. He seemed unaffected by the near attack, but Raelyn stayed rooted.

"I think you should tell us what's going on." Raelyn inwardly cringed. Her voice sounded small and strained. "Gabe didn't say anything about dangerous . . . dogs." The same dogs she had already seen. Her fear pushed to the surface, straining her slender thread of composure. She wasn't moving an inch until he said something.

"Raelyn, daughter of Fulton and Virginia." Hearing her father's name, and even more so, her mother's, coming from this man sent a jolt through Raelyn, sinking her further into a swirl of confusion and fear.

"I will give you all the answers I can. Joshua, son of Theodore and Ella,"—he dipped his head to Joshua, then addressed Gabe—"and Gabriel, son of Benjamin and Ashley. The varga will return in greater numbers. They are becoming bolder. I will lead you to shelter." He hurried around the monument and started up a hill without looking back.

Gabe took one glance in the direction of the dogs before jogging after Kade. He threw a look behind. "C'mon!"

Raelyn paused. This was what she had come for, wasn't it?

"Wait." Joshua grabbed her arm. "We need to be careful." His Texas accent was especially pronounced.

Raelyn glanced at Kade walking up the hill, then back to Joshua. "A little late for second thoughts. Besides," she eased her arm from his grasp, "we can't stay here." His caution was as understandable as it was irritating.

Joshua scanned the trees, then watched Kade's retreating figure. He ran his hand over his short hair before giving a single nod.

They hurried to catch up and crested the top of the hill. Tucked away in a parched valley was a dilapidated stone structure. A few beams of wood created a roof. It would have appeared abandoned but for a tendril of smoke snaking out of a crooked chimney stack. Like Hansel and Gretel's gingerbread house with the hag waiting inside. With no alternatives, and anxious for answers, Raelyn and her companions continued down the hill to the shack. The rippling effect was stronger than ever, making it impossible to focus. She trained her eyes entirely on the house and let Joshua, Gabe, and the stranger fade to her peripheral vision. A roar, much like the wind before, filled Raelyn's ears. Just beneath the noise, she thought she heard a crowd of voices calling out.

Raelyn stopped as Kade pushed open the wooden door, ushering Gabe through before ducking inside. Joshua, his jaw set, glanced back at Raelyn and entered next. With a deep breath, Raelyn stepped into the dark house. The cacophony grew. A single cry rose above all the noise. It sounded like Peter. But as the door clicked shut behind her the cry was cut off.

Raelyn's heart hammered. As her eyes adjusted she expected to see Peter cowering in a corner of the cramped room. Instead, a fire crackled in an ash-filled fireplace, casting flickering light into the shadows.

She glanced at Joshua who was breathing hard and blinking rapidly. Gabe rubbed at his eyes. The waves in Raelyn's vision slowed to a pulsing haze. She scanned the room, her fists clenched and her body tense, ready to bolt back out the door. A small round wooden table in front of the fire was flanked by two chairs. A slight girl perched on the edge of a long bench and watched the newcomers. She was just a teenager, with smooth black hair and porcelain skin. She cupped a small ivory mug on her knees and her dark, slanted eyes darted between the three of them, as though making a judgment on each before moving to the next. Her gaze fell to Kade. She was apprehensive, but not fearful. Based on her clothes, a short floral dress over black tights, ending in short boots, Raelyn guessed she was one of the others Gabe had mentioned.

"Now, where shall we start?" Kade rubbed his hands together as if warming them. He smiled, a slight twinkle in his eye. He seemed oblivious to their panicked state. The golden hue that surrounded him was subdued, but stark in the darkness. It wasn't light exactly, but a movement of the air around him, casting a gilded halo around his head and his shoulders, moving off his hands at every gesture. No one spoke. Shock, disbelief, fear, all jostled for attention in Raelyn's mind. She opened her mouth and took a breath, not even sure what she would say—

"Tea!" he exclaimed, pointing a finger upward as if this brilliant idea had just struck him. "Tea will refresh you."

He swept his cloak to one side as he quickly gathered mugs matching the girl's and handed out one each. He lifted a large kettle suspended in the fireplace and filled their mugs with a steaming, amber liquid. The air was filled with a soothing aroma. Something like honeysuckle and lavender, spring rain, and freshly fallen leaves. Raelyn peered into her mug then glanced at the others. No one drank except the girl, who took a small sip, still looking at Kade expectantly. Gabe kept his eyes on her as he tipped the mug and swallowed. He took a deep breath and blew it out slowly with obvious relief. Raelyn brought the cup to her lips, breathing in the intoxicating smell. Her headache eased and her stomach settled. An antidote? She hesitated for just a moment and then drank. The liquid ran down her throat and seemed to spread into her fingertips, down into her legs to the ends of her toes. Her shoulders relaxed and her mind cleared. She was at once calm and alert. Her senses both subdued and awakened. Her vision sharpened.

Joshua leveled his gaze at Kade and took a defiant swig. His shoulders relaxed and he looked into the mug. Kade smiled, clearly pleased with the effect.

He nodded solemnly. "The tea, seripyn, is made from special leaves, from a sacred tree. But more of that later."

He lowered himself into one of the chairs near the fire, his eyes settling on the trio, who had not moved from the doorway, with a strange, joyful eagerness. "Let me introduce Raelyn and Joshua. Gabriel, you have met." Kade held an open palm out to each in turn introducing them to the Asian girl.

Gabe cleared his throat. "Gabe," he corrected. Kade nodded and smiled.

"This," he continued, holding his hand out to the young woman, "Is Lee Chin-sun, daughter of Lee Johoon and Heejin."

"Jinny," she said, her gaze lingering on Gabe. A tiny smile lifted the corners of her lips.

When no one responded, Kade leaned forward and placed his hands on his knees. His expression turned serious. "Welcome to Alnok. I am truly sorry for the way in which you were brought here." He dropped his gaze to the wooden floor as though searching for a place to start. "So much to tell you."

"What were those things?" Joshua's gruff voice broke the silence.

"What about what you said in your letters?" Raelyn added.

"Why does it look like we all jumped in a lake with our clothes on?" Gabe asked.

"The varga are a part of the horde of our enemy, Cosyn. He commands them both here and in your world, Earth Apparent. As a guardian, I serve Arkonai in the protection of Alnok, and now, to protect you, your loved ones, and all of Earth Apparent." Kade's voice deepened, commanding total attention. "Alnok is at war with Cosyn. He is bent on one thing: domination of Earth Apparent and destruction of all its inhabitants. The ruin from which you just came was Durnoth, once a flourishing kingdom set aside long ago for a faithful group of temporals. There were five other such kingdoms. Now gone. The varga are only a part of Cosyn's legion."

He looked at Raelyn. "What I promised in your invitations I hold to. It is our war, but it is also yours." He fixed her with an unwavering gaze. "A long, dangerous journey lies ahead. But you have been chosen to follow this path. And as such, you are equipped."

As he spoke, everything faded to the background. As though only she and this strange man from another realm existed. Kade's voice filled the room. Raelyn met his eyes, deep blue, luminous, and captivating. His gaze pierced her heart. She closed her mouth and looked into her mug, swirling the contents as Kade continued.

"Your dedication to those you love is of greater value than you know. As are you. When you acknowledge this, use it to your advantage, you will find nothing can oppose you. In the meantime, your physical state is not designed to function within this realm. The seripyn alters your state of being, allowing you to remain in this world. Distance, depth, height, even time, to some extent, behave differently here. The seripyn will help you interact in the linear sense to which you are accustomed." Kade stopped and looked at each of them.

"At one time a blessed group of temporals were rescued from a devastating plague long ago. They called Alnok home. But that was ages past. There has been no access from Earth Apparent to the Periferie . . . until now. I brought you to Alnok through our sacred lagoon, the Silom Pool, hence the wet clothing. Although," Kade frowned, "you should have been taken immediately to the kingdom of Malvok."

"But that didn't happen?" Raelyn asked.

"Nay." Kade shook his head. "I do not yet know why." He stood and crossed to a small window. "I will have more answers when we reach Malvok." He looked outside before returning to his post at the fire.

Raelyn took another sip of the comforting elixir. "Kade, what happens if we stop drinking the tea?"

He offered a soft smile, gentle, loving, fatherly. *The way I've wished my father would look at me.*

The thought caught her off guard and her heartbeat quickened. A gust of wind rattled the wooden roof. The door shifted on its hinges. Kade's face tensed as his eyes darted to the door. Everyone waited.

He finally looked away from the door to Raelyn. "Without the seripyn your bodies would no longer function properly. Eventually, you would fade, losing sight of Alnok without fully returning to Earth Apparent. You would become a shell, a ghost of your former self."

The wind rocked the house again. Ash in the fireplace swirled. A commotion came from a distance. Rhythmic grinding of the gravel road. Wheels. The group was motionless. Joshua's mouth was half open, his next words frozen. Raelyn half rose, ready to flee at the slightest threat. Only Kade remained relaxed. He placed his mug next to Joshua's, strode to the door, pushed it open, and walked outside, leaving the door ajar.

Filtered sunlight broke through the heavy gloom. Jinny exited behind Kade without looking back. Gabe took an ambivalent step toward the door. He shoved his hands into his pockets, paused for a moment, and then marched outside. Raelyn peered out. The sun had barely dipped in the sky.

A wooden cart, harnessed to two massive horses, one chestnut, the other blond, lumbered to a stop at the entrance to the house. Two additional horses, as large as the others, were tied to the back of the carriage. A slim, brown-skinned man sat in the upper seat. His sleek dark hair touched his shoulders and framed a long face and sharp, blue eyes. A leather jerkin was visable beneath a layer of short chain mail. His long legs, bent high enough on the wooden platform to prop his elbows on his knees, showed similar leather pants and laced boots. Like Kade, radiating about his shoulders, even his arms, and legs, was a light, or glow. Though his was paler, less golden.

Like an aura.

That didn't entirely fit. But it was close.

"Captain Ditimer!" Kade cried. "I trust there is good reason our visitors did not arrive in Malvok as intended?"

"Kade," Ditimer said in a low voice. "There were . . . complications." His eyes darted around at the four newcomers and his face hardened. "Your warriors still need such accommodation?"He jerked his head back to the wagon.

Raelyn looked at Gabe and Jinny. *Warriors?*

"For now," Kade said firmly. "They have come a long way and still have much to discover. We can address the . . . complication . . . when we are safe." He turned back to his charges and again rubbed his hands together. Before he could speak, the now-familiar screech came from deep in the forest. It was followed by two closer, rising to a shrieking clamor. Then silence. Raelyn's heart pounded. They all stared into the trees.

"I will need to continue my account at a fortified location," Kade resumed, his words rushed. "I have the power to overcome the varga for a time, however, they grow stronger. Ditimer is the captain of the guard." He gestured to the grumpy man on the carriage, who touched his forehead with his fingertips. "He will take us to Malvok where we will have greater protection."

"I have horses for those who would prefer to ride," Kade said walking to the back of the cart. "Or the carriage if you would be more comfortable in there."

Gabe waited for no further invitation. "I'll take the carriage," he said, before clambering into the back of the cart and sitting on one of the two wooden planks.

Jinny walked to Kade and frowned up at him. He stood a solid foot above her slender frame. He looked down with a tender smile and held out his hand. She took it and climbed into the cart, settling next to Gabe.

Joshua leaned toward Raelyn, his arms still folded. "What do you think?"

Raelyn shook her head. "It's terrifying. But then so is what I'm dealing with at home. It's worth seeing how far this rabbit hole goes." She looked at Joshua's profile. A muscle tensed in his jaw.

"Right," he exhaled. "But keep your guard up." Raelyn nodded as Joshua stalked off to one of the two horses behind the carriage. He hiked his leg up, barely able to wedge his toe into the high stirrup, and swung his leg over. As he settled in, he looked stoically down at Kade.

Raelyn hesitated between the second horse and the carriage. She had not been on a horse since a middle-school field trip. And this animal was larger than any she had ever seen. The carriage was safer. Raelyn walked past Kade and joined Gabe and Jinny. As he secured the wagon, Raelyn studied Kade's face. His tanned skin was worn but soft, and his dark beard, streaked with gray. Guessing his age was impossible. Of all his features Raelyn was struck by how he could look so jolly yet imposing. How his eyes were at once kind and fierce, his voice commanding yet gentle. Kade gave a fleeting smile to the three passengers. A copper medallion on a leather cord glittered around his neck as he turned and moved with sudden speed and dexterity. He leaped into the saddle of the last horse and prodded it to the head of the caravan.

"Hi-ya!" Ditimer called snapping the reins. The carriage rolled forward and climbed back over the hill to the roadway. Raelyn turned to look at Joshua, who continued to scowl but nudged his horse to follow. Shadows seemed to shift in the trees, suggesting the beasts were nearby.

The jostle from the cart had worked Gabe's glasses down his nose as the cart rocked rhythmically along the roadway. The sun sank to their right casting rich, brilliant beams of light across the colored stones which glittered all around them. But the beauty was sullied by the distinct feeling of being watched. Raelyn held the side of the wagon to steady herself but Jinny somehow maintained a perfect posture, her hands resting on her knees.

Raelyn shifted to find a more comfortable position. "Um, Jinny. Did you know anything about Alnok, these dimensions, before you met Gabe?" She inwardly groaned. It was like asking 'So, what brings you to Alnok?'

Jinny shook her head. "I'm not a mathematician or physicist. But my father wanted me to go into engineering. My older brother studied physics in Seoul and I picked up a little from him. Then the discoveries were all over the news. I was in Houston, one of Seoul's friendship cities, visiting a pen-pal when Kade approached me. I never would have imagined there to be *life* in the fifth dimension."

"So he gave you a —" A screech came from the eastern forest. Closer.

"You may not have been aware of us," Captain Ditimer commented over his shoulder, "but we have most certainly been aware of you."

Again, several screeches rose from the trees. The gurgling trailed off but was followed immediately by more screeches.

Kade urged his horse to a gallop. The horses pulling the carriage followed suit. The violent bumping of the cart jarred Raelyn in unforgiving wallops. She gripped the side of the wagon and held on. Joshua leaned forward and matched the pace, maintaining a consistent distance from the cart. Joshua met Raelyn's eyes. Hers were wide with fear; his were narrowed, determined.

A legion of varga poured out of the dead forest behind him with a cacophony of screeches and sickly growls. Dust swirled into the air. Too many creatures to count. They were a throbbing mass of gray, hairless skin, bent on reaching their prey. And they were gaining.

Two broke away from the pack, speeding faster. One caught up to Joshua, nipping at his horse's flank. The other sped next to the wagon. Raelyn looked at Gabe and Jinny, both clutching the sides of the cart. A hound leaped at them, its slobbering mouth nearly at eye level with Raelyn. She looked frantically around the inside of the cart. A smooth wooden pole rolled between the two benches. She snatched it and turned to the hellhound. She held the pole at the ready, balancing on one knee, and braced herself with her other leg against the side of the cart, her stability precarious at best.

Lightning fast, the varga struck again. Raelyn jabbed the pole forward with all her strength. It caught the beast in the side of the mouth and the hound dropped, rolling onto the gravel road.

"Kade!" Ditimer roared. Immediately Kade fell back and shot a glance at the three in the carriage. Raelyn remained on her knees, holding the pole in one hand and gripping the side of the carriage with the other. Kade pulled up next to Joshua, who was kicking at the other varga, its teeth latched onto the stirrup.

"Make for the river!" Kade yelled to Ditimer, who nodded and whipped the reins, forcing the horses faster. Kade wrenched his horse around to the side of Joshua's and planted a boot to the varga. It released with a snarl and tumbled onto the road. Just past Kade and Joshua, Raelyn watched as hundreds more poured out of the forest. The enormous horses galloped faster than seemed possible as they careened down a steep hill, but the varga were closing.

At the bottom of the embankment, a stone bridge spanned a wide, swollen river. As they closed the distance to the water Ditimer bellowed "Hold on!" Unlike the ruins, the bridge was massive, flanked by imposing stone arches on one side and tall towers across the river.

The wagon hit the lip of the bridge and bounced violently. Raelyn lost her grip. Her back twisted with the jolt as she was flung from the cart, landing hard against one of the pillars. She heard Jinny scream and Kade and Joshua's horses race past. Across her mind an image of Peter arose, crouched in the corner of the shack. His head bowed as great sobs echoed through the room. She heard screeching and snarling as the pack of varga approached. Her world spun and went black.

CHAPTER SIX

Kade spurred his horse faster as the wagon's wheels hit the bridge's threshold and the vehicle tipped to one side. Raelyn, already unstable due to her stance against the varga, tumbled over. For all the authority and powers Arkonai had bestowed on Kade, at this vital moment, he was utterly helpless. Gabe jerked Jinny back when she grabbed for Raelyn or she would have fallen from the carriage as well.

Ditimer did not slow down and they were halfway across the bridge when Kade pulled up on the reins and his horse skidded to a stop just past Raelyn's crumpled body. Joshua pulled up hard beside him.

"Go!" Kade commanded. Joshua hesitated. The varga were right on top of them. From the far side of the bridge a volley of shimmering arrows arched across the river and descended into the pack of wolves. They scattered and with another volley the varga reversed course. Some were pierced and dropped to the ground as the others scrambled past. The screeching and harsh, frantic gurgles intensified, then faded as the creatures disappeared into the woods, leaving only the roaring river to fill the silence.

"Follow the others, Joshua." Kade softened his voice, but gave Joshua a hard, unwavering stare. Joshua lingered a moment longer, looking from Kade to Raelyn and then back. He jerked his reins, turned his horse, and galloped across the bridge.

Kade jumped from his saddle and rushed to Raelyn, who lay curled on her side.

"Arkonai, please," Kade whispered as he reached her body. He knelt and gently rolled her onto her back, moving her as little as possible. Her chest rose and fell shallowly. Alive. For now. Their bodies were fragile, these temporals. All could pass on, but the inhabitants of Earth Apparent so easily.

Kade stroked her cheek. He was surprised to see such a resemblance to her ancestors. He grasped the amulet around his neck, feeling the warmth radiate into his hand. He held his other hand over Raelyn's face.

Kade closed his eyes and whispered, "Gã innen gaihala hai. Arkonai, heal her." He remained kneeling over Raelyn until she stirred.

With a mighty sigh, he touched his hand to his forehead. He gathered Raelyn into his arms, stood and carried her across the bridge. His horse snorted and followed obediently. The river pounded beneath his feet and drowned out all other sounds as a fine mist rose around him. The bridge, once a busy thoroughfare, now served as a barrier, surrounded by watchtowers. Repeated attacks had left gaping fissures in the stone railing. The once gleaming, colorful stones spanning the bridge were now dull and dust covered. Kade approached Gabe and Jinny who stood anxiously beside the carriage. Joshua had dismounted and walked up behind them.

Kade cradled Raelyn and looked at their frightened faces. *How will I help them see?*

He addressed Joshua. "If you would please help me get her into the carriage." Joshua leaped into the cart without comment.

"Is she okay?" Gabe asked, peering over Kade's shoulder.

"By the grace of Arkonai, she will be," Kade replied. He lifted her to Joshua who took her shoulders, bracing her head with his arm. Together they laid her down.

"Jinny," Kade said, smiling, intentionally using the name she preferred. "Would you be so kind as to ride next to Raelyn? We will enter the city of Malvok just through those trees."

"Welcome, Kade!" a voice called from the top of one of the sentinels. A dark-skinned man leaned over the turret, dressed like Ditimer, but a helmet stood askew on his head and a bow was casually slung over his shoulder.

"Thank you, Erye!" Kade called. "Not a moment too soon!"

"There were more this time," Erye exclaimed.

Kade sighed. "Indeed." He walked to Captain Ditimer, who had not left the cart. More and more frequently Kade had watched, not just varga, but other evil creatures reveal themselves, taunting, reveling in their darkness. But the time had come. The destruction of the temporal strongholds, long ago, was only the beginning. The battle waging in Alnok had finally reached a breaking point, infiltrating Earth Apparent.

"Gently now," Kade said to Ditimer.

Ditimer nodded. "Bastila has run ahead to the sanctuary to prepare the healers."

"Of course. See that Abigail tends to Raelyn immediately," Kade said frowning. Ditimer nodded and flicked the reins.

Kade kept his eye on the cart as it rolled away, knowing the newcomers watched him, awaiting answers, assurance. The answers were easy, but the assurance . . .

Raelyn awoke, again in an unfamiliar place. Instead of on grass, she lay on a soft bed with a light blanket pulled to her chin. She tried to force her heavy eyelids open. Every muscle howled and, as she struggled to shift positions, her back pinched. She winced, settling back against the pillows.

"Lie still, daughter." A deep melodic voice. Kade.

Raelyn looked over and her eyes gradually focused. "Wha —" Her throat constricted. She coughed and tried again. "What happened?"

"Much." Kade sat in a chair next to the bed, draped in an ivory cloak. His shining, dark hair lay on his shoulders. His face was relaxed and his eyes ever kind. "But first, you must recover. When your strength returns we will speak."

He looks like an angel. Raelyn, startled by the sudden thought, couldn't deny the wave of affection. Kade's gentle ways and strong presence were calming, welcoming.

A short, stout woman, with a loose bun of brown hair planted on the top of her head, bustled into the room. A white apron covered a gray dress. A pale, pulsing glow, the color of fresh apricots, hovered around her as she moved.

"That's our girl!" she said as she fussed with the blanket and pillow. "How are we feeling? Like you were trampled by a stampede of horses I reckon. And you nearly were mind you!"

"This is Abigail," Kade said, smiling at her fondly. He rose from the chair and took a step toward the doorway.

"Kade, the others. The varga. What happened? Peter . . ." Raelyn, pushing herself onto her elbows, rushed out the questions before he could leave.

"The others are safe and patiently awaiting your recovery. The varga were driven off. And Peter's condition has not changed, for now. I understand you have many questions. It is important for you to mend quickly. When you have regained your strength I promise I will provide you with all the information I can."

Raelyn lay back on the pillow, but her body remained tense.

"I leave you in Abigail's capable hands. I suspect you will heal quickly under her care." With that he swept out of the room.

Abigail beamed as she looked at Raelyn, Kade's compliment obviously not lost on her. With full rosy cheeks, and ruddy complexion, she had all the air of an overprotective grandmother.

"Before you know it you will be out and about." She continued to fuss with the sheets, then stopped and gazed at Raelyn. "Not to worry, child. You are safe. Arkonai watches over us even as we sleep."

Over the course of several hours Raelyn was given a regimen of hot broth, warm compresses and, best of all, more seripyn.

After a while, Abigail helped Raelyn out of bed. Gauzy, white drapes hung from the carved wooden canopy. Matching window coverings fluttered in a fragrant breeze from an open window. Raelyn, leaning on Abigail's shoulder, limped to an adjoining room. Steam rose from a copper tub. Raelyn eased into the water and let the heat melt away the knotted muscles and loosen her tense shoulders. Abigail brought towels and Raelyn considered asking about the others and for details about their escape from the varga. Instead she sank further into the hot water, deciding to heed Kade's advice and focus on getting better, allowing her questions to go unanswered.

But throughout the day she became more restless. Sitting in a castle tower got her no closer to saving Peter. Abigail continued to care for her but offered no insight and Kade did not visit again.

As night overtook the room Raelyn drifted into an uneasy sleep. She had promised to find Peter's cure. But it wasn't as simple as she had thought.

At dawn Raelyn pulled a matching robe over her blue nightdress and made her way to the window, massaging the small of her back which remained stiff and sore. She pulled back the drapes and gasped. The castle wall dropped from a dizzying height. Gone were the charred trees, gravel roadway and imposing cliffs. Instead a dazzling morning sunrise swept across a lush, green field to the shimmering river that flowed into a lake and passed out of view. Rows of thatched roofs lined a network of roads in the distance.

The radiance and calm surrounding Malvok contrasted with the outer reaches. Nearly beyond sight the sky smoldered black, a hulking shadow hovering over a distant, deep green forest. Raelyn stared into the darkness and even as a sick foreboding grew, she could not pull her gaze away. Her chest constricted in a dull panic. Disoriented, confused, a chaos clouded her mind and her eyes filled with tears. She blinked them back, willing herself to look away. Amid the swirling mass a light pulsed and the cloud swelled, like the deep breath of a great beast. Then it went still.

"The Peostrum," Abigail said behind her. Raelyn startled and spun around.

Abigail looked past Raelyn out the window and fiddled with the lace on her collar. "A reminder of the evil residing in Theurham Forest." Her eyes, dark brown and fiery met Raelyn's. "A reminder that a threat must be answered. Cosyn has made the forest his lair." Her face softened as she walked to Raelyn and took her hand, guiding her away from the window. "The answer must come soon." She smiled. "The others are anxiously awaiting your presence. They will be so relieved. And Kade is there. He has much to tell you."

"Thank you, Abigail." Raelyn took one last look at the distant darkness. "You've been such a comfort."

Abigail blushed. "Oh, my dear. It is you we have been so longing to meet." Before Raelyn could ask her about this strange comment Abigail continued.

"In the wardrobe you will find suitable clothes. I will leave you to change and have someone come to lead you to the drawing room." She patted Raelyn's hand and hurried out.

Raelyn sighed and limped to the elaborate wardrobe made of the same carved wood as the bed. Her recovery allowed her to put off dealing with what would come. Whatever the answer was to the threat of which Abigail spoke, Raelyn suspected she was in some way part of it.

She pulled on the doors which opened soundlessly on heavy iron hinges, revealing rows of shelves. There she found a pair of leather pants similar to Ditimer's. She pulled them on under her nightgown. The dark-brown hide was supple, soft, and a perfect fit.

She removed the nightgown and pulled on an indigo tunic, the same shade of Kade's robe, that fell just above her knees. It was soft as brushed suede, but as light and cool as linen. The long sleeves were snug and the neck and hem were embroidered with a fine gold thread. A wide leather belt cinched her waist. Finally, a pair of knee-high lace up boots completed her new uniform. There was no mirror in the room and she felt a little silly, like she was dressing for a medieval fair. But the sturdy fabric supported her sore back, and made her arms feel strong and her feet light. She quickly put a French braid in her hair and finished it off with a leather strap from another shelf. As she finished tying the ribbon there was a knock at the door.

"Miss?" a young voice called on the other side. Raelyn opened it to find a young girl, about twelve years old. Raelyn's throat tightened. Her resemblance to Harlan was jarring. The palest blue wisps of light diffused from her white-blond hair and her aquamarine eyes sparkled. A sprinkle of freckles gave her a mischievous look. Raelyn's mind flashed to the last time she had seen her little brother; blond hair peeking from beneath a ball cap, cheeks red from the cold spring wind. He raced past her, shouting and jumping, celebrating his first baseball win.

Raelyn shook her head and peered around for anyone else. She couldn't help smiling at the girl, who was grinning from ear to ear.

"You are as beautiful as I was told," the girl breathed. Then she cleared her throat and straightened her back. "I'm here to escort you to the drawing room," she said, then grinned again.

Raelyn chuckled. "What's your name?"

"Lydia." She reached for Raelyn's hand with a surprisingly strong grasp.

Raelyn left her room for the first time, relieved her back only felt tight, the pain gone, at least for now. The hallway, showcasing perfectly cut stonework, was high and arched, the walls lined with opulent tapestries of reds, blues, greens and gold. Some were just patterns. Others had woven inscriptions. As she passed, the designs shifted and changed. She stopped to take a closer look at a large crimson hanging. The patterns rippled, faded and pulsed, altering shape and color.

"You will find much is not as it appears," Lydia commented and tugged on Raelyn's hand.

"I —" Raelyn began, but shook her head. She didn't even know what to ask.

They approached a wide staircase. The railing, seemingly carved from a solid piece of stone, curved away to the lower level. It glimmered as though inlaid with crushed diamonds and glowed with its own light. High stained glass windows filtered the morning sunlight splashing the steps with deep reds and blues. Women, dressed like Abigail, bustled up and down the hall, a few stopping to curtsy to Raelyn. Quiet, but purposeful activity was everywhere. The castle was at once imposing and inviting.

Lydia tugged on Raelyn's hand, leading her down the stairs. They passed through a grand entrance where two massive arched wooden doors were propped open. Raelyn caught a glimpse of a courtyard with a large fountain, its iridescent water spilling into a large pool. She slowed to get a closer look but Lydia pulled her down a hallway to a small doorway and into a wood-paneled room.

Light filtered between heavy, drawn drapes from a far window, unable to keep the deep and depressing shadows filling every corner. Kade stood near a carved wooden mantel where embers burned in a fireplace. As before, he was enveloped in soft, golden light.

"Come in, Raelyn." He smiled tenderly. "I see you have mended well."

"Yes, I uh —" Raelyn, still holding Lydia's hand, froze in the doorway. Gabe and Jinny sat on a red sofa in the middle of the room. Joshua leaned back in a chair at a small round table. All were dressed similarly to Raelyn - Joshua in gray, Gabe in dark brown and Jinny in beige.

Raelyn took a deep breath. "I'm feeling better thanks."

Lydia let go of her hand. "Perhaps I will see you later Miss Raelyn." Her blue eyes gazed up expectantly.

Raelyn offered a smile she didn't feel. "Sure." She could think of no other response. Lydia turned and skipped away, blue tendrils bouncing behind her.

Anticipation hung heavy in the room, the castle activity muffled by the drapes, rugs and upholstered furniture. The effect was both calming and disconcerting.

Kade cleared his throat. "We have much to discuss, but first . . ." Kade looked behind Raelyn to the open door. She turned just as a short man with black, wavy hair stomped in.

"I would like to know where my bloody clothes are! And my phone!" he shouted in a thick, Yorkshire accent as he brushed past Raelyn. He wore similar leather pants to her but in black and a long-sleeved shirt untucked, buttoned only part way up. He was barefoot.

"I would like to introduce you to Avery, son of —" Kade began.

Avery swatted the air. "Yes, yes, we know. Son of John and Martha." He looked Raelyn up and down. "Glad to see you're up. Maybe now we can get some answers."

"Yes," Kade said nodding. "I felt it best to speak to you all at once. Raelyn, please come in and have a seat." He gestured to a plush chair next to the sofa. Avery stalked to the window buttoning his shirt and leaned against the frame, crossing his arms. Raelyn took one more survey of the room and eased herself into the nearest chair. Though he was what her dad would have called a blow-hard, she shared Avery's concern. It was time for answers.

"You are in the realm of Alnok," Kade said, "of the Periferie."

"As you've said—" Avery objected.

"The Periferie," Kade continued, unfazed, "exists parallel to Earth Apparent. But this was not always so. In the beginning all was one, harmonious and peaceful. Long after the fracture when the temporals were rescued from Earth Apparent they were given six royal cities in which they lived and prospered: Shaldon, Galdor, Boiland, Tor-Barnoth, Deshill and Durnoth." He paused and looked into the dying fire.

"Then Cosyn," he continued, his voice quiet, "one of the two sons of Arkonai, waged war on the temporals."

"Why?" Jinny breathed, clearly caught up in the story.

Kade looked at her, tears glimmering in his eyes, and smiled. "His heart was twisted by jealousy, pride, hate. The temporals, you"—he swept his arm, motioning to them all— "are the object of Arkonai's love and his most treasured creation. Cosyn coveted that affection and desired Arkonai's power, so he set out to take over the cities. Set up his own rule. When he failed, he attacked. One by one each fell. Durnoth became the final stronghold. Raelyn, Joshua, Gabe and Jinny found themselves in the ruins of that city when you first arrived here."

Kade paused, his eyes on the floor, seeming to relive the long-ago betrayal. "With all the royal cities destroyed, Cosyn and his followers turned their attention to the fortresses of Alnok. All those in this realm have battled against his influence." He shook his head sadly and looked around the room.

"I'm sorry, but I came here for one thing." Avery's voice shook.

"The war began with the temporals, the most hated by Cosyn. What he began here, he has continued in Earth Apparent. In your cities. And your homes."

Joshua and Avery began talking over one another.

"Who is this—"

"Why are we —"

"I need to call home —"

Raelyn listened as the questions gave way to objections and as Gabe joined, a rising chorus of confusion broke out. Kade's invitation had said Peter's cure was in Alnok. But it seemed Kade might be saying his illness began there too. What kind of danger was he really in? A lump swelled in her throat. As the arguing continued Raelyn squeezed her hands together, fighting the impulse to cover her ears.

Joshua was on his feet, his voice rising above the others. "I don't care what happens here! I only care about my daughter!"

Complete silence followed. They all looked at Joshua. He didn't take his eyes off Kade, who quietly returned his gaze.

"Perhaps," Kade said softly, "you will find those around you to be worthy of your care." He stood abruptly. "Come, follow me." He crossed the room in three brisk steps and was out the door before anyone could respond.

Gabe and Jinny followed without objection. Raelyn stood and looked at Joshua. He gave a heavy shrug, suddenly looking worn and defeated.

"If you don't think Kade can help, why are you here?" Raelyn kept her voice quiet but didn't try to mask her accusation. Joshua opened his mouth to respond.

"It could be rubbish," Avery cut in as he stalked by. "But I'm willing to give it a listen."

Joshua gestured to Avery and shrugged again. "I'm . . . looking for answers. I just don't know if this is it."

Raelyn nodded. His reasons for being here were his business. She and Joshua followed Avery, joining Kade and the others who were gathered around an emerald-green tapestry at the end of a long hall. An illegible gold script drifted and swirled across the fabric, as though caught in the flow of a peaceful river. The script slowed its movement and settled into words.

Kade was talking. "This tapestry records Alnok's entry into Earth Apparent. In the beginning there were . . . openings, if you will, at each of the temporal villages and kingdoms. They allowed the guardians from Alnok to come and go from your world. We called these openings 'prescails'. But we discovered Cosyn using these entry points to send his horde into Earth Apparent."

Raelyn read a few lines of the script:

The Prescail, our entrance to Earth Apparent, opened for the heralds, the protectors, and the soldiers. We hold back the darkness and usher the temporals into the light . . .

Before she could read on, Kade was leading them further down the soaring hallway. The script went back to its flow and ripple of unintelligible marks.

They came to a high-ceilinged alcove where the hall branched off in two directions. Multicolored glass glittered in an arched window high above their heads. Kade stopped below the window and pointed. The light took on a more uniformed look and then figures began to appear. One shadow took the form of a man. He stood in the midst of a dense forest before an circular gateway, the center of which held an empty void. The shadow man raised a scepter, slender and shining, and pointed it to the archway. A flicker and then a glow pulsed as a pale blue light grew at the center, part of it peeling away, as though from a page in a book. With a disconcerting crackle, streaking shadows poured from the dense forest surrounding the man and disappeared through the opening, behind the folded layer. As they did so, a cold gust of wind passed from the far hallway through the alcove. Then the shadow man walked through the doorway and was gone.

The scene dissolved and became a multicolored window once again.

"One by one we destroyed the prescails, impeding our own access to Earth Apparent, but eliminating Cosyn's." Kade paused. His face fell and his eyes held so much sadness Raelyn's throat constricted in response.

"Or so we thought." Kade shook his head. "Cosyn constructed his own points of entry, though poor mimicries of the prescails. They are plyes. Distorted, warped, but serving his purpose."

Kade silently walked back the way they had come, his hands folded behind his back and his steps measured. They all followed without comment.

As they reached the wood-paneled room, Gabe and Jinny whispered furiously to each other. "Dark matter . . . bosonic string theory . . . Calabi-Yau." Words Raelyn barely recognized, drifted from their conversation as they made their way back to the sofa. Raelyn, Joshua, and Avery stood silently, just inside the doorway.

Kade resumed his position in front of the fireplace before he spoke. "There have been occasions, instances when the Periferie has been revealed to temporals. But most do not have the capacity, nor the desire, to see." He looked pointedly at Avery. "As I am sure Gabe has explained, technology from Earth Apparent, all of which Cosyn has distorted, misused, manipulated, and spoiled, does not work in Alnok."

Raelyn took a firm step forward. "What does this have to do with what you promised?" Her hand shook as she pushed a strand of hair back and touched the scar on her cheek. Kade's eyes flitted to the scar then held her gaze. There was no trace of his usual smile.

"You have a connection to Alnok. And because of this, Cosyn has targeted you. And your families."

"A connection?" Jinny whispered. "How?"

Kade smiled. "In time." He brought up his hands and the golden light from his shoulders and arms rushed to his open palms. It cast a warm hue throughout the room, breaking up the dark corners and illuminating their faces. "There is hope. A light penetrating the shadows. Trust me when I say you were chosen long before Earth Apparent even came to be. And because of this, you have been made a target. You and your families. Perhaps particularly your families. But do not doubt that those called are also equipped."

Gabe stared into the light in Kade's hands. "Equipped for what?"

Kade glanced at them one by one. "We in the Periferie were tasked with guarding Earth Apparent. But you must break Cosyn's link to your world. There are three known plyes, heavily guarded by Cosyn's horde. One is in the city of Olyaund, near the kingdom of Shalhala. Through this portal he has located and launched his attacks against you and your families. With it destroyed, his hold will be loosened."

Raelyn, whose stomach had not stopped its steady loops, eased back into her seat. Joshua returned to the little table. Avery remained in the doorway.

"Kade," Raelyn began, keeping her voice low and steady.

"Yes, child?"

"Why us?"

Kade looked deep into her eyes. "You were chosen because of your unique connection to the Periferie. Because only you are equipped to reach these plyes." Then he smiled. "And because you are the last warriors Cosyn would ever expect."

CHAPTER SEVEN

Lydia and a group of Malvokians brought a lunch of cured meats, bread, and vegetables. After a few days of only broth, Raelyn's stomach growled. As they ate, Kade excused himself to meet with the ruler of the kingdom of Malvok.

"Lord Talmond and Lady Ryla have planned a banquet in your honor tonight," he said as he stopped in the doorway. "Know this, we must act soon. Raelyn, Gabe, and Joshua's arrival in Durnoth has exposed your presence. I do not believe the varga attack was by chance."

Raelyn glanced around the room and saw her apprehension mirrored in each of their faces.

With Kade gone, they picked at the food in silence. The weight of the information blanketed the room, heavy and stifling. After a few minutes, Joshua slipped out without a word. Raelyn glanced at Avery, Jinny, and Gabe, but no one had noticed.

"Do you suppose our families are in real danger?" Jinny finally spoke, her voice tense.

"There was always danger," Gabe said. "It hasn't changed now that we know why."

"Aye," Avery chimed in. "We all have people we want to protect. But I question if this is the correct course."

Joshua, his hands on each side of the door frame, leaned into the room. "You need to see this," he said to Raelyn then gave the others a sweeping glance. "All of you." He pushed himself back through the doorway.

Raelyn glanced around at the others. Without comment, they made their way out to the hallway and found Joshua already at the end at the alcove with the high window.

Raelyn looked at the muted panes as she caught up. Light danced quietly, spinning and turning the colors. But Joshua wasn't looking at the window. He was studying a massive blue tapestry on the adjacent wall, twice the size of the green one, and nestled into a recessed niche flanked by torches. Gold markings flitted from top to bottom. Joshua took two steps back to join Raelyn.

"Well?" Avery finally asked, not masking his impatience.

"Just wait." Joshua's eyes scanned the hem of the hanging. "Here." He hastened forward, pointing to the lowest portion of the drape. Raelyn joined him and inspected just above his finger. The script glowed, pulsed, and settled into two names.

"Joshua Samuel," Raelyn read aloud. "Joshua — wait, is that you?" She looked up at him. He gave a short nod.

"Yep, and here," he said, pointing to another location on the tapestry.

"Raelyn Angeline," Raelyn murmured. She followed a delicate thread and two other names appeared: Fulton and Virginia. The thread continued like a meandering vine, tiny green leaves shooting off at intervals. More names, dates, grandparents, leading to names she didn't recognize.

Gabe and Jinny joined, searching for their own names and tracing their parents and beyond.

Avery stood rooted with his arms tightly crossed. "This must be some kind of coincidence."

Raelyn returned to the bottom row of names. "Avery Waightstill," she called and turned to Avery. "Is that you? Unusual name for coincidence."

Avery bolted forward and studied his name. They all traced their lineage to the middle of the tapestry but the light was too dim and the tapestry too tall to read further. Stunned curiosity had taken over. Joshua dragged a stately table from the opposite side of the alcove and gestured to Gabe. "Give me a hand?"

Gabe nodded and steadied it as Joshua climbed on top. He raised onto his toes and began calling out names.

"Mikah, Joash . . ." He moved his finger to the left. "Mattias, Rachel . . ."

He shifted to his right and continued. "Ichabod, Phineas, Obediah . . ." He craned his head to look at the topmost names leaning back as far as he dared.

"Moses and Nahor," he finished, before easing back to the floor.

"You're telling me——" Avery began.

"We're all related," Jinny finished with a laugh.

"There's something else," Joshua said, his voice low and humorless, evaporating Jinny's chuckle. He glanced up and down the hall. "Not here," he whispered and marched back to the drawing room.

Once they had shuffled back into the room they stood in a semi-circle around Joshua. He looked at them sternly. "The tea."

Raelyn took a sharp breath. Poison? Hallucinogen? Both?

"It's like Kade says," he continued.

"What do you mean?" Jinny asked, narrowing her eyes.

"I stopped drinking it after I got to the castle."

Gabe looked him up and down. "But you're still here. You look the same. I thought Kade said you'd . . ." He looked around as though searching for the word.

"Fade," Raelyn finished.

"Right!" Gabe said pointing at her.

"At first," Joshua said, "I felt the dizziness, the blurred vision. But after Kade's explanation, it made me wonder."

"And?" Avery asked.

"I don't know if it's been long enough, but I've caught . . . glimpses. A noise I recognize. I've even caught sight of — well of someone I recognize. From home."

"You're kidding," Gabe breathed.

"And"— Joshua continued looking at him and then around the group— "I think they knew I was there."

"So we shouldn't take another sip of that stuff." Avery crossed his arms.

"I'm not saying that. The longer I go the less I can focus, even walk straight. The headache and nausea are coming back."

"But if it's possible . . ." Avery studied the floor as he wandered to a chair and sat down.

"We might be able to see our families?" Jinny asked as she twisted at a corner of her tunic.

Joshua shook his head. "I don't know." He walked back to the fire, massaging the back of his neck, and slumped into a chair. Raelyn wondered how long she could go without drinking the seripyn. She glanced around the room. She had heard cars, voices. Would she see her apartment? The coffee shop? Her dad? Peter?

Lydia bounced into the room, followed by a woman and three men. The blue tendrils drifted from her hair, her shoulders, even her feet. Raelyn's heart ached again at the similarities to her little brother. Contagious joy. Impish smile. She eyed each of them and then addressed Raelyn. "Kade has sent me to gather you all for the banquet."

"Bah, good Lord," Avery said. He rolled his eyes as he heaved himself out of the chair and stalked out of the room. One of the male attendants hurried after him.

Gabe looked from Joshua to Raelyn. His face was tense, but his eyes were bright with eagerness. "I came here for one thing, but we're not going anywhere tonight. Maybe meeting others in this dimension will be helpful." He shoved his hands into the back pockets of his leather pants, waiting for Jinny before they both walked out, followed by the second man and the woman.

Lydia looked back at Raelyn, who didn't move. A party was the last thing she wanted.

Joshua took a deep breath. "How did you put it? Let's see how far this rabbit hole goes." He smiled, although it seemed forced. She returned the smile and nodded. He looked as though he might say something, his gray eyes holding hers for a moment. Then he turned and took a few unsteady steps to the door. The remaining attendant, tall and lean, held out his hand for Joshua, who glanced at it before walking past.

Raelyn waited until he disappeared into the hallway and then looked at Lydia. Her glowing face was an unexpected source of calm. Raelyn sighed and took her hand. What was she thinking? She was way out of her depth.

CHAPTER EIGHT

Hanging lanterns glowed throughout the castle, flickering light across the walls, tapestries, and marble floors. Soft choral music filled the corners of every hall. The usual flurry of activity was replaced by a quiet, somber mood.

As soon as Raelyn entered her room, Lydia curtsied and dashed away. Candles and oil lamps had been lit and peaceful light danced and mingled with the orange blaze slanting through the window from the setting sun. Across her bed lay a long deep-blue gown, simple and unadorned but elegantly made of soft, fine velvet with matching slippers on the floor. She walked past them to the window and watched the black cloud envelop the sun sinking below the horizon. Raelyn shivered and turned her back to the window. But the cloud seemed to press in directly behind her.

She returned to the dress. Getting ready for a banquet was better than watching the darkness. Like the pants, the dress fitted perfectly. As soon as Raelyn had slid the shoes onto her feet, Lydia returned with a tray bearing a plate of crackers and fruit and a teacup full of caramel-colored liquid. She was followed by a raven-haired woman.

"I'm Samaria." The woman's voice was soothing and deep. She pulled a chair to face the wardrobe mirror and guided Raelyn into it. The light that drifted around Samaria's hair and trailed after her moving hands, unlike Lydia's bright wisps, smoldered like molten pewter.

Lydia placed the tray on the bed within Raelyn's reach. Samaria fashioned Raelyn's braid into a bun on top of her head. Raelyn picked up a cracker and nibbled on it, eyeing the tea.

Samaria asked Raelyn about her home and family. Raelyn was surprised at the ease with which she talked about her classes, her job, even her brother. Like Kade, Lydia, and Abigail, Samaria's serene presence eased Raelyn's apprehension. Lydia stood next to the bed and watched Samaria work.

"You have much at stake," Samaria commented.

Raelyn looked up at her in the mirror and raised her eyebrows. She had said nothing about Peter's condition since waking up in Alnok. She wasn't trying to keep her brother's illness a secret but a strange reluctance prevented her from speaking about it. She cleared her throat, but her words were little more than a whisper. "What do you know?"

Samaria opened a box on the nightstand and sifted through the items. "Only that you are here at great cost. That you are a protector, a warrior, and a target of Cosyn." She retrieved a bottle and dabbed the opening onto her finger. She leaned forward, applied a balm to Raelyn's eyelids, and stepped back. Looking Raelyn over, she smiled and nodded.

"You will find the truth you seek. For now, enjoy the banquet, daughter. Tonight is for you." She scooted Lydia out of the room and followed, leaving the door open. Raelyn looked at her reflection. The transformation was shocking. Shimmering eyelids, dramatic hairdo, elegant ball gown. She relaxed her shoulders and took a deep breath. She tried to smile but with a small twist in her stomach, it faltered. She was no princess. Not even close.

Raelyn sighed and looked at the remaining food on the tray. She plucked a piece of fruit and chewed slowly as she regarded the tea. Seripyn. It helped her adjust to Alnok, and seemingly blocked her glimpses of home. Raelyn grabbed the cup and strode to the washroom. She paused for just a moment before dumping the contents into the basin and watched it disappear down the small drain. A rush of triumph swept over her. She would close the plye, if that's what it took to save Peter. She would do battle with whatever forces stood in her way in Alnok. But no one could make her drink the tea.

A small tap on her open door made her jump. She slid the teacup onto the counter and it clattered as her hands shook. She peered into her room and saw Jinny's head poking through the doorway.

"Hi there." Jinny's pale-peach dress, shorter and more fitted than Raelyn's, was strikingly modern against the traditional clothing of Malvok, as were her fingerless lace gloves. Her shiny, ebony hair sparkled with gems. Jinny smiled at Raelyn and shifted her weight, tugging at her skirt.

Raelyn realized she was staring. "I'm sorry. Your dress, your hair, the gloves. You look like you belong in a fashion magazine."

"I added a few of my own touches." Jinny's smile widened as she held out a hand to admire one of the gloves and then looked up and cocked her head. "Would you like to go down together?"

The fruit and crackers had done little to stave off Raelyn's appetite. "Absolutely." She followed Jinny out, her dress swishing across the floor as they walked down the corridor.

Jinny looked at her feet, clad in white shoes with tiny buckles. "Are you married?" She cast an uncomfortable glance at Raelyn. Small talk didn't seem to be Jinny's forte. But then, neither was it Raelyn's.

"No, no. On my own. I'm finishing my MBA in English. I have an older brother. You?" There was no way to make this conversation feel natural as they strolled down the corridor of a castle in the fifth dimension on their way to a medieval banquet.

Jinny ran a hand down the sparkling stone wall. "I'm . . . a student as well. I live with my parents and brothers outside Seoul."

She stroked the fabric on her sleeve. "Well, with my father. My mother, she . . . um has not been well."

Raelyn nodded. "My brother's in the hospital." But Jinny was shaking her head.

"Her body is healthy. Her mind . . . she sees things. Has fits. Has forgotten her family." She slowed and looked at Raelyn, her dark eyes glittering with tears.

"I'm so sorry." Raelyn touched Jinny's arm. So it wasn't just physical health that was affected. They continued in silence for a moment and Raelyn's thoughts drifted to Peter. An artist. A thinker. If he was in some kind of personal battle, he was losing. What made her think she could do better?

"I don't think —" Raelyn stopped and grabbed Jinny's shoulder again, this time to stop her. A dark-haired man in a trailing crimson cloak hastened across the end of the hallway, just past the stairway followed by two soldiers. A flash of orange light burst from their wake.

"Who —" Jinny began but Raelyn dashed after them, holding up her skirt with one hand. A strange compulsion to follow the soldiers overpowered common sense or fear. Perhaps it was their determined march. As though on their way to a critical decision. Having rejected the tea, a recklessness overtook Raelyn. She came to the crossway and peeked down the hall as they disappeared around a corner at the far end. She held her breath and darted from shadow to shadow as Jinny trotted close behind.

The music died away as they followed the men, just out of sight. Up a set of stairs, down another hall. Raelyn started around the intersection but ducked back behind the wall, bumping into Jinny. An ornate door stood ajar midway down the hall and one of the soldiers, whom Raelyn recognized as Ditimer, stood sentry outside. She dared not take a second look, but she did not need to. With the door open she could clearly hear the conversation.

"Kade, these temporals have no chance of battling Cosyn's horde!" a man bellowed.

"My lord, I understand Arkonai's ways are not always discernible. But his ways are higher than ours. It is not our duty to question —"

"Of course I am not questioning Arkonai's will." The man threw his words like scalding water. "I am, however, questioning . . ." The door slammed shut, cutting the conversation off.

Raelyn turned to Jinny, her heart pounding. Jinny's eyes were wide. They made a hasty retreat the way they had come until they were standing at the top of the grand stairway.

"What did that mean?" Jinny whispered.

"I have no idea," Raelyn said breathing hard. She put her hand on the stone railing. They were each there to, in some way, protect their families. But even those in this world doubted their ability.

CHAPTER NINE

"Kade, these temporals have no chance of battling Cosyn's horde!" Lord Talmond bellowed.

Kade tensed, but he had known this was coming. "My lord, I understand Arkonai's ways are not always discernible. But his ways are higher than ours. It is not our duty to question —"

"Of course I am not questioning Arkonai's will," Lord Talmond shot, his pale blue eyes flashing. Ditimer entered the room and closed the door. "I am, however, questioning your faith in the temporals." Lord Talmond strode to the back window and looked out, his hands clasped tightly at the small of his back.

Kade walked past a heavy wooden table littered with maps and letters. He joined Lord Talmond at the window overlooking the front lawn, now in deep shadow. Several soldiers passed beneath a pair of torches, briefly illuminated before disappearing back into the night. Malvok was as it had ever been, in sleepy anticipation. Napping with one eye open.

Kade faced Lord Talmond directly, gleaming armor on display behind him, with a variety of highly polished swords mounted in stands and shields on the walls. "You would have them escorted by our soldiers."

"Arkonai did not forbid reinforcements."

"Nor did he specify them."

"Arkonai gives tactical latitude."

"At times. At others, the path is hidden until we walk upon it." Kade searched the leader's eyes. He did not discern deceit. But pride? Perhaps it was Lord Talmond's trust in his own capability that led him to question Kade's interpretation of the prophecy.

"You know, I once led our army in hand-to-hand combat," Lord Talmond said in a smooth voice as he walked around the table. He took a seat and looked at Kade expectantly.

"You are a brave and able soldier, my lord. I am happy you are aiding our appointed warriors." Kade kept his voice even.

"But?" Lord Talmond raised his eyebrows.

"But," Kade began slowly, "the prophecy specifies the coming of the temporals. Only they are called to close the plyes." He turned to Ditimer, standing silently near the door. "Why did you not take the temporals to Malvok from the Silom Pool? What was the complication?"

Ditimer lowered his head, his voice deep and quiet. "I waited with Raelyn, Joshua, and Gabriel as you instructed when you returned to Earth Apparent to retrieve Chin-sun. But I perceived a threat from the forest. Before they awakened, I set out for Malvok along the Beorean River. The varga blocked my way south and forced me to bypass the kingdom. I crossed the river into the ruins, but hid the temporals separately so they would be less visible and I could return to the pool for you."

"But you did not return for me." Kade watched Ditimer's normally stoic face. It was creased with remorse. Kade's suspicion was swept away in a rush of sympathy. Ditimer was a loyal and trustworthy friend.

"Nay," Ditimer continued, "again I was intercepted and forced to return to Malvok. When the varga passed I retrieved the carriage and went back to Durnoth." He paused and finally met Kade's eyes. "How is it you came there?"

"Just before I reached Malvok I heard the temporals voices as they called to each other. I hastened to the cottage with Chin-sun in time to thwart the varga."

Silence followed the exchange. Kade gazed at Ditimer a moment longer.

"Cosyn must know the temporals have returned to Alnok," Lord Talmond finally said.

"Aye. I fear it is so." Kade scratched his beard and began pacing. "However, Ditimer's detour may have given us an advantage." Ditimer seemed to snap to attention. Kade hoped the possibility of salvaging the situation eased his guilt.

"Oh?" Lord Talmond glanced at Ditimer.

"Cosyn may know the temporals have returned," Kade said, a smile creeping across his face as he stopped pacing, "but he would not know for what purpose. Four temporals discovered in the ruins of Durnoth may lead him to believe we are once again establishing the temporal cities."

"Perhaps." Lord Talmond seemed not to share Kade's sanguinity.

Kade rubbed his hands together and continued. "I recommend sending a unit into Durnoth as though to fortify the city. Rebuild some of the structures."

"A ruse." Lord Talmond nodded slowly, the corners of his mouth turning up.

"Kade." Ditimer took a step forward. "The Peostrum in Theurham Forest. The shadow has grown. Before the temporals even entered the Periferie. Perhaps this is not the time —"

The door opened and a woman entered, her slender form fluid and graceful. Pale blue eyes, like Lord Talmond, auburn hair that flowed down her back and a crimson glow contrasted sharply with her cream-colored gown, glittering as though woven with diamonds. She took up a position behind Lord Talmond, her movements commanding a quiet respect.

"Do not let me interrupt," she said, her eyes twinkling.

"Lady Ryla." Kade bowed his head. Ditimer did likewise and Lord Talmond looked up at her with a soft smile.

"Now is not the time for what?" she asked, looking at Ditimer.

He shifted his gaze from Ryla to Kade and back, then cleared his throat. "Time for the temporals to enter the Periferie."

"Nonsense." She flicked her hand. "Arkonai's timing is perfect."

"Of course." Kade dipped his head toward Lady Ryla. "However"— he looked at Lord Talmond— "I am uneasy regarding the timing of the banquet. Is it wise to expose the temporals in such a way?"

"What could harm our champions within the walls of Malvok?" Lord Talmond smiled, perhaps to reassure, but there was a challenge in his eyes.

Kade knew he must tread lightly. "Agreed. Nonetheless, the threat lies not far outside these walls."

Lord Talmond's chin rose slightly. "We have long defended the kingdom of Malvok. The temporals are perfectly safe here. Is it not important to show our support, encourage the temporals and celebrate the prophecy coming to its fulfillment?" Lord Talmond eyed Kade steadily.

Kade took a deep breath. "Very well." Lord Talmond had a point. If only to show the temporals their support, the banquet might be worth the risk. And they rarely let pass an opportunity to celebrate.

"There is one additional item I would like to discuss," Kade said.

"Only one?" Lord Talmond's smile was wide and genuine.

Kade relaxed and returned the smile. "For now. Our tactics. We must keep our journey to Shalhala secret."

"Your suggestion?" Lord Talmond gestured for Kade to sit in the chair next to him.

"Should the need arise, I would like to consider using the Aldhale Tunnel." Kade waited for the lord's reaction, but his face was unreadable.

"I see." Lord Talmond nodded slowly. "Opening the tunnel would expose Malvok. Cosyn's use of it nearly destroyed our kingdom. It has been sealed since the temporals left the Periferie. "

"There would be no reason for Cosyn to believe we had opened it."

"Access to the tunnel not only leaves Malvok vulnerable, Cosyn's evil filled that space. It became a den of malice and hate."

Lord Talmond was right. Even a residual evil may be more than the temporals could handle this early in their quest. Kade dropped his gaze to a map of the city spread across the table. Lord Talmond had been Malvok's ruler for ages. His commitment to and passion for serving Arkonai was unwavering. But there was a time when he and Kade were at odds. Lord Talmond resisted the temporals being brought to Alnok in the first place. He did not share Arkonai's, nor Kade's, love for the frail beings. But in the end, he had been gracious in his treatment of them.

"We could ready it for an extreme situation?" Lady Ryla spoke softly to Lord Talmond as she walked around the table to face him. The two looked at each other for a moment.

Lord Talmond nodded and turned to Kade. "I will dispatch a unit to prepare the tunnel." He leaned over the table with a piercing gaze. "For only the utmost need." He stood and crossed the room to a cart near the wall. "They have been briefed on the task?" He poured three silver goblets of wine and brought them back, giving one to Kade and another to Lady Ryla.

Kade accepted the drink "Not entirely."

"Oh?"

"Overall, they are eager to save and protect their loved ones. They do not yet realize the full ramification of the plyes."

Lord Talmond shook his head. "A band of weak, fickle temporals pitted against the enemy of all creation."

Kade knew where Lord Talmond was going. "Great odds produce even greater victories. Where you see weakness, perseverance overcomes. Moments of faltering become opportunities for faith to bloom. Do not be so quick to dismiss what has been put in motion."

"And now, my lord," said Lady Ryla as she took Lord Talmond's goblet and placed it on the table, "it is time to welcome these fickle temporals." She pulled his arm gently.

Kade bid Lord Talmond, Lady Ryla, and Ditimer farewell and made his way across the castle to his quarters to freshen up before heading to the banquet. They would need to make for the plye soon. But the path was uncertain. And Arkonai was silent.

CHAPTER TEN

Raelyn and Jinny followed the music down the stairs and past the castle entrance as the volume rose. They entered the banquet hall beneath a high arch. The room glimmered with intermingled light from the dancing and laughing Malvokians, who were dressed in similar fashion to Raelyn. The aura that radiated and swirled from each of them - bright golds, muted blues, soft greens - created a prism of light. Kade passed through a side doorway dressed in a royal-blue cloak with a small rounded collar.

He opened his arms to the women, the aurelian glow rising from his fingertips. "Raelyn, Jinny you look lovely!"

Raelyn's face grew warm at his paternal voice and offer of acceptance, love, tenderness. A budding desire to believe this was her life, that she was specially equipped for this quest, kindled warm and hopeful, deep in her heart. Startled, she extinguished the unexpected yearning.

"Hi, Kade. Thank you." She fought the bizarre instinct to curtsy.

"I agree." At the voice behind her, Raelyn spun around. Joshua was wearing a burgundy tunic and black pants, cinched by a leather belt. His gray eyes seemed to assess the room, shifting from one corner to another, then to Kade and Jinny before settling on Raelyn. "Shall we?" He held out his elbow for Raelyn as Kade did the same for Jinny.

"I feel silly," Raelyn whispered, not entirely meaning it. There was a certain magical, ethereal current on which she felt she could be swept away. Fears of the varga, alternate dimensions, and evil horde faded as they crossed the grand ballroom.

Three endless dining tables, set for hundreds of people, took up the center of the room. Gleaming candelabras illuminated rows of stately place settings. A few Malvokians, dressed in simple but elegant attire, sat casually, but most chairs were empty as the guests milled about the room. Two women played large harps in a corner, filling the room with a soothing melody.

As Raelyn passed through the room, various groups bowed their heads slightly toward Kade and Jinny and to Raelyn and Joshua. She tried to nod back but it felt more like an awkward head jerk. At the far end of the room a soaring arched doorway opened onto a lavish courtyard and against an adjacent wall a man and woman, seated on elegant chairs, overlooked the crowd from a circular dais. The dark-orange light radiating from the man and the crimson light from the woman blended and diffused to a copper glow between them.

Raelyn and Joshua trailed Kade and Jinny as they joined Gabe hovering close to one of the tables. Gabe's red hair, in flaming contrast to his short green jacket and pale green pants, was combed but looked as though it may rebel at any moment. Jinny released Kade's arm to stand next to Gabe.

A man offered goblets from a silver tray. They each took one and Raelyn stared into the contents. She didn't trust it not to contain the seripyn. And if it was just wine, she shouldn't drink it anyway. A year of AA had taught her that.

Kade glanced at the doorway. "Avery should be along soon. Lord Talmond and Lady Ryla would like to greet you all together." He gestured to the man and woman on the platform.

As if on cue, Avery scurried into the room, his eyes darting in every direction. He had changed into purple linen pants and a long, lavender silk shirt.

Kade offered Avery a goblet. "Welcome my friend." Avery took it and inspected the jewels.

"Now that we are all here, allow me to present you to our hosts." They crossed to the dais. "May I introduce Lady Ryla." Kade swept his arm to the woman. Her ruby lips, stark against her pale skin, curved in a small smile. A circlet of delicate gold sat atop her long auburn hair. She tilted her head forward. "And Lord Talmond." The man inclined his head down to them.

Raelyn caught Jinny's eye. He was the man they had overheard from the hallway. He looked as though he could have been a direct relation of Lady Ryla, but with a chiseled jaw and long nose. His blue eyes took them in with a shrewd gaze. He wore a similar crown to Lady Ryla, barely larger than hers.

"Welcome!" Lord Talmond boomed. He smiled and stood.

Lady Ryla followed suit. The room hushed; the harps quieted. On sudden display, Raelyn was glad she was facing away from the room.

"We have long awaited your arrival," he continued. "There will be much to prepare, and to discuss." He paused, studying the room. For the first time Kade, while not appearing angry, was unsmiling.

"But tonight, we celebrate our fellowship. We toast!" Goblets were brought to the Lord and Lady. "To peace. To love. To Arkonai. And to our Cord of Five. May they find unity, guidance, and victory!" At the last word, he raised his voice and his cup with everyone else and the room exploded with "The valor of Arkonai!" before they drank.

Raelyn held her drink close to her chest, neither toasting nor drinking. Unity and victory. The words made her homesick. The hum of the hall resumed, and everyone hastened to the tables.

"You have seats of honor," Kade said, breaking into her thoughts as he ushered them to the far end of the first table.

Lord Talmond was seated at the head, with Lady Ryla to his right and Kade to his left. Joshua pulled out a chair for Raelyn and Gabe watched him before doing the same for Jinny. When they were all seated, the hall again fell quiet, and even the harps were silent. Everyone bowed their heads. Raelyn did too but scanned the table through squinted eyes. *A prayer?*

Kade spoke, his voice melodic, the words rhythmic. "We pray you bless this night. We ask for favor, for friendship, for love. Above all, we bring you glory in all."

"The glory of Arkonai," the hall murmured in unison.

As food was served, Lord Talmond asked an unending series of polite, but acute questions. "What work do you attend in Earth Apparent? Who are your families? Have you enjoyed the hospitality of Malvok?" He asked each question between bites of food. He seemed most interested in Joshua and his military background, asking him details of his assignments. Of the five, Joshua was the least forthcoming with answers. When Lord Talmond asked about his family, Joshua stopped talking altogether.

Kade intervened. "Our hope, gracious host, is that our Cord will spend the evening enjoying our hospitality."

Lord Talmond's eyes narrowed for a split second before he smiled. "Of course." He waved a hand and a procession of servants brought silver trays filled with an array of desserts. Kade's eyes remained on Lord Talmond. Raelyn glanced at Lady Ryla who was watching her husband, her mouth drawn. Her gaze flitted toward Raelyn and her smile returned. But it seemed sad and guarded. Raelyn looked away quickly, feeling she had intruded on the lady's secret thoughts.

The remainder of the night was a dizzying display of food, music, and laughter. They heard stories of hard-fought battles, beautiful lands, and deep friendships.

Lord Talmond reclined in his seat. "Tomorrow will usher in the start of your journey."

"What?" Avery sat up. "We're leaving tomorrow?"

Lord Talmond chuckled. "Nay. Soon. But we would not send you so defenseless."

Joshua sat up. "Weapons?"

Lord Talmond nodded but said no more.

The night wore away, and the weight of the day grew heavy. Raelyn's back ached and a longing to be home reinforced her weariness. The others leaned in to hear Lord Talmond's next tale of heroism, but Kade glanced her way.

"I believe I will escort our daughter Raelyn to her room. Her injury requires further rest, does it not?" Kade directed the question to her but was already standing.

Raelyn nodded and stood as well. Joshua moved to join her but Raelyn put her hand on his shoulder. "Please, stay. I just need some time to rest. Good night, everyone." They all bade her good night and went back to their stories.

Kade put his arm gently around her shoulder and escorted her from the dining hall. "You are still mending, it seems." He didn't look at her and Raelyn sensed he had more to say.

"We will need you to be fully healed for the coming journey," he continued to prod.

"It's like a dream and a nightmare all at once." Raelyn stopped and looked at him.

His eyes were kind. "So is often the case when we are called to great and dangerous quests."

"You keep saying we were chosen."

"That you were."

"But why me? Who am I? Can I really save Peter? I've done nothing but —" her throat caught and tears burned her eyes. She meant to push a stray hair back from her forehead but instead touched the scar on her temple. Kade's eyes followed her hand.

"How long will you punish yourself?" he asked softly.

"What do you mean?" She jerked her hand to her side.

"You will find no judgment here."

Raelyn's stomach flipped. He knew. Every detail of the accident that took her mom and youngest brother, Harlan, raced through Raelyn's memory as though it had happened yesterday. The sound of squealing tires. The momentary feeling of weightlessness as the car flipped. The final shatter of glass and hiss of steam when the car came to rest along the embankment. Raelyn's head spun for a moment. Perhaps due to the lack of the tea, or simple fatigue. But it felt more like a residual part of the memory.

"Now that I'm here, it seems impossible," she whispered.

"More will seem possible when you learn to forgive." Kade continued to smile.

"Forgive who?"

"Yourself."

CHAPTER ELEVEN

Raelyn stood at her bedroom window taking in the beauty of Malvok. The eastern forest, little more than a mass of green at such a great distance, slumbered in a cool dawn mist. The trees shook all at once, as though a deep shiver ran through the branches. The hovering dark cloud lifted from the canopy and drifted toward her, but as it approached there appeared a swarm of massive black birds. They swept over the castle. Movement on the castle lawn caught her eye.

Peter!

She called out, but her voice was swept away on a gust of wind. He limped through the eastern gate. His brown hair was matted with blood. He looked up and met her eyes. Horror and despair overcame her, pain wracked her body, but somehow she knew these feelings belonged to Peter. She tried to scream his name again, but her voice locked in her throat. She jerked away from the window but her feet were bonded to the floor. One of the birds returned and dove at him, pecking at his face. He waved his arms, trying to beat it back. Raelyn watched as bird after bird descended on her brother, picking the flesh from his hands and arms. Finally, he fell forward as though in slow motion. Raelyn's scream burst from her throat as he hit the ground.

She jerked awake, kicking the blankets in all directions. Sweat drenched her sheets and her throat felt like sandpaper. She drew up her knees and sobbed into them.

The feeble early-morning gleam gradually filled the room with light. Raelyn sat up just as there was a tap at the door.

"Come in," she called, her voice scratchy and raw.

Lydia breezed in, as bright as the sunshine. "Kade has something to present to you today." She set a heavy mug on the nightstand before she opened the wardrobe and brought out Raelyn's Malvokian clothes. She laid them across the bed and looked at Raelyn. For the first time, a frown crossed her smooth face. "You did not sleep well."

"Nightmare." Raelyn rubbed her face with open palms to wipe away the gloom.

"The journey will not be easy." Lydia's expression was solemn. "Drink." She gestured to the mug and walked to the window. "Your triumph will bring healing and hope to many." She turned to Raelyn, her face soft, her eyes wise and compassionate. "Not only your brother." She smiled and was once again cheerful. "Use today to find peace and restoration. Kade will meet with all of you this afternoon."

Raelyn nodded as she climbed out of bed. She grabbed her clothes and picked up the mug before heading to the washroom. She could hear Lydia's sweet voice singing as she made the bed and freshened the room. Raelyn dressed and, with a twinge of guilt, dumped the tea down the sink before she returned to the bedroom.

Lydia led Raelyn on a meandering stroll through the castle. Raelyn listened as the girl chattered about the purposes of each room. But it was Peter who consumed her thoughts. More than ever she wanted to be home. She tried to focus on what Lydia was saying and on the light that glistened from the girl's hands and rose from her hair.

"What's Malvok village like?" Raelyn asked as they climbed a narrow circular staircase to an upper turret. Just as with all the walls in the castle the stone shimmered with its own light.

"It's beautiful. Tranquility amid discord. Filled with farms, cottages, shops. Anything you could want."

"But you live here in the castle?"

"Yes. I serve in the castle. But we are warriors first and foremost. At our coming-of-age ceremony we are allowed to choose our area of training - sword, bow, or staff." She stopped at the top of the stairs and looked over her shoulder. "I chose the staff." Her face was serious, but her eyes twinkled.

"Staff, huh?" Raelyn said. "So coming-of-age, how old does that make you?"

"Oh, I don't know," Lydia said, shrugging as she entered the top-most room of the tower.

"Don't let our appearance fool you. All of Alnok is older than Earth Apparent. Even the youngest of us have served Arkonai beyond memory."

"Served?"

Lydia stopped in the middle of the round room and looked directly at Raelyn. "We serve one another. We serve to protect Earth Apparent. Your enemy is our enemy. We are called to a battle that was waged long ago." She frowned. "And Cosyn grows stronger." She gestured toward an arched window.

Raelyn looked out. The cloud was closer. Or seemed so from this vantage. She could almost imagine the birds from her dream in the dark mass.

"Now you are here, you will find victory," Lydia said behind her.

Raelyn sighed. "I appreciate the vote of confidence." Her head began to throb. "But I'm no warrior." She held out her hands as though to prove her inadequacy.

"So have said many temporals who have been called to engage in the war. No one is called without being equipped," she said. "They all found they were capable, in one way or another."

"Temporals. From our world."

"Our world is your world. You just never knew it until now. Temporals have not been a part of Alnok for a very long time. But when you hear of ghosts, demons, and aliens, those are Cosyn's forces revealing themselves."

"But what about you? And Kade? Do you enter our world?"

Lydia smiled, grasped both of Raelyn's hands, and stared up at her. Suddenly this young girl was not young at all. Nor was she old. She was ageless, timeless. Wise and fierce. A warrior and a protector. The blue light diffused and filled the room. "All the time," Lydia whispered.

Raelyn's head cleared. A deep desire to fight back against the enemy of her world started in her gut and welled into her chest. She took a deep breath.

Lydia grinned and she was the jovial child again. "Come." She pulled Raelyn from the room. "I believe it is time to meet with Kade."

Raelyn said nothing. Her headache had returned in full force and with it the blurred vision. She welcomed the sensations if it meant she could see something from home. Maybe even Peter.

Lydia led her back down the stairs to the back of the castle and out through a set of heavy doors that opened into a grand conservatory. Iron supports, intricately wrought yet thick and substantial, framed four glass walls and an arched ceiling. Pale, luminous marble paved the floor. Trees grew tall in sunken gardens, their pale-green leaves glistening with silver light. Multi-colored ferns surrounded them, and a fountain gurgled in the center. A few of the glass doors were open and Raelyn caught a waft of recent rain.

"Kade will join you soon," Lydia said and skipped back through the doorway.

Raelyn wandered to the far end of the room and found Jinny looking out the window, wearing her tan vest and pants with her hair in a high ponytail.

Raelyn slowed her pace. "Jinny?"

Jinny turned, her face wet with tears. "I can't do this," she cried and covered her face, her shoulders shaking.

Raelyn touched her shoulder. "Is it your mom?" She kept her voice soft as she gently pulled Jinny's hands from her face and looked into her deep brown eyes, " Remember why you came here. I have a feeling you're made of tougher stuff than you know."

Jinny shook her head. "Not just my mother. My father is proud for me to follow his footsteps. After what has happened . . ."

In her distress, Jinny's normally articulated English slipped. She took a deep breath. "I quit school. My grades were slipping and I knew I would lose my scholarship. He doesn't know." Her voice had risen an octave. "I'm not smart like everyone thinks I am. Like I'm supposed to be."

"I don't think that's true. And besides, this seems to be something that requires not only knowledge but heart. And you have plenty of that." Raelyn offered what she hoped was an encouraging smile.

Jinny didn't look convinced. "The letter from the school will arrive any day. I thought I could make it back before my father saw it. If he finds out . . ." Jinny winced and shook her head. She gazed back out the window.

"If we succeed, he'll see things differently." The words might have been more for her than Jinny, but they sounded hollow.

Jinny wiped her eyes and said something else, but Raelyn didn't hear. The room did a quick spin and she closed her eyes, gripping Jinny's shoulder. A roar of voices rose and subsided. Raelyn opened one eye. The room had steadied but Jinny was staring at her with wide, frightened eyes.

Raelyn took a deep breath. "I haven't been drinking the tea," she whispered.

Jinny gasped. "Is it the same as Joshua?" she breathed back.

Raelyn shook her head. "Just like when I first got here. My head's killing me. And my vision comes and goes."

Joshua entered the conservatory and joined them. "Mornin'." He raised his eyebrows. "Everything good?"

Raelyn glanced at Jinny. "I've uh —"

Avery and Gabe strode through the entryway, Gabe going to Jinny's side. He gave her a quizzical look. Jinny shook her head and gave him a small smile.

"Well here we are," Avery announced loudly, opening his arms in an exaggerated gesture.

Gabe nodded and smiled at all of them. "Yes, the Cord of Five."

"Not so fast." Avery put up his hands. "I haven't agreed to any of this."

"Then why did you come?" Gabe shook his head. "The tapestry . . . all of us on it."

Avery narrowed his eyes. "Just because we all share long lost ancestors doesn't convince me this place has . . . answers."

Before the conversation could continue Kade swept into the room.

"I'm glad you are all here," he called as he walked up. He clasped his hands and rubbed them together. Light swirled from them. "Today I present your weapons to you." He paused and swept his eyes over them in their rigid semi-circle.

"You will find them to be . . . unconventional." He smiled.

"This should be interesting," Avery mumbled as they followed Kade to the center of the conservatory.

Kade motioned for them to spread out. "The items have been created by the most skilled craftspeople of Alnok and are perfectly suited both for your quest and for each of you personally." His smile dropped slightly. "The threat grows. You have seen the Peostrum, the shadow rising from the forest?" When Jinny, Gabe, and Raelyn nodded, he continued. "Ever has it hovered at our borders, a watchful menace. Two days ago, it doubled in size. We do not yet know its purpose. But to ensure our success, we must embark soon."

Raelyn shuffled a few steps behind her comrades. Unconventional weaponry sounded dangerous. And she didn't like the idea of being responsible for guns or swords, neither of which she had handled. She felt a flutter of panic take hold of her stomach. It was all too fast. The room did a slow spin before her vision cleared, but she held her place.

Kade turned as another young woman entered the room wearing similar armor to some of the sentries, but more ornate. Long blond hair spilled from a shining silver helmet, detailed with copper engraving. Sage green filaments rose from her shoulders. She might have been a taller, older sister to Lydia. But her blue eyes, steadily trained on Kade, were solemn. She handed off an item wrapped in silvery, velvet fabric.

He bowed. "Thank you, Emaline." She returned his bow and marched out of the room.

Kade turned and called, "Gabriel Michael McKaney!"

Gabe, standing next to Raelyn, jumped. He paused and looked over to Jinny, one brow raised, then took a few slow steps forward. Kade held out the item, keeping it wrapped until Gabe closed the gap between them, then let the fabric fall away. "The Leohfaet."

It resembled a torch of brightly polished metal, with a slender center and flared base. A vine-and-leaf pattern adorned the top where a large flame-shaped globe was held in place by a metal fitting.

Gabe took it and drew a sharp breath. He looked at Kade and stalked back.

"Did anyone else think we might be getting Rugers? Or rifles? Or even swords?" he whispered.

"Avery Waightstill Montgomery." Kade's voice carried across the room. Avery moved forward, his chin jutting out and his short legs taking long strides. This time a tall, powerful man with a pensive frown and a slate-blue light entered the room. He carried a large velvet pouch which Kade plucked from his hands, giving him the same bow. "Tilman."

"Hold out your hands, Avery," Kade said ceremoniously. Avery did as he asked without comment.

"Rocks!" he shouted, his accent heavy with sarcasm. He spun around. "Ye can all rest easy now!" he bellowed. "I have the magic stones of Alnok!"

He stomped back to the group. Raelyn peeked at his hands cupping five smooth stones, each no bigger than a half-dollar. Kade had said 'unconventional', but obnoxious as Avery could be, Raelyn understood his confusion. What were they expected to do with a torch and some pebbles?

"I beg your patience." Kade focused on Avery, his voice unusually stern. Avery quieted, his knuckles white around the rocks. Kade's face softened, but his words remained firm. "If you recall, your physical bodies require adaptation . . ." Raelyn winced. *Does he know I stopped drinking the tea?* ". . . the roads we travel do not cover linear distance, therefore do not require speed. Likewise with clocks, electricity, and propulsion. You are in an alternate realm. The fabric that makes up the physical rules in Earth Apparent do not apply." As Kade was speaking, the first woman, Emaline, returned, this time carrying a small chest. She handed it to Kade and remained in the room.

"Lee Chin-sun," Kade resumed and smiled warmly. "Jinny," he corrected himself. Jinny inhaled deeply and took tiny steps to Kade, her arms glued to her sides.

Raelyn's heart went out to her. Jinny had just confessed to desperate feelings of inadequacy. Raelyn fought the impulse to touch her scar, the constant reminder of her own incompetence. *Uselessness.*

Kade was holding the chest out and opened it to her. She reached in her dainty hands to lift out a delicate circlet of fine metal.

"The Seon," Kade announced.

Woven into a vine pattern, the leaves glinted and shone between golden pearls and tiny pink flowers. Jinny held it in her open palms and looked up at Kade. She turned, and to Raelyn's surprise, a tiny smile played on her lips. She walked back and took her place with the others.

"Joshua Samuel Spurgin," Kade called. Tilman didn't return with something so mysterious to be cloaked in silvery cloth or in a chest. It was clearly a sword in a leather scabbard.

"Bloody brilliant," Avery said, watching Joshua stride to Kade. "He gets a sword. I get a bunch of oversized marbles, but he gets Excalibur." Avery continued to mutter, but no one seemed to hear him. All eyes were on the sword Kade was holding out for Joshua.

Joshua gripped the scabbard.

"The Ruah," Kade called out.

Joshua took the sword but didn't attempt to draw it. Without looking at Kade, he spun around. He eyed each of them intently, his mouth drawn tight. Again, Raelyn had the impression he was assessing, weighing, considering. With an almost imperceptible nod, he strode back to the group.

"Raelyn Angeline Witt." Kade finally called her name. She straightened her back, but her knees were weak.

A different soldier, a woman with smooth ebony skin and wide-brown eyes handed Kade a thin journal. She looked up at Raelyn and flashed a quick smile before stepping back with the other soldiers, a glow of fresh yellow trailing her.

Raelyn walked up just as Kade turned to present the book to her on his open palms.

"The Bokar."

It was tied closed with a leather thong, and the rich brown leather cover was inscribed with the vine-and-leaf pattern. Raelyn took it, resisting the temptation to open it. She expected to feel something, a spark or buzz. Everyone seemed to be enthralled, or at least affected, by their gifts. Raelyn felt . . . nothing. She looked into Kade's deep-blue eyes, two wells of an unending fountain, and saw the glow illuminating his face. He smiled at her, as though he held a wonderful secret. She looked at the journal and then walked slowly back to the others.

"We will instruct you in the use of your weapons," Kade said, as though making a proclamation. "They were designed, fashioned, and created for you alone. Some of you will have the pleasure of exercising their powers right away. Others"— he glanced at Raelyn —"will need to be patient. Those standing behind me have been thoroughly educated in the use of each of your weapons. They will guide you in their handling and techniques, but only you can wield their powers."

Raelyn looked at her journal. No longer able to resist, she untied the leather strap. Her heart pounded. Instructions, insight, revelation. This book could help everything fall into place in her mind and her heart. She opened the book. Her chest tightened and tears of frustration stung her eyes. The pages she had hoped would give her direction were absent. There were no pages at all. The book was empty.

CHAPTER TWELVE

Raelyn closed the journal and reopened it quickly. She flipped it over. Inspected the cover. None of it made sense. The dark leather was inlaid with trailing emerald vines and leaves. One small pale pink flower bloomed at the top.

As the soldiers left the room, Kade gave the group a sweeping glance. "Take the day to consider, pray, meditate. Tonight, we will discuss our next move."

"Kade." Gabe rushed up to him, the torch dangling at his side. "I need to ask you some questions . . ."

Raelyn didn't wait to hear the rest. Without looking back, she marched from the room. Back to the front of the castle and through the front doors. Her headache threatened to blind her. Bile hit the back of her throat.

Outside.

Fresh air.

Just get away.

She breathed in the sweet smell of late-summer grass. Slowly the pain in her temples eased. Her stomach settled. But her vision remained unclear. She could hear the muted clop of horses, distant chattering of people, and chirping birds. A rush of wind blew against her face and shook nearby trees. The rustle took on the sound of a distant drone. A plane. Airplane! She searched the sky, but only blurry, billowing clouds drifted in a late-afternoon sky.

Raelyn continued down a path that cut through the castle lawn, clutching the journal to her chest and focusing on each step. She passed the outer gate with no idea where she was going, just a desperate need to escape. She was dangling from a pendulum, swinging between a frenzied need to save Peter and a paralyzing fear.

A gravel roadway wound to the right. She gripped the bookbinding and kept her eyes down, forcing her unsteady legs to carry her further. She couldn't go without the tea much longer.

A hub of activity centered around a town square. Pottery was stacked on tables next to one shop, books on another. The smell of freshly baked bread wafted through the open window of a third. She ducked inside the store and a short man in a white apron offered her a small loaf and a piece of fruit. She shook her head, but when he insisted she took the food and mumbled a thank you as she put her head down and turned to leave. The smell of brewed coffee filled the small shop. She jerked her head up. Not the bakery. A coffee shop.

My coffee shop.

With wide eyes, she took in the scene. Some of the regulars clustered at tables near the window sipping their lattes. Cindy, the barista that worked Saturdays, filled a mug at the counter. Raelyn took a step toward her. A black mass, a smaller version of the one above the forest, overtook the scene. It ate up the tables and chairs as it pressed toward her. She staggered backward and found herself in the Alnok bakery again. Her vision was clearer than before and she glanced at the baker who gave her a wary smile. She looked down. Her fingers gripped the bread, crushing it against her chest.

"Sorry," she muttered and fled the shop.

She continued down the road, determined to find a place where she could be alone. She felt eyes on her. Conversation hushed as she walked by. She was greeted with smiles, nods, and even a few curtsies, but no one approached her. She eventually left the roadway and followed a winding path to the outskirts of the city. Within minutes she came to the immense lake of which she could see a portion from her room. The sun peeked from behind tall evergreens and warmed her face and shoulders. Beyond the lake, mountains rose to snowy peaks. A wide tree dipped its exposed roots into the water, its smooth, translucent bark rippling with a pale-gold luster. Raelyn stumbled to it and dropped beneath the outstretched branches whose blooming yellow flowers floated in the lapping waves.

After a few bites of bread, her head cleared a little. She finished off the food and stared across the glassy lake. Drained, frustrated, and more confused than ever, she pulled her legs up to her chest and took a huge breath. The dream flashed in her mind. Peter, picked apart by the massive crows. She focused on his face. Willing herself to be near him. If she could hear an airplane and see the coffee shop, surely she could catch a glimpse of her brother.

Nothing happened.

Each of the others seemed to have something to offer. Gabe and Jinny with all their scientific knowledge. Joshua the soldier. Avery, well, Avery had himself. *Compared to any one of them, I've got nothing. Nothing to offer.*

She gazed into the water. Iridescent ripples fanned out from the flowers. The water grew murky, then black until it was gone entirely. The lake, the tree, the mountains: All gone. She was sitting on the living-room floor of a dark house. Her father's house. A single light glowed from the kitchen. The scent of cinnamon and fresh laundry brought rushing memories of family game nights. She looked down at her hands, the journal still cradled in them. But it might as well have been a solid brick. She brought it to her chest as she stood and tiptoed across the room until she stood on the kitchen threshold. Beneath a single light her father hunched at their small round table - still, silent, and brooding.

The light sputtered. Black smoke billowed from the ceiling. Raelyn gasped and took a step forward. Fulton lifted his head and met her eyes as the blackness overtook him.

"Raelyn?" His voice echoed.

"Raelyn?" She spun and saw Joshua standing just inches from her. His wet face intense. His hair dripping. She was back in Alnok.

"You've stopped drinkin' the tea." He looked her up and down. She nodded and her knees gave out. He grabbed her and eased her to the ground, then plopped down next to her. "You saw something?"

"Yeah." Raelyn took a shuddering breath. "My dad." She looked up at Joshua. "I think maybe he knew I was there."

Joshua gave a short nod and gazed across the lake.

Raelyn leaned back and looked him over. "Why're you all wet?"

He shrugged. "You bolted out so fast you missed the food they brought." He held out a cloth-covered bundle. The sword lay on the ground next to him.

"When I couldn't find you I decided to take a swim. Clear my head." He gestured to the lake. "The water here, just like everything else, it's different. It's wet of course"—he shook his head, droplets of water flying—"but light as air. Almost like I could've breathed underwater."

Raelyn nodded. "Have you started drinking the tea again?"

"Nope. The swim helped."

"The cloud from the forest . . ." Raelyn gazed over the water before looking at Joshua. "It was in my coffee shop."

He nodded. "Yeah."

"And it spread over my dad," she finished in a whisper. Joshua remained silent. "What are you seeing?"

"At first?" Joshua squinted. "The barracks. The house I lived in with my ex. But . . . also the building where we escaped the varga. And, well other places I don't recognize - towers, an ocean."

"Visions from Alnok?"

He shrugged again. "So, your dad, huh?"

Raelyn looked at her hands. "We only recently began speaking again. When Peter, my brother, went into the hospital."

"Sorry," Joshua said. "Didn't mean to pry."

"No, no, it's okay. My dad and brother. They're the only people left in my life who I really care about. But, it's complicated."

"It always is."

They sat in silence for several minutes. Raelyn, grateful for the reprieve from the headache, watched the flowers fall from the tree.

"When Kade gave me the sword," Joshua said softly, "it all hit me." He finally turned to Raelyn. "I was married, had a baby girl. But when her mom and I split up, I committed everything I had to the service. But I realized, when I held that sword, this is my new assignment." He paused and frowned as he dropped his gaze to the ground between them. Then he cleared his throat. "Anyway, Kade wants us to join him at the pub in town this evening."

Raelyn ran her hand over the grass. "Even now, this all seems surreal." White birds, the size of eagles, soared across the surface of the lake.

"Yep," he said, watching the birds dip and soar. "But now that we're here, there's this feeling . . . like it's always been here. Just out of sight."

Raelyn looked at his profile. A dark stubble had grown over his chin and cheeks. He looked tired but unguarded. He met her gaze with unwavering gray eyes. "It's all strange. A quest to banish evil. And our unit"—he gave a sad, half-grin and raised an eyebrow —"not exactly soldier material."

Raelyn smiled. "I wonder what the others think." She shifted to look back across the lake.

"Well, we know what Avery thinks," Joshua said, chuckling.

Raelyn relaxed against the smooth tree trunk. Joshua's commitment brought a comfort she had not felt since waking up in

Durnoth.

The sun had slipped from the sky, smoldering on the far side of the forest. Raelyn turned to ask Joshua if they should make their way to the pub but something in the shadows of the viridian forest caught her eye. She was immediately reminded of the ripple the varga had made before they launched out of the blackened trees in Durnoth. She shot a glance at Joshua. He was laser-focused on the trees. A legion of giant crows burst from the forest and flew straight into the blue sky. In unison, they sped across the lake, directly toward them. Raelyn jumped to her feet. Joshua drew his sword and stood next to her.

It was just like her dream. The birds that attacked Peter. Her pulse pounded in her ears and her headache immediately returned. Her mind locked. Stay here or run to the castle? She glanced at the Bokar, thin and useless, still laying where she had tossed it. She grabbed it and looked back to the sky.

"These birds," Raelyn said, taking a step backward as the flock approached, "I've seen them before."

"A threat?" Joshua asked.

"I don't know. They were in my — dream."

"I wouldn't take anything for granted." Joshua sheathed his sword. "Let's get back." He grabbed her elbow and Raelyn didn't resist.

Stealing furtive backward glances, they jogged back up the path to the main road. They weren't the only ones to have seen the birds. The townspeople were rushing in all directions, pale light streaming behind each of them. Joshua and Raelyn worked their way around the scramble of people toward the castle. But the Malvokians weren't scattering in fear. Some climbed stairways to platforms at the tops of the houses. Others gathered in the road with bows, watching the skies. There were no cries for help. No one cowered in despair. In fact, no one seemed frightened at all.

Raelyn and Joshua reached the castle gate, gasping for breath just as the murder of crows passed overhead like a rush of wind bringing on a devastating storm. Their call like the horn-blast of a hundred freight trains. Raelyn ducked and covered her head, pressing her arms over her ears. Joshua grabbed her arm as though to seek cover. But the birds didn't swoop down to peck apart Raelyn's arms or face. They continued on their eastern course. And as fast as they had arrived they were gone.

Raelyn continued to peer into the sky, but all was calm. With dusk approaching, they returned to the town to find the pub. Everyone had resumed their normal duties, but Raelyn sensed a heightened tension. Inside, the tavern was crowded and noisy. Sweet tobacco smoke lingered in the air, muting the already soft glow lingering around every patron. Raelyn and Joshua made their way to the back of the tavern and, to Raelyn's relief, were largely ignored. As they passed through a wide doorway into an adjacent room, they found the others at a long table beneath an opaque window. The pub noise became a lively backdrop. Raelyn took a seat beside Jinny and set the Bokar on her lap under the table. Joshua sat across from her next to Avery, who was in the middle of lecturing Gabe and Jinny.

"I've had enough of this nonsense. I spoke with several of the guards. This fight has been going on for ages. It has nowt to do with us —"

"You're wrong." Gabe jerked his hand, hitting the torch laying on the table, sending it rolling to the edge. Jinny caught it and set it back on the table.

Avery sat back with an aloof stare at Gabe. "You think so? Or do you just feel responsible?"

"So what if I do?" Gabe cocked his head and met Avery's eyes. "This gateway was opened by my company. Kade came to me. I sent you all through the portal."

"Just because you're all in . . ." Avery barked.

Gabe glanced around the table. "Our ancestors were all here before —"

"Could be made up," Avery countered.

Gabe leaned over and looked Avery full in the face. "You're here."

Avery scowled and looked away.

"Look, I'm just as much at risk being here as any of you," Gabe said, lifting his voice above the tavern din. "My dad . . . he was accused of something. Something bad. And now he's in prison. The last time I saw him, we fought." Gabe's gaze had fallen to the table as he pushed his glasses up his nose.

Jinny touched one of the leaves on the Seon. It was resting on its brown fabric that she had spread neatly on the table. She turned to Joshua. "Have you seen anything more of our dimension?" Her voice was barely loud enough to be heard over the tavern chatter.

"Yes." His eyes flitted to Raelyn.

Raelyn took a deep breath. "I have too." All eyes swung to her. She told them about the visions in the Malvok village. About the flock of birds. Even the conversation she and Jinny had overheard.

"What does it all mean?" Jinny asked.

"Whatever it means, Kade has made it clear we have a choice," Avery said. "I came 'ere because I was promised a solution to my problem. Even if you could convince me of a portal where a supposed boogie man sends his spookables into our lives, I can't imagine fighting 'em off with a bunch of rocks." He stabbed a finger at the pouch on the table.

"I'm glad to see everyone is here," Kade strode into the room, his boots clunking across the wooden floor. He looked at each of them. The tension at the table was palpable, but Kade did not comment. Instead, he called over his shoulder through the entryway. "Ashbury!"

A harried but smiling older man behind the bar looked up from the glass he was polishing.

"Seven olumens!" Kade stepped closer to the table. "I think you will enjoy this particular ale. And not to worry my young friends"— he eyed Jinny and Gabe— "there will be none of the intoxicating effects. It is brewed using the seripyn leaves." Raelyn thought she saw his eyes flick in her direction.

"I hope you have enjoyed exploring Malvok. It is an altogether enchanting city. While well-protected, I have word from the sentries —"

A man cleared his throat behind Kade.

"Ah," Kade said, turning, "I am glad you could join us." He stood to one side and ushered Lord Talmond and Lady Ryla to the table. Raelyn was startled, but Kade seemed genuinely pleased by their arrival. The lord took the head chair and the lady sat on his right, next to Avery.

Kade stood behind Raelyn's chair. "As I was saying, the evil surrounding Malvok grows. I fear news of your arrival has spread."

"I don't see how —" Avery began, glancing at the lord and lady, but Kade held up his hand.

"I am confident they have not identified exactly who you are, only that temporals are here. I trust you saw the hyram this afternoon. The ravens —" He waited as Ashbury brought and distributed large ceramic mugs to each of them. Then he took the last seat opposite the lord and lady. "The ravens are ever watchful over Malvok. We have been aware of their presence, but their flight to Theurham Forest suggests a renewed interest by the enemy. We have no more time." His voice had become strained and urgent.

"You are absolutely right," Avery said, his voice cold. "The time has come for me to go 'ome."

Kade turned to him with a penetrating stare. "What you love most is no longer safe. Closing the plye here will protect what you have there."

For the first time, Avery squirmed. He looked at Kade, at the others around the table, and then back to Kade. He opened his mouth and closed it again.

"Why do you wish to return?" asked Lady Ryla.

Avery stared at her, though Raelyn couldn't decide if he was considering the question or scrutinizing the lady.

"The future of my company depends on a merger that will take place in fifteen days. If I 'm not there, all I 'ave worked for will be ruined." Avery narrowed his eyes at Lady Ryla, but she offered no objection.

"Kade," Jinny said. "I only speak for myself, but I do not know how to fight this evil. I am not old enough, skilled enough. I do not have the knowledge to do what you ask." She voiced all that Raelyn had been thinking over the last two days.

"It is neither age, nor skill, nor knowledge that will prove victorious," Kade said. "You are chosen. This battle is yours. You will claim victory. But do not look to your own ability."

"Where do we look?" Gabe spoke up.

"Ah, there are powers beyond our understanding. You will come to know, and learn to use, those powers."

Joshua picked up his tankard, keeping steady, resolved eyes on Kade. He took a large swig from his mug and thumped it back onto the table. "I'm in," he said and wiped his mouth with the back of his sleeve.

"Me too," Gabe joined in.

Kade turned to Jinny. She nodded her head as she looked steadily into his eyes.

He reached out his hand and placed it over hers. "I will be with you," he said.

Avery looked around the table shrewdly. But something had changed. "All right," he said slowly. His gaze moved from Lady

Ryla to Lord Talmond and settled on Kade. "I'll wait. For now. But I make no promises to fight. Power or no power."

Raelyn stared into her ale. Her gut fluttered. She was no Laura Croft, Black Widow, or Wonder Woman. She had nothing to offer. But whatever she had, she would use it to save Peter. Afraid her voice may fail, she simply nodded and raised her mug. She stared into Kade's warm eyes. He raised his mug and one by one the others joined. All but Lord Talmond and Lady Ryla.

"The Cord of Five," Kade called and they all drank. Raelyn put the mug to her lips and tilted the liquid into her mouth. The cool ale filled her every fiber. She gave in to the overwhelming relief as her vision cleared and the throbbing in her temples abruptly stopped. She felt sharp, alert. Even strong.

"So, now what?" Gabe asked.

"Sleep, my friends," Kade said rising. "Tomorrow your training begins."

CHAPTER THIRTEEN

Just before dawn, Raelyn stood in the same conservatory as where she had been the day before. The same clothes. The same people. The same empty book. And yet everything was different. She was now part of a team. A Cord, they were called. And she was on her first day of training. She wandered through the solarium shaking her head.

What am I doing?

The woman who had brought Raelyn's journal to Kade strode through the entrance toward her. "Miss Raelyn." She bowed her head, a curt movement. "I am Altizara." She was Raelyn's height with eyes like two deep inkwells of wisdom and mystery. Her dark skin was smooth and luminous. The light around her swirled the color of daisies.

"The Bokar." She nodded to the journal. Raelyn held it out, trying to form questions but with so many, she couldn't articulate one.

"Kade will explain." Altizara paused before touching Raelyn's arm. "Patience."

They both looked over to Kade, standing with his arms pulled behind his back between Gabe inspecting his light and Jinny studying her tiara. Emaline was gesturing as she explained something Raelyn couldn't hear.

"In the meantime"— Altizara resumed her brusque demeanor— "I will teach you the bow."

Raelyn trailed Altizara as she marched through the back doors of the conservatory onto an expansive courtyard. Tufts of white pollen floated on a cool, pale-morning breeze. A stone patio met a lush green lawn surrounded by tall hedges which barricaded the towering evergreens of a dense forest. Three hay bales spaced at intervals roughly one hundred yards away were draped with bullseye targets.

A rack against the castle wall held three bows of varying shapes hanging horizontally. Without a pause, Altizara removed her helmet and grabbed a bow. Raelyn followed, as Altizara tromped through dew-covered grass to a tall wooden bucket holding a dozen arrows, most of which looked as though they had seen several battles. Altizara planted her helmet on the ground and grabbed an arrow. As she loaded it into the bow it transformed, as though shedding an old skin, becoming shiny and new. She aimed fairly high, pulled back, and let it fly. The arrow hit the dead center of the target. She grabbed another and in one motion loaded, aimed, and fired. Over and over she shot the arrows in the air in graceful, fluid movements.

"I'll do it slower." Altizara took another arrow and aimed again. She glanced sideways at Raelyn. "Right-handed yes?"

"Um, yes." Raelyn nodded.

"Watch closely." Altizara held her position. Her left arm locked into place, holding the bow at eye level. Her right forearm was perfectly in line with the arrow. She held the string with her index and middle finger and then casually loosed the arrow. Another bullseye.

"My feet." She stamped each foot into the grass showing their position. "Don't rest on your back leg. Keep balanced between front and back feet."

Raelyn nodded again.

"My back"— she pulled the bow up to eye level—"is straight. Everything faces forward. Only your head turns to look to your target." She eased the bow down and looked at Raelyn. "Of course in the field you can't always depend on having a perfect stance, so you will need to be flexible."

"Got it." Raelyn didn't get it. Not at all.

"Now," Altizara said, raising the bow again, "when you nock the arrow, placing it into the string, let it rest between your middle and index fingers." She pulled the string back. "Let the front of the arrow rest on your left index finger." She wiggled her left finger under the arrow. "Shoot where you look. After some practice, you will learn to aim. Take a deep breath." Altizara inhaled slowly. Raelyn found herself doing the same. "Let it out." Altizara blew out between pursed lips and let her fingers relax, releasing the arrow. Bullseye.

She faced Raelyn and held out the bow. "Your turn."

Raelyn looked at the journal in her hands. Altizara made no move to take it, so Raelyn tucked it into the back of her belt and grasped the bow in her left hand. Altizara wordlessly handed her an arrow. Raelyn took it in her right hand and looked at her teacher who simply gestured for her to take her place at the firing line. Raelyn walked up and tried to place the unruly arrow onto the bowstring between her index and middle fingers. The shaft waved wildly, refusing to rest on the bow. When she felt she had it somewhat under control, she pulled back and the arrow tumbled to the ground five feet in front of her. Altizara threw back her head and laughed.

"Wonderful try, Raelyn!" she cried.

"What?" Raelyn shook her head. "I didn't even shoot it. It fell forward more than anything." But she chuckled along with Altizara who was already reaching for another arrow. An hour passed, then two. Raelyn lost herself in the lesson. Altizara was patient, detailed, and jolly. Lydia skipped in and replenished their supply of arrows. She grinned at Raelyn but did not linger. Otherwise, no one else joined them. Halfway through the morning a tray of biscuits, tea, and fruit was brought out. The women stopped long enough to inhale the food and went right back to the instruction.

By the time Altizara handed over the last arrow, Raelyn had managed to put a dozen of them into the hay bale, a few coming close to the target. Her last attempt landed in the ten ring. Raelyn took a breath of weary satisfaction. Her fingers were raw, her shoulders burned, and her back ached where she had fallen. The sun had risen in the sky, warming the afternoon air.

Altizara looked at her. For the first time, her face was serious.

"We will need many lessons and time is short. Your journey will begin soon." Then a smile broke across her face. "We need for you to be able to hit at least a stationary target." She burst out laughing. "I will see that you are given a glove to protect your fingers."

Raelyn, already used to her teacher's good-natured gibes, chuckled. But now was her best opportunity to ask what she had wanted to all day.

"Altizara, what about the book?" She pulled the Bokar out of her belt. "Why was I given a book with no pages?"

"The pages are part of our quest," Kade's deep voice said behind her. He stood back a few paces behind them, and Raelyn suspected he had been there for a while.

"The book you hold is simply the vessel. It is special. Altizara oversaw the crafting of it herself. But the power lies in the pages, and more specifically the words on the pages. Therefore, until now, we have kept them separate from the book. We will retrieve them in Shalhala." He fell silent for a moment and as Raelyn was trying to pin down which question to ask next, he added, "Your work with the bow is coming along."

"She's a natural." Altizara winked at Raelyn, slung the bow over her shoulder, and walked to the conservatory. Raelyn watched her go. The lesson had distracted her from her anxious thoughts, but the twitter of uncertainty took flight again.

"Kade, I —" Raelyn began, her voice faltering. "I know you say we're chosen. And I know you somehow think I have the ability to fight against this evil. But I don't think you know who I am. Who I really am," she mumbled as she looked at the journal.

Kade moved closer and lifted her chin. "Daughter, you are a magnificent work of art. Chosen for the special abilities only you possess." His smile was soft. "You cannot trust your own understanding. The Periferie lies outside what you can comprehend. You must trust."

"Trust what? Who?" Raelyn's voice shook. Tears stung her eyes. No one had ever talked to her like that. So cryptic and incomprehensible, yet penetrating her heart with love and truth.

"Trust the path before you."

Raelyn searched his blue eyes, oceans of peace and comfort. Gabe and Jinny strolled up, each carrying their battle gear: a torch and a crown. They had their own path to travel for different reasons, but there was no doubt in Raelyn's mind that, if any one of them failed, they all would.

"So"—Raelyn gestured to Gabe's torch—"how'd it go?"

Without a word, Gabe thrust the torch in the air, like an Olympian lighting the flame. The crystal globe flickered weakly. He repeated the motion and a steady glimmer fluttered at the center.

Kade smiled approvingly and led them into the conservatory. "Come, let us see how the others fared."

"I'll see you tomorrow, Rae," Altizara called as she jogged after Emaline. Only Peter and her dad ever called her that. But somehow it seemed right coming from her fierce but friendly trainer. Raelyn shrugged her tight shoulders, a testament to all she had learned.

Joshua, sheathing his sword, met them in the doorway. His dark hair was windswept, and his face flushed. Avery sauntered up, a sly grin on his face. He held the velvet bag with his stones. Over his shoulder . . . a shield. He offered no explanation, but he looked like the cat who ate the canary.

Kade clapped his hands and rubbed them together.

"I believe we should all have lunch," he said happily. They agreed the morning's events had left them starving. A small dining room was located just off the conservatory. Roast chicken, toast, boiled eggs, fruit, tea, and water were laid out across a table. They carefully placed their weapons on a bench along the wall, and Raelyn left her book tucked into the back of her belt.

For a full hour, they shared their experiences between mouthfuls. Avery kept silent as he sipped his tea, peering over the rim. He placed the cup on the table and casually turned the handle away from him. Raelyn knew he was thoroughly enjoying the mystery, but everyone waited for his explanation. Finally, he drew a deep breath.

"The shield, the Cieskild"—he pronounced the word slowly —"is quite ordinary." He waved his hand dismissively. "It's the five stones, plucked the Beorean River at the base of the Bastillion Cliffs, that carry the real magic." He leaned forward, scanning the table.

"Not magic, Avery," Kade corrected. "The weapons are imbued with powers that you can command. Magic is a trick. Sleight of hand. Use of deception."

"Yes, yes," Avery said impatiently. "There are impressions in the shield that hold each of the stones. As soon as I inserted them, I felt . . ." He frowned, and Jinny picked up his explanation.

". . . a tiny spark of electricity." Her voice was quiet, but her eyes shone with contained excitement. "That's what the Seon feels like."

"Yes!" chimed in Gabe. "And when I concentrate on the light I can feel it all the way to my chest. Emaline said not to concentrate with my mind, but with my heart." He hesitated, looking around as though they might find the statement funny. But no one was laughing.

Raelyn wanted to feel happy for the others, but with nothing to share, she was an outsider. The glimmer of hope, the rise of worthiness extinguished in an instant. She sipped her tea, listening to Joshua describe his short sparring session with Tilman.

"He's a good teacher. I've never worked with a —"

"What about you?" Avery cut Joshua off, looking at Raelyn. She choked back her tea.

"I uh, well, Altizara was training me to use the bow," she began.

"But Kade gave ye a book," Avery pressed and looked at Kade.

"Ah, so much to learn and yet, the day grows late." Kade pushed back his chair as he stood. "Raelyn will learn to use the Bokar, just as you are all learning. In the meantime, I think you will find she is a natural archer."

"Yes, well, I'm not that good." Raelyn smiled, grateful for the redirect.

Kade stood with a wide smile. "And now that we are well fed, we will begin part two of the training. Please join me on the front lawn in an hour." And with that, he was gone.

Raelyn glanced at Joshua. *Part two?*

The castle's front lawn was surrounded by a fifty-foot stone wall with sentries stationed at regular intervals. Now that Raelyn was drinking the tea and her body had adjusted to Alnok, she took in the details she had missed the day before. The Cord followed the pathway Raelyn had taken to the Malvok village, which ran straight through the middle of the lawn to a towering arch housing a massive wooden gate, now closed. It appeared to be the only opening in the entire wall. Two small paths split from the main one, leading to a garrison in one direction and a small chapel in the other. From her bedroom window, Raelyn had seen steady activity across the lawn. Today it was quiet and nearly empty.

She tilted her head and let the afternoon sun warm her face. The sky was an ocean of brilliant blue in which billowy clouds sailed. A cool breeze whispered of a coming autumn. They walked to the far side of the lawn where Altizara, Emaline, and Tilman stood to attention, their armor replaced by simple leather pants and tunics. Raelyn smiled at Altizara.

"This afternoon you will be shown a few techniques in hand-to-hand combat," Kade began. "Your weapons are your first line of defense. However, we must be prepared for any encounters."

He turned to the soldiers. "Emaline, Tilman, come forward please."

Altizara put her hands on her hips and smiled as the other two approached Kade.

Raelyn heard Avery snort. Emaline, willowy and delicate was entirely outmatched by Tilman, who flexed his shoulders and lifted his chin. But she was grinning and had eagerly taken a wide stance facing Tilman with her arms up and her hands in front of her face. Tilman's mouth tugged with a suppressed smile.

"Watch closely," Kade said as Tilman took a similar stance to Emaline. Kade shouted "Begin!" and Emaline rushed forward. With a series of sharp movements, she had Tilman on his back. Raelyn shot a glance at Avery, whose mouth gaped.

Emaline held out her hand for Tilman. They were both laughing.

"They have demonstrated a point," Kade said. "Height, girth, and strength mean nothing. Skill, technique, and confidence serve better. Today we will work on the same maneuver with which Emaline here handily put Tilman to the ground."

For the second time that day, Raelyn learned a new skill, a sparring method similar to Harlan's Taekwon-do lessons, but with more fluidity and fewer movements. Altizara instructed Raelyn on basic moves, form, and style. Emaline worked with Gabe and Jinny while Tilman worked with Joshua and Avery. Raelyn sneaked glances at the others when she was supposed to be watching her trainer.

Avery, who was closest, yet still several yards away, seemed to be the most frustrated, having been bested by Tilman. He stood up, face red, jaw clenched, and took a step back to make room for Joshua's attempt. Joshua executed the moves with precision and laid Tilman out within seconds.

"Raelyn," Altizara said sharply, bringing her back to her own training.

"Sorry." Raelyn's cheeks flushed as she pressed her lips together.

The sun had dissolved into the horizon by the time Kade called for the end of the lesson. Raelyn had performed the same move several times and had overcome her trainer once or twice, although she had no doubt Altizara had let her.

As a blue twilight took over they retreated to the same dining room, sweaty, and too exhausted to talk much. A simple dinner was served and Raelyn slipped away to her room for the night.

The next morning, the Cord resumed training on their weapons. Altizara strapped a quiver onto Raelyn's back and Raelyn learned to reach for an arrow, nock it, and fire in one motion. During the afternoon sparring session, Altizara was relentless. Raelyn's muscles throbbed in protest as Altizara pushed her harder, her critiques more pointed.

"Focus, Raelyn," she shouted when Raelyn hesitated a moment and Altizara's foot connected with Raelyn's gut. Raelyn sprawled on the grass breathing hard and glaring at her trainer. She jumped up and readied herself again without comment. This time she blocked Altizara's foot and countered with a swift jab. They learned new moves and practiced until well past dark.

The following morning Raelyn dressed and stood at her window waiting for Lydia. By now Raelyn could find her way around the castle, but she lingered, eager for Lydia's sweet chatter as they walked together. The girl's likeness to Harlan brought a familiar and comforting sense of home. And the similarities served as a bittersweet reminder as to why Raelyn was there.

The dark cloud, silently brooding in the east, drew Raelyn's attention. Something was different. It wasn't closer but was definitely larger. It rose into the sky like a pillar of smoke. And from the center, daggers of light pierced the mass. From the corner of her eye, she caught movement from the north. She fixed her eyes across the river to the black trees of Durnoth as she leaned through the window, straining to see. She gasped and pulled back. Varga. First a few, then a dozen, then two dozen. They slunk from the charred forest onto the roadway near the bridge where, not long ago, Raelyn had fled with Kade and the others. They made no move toward Malvok, but stood stone still, watchful. A line of sentries filed along the wall, facing the river. Raelyn looked back at the mass and then to the varga. She took a backward step just as someone tapped on the door.

Lydia entered and joined Raelyn at the window. "Yes," she acknowledged, "it seems our time may be up. We must hurry." Lydia tugged at Raelyn's hand and led her out of the room.

Altizara pushed her even harder that day. Raelyn lost count of the number of arrows she fired. Hundreds. By mid-morning, she was able to nock her arrow quickly and more times than not, find its mark on the target. During a water break, Altizara announced Raelyn would be aiming at a moving target.

"You'll be using these." She gathered a handful of arrows from the bucket and held them out to Raelyn. Raelyn took them, inspected the blunt, padded tips, and cocked her head at Altizara.

"What'll I be shooting at?"

"Me." Altizara winked and strode toward the targets.

"Wait! I can't shoot at you! What if I hurt you?" She made no move to prepare her arrows.

"Who says you'll hit me?" Altizara said over her shoulder and chuckled.

Raelyn dropped all but one of the arrows into her quiver. She fired the first one. Altizara ducked and it sailed over her head. Raelyn shot another. Then another. Each time Altizara dodged the shots with ease.

"I don't know how to do this!" Raelyn cried after she had fired every arrow.

"Don't just aim," Altizara called as she collected the spent arrows and walked to Raelyn. "Use your instincts. Anticipate my moves. Aim where I am going, not where I am." She handed the arrows over and paused with her hands on her hips. "Again!" she yelled and sprinted toward the targets.

Raelyn snatched another blunt arrow from the bucket. She loaded it and leveled the bow, aiming at Altizara's chest. She breathed and then noticed Altizara lean slightly onto her right leg. She was going to run right. Raelyn shifted her aim right and let go. Altizara was already moving but the arrow connected with her left hip. She staggered but recovered, laughing and jumping in the air.

"Yes! Yes! Again!"

Raelyn's heart pounded and a surge of adrenaline made her hands shake. She missed the next shot. But she was already going for the next arrow and fired again. This time she hit Altizara on the shoulder. Raelyn fired another dozen, refilling her quiver once from the bucket before Altizara raised her arms in surrender.

"Excellent!" she yelled as she walked back to the firing line, rubbing her arm where Raelyn's final arrow had struck. "That was a good start. But I fear you will have few opportunities to practice further."

Raelyn nodded. What she had seen from the window told her that.

Altizara filled Raelyn's quiver with arrows before sending her to lunch. Raelyn trudged through the doorway. She was about to enter the small side room where they had been taking their meals and was nearly knocked over by Jinny rushing by.

"Hey, what's —" Raelyn called but Jinny sprinted out of the conservatory.

"What in the world?" Raelyn asked Gabe, who was sitting at a small side table. He shook his head, his mouth hanging open in shock. Raelyn set her bow and quiver against the wall.

His eyes darted over the table, as though looking for an answer in the wood, or calculating something in his head. "I don't know. I told her she was a natural fighter."

"Yes?" Raelyn took slow steps to the table.

"Then I asked her about the Seon."

"And?"

Gabe screwed up his face. "She kind of seemed annoyed but she hasn't really tried it."

"Gabe?" Raelyn put a hand on her hip and faced him.

He ducked his head. "I just said she seemed afraid to."

Raelyn raised her eyebrows and nodded.

His shoulders slumped. "And that it didn't seem to fit very well anyway."

"Didn't go over so well, huh?" She shook her head and began filling a plate with roast beef and potatoes. "Maybe you need to apologize."

"But I wasn't trying to hurt her feelings. She does seem afraid, and the Seon *is* a little big."

Raelyn eased into the seat across from him as Joshua marched in, followed by Avery.

"So, you're the expert now," Avery was saying, waving his arms in exasperation.

"No, but I think I know a bit more than you." Joshua, several inches taller than Avery, frowned down at him. He began spooning potatoes onto a plate.

"This isn't your unit and I'm not one of your soldiers." Avery glared at him, his voice quiet and icy.

Joshua sighed and put down the plate. "Look, I just made a few suggestions —"

"Like I said," Avery cut in, "ye have no more understanding than the rest of us when it comes to this place. Just mind your own business."

Joshua's jaw flexed as he turned fully to face Avery. "This is everyone's business." His voice was low and tense. "There's too much at stake to risk —"

"Stakes?" Avery's face was nearly purple, his eyes slits. "I know plenty about stakes!"

Joshua took a step forward, putting himself nearly chest to chest with Avery. Raelyn stood, her plate of food forgotten.

"Don't talk to me about what I have to lose. You couldn't possibly know —" Avery's voice caught. Without another word, he stalked from the room.

Raelyn let out a long breath. "Was that really necessary?"

Joshua did not respond but resumed piling more potatoes onto his plate

Kade entered. He glanced at each of them. "It seems we are missing a couple." Raelyn had the distinct impression he knew exactly what had just transpired. He didn't wait for a response. "The time has come to train together."

Raelyn winced. "Kade, maybe now isn't the best time to get us all together. Especially with weapons." She fought the impulse to look at Joshua.

"Unfortunately we are running short on time." He turned to leave. "Meet on the lawn in fifteen minutes."

Raelyn sighed and gulped down a few bites of food before following Kade. She glanced back at Gabe. His pained expression washed away some of her irritation, but she had no words of comfort. She walked out, leaving him to his chagrin, and Joshua to his potatoes.

CHAPTER FOURTEEN

Raelyn paced on the lawn that had become their training spot. Jinny, her crown hung loosely in her hand, stood nearby. The afternoon sun set the tall, defensive walls aglow and glinted off the armor of the sentries who stood at regular intervals. The menacing black cloud, the Peostrum, swelled into the far sky, overshadowing the radiant sunset. It gave a palpable rumble, a distant warning. Raelyn clutched her bow and glanced at Jinny. The rumble faded as Gabe trudged out of the castle, his eyes on the ground. He was followed by Joshua, his sword fastened at his waist and a few strides behind was Avery, the shield slung over his back. All tense and angry. For the next few minutes, they stood in an awkward clump, making no eye contact.

Finally, Kade strode across the grounds, his cloak flapping behind him; the golden light around him a steady blaze. Though unsmiling, his face was gentle. His eyes were fierce but shining with unspoken love.

He passed them and turned, like a general about to address his troops. "Your trainers will join us soon. For now, I have a few exercises of my own." He looked at each of them with a fatherly sternness. "Joshua, Avery, stand here." He pointed directly in front of him. "Face each other." Both did as they were told, both keeping their eyes on Kade. "Ready your weapons."

Joshua immediately unsheathed the Ruah. Avery felt over his shoulder for his shield and brought it in front of him.

"Joshua, make one strike. Avery, deflect the blow."

Without hesitation, Joshua took a large step forward, raised the sword, and brought it down. Avery ducked behind the Cieskild. Light flashed from the Ruah. The ringing metal echoed.

Avery glared at Joshua. "Is that all you have?" he asked through gritted teeth.

Joshua advanced again and struck. Avery barely had time to step back and bring the shield over his head. The light flared stronger. Raelyn glanced at Kade, her heart pounding. Kade watched intently but did not intervene.

Joshua brought the sword down again, forcing Avery onto one knee.

Raelyn squinted against the flash. "Joshua!" She started toward him but felt a firm hand on her shoulder. Joshua glanced at Raelyn as she called out, and Avery used his leverage from the ground to launch himself at his opponent, slamming the shield into his chest. Joshua staggered back, dropping his sword. Avery shot him a satisfied smirk.

Raelyn looked at Kade, who still held her shoulder, while he continued to observe the two men without comment.

Joshua grabbed his sword, already moving toward Avery, whose smile vanished as he deflected another blow. Then another. Each strike was punctuated by a deep shout from Joshua and a flash of light.

Joshua raised his arm once more, but his hit never came. Avery let out a guttural scream and brought his shield in front of his face. A force, driven from the shield, knocked Joshua off his feet. Raelyn's hair blew back from her face. Avery's cry echoed across the lawn, followed by a stunned silence. His mouth hung open as he stared at Joshua, who looked equally shocked.

"Well done!" Kade clapped as he walked to Joshua and offered his hand. Joshua accepted it and stood for a moment. Without looking at Kade he strode to Avery, who took a step back, his jaw clenched. As Joshua approached, his sword in one hand, he held out the other. Avery looked at it suspiciously but lowered the Cieskild to his side. He finally reached out and took it, pumping once in a quick handshake.

Joshua let go and sheathed his sword without a word. He seemed thoughtful but less angry. Avery gave a curt nod as though he had decided something. Raelyn let out a long breath and relaxed her shoulders as Kade released his grip.

"That's what your shield does?" Gabe asked Avery, his eyes wide.

Avery looked at him and then down at the shield. "It's the first time that's happened."

"Indeed." Kade ushered Joshua and Avery back to join the others. "You each possess unique abilities. But you will find your greatest strength in unity."

Raelyn's thoughts flashed to the journal, tossed in a drawer in her room. There was nothing unique about an empty book.

Another rumble came from the sky and they all turned their heads toward the cloud. All but Kade. He was looking behind them. Raelyn glanced back and saw their trainers crossing the lawn, Altizara leading with her confident stride. They lined up behind Kade, standing at attention.

"Raelyn," Kade said, "please walk twenty-five paces in that direction." He pointed toward the castle. Raelyn darted her eyes at Altizara before she walked away from the group, counting her steps, then turned. The others stared at her from what seemed a longer distance than just a few yards. She waited as Kade gave instructions she could not hear. Avery walked halfway to her then stopped and turned back to the group. Altizara joined Kade. He dropped something into her hand. She stepped and hurled whatever

Kade had given her towards Raelyn. Raelyn squeezed her eyes shut and ducked. Nothing struck. She opened one eye and peeked at a sizable stone hovering over Avery, who had raised his shield over his head. He stepped out of the way as it thumped to the ground between them.

Raelyn let out a shaky laugh and shook her head.

Kade waved them back in. "Though some may say firearms"—he glanced at Joshua—"or advanced technology"—a look to Gabe — "are superior, you will find the uses of your weaponry far exceeds any modern device. You supply the power. The source of that power, unlike many conventional weapons, comes from a pure desire to overcome evil. A commitment to serve, defend, even love one another. The more you trust your calling, and each other, the more powerful you will become." He took a deep breath. "For the remainder of today's training, you will use your weapons both defensively and offensively."

They separated with their trainers. For the rest of the afternoon, Raelyn tried to focus on her own training. It hadn't really changed from what Altizara had already taught her, except they were in an open space and Altizara used a shield to deflect the arrows. Raelyn stopped to watch Kade place the Seon on Jinny's head. Emaline tied a blindfold over her eyes. She checked to make sure it was secure and then dashed ten yards away from Jinny before skidding to a stop, turning and running headlong back at her. Jinny stood with her hands at her sides as Emaline closed the distance within seconds. Just as it looked as though Emaline would collide into her, Jinny dodged to her left. Not only that, she also caught Emaline's arm as she sped past, spun her once, then let go with a surprised shout and tore off the blindfold. Both girls stared at each other and then burst out laughing.

Raelyn looked at the bow in her hand; a twist of envy dissolved into a wave of shame.

"Raelyn," Altizara said, and she started, even though her trainer's voice was quiet and tender. She looked into the woman's dark eyes. "If you crave another's gift, you will never truly discover your own." Altizara brushed Raelyn's cheek.

Raelyn nodded. "I just wish —"

What? What do I wish?

But Altizara was shaking her head. "Don't wish. Trust."

Kade called for a halt to their training as early stars winked in the dusky sky.

"In three days, we will embark for Shalhala. It will be a long and dangerous journey. Thus, you must give your final lessons your greatest effort as we have more to add to your arsenal. Tomorrow we will begin here. Sleep well." He gave a quick bow and walked away.

"Greatest effort," Avery said as they ambled to the castle. "What was this, a play date?"

Gabe rolled his shoulders. "I'd hate to see it get harder." The flashes of light from the Leohfaet hadn't exactly revealed how it could be used in an attack.

They climbed the stairs together, then parted to their own rooms, mumbling "good night" but not lingering. If there were more challenging days to come they had a long way to go. Raelyn crawled into bed and was asleep as soon as her head hit the pillow. But her dreams were dark and disturbing.

She stood alone in the charred Durnoth woods, listening to the varga's screeches echo around her. Out of the forest advanced a hulking shadow. She lunged as a fighting instinct took over, intending to put the intruder to the ground. But she grabbed at smoke. Again and again, the shadow moved toward her. Each time she dove forward and each time she missed. Panic took over her mind. Her arms refused to lift again. Now the shadow approached slowly. She could no longer move. Her arms were like lead and her feet fixed to the ground. She waited as a form took shape, human but tall and terrifying. Eyes of burning coal, pallid skin, clumps of black hair dangling from a mottled scalp. Dark vapor rose from his skin. A sour smile twisted his thin lips.

"There is no hope for you." His voice resounded in her ears. "You will die. You will all die." The words faded to a hiss.

"Raelyn . . ." He said her name and it sounded foul, uncouth. Her knees buckled.

"Raelyn . . ." Again, louder, menacing.

"Raelyn . . ." Now higher-pitched, younger.

"Raelyn . . ." Not the beast, a girl.

Raelyn forced her eyes open. Lydia was leaning over her holding a lantern above her head.

She bolted upright. "Lydia, what's wrong?" Her throat was raw and dry.

"Kade has called you all to the entry." Lydia stepped back, no longer in the white dress, but wearing a white tunic and pants, a thin staff in her other hand. She was once again the commanding warrior. "You must dress quickly."

"Why? What's happened?" Raelyn threw off her blankets and began to dress.

"Evil, Raelyn. Evil has entered Malvok."

Raelyn shoved the Bokar into the back of her pant belt beneath her tunic. She strapped the quiver full of arrows to her back and grabbed her bow on the way out the door. Equipped and sickeningly terrified, Raelyn raced down the stairs with Lydia leading the way.

The castle thundered with activity. Pounding footsteps and shouts commanded readiness. Controlled urgency hummed, but had not swelled to panic. The Malvokians were prepared. Everywhere light blazed. Lanterns, torches, even the castle walls pulsed with diffused light. All around the Malvokians shone a fierce radiance. Already the other four, fully dressed, huddled around Kade at the bottom of the stairs. Gabe's torch dangled in his hand and Joshua's sword was sheathed at his waist. Jinny's crown glinted where she had hooked it onto her belt. Avery's shield was lashed to his back. Altizara, Tilman, and Emaline stood along one wall.

As soon as Raelyn reached the foot of the stairs, Kade spoke. "Cosyn has sent a horde of sibukyn through the city gate. The varga have crossed the bridge. Guards are holding them off, but I fear not for long. We must leave now."

Kade hastened through the massive front entrance of the castle and they followed. Lydia jogged next to Raelyn. Altizara and the other trainers marched alongside.

The night was deep in darkness. The full moon, already high in the sky, was obscured in a mist of clouds, offering only dull light. Torches lit the expansive wall. The air was heavy with smoke and the acrid smell of burning wood.

Something black and sinewy darted from the shadows. Avery swung his shield at it and thumped Gabe in the back of the head. Tilman advanced and it scurried away even as he sliced at it. Kade continued to lead them along the castle wall. Raelyn tried to pull an arrow from her quiver, but she couldn't seem to close her fingers around one. Emaline, like Lydia, held a staff. As one creature after another attacked, she sent them back with a flash of light.

"We're going to Shalhala?" Jinny asked between gasping breaths as they approached the outer wall.

"Aye." Kade yanked a lantern off the wall and pushed open a small door hidden in the exterior wall. Lydia grabbed Raelyn's hand.

Altizara spoke low in Raelyn's ear. "Remember, steady your breathing when you aim." She stepped back and held Raelyn at arm's length. "You are a soldier of Alnok. A strong warrior. Stronger than you know." Altizara hugged her quickly and dashed away as she shouted, "For the glory of Arkonai!" and disappeared into the night, followed by Tilman and Emaline.

Kade ushered them through the doorway. A dark road stretched the length of the stone barricade into the forest, beyond sight. A wagon, identical to the one that had brought them from the Durnoth ruins to Malvok, awaited them. An attached lantern flickered light on Ditimer, once again perched in the upper seat, his face set and stern. His hands gripped the reins, and his eyes were fixed on the road ahead. Lydia squeezed Raelyn's hand. Raelyn squeezed back.

Kade waved them into the wagon. "Ditimer will take you down a secret road," he whispered urgently. "There are supplies within the wagon. A two-day ride will take you to an outpost we believe to be safe for the time being." Ditimer grunted, still not looking at the group.

Gabe, Jinny, and Avery had boarded the cart when shouts came from inside the castle wall. "The outer gate is breached!"

Lydia pulled away from Raelyn's hand. Raelyn shouted "Wait!" as Lydia ran back to the castle. Torchlight shone on her blond hair and illuminated her white uniform. Lydia stole a glance behind and Raelyn saw not terror, but determination in her face as she raised her staff. She turned as a jet-black creature with long legs and arms, mouth wide with sharp teeth, skittered from the shadows. Lydia dropped the lantern and struck the creature. But as it fell, a second one launched at her and buried its fangs into her neck. White light flared from her body, sending the demon flying back. Then Lydia was gone.

"NO!" Raelyn screamed and started back through the doorway. Kade grabbed her arm and pulled her back. He pushed her toward the others.

"Go!" he bellowed.

Joshua shoved Raelyn into the cart and jumped in after her. Ditimer let out a rough "Hi-ya!" and the cart lurched forward.

Raelyn gripped the sides and watched as Kade's cloak, a fading shadow, disappeared back through the doorway.

They made a sharp right turn and rumbled onto a wooden ferry, hidden by branches and brush, docked on the river. Ditimer leaped from the cart and began pulling at a rope. The water rushed beneath them. Once on the other side, Ditimer climbed into his seat and whipped the reins. The horses pulled the cart at what seemed an impossible speed.

Raelyn's mind flashed through fragmented memories. Lydia's happy giggle. Her blue eyes still watching her as the creature took her life. Harlan's whooping celebration at his last baseball game. Pulling his limp body from the car. She had lost Harlan. Now Lydia. She looked at her hand that had only a moment ago held Lydia's.

Ditimer slowed the horses to make a sharp left turn and she bent forward, a rasping cry tearing through her throat. Low tree limbs from the forest on their right reached out across the roadway, scraping at her arms, but she barely noticed. She was vaguely aware when the horses picked up speed and angled right, entering the forest. The road there took a sudden, steep drop. Raelyn's stomach lurched as she was lifted off the seat and down the hill they sped. Through her tears, she could see they were headed toward what looked like a dark opening.

They rushed at full speed into a tunnel entrance. Raelyn looked behind as gates slammed shut behind them and they descended into thick darkness. The lantern shone on a low stone ceiling streaking above her head. Joshua clasped her hand, his harsh breathing near her ear. The tunnel went on, for how long Raelyn couldn't guess, but just as she felt her teeth would chatter out of her head, the carriage slowed. Avery let out a relieved sigh.

The chill tunnel smelled of damp earth, reminding Raelyn of her grandparents' storm cellar. The lantern grew brighter, illuminating each drawn, weary face. A halo shone across the ceiling from the lantern, but unlike the shimmering stone of the castle, it was dull and dirty.

"The tunnel continues far outside the city's borders and bears south." Ditimer kept his voice low. "We will stop once to rest the horses. This was once a nest for the sibukyn, a part of Cosyn's horde. It was shut long ago but Kade had the foresight to make it available for just such an occasion. Whether Cosyn knows this or not, I do not know."

Raelyn listened, but his words dissolved before she could grasp their meaning. She bent her head and sobbed quietly. No one asked why. No one spoke.

"Sibukyn," Raelyn finally croaked without looking up. "Is that what killed Lydia?"

Ditimer ignored her entirely. "Below your feet is a hatch. You will find provisions." Raelyn glared at him through stinging tears. He turned halfway, holding the reins with one hand. "Much was risked when you came here." His gaze was stern in the dim light. "Loss is part of war."

"You care nothing for your children?" Jinny asked.

"It is our duty to battle and defend. Lydia was no exception. She will pass on to a better realm. Weep for your loss, but not for those who depart." Ditimer turned back and clicked at the horses.

Raelyn peered around at the others. Each was lost in their own thoughts. Jinny fiddled with the Seon, still hooked onto her belt. Gabe picked up the torch between his legs and let it drop back onto the wagon's floor, again and again, until Jinny glared at him. The Bokar pressed uncomfortably against Raelyn's spine. She felt equally empty and useless.

The wheels of the cart lumbered further into the gloomy, sodden tunnel beneath the forest. The confined space was stale and oppressive. Raelyn's chest tightened with bitter sorrow and continuing fear. Joshua had let go of her hand. Everyone nursed their own heartbreak. No words. No comfort. No hope.

CHAPTER FIFTEEN

"She was a brave girl." Jinny sniffed.

Joshua nodded. "We'll remember her loyalty and sacrifice"— he paused with a deep breath— "and we will avenge her death in whatever way we can."

Raelyn couldn't speak through the aching knot in her throat. She listened as Joshua, Gabe, and Jinny discussed what had happened in halting, confused whispers, the soft clopping of the horses' hooves a rhythmic backdrop. Soon their hushed conversation turned to what lay ahead.

Jinny pulled the Seon from her belt. "When I put on the Seon I see . . . things. Not see exactly. More like an awareness."

"Of what, exactly?" Avery asked.

Jinny shook her head. "Like I could see past the air in the room. Down to the molecules, atoms even. And between those spaces, I could discern people, other beings, angels maybe. I don't know."

"You strike closer to the mark than you know," Ditimer shot over his shoulder. "Alnok holds beings both known and unknown. Good and evil."

"Dokkaibi," Jinny said.

"Aye, each culture and each generation give their own names to the sibukyn they encounter. In Korea, dokkaibi, in other cultures, goblins and the like. This is the deception of which Kade has no doubt spoken. Evil enters your world from Alnok and, for lack of understanding, your world names these things according to what they fear, and even what they wish for. Giving the evil substance and power. The acceptance of many gods, the search for the spirits of temporals, and so on." Ditimer flicked a dismissive hand in the air. "These are all beliefs derived from the trickery of Cosyn. Temporals exchanged truth for a lie." The bitterness in Ditimer's tone was unmistakable.

The cart jerked to a halt and Raelyn leaned around Ditimer. Stones had crumbled from the ceiling in a heap, blocking their path.

"Oh no," Jinny cried. "What now?" Her voice rose an octave. Ditimer leaped from his seat and walked to the collapse. Raelyn followed Joshua out of the back of the cart, the others right behind. They approached Ditimer inspecting the pile.

Joshua squinted close, as though trying to see between the rocks. "How deep d'you think the blockage goes?"

Ditimer picked up a smaller rock. "Moving the stones may cause a larger problem." He sighed as he tossed it in the air and caught it. "We cannot risk the tunnel collapsing. And it is too dangerous for you to return to the castle. I will take one of the horses back. Alone I can cover the distance faster. I will return with reinforcements to clear the path and brace the opening."

"Can't we use something here?" Gabe asked, inspecting the wagon.

"You have suggestions?" Ditimer asked. Gabe shrugged and thrust his hands into his back pockets. Ditimer unharnessed the horses and mounted one.

"Gather your strength," he said, steadying the horse. "I will return as soon as I am able." With that, he spurred his horse and bolted back through the tunnel.

As soon as the galloping was out of earshot Gabe climbed back into the cart and opened a hatch in the floor. He retrieved a canvas rucksack and tossed it down to Joshua. Then one for each of them.

Raelyn caught hers and surveyed the contents: a slim, rolled blanket and a cloak, a canteen of water, some dried meat, bread, cheese, and fruit. She shoved the Bokar into the bottom.

They each chose something to snack on, huddled around the cart, and ate without speaking. The lantern light cast a ring around their feet and heavy shadows on each of their faces. Raelyn shivered as she packed away her food. A skittering echoed from the furthermost end of the tunnel from which they had come. Ditimer already returning? Closer, a stealthy swish and the clicking of tiny, tumbling pebbles. Whatever was there, it was no horse. A wet gurgle, like a breath taken through sickly lungs. A knot formed in Raelyn's stomach as she drew closer to the others.

"I don't know about ye," Avery whispered, "but that did not sound friendly."

Joshua hoisted his pack on his shoulders "Agreed." He adjusted the belt that held his sword around his waist.

More swishing, the echo making it impossible to tell how close.

Raelyn shuddered. "Gabe," she whispered over her shoulder.

He stumbled up next to her. "Yeah," he whispered back, both peering into the darkness.

"You have that torch, right? The um —"

"Leohfaet, yeah."

"Right." Raelyn finally looked at him. He had his rucksack strapped high on his back. "You think you could shine it down there? See if we have company?"

"Yeah, sure, sure." He broke away and rushed back to the cart. When he returned, he tripped over a large rock, nearly knocking Raelyn over.

He eyed his torch uncertainly. "I don't know how much I can get it to light."

"It's okay." Raelyn squeezed his arm. "Just see what you can do."

Gabe took a deep breath and held up the torch as he had before. Nothing. The swish came again. Not close, but closer. Gabe tried again. Still nothing.

"You remember what Kade taught?" Jinny said behind Gabe. "About focusing your heart?"

Gabe glanced at her then back to the Leohfaet. "Yes, but I didn't even get that good with it in training," he murmured. "I'm sure Emaline thought I was hopeless."

Joshua put his hand on Gabe's shoulder. "The Ruah might seem ordinary, but it's more than my movements. I would say it anticipates my thoughts, or feelings. Look at it this way. You can see light in your mind, right?"

"I suppose."

"See it move to your chest. Then down your arm and through your hand."

Gabe nodded, though he didn't seem any more encouraged. But he raised the torch again. A weak glow appeared. Just enough to illuminate his face. He let out a surprised laugh and then clapped his hand over his mouth. The light went out.

More rocks tumbled. The swish and gurgle became constant.

"Try again." Raelyn forced her voice to stay steady.

Once more Gabe lifted his arm. A blue light flashed from the Leohfaet, filling the tunnel, then quickly extinguishing.

Gabe dropped his arm. "It's no use. It's too far."

But it was enough. The knot in Raelyn's stomach clenched. A mass of glistening movement crept from the distance.

Raelyn shoved Gabe back toward the cart. "Move!" But they were already moving. Joshua and Avery pushed the cart, still several yards from the cave-in, perpendicular to the tunnel, creating a blockade. They all bolted behind it.

"Did you see the — something moving this way?" Raelyn stammered ."Maybe more of those animals . . . the same that . . ." As Lydia entered her thoughts, Peter, Harlan, and her mom all flashed through her mind. Anger boiled from her gut into her chest and she took a sharp breath. "The same that killed Lydia." Her voice shook with hot rage. She yanked her bow off her back. "We were given these weapons for a reason."

"But we've only used them in training." Avery countered.

"We know what they should do," Joshua said. "We have two directions. Through whatever is down there —"

"Or through the blocked tunnel?" Avery asked, waving his arms at the pile of stones. The gurgling echoed louder, the rocks continuing to clatter across the cave.

Avery opened his mouth, but Joshua cut him off. "Avery, the shield —"

"The Cieskild," Avery corrected.

"Could you do more than block?"

Avery's eyes darted between Joshua and the pile of rocks. "I, I don't know. Moving isn't the same as blocking."

"You didn't just block me." Joshua's voice was low. He gestured to the cave-in. "Let's give it a try."

Avery nodded slowly, chewing his lip. The horse snorted and stamped his feet.

Joshua turned to Gabe. "You think you could give Avery some light?"

"Yeah, I'll try." He raised the Leohfaet, and it sputtered into a thin, blue glow. He and Avery stumbled to the cave-in and surveyed the blockage.

"We could use the light to keep an eye on what's coming." Raelyn glanced over her shoulder. Jinny, lit by the lantern's halo, was peering over the cart into the darkness.

Joshua nodded his head to Jinny "You think she could see what's down there?"

"It's possible."

"She trusts you."

Raelyn nodded, and they both approached Jinny. Raelyn put a hand on her shoulder, and she startled like she'd been shocked.

"Hey." Raelyn smiled and held off her own panic. "Joshua, well, *we* thought it'd be helpful to know how close those things are."

Jinny tore her eyes from the tunnel. She looked at the delicate crown hanging from her belt. "I won't see them," she said as she unhooked the Seon. "But I'll try to help."

"Atta girl." Raelyn patted her back.

Jinny lifted the Seon onto her head and took a sharp breath through her nose. "The dokkaibi. They are there"— she shuddered — "and moving closer."

Joshua nudged Raelyn and pointed to the exposed side of the cart. "We've got the weapons." He moved around to stand between the open tunnel and the cart. Raelyn followed and pulled an arrow from her quiver.

From behind them, Avery let out a heavy grunt followed by a clattering of rocks. Then another.

But more clinking rocks came from ahead.

Jinny whimpered and Raelyn looked back at her. The Seon glittered just above her eyes.

Joshua took a step back without taking his eyes from the darkness. "How close, Jinny?"

"I — I'm not sure. I don't really see them like I see you."

"Guess."

She shook her head, frowning, and blurted, "Twenty meters."

Raelyn's heart jumped. So close. The swishing filled the tunnel and was now accompanied by a rasping, wet hiss. A thousand angry snakes.

"Avery?" Joshua called.

"Yes, yes. Let me concentrate," Avery shouted.

Joshua drew his sword. "Raelyn, have your bow ready."

A growl erupted just a few yards to their right. Another to their left. Then the tunnel was filled with a deep, angry roar. Jinny screamed and gripped the Seon, squeezing her eyes shut and ducking her head. Raelyn put all her focus on what was coming. It was as if the creatures were part of the darkness, welcomed and aided by the shadows. But that darkness was now an undulating mass. A swarm of shadowed movement rushing at them.

"Avery!" Joshua yelled.

One of the shadows launched itself at Joshua. He swung the sword in an arc and managed to cut down the first creature. A burst of light flashed from the contact. Raelyn recoiled. A hairless black body; its taut skin shiny with a mucous-like substance. Elongated arms and legs ended in sharp claws, its face devoid of anything but large yellow eyes and a wide mouth full of sharp teeth. And more were coming. Showing themselves in the light.

Raelyn dropped the arrow she was holding and fumbled for another. She tried to place it on the string, but it seemed to fight her. Her fingers were stiff, her breathing too fast. All Altizara had taught her evaporated.

"Avery!" Joshua howled and sliced again. Three more creatures dropped. Raelyn continued to fumble with her arrow. Something grabbed her arm. She yanked away and was shoved backward as a bright blue light shone across the tunnel, revealing hundreds of the goblins. They drew back, away from the light and Raelyn looked up. Gabe, his eyes wide, held the Leohfaet in the air.

He swallowed. "Come on. Avery did it." He ran around the cart and grabbed Jinny's hand.

Without Gabe's light, darkness rushed back at Raelyn. She scrambled after him and met Joshua at the cart. He grabbed the horse's reins and they rushed after Gabe who darted into a gaping hole with Jinny. At the center, Avery hunkered beneath his shield, mouth drawn, and eyes shut. The stones from the shield hovered above it in an arc, apparently holding back the rocks from the cave.

"Take the horse!" Joshua shoved the reins into Raelyn's hand.

She skimmed around Avery, pulling on the reins as the horse ducked its head and the saddle scraped the ceiling, showering her with tiny pebbles. Ten paces and she was through. Joshua shouted behind her and slobbering growls echoed through the tunnel. Then a fiendish roar. Gabe shone the light through the cave but the beam didn't reach the other side.

Joshua bellowed, "Avery, NOW!" He raced past Avery, who followed, holding the shield over his head.

The rocks began to fall, the first few sealing them off from the sibukyn. But the stones pounded against Joshua's shoulders and Avery's shield. Joshua reached the end and rolled out. Avery lunged forward as the final boulder fell, crushing his right leg. He let out a raucous shout.

Joshua dropped his sword. "Give me some help here!" He rushed to the boulder, already pushing against it by the time Raelyn joined him. She pushed one side, while Jinny and Gabe, braced shoulder to shoulder, pulled the other. The Leohfaet, tossed on the ground, dimmed.

"On my count," Joshua said. "One, two, three!" Nothing. "Again! One, two, THREE!" Raelyn pushed with everything she had. She felt a slight give. It was enough. Avery shifted his leg out of the way and the boulder rolled back into place.

Jinny rushed around and crouched beside him. "Can you move your leg? Wiggle your toes?" she asked.

Avery let out a harsh breath and shook his head. The sibukyn squawked and hissed just a few yards away.

Raelyn glanced at the pile of stones, imagining their sharp claws digging at the rocks. She bent down. "Avery, we have to move. We need to get some distance from those things." She was getting used to forcing a calm she didn't feel.

He nodded and grimaced as he struggled to sit up with Jinny's support. Sweat dripped from his forehead.

Joshua knelt next to him and looked at Gabe. "Let's get him to the horse. If he can ride, we'll make better time than carrying him."

Gabe and Joshua hoisted Avery onto the horse. Avery groaned as they lifted his leg over the saddle, but he settled in, and then they were moving. Gabe lit the way with the Leohfaet, dispelling the shadows ahead of them with Jinny next to him. Joshua and Raelyn flanked the horse in case Avery slipped off. No one spoke. Raelyn glanced back every few paces. The scratching and grating echoes faded as the creatures continued to burrow at the rocks. They were creating some distance, but the sibukyn could break through any moment. And the Cord had no idea what lay ahead.

CHAPTER SIXTEEN

The Cord plodded down the dank tunnel as fast as they dared. The shaft was wide, but the rock-strewn ground was uneven and unforgiving. Jinny and Gabe led, the Leohfaet casting a cool swath of light over the shining, black stone. Raelyn took a deep, shaky breath as the creatures' echoes faded.

The silent hours slipped by, interrupted by the hollow crunching of gravel beneath the horse's hooves and an occasional sniff or cough.

Finally, Joshua spoke. "Kade said a two-day ride to the end of the tunnel."

"I don't remember," Raelyn whispered back. The escape was a blur. "But when we come to the end, what then?"

Jinny glanced over her shoulder. "Maybe Ditimer will try to reach us on the other side." Raelyn shrugged and shook her head. Hope was little more than a dwindling flame.

"I don't hear the goblins anymore," Jinny continued.

"It doesn't mean they're gone," Joshua said grimly. "We're creating distance, but if they find a way to burrow through, I don't know if we could hold them off a second time."

"Great job with the shield, Avery," Raelyn offered, and she meant it. Avery grunted in response, his head still bobbing on his chest. Everyone handled their weapons in a way that allowed their escape.

Except her.

A flush of frustration rose up her neck and into her cheeks. She had done nothing. Nothing to help. Despite the imminent danger, and unknown destination, Raelyn's chest tightened with self-pity and anger.

"We all did a great job," Joshua said. "If we hadn't been able to work together there's no way we would've made it." Raelyn didn't answer. The reassurance did nothing to penetrate her self-loathing.

Chosen. Chosen for an empty book and arrows I can't shoot. Peter's pale face, eyes closed, monitors surrounding him surged to the front of her thoughts. What if they couldn't close the plye? What if those sibukyn, goblins, whatever they were, got to him? Or to Dad? She would fail them. Again.

After another spell of silence, Raelyn's stiff legs threatened mutiny. She stumbled and reached out for balance, gripping the side of the saddle.

Joshua glanced at her. "I think maybe we should take a break. Rest a little."

"Yeah," Raelyn croaked. "And eat something."

"Hey, y'all!" Joshua called. "Hold up." The horse snorted and stopped as he put a hand on its neck. "No matter what's ahead, or behind, if we don't get some rest we'll be no good with any defense."

All agreed.

Joshua and Gabe eased Avery off the horse and propped him against the tunnel wall. They dug through their packs and ate in silence. Avery even ate a few bites and took some water. Joshua and Gabe agreed to each take a turn listening for any threat.

Raelyn helped Avery get comfortable, careful not to move his leg. Gabe propped his torch between him and Jinny and they slumped over, resting against a cluster of boulders. Raelyn managed to find a dry patch, free from the sharper rocks. She lay on her side as Gabe let his torch's light dwindle so that the lantern bathed them in a yellow glow. To the steady rhythm of water plunking into nearby puddles, Raelyn succumbed to sleep.

"Hey, Raelyn." Joshua shook her shoulder.

Raelyn took a sharp breath and sat up, grimacing as every muscle howled at once.

"We should get going," Joshua said, kneeling next to Avery, who moaned as he was helped to his feet. Even in the dim light his face was pasty and coated in a sheen of sweat.

They packed away their gear and after a successful, if awkward, attempt to get Avery back onto the horse, they continued their trek in the same order as before. It was as though they would never come to the end. And the longer they trudged through the gloom, Raelyn's stomach churned in rising fear. There was no way to know Peter's condition. She had only Kade's promise that he would be okay until they reached the plye. What if Kade was wrong? He hadn't accounted for a delay like this. Perhaps the early escape from Malvok would counter their slow journey through the tunnel. There was no way to know —

Jinny. Could she see what's ahead?

Raelyn elbowed Joshua, who jumped, as though he had been asleep on his feet. "I have an idea."

She jogged ahead and touched Jinny's shoulder. "Jinny?"

The girl gripped Gabe's arm and continued to stare ahead with glassy eyes.

"Jinny," Raelyn repeated, louder. Jinny stirred and turned her head to Raelyn as she continued to walk. She had said almost nothing since escaping the sibukyn.

"I —" Jinny swallowed. "My uncle told us stories about the dokkaibi. My grandmother knew they scared me and told me they were not real." Jinny shook her head and glanced over her shoulder.

"I know Jinny, but they still aren't real."

"But we saw them. We fought them." She shivered. "They are still there."

Raelyn nodded. "Think about what Kade told us. Cosyn is a liar. His weapon is deception. Whatever is back there, they came from Cosyn. They were meant to scare us. But we made it through. You were able to look down the tunnel and see them. To give us a chance to get away. You were very brave." Jinny shot her an uncertain glance, but Raelyn couldn't spend any more time consoling her. "Look." She kept her voice gentle. "We need to know how far we have to go. I don't know how it works, but if you could use the Seon—" Jinny was already shaking her head vigorously.

"If there's something ahead, we need to know," Raelyn pressed. She sounded like her mother. But afraid or not, she needed Jinny's cooperation. Raelyn looked at Gabe for backup. He glanced down at Jinny, who had resumed her blank stare down the tunnel.

"Jin," he said.

Jinny responded by closing her eyes briefly and taking a deep breath. She stopped short. "Okay, okay."

Raelyn dropped back and explained to Joshua what they were going to try, and they all came to a halt, huddling around Jinny. The horse snorted and Avery stirred.

Jinny unhooked the Seon from her belt. She looked at it and then lifted it with both hands, placing it onto her head as she gazed down the tunnel. In the silence, the horse's breathing became magnified, as did the water droplets hitting the puddles. Jinny continued peering into the distance.

She shrugged. "I see nothing. Just darkness." She brought her hands to the Seon, about to remove it, but stopped and gasped.

"What? What do you see?" Gabe asked.

"Light," Jinny said. "A single light. An opening."

"Like an exit?" Joshua asked.

"Yes," she said slowly, squinting her eyes in concentration. "I think so. And movement. Maybe."

"That could be good or bad," Gabe muttered.

"We can't go back," Raelyn said. "We'll have to take our chances. But be prepared."

Jinny didn't remove the Seon. "I don't think this is bad. I can . . . well, I feel no threat." She took off the crown and fastened it back to her belt. No one questioned her assessment and the knowledge heartened Raelyn. There was an end in sight.

Joshua pulled out his sword and started forward. "So we should get moving,"

A small spark of hope erupted in Raelyn's heart. She got her bow ready. They continued faster, risking missteps in the faint light, and staying grouped together. Avery groaned, the new pace rocking him in the saddle.

"Hold on there, Avery," Raelyn called. "We think we found the exit."

"Any way to tell how far?" Gabe asked Jinny.

"It's some distance. Too far to tell. Just an impression. I can't feel distance." She smiled for the first time since before her argument with Gabe.

The creatures behind them were momentarily forgotten as all their focus was on the opening, seemingly a consistent distance ahead. Their excitement waned, replaced by fatigue. Even the horse showed signs of weariness with a drooping head and labored gait.

Just as Raelyn was about to suggest another short break, Gabe called back. "I see something!"

Raelyn strained her eyes and caught a pinpoint of light. There was definitely something down there.

Steadily, the pinpoint grew to an orb. Then an arch. Rapidly moving shadows crossed the light and the sound of unintelligible voices, calling and shouting, echoed down the tunnel. Joshua held his sword in front of him. Raelyn slid an arrow from her quiver. She nocked it, ready to fire the moment she sensed a threat.

"Hellooo!" One voice rose above the others. Raelyn could see a shadow advancing, waving one hand. *Kade?*

"Kade!" Jinny cried and ran ahead.

"Jinny, wait." Gabe grabbed for her, but missed and sprinted after her.

It sounded like Kade, but that didn't mean it was.

"Jinny!" Raelyn bellowed. Jinny stopped and turned, her smile faltering. But it was too late. The man had reached her.

Kade scooped Jinny up and hugged her tightly, spinning her around, laughing, filling the tunnel with his golden light. He set her down and embraced Gabe. Raelyn felt the impulse to run at him, full speed, and leap into his arms, bury her head in his dark hair, and cry. Instead, she released her bow and stowed her arrow, waiting for him to approach.

"Daughter." He cradled her face in his warm hands, looking deep in her eyes, with all the tenderness of a loving father. He pressed his forehead on hers. She closed her eyes and breathed deeply, willing herself not to cry. When she opened her eyes, she was looking at the amulet hanging around his neck, colors swirling around a tree at the center. And then he was greeting Joshua and Avery.

"Ditimer? Where is he?" he asked, looking down the tunnel.

Joshua gave a hurried report of what had happened as they made their way to the mouth of the tunnel. Kade's brow furrowed deeper, and his face darkened.

"We had hoped he might be here waiting," Jinny finished.

"I have had no reports of what happened." Kade gave the shadowed passage one last glance. "Let us go." He took the horse's reins and led them all from the tunnel.

They had traveled along a wide but overgrown path for what felt like hours, under a low sun. Falling leaves fluttered gold, orange, and crimson. The same glimmer was present in the stones, the water, and the trees. Spinning and twinkling like confetti, the foliage covered their path, muting their footfalls in rich, glistening color. Kade led the horse with Gabe and Jinny flanking him like children, afraid to let their father out of their sight. The few words they spoke were muffled by the dense trees. Raelyn settled into the march, anxious about what might follow out of the tunnel, but trusting their guide to protect and escort them to safety.

Kade circled around a tall cluster of shimmering trees. "Welcome to Tegre," he announced. "This way."

As they drew closer the outline of a stone building came into view. It resembled one of the Malvokian outpost towers, though smaller, older, and overgrown. It might have been abandoned, but for a sedulous watchfulness.

"Here we are." Kade stopped in front of two trees. Behind them, a pair of substantial wooden doors were mounted into the stone, like doors to a cellar. He pulled a large weight that hung from the wall. The doors creaked up and out, before sliding back and disappearing entirely into a wide opening. A ramp descended into darkness but still, there were no signs of life. Without another word, Kade led the horse down the ramp as Avery ducked his head beneath the threshold. Jinny shot a glance behind before following.

Raelyn plodded down into the underground outpost, expecting a cold and musty basement. Not only did the temperature warm, the smell of tanned leather, tilled earth, and sweet hay filled the space. They approached an expansive, circular room with a dozen stalls, horses peeking out of a few. A lanky soldier, with a wide grin and blond curls tumbling over his tanned face, rushed to Kade and embraced him.

"Pai-gretan," he said, and turned to the others with a bow. "Peace and welcome friends. I am Griseld. We have prepared a place for you to rest"—he looked at Avery as Kade helped him off the horse—"and heal."

Leaving the horse in Griseld's care, another soldier led them to the interior of the citadel, which was tidy and full of activity. Rows of torches and lanterns illuminated the passages, chasing away the shadows. Soldiers hurried down hallways, some greeting Kade or giving a quick bow to the Cord before continuing. They passed an enormous armory before reaching a circular inner room. A round table in the middle held bread, fruit, cheeses, and dried meat. They pounced on it without comment.

"We will stay but one night." Kade tore a piece of bread from a loaf. "With no word from Ditimer, I do not know what we will encounter."

As soon as he had eaten, Avery was taken to a separate room. When he returned his leg was dressed and bound. A slender soldier, a woman with long, blond braids and soft, blue eyes, led them to two separate, windowless rooms. The men in one and the women in the other. Down mattresses, pillows and blankets were piled against the wall. Raelyn and Jinny rinsed off in a connecting bathing room with basins of warm, herb-scented water. Long, cream tunics and matching pants were folded on the beds. Raelyn changed, arranged her bow and quiver next to the mattress before falling into it, and was soon asleep.

Scratching, like claws on a door, and a far-away screech was followed by the echo of tumbling stones. Raelyn couldn't move. She could only await whatever might break free. She woke with a start, beaded sweat on her forehead, and her heart pounding. The room was dark but for a small lantern hanging in the corner.

"You okay?" Jinny whispered from the adjacent mattress.

Raelyn lifted onto her elbow. "Bad dream. You can't sleep?"

"No. I fear we are not prepared for what is ahead." She sighed and her blankets rustled in the dark.

"Is it something you see?"

"No, but I am concerned for Ditimer."

"I'm sure he's fine," Raelyn whispered, without conviction. In truth, it was suspicious. Shortly following Ditimer's disappearance the creatures had attacked. She closed her eyes, willing sleep to come. Images of Lydia played in her mind. The girl laughing, chattering, skipping down the castle halls. The attack and the flash of light that took her. Raelyn squeezed tears from her eyes and pushed the thoughts away.

"Try to sleep, Jinny. I have a feeling we've only scratched the surface."

CHAPTER SEVENTEEN

Morning came quickly. High windows shone a cool gray, suggesting early dawn. Raelyn and Jinny dressed in their Malvokian clothes, which had been cleaned and laid out. A clamor of rushed footsteps passed outside the closed door. Raelyn glanced at Jinny who had stopped lacing her boots to listen. They bolted out the door, dodging several soldiers who passed them in the opposite direction, and made their way to the room where they had eaten the night before. A steaming kettle, porridge, and fruit awaited them.

Raelyn filled a bowl, glancing through the doorway as a rumble of activity echoed around the citadel.

Joshua and Gabe shuffled into the room. They all mumbled distracted good-mornings.

"Where's Avery?" Raelyn asked, looking past Joshua.

"He was gone when we woke up. Thought he might be here." Joshua shrugged and spooned a mound of porridge into his bowl. They ate in silence. After a few bites, the food sat heavy in Raelyn's stomach and she pushed the bowl away.

Avery limped in, pressing his hair down and keeping his eyes on the table.

"Where'd you get to?" Joshua asked.

Avery shifted his eyes to Joshua and shrugged. "Exploring." He filled a bowl, dropped into a chair, and began shoveling the food into his mouth.

"How's the leg?" Raelyn asked.

Avery shrugged again and took a bite of a yellow strawberry. "Not bad," he mumbled around the fruit.

Kade swept through the doorway, golden light spinning into the room with him. "Eat quickly. We had hoped for a longer reprieve, but we must continue without delay. The longer we tarry, the more we are in danger. The tower is strong. However, even with the might of our warriors, we would be hard-pressed to escape should the enemy discover this outpost. Our scouts are wary. There has been a surge of movement in the direction of Aldhale Tunnel and they are preparing to seal the exit." He took a deep breath. "Your victory at the tunnel was most spectacular. Well done." He smiled but his face was drawn and preoccupied. He looked at each of them, and Raelyn braced herself for bad news. This was where the 'but' always came in. The victory seemed ages ago, fatigue and fear sapping the gratification.

Several shouts sounded nearby and Kade hurried back to the doorway. "Gather your packs and meet at the entrance." He glanced down the hall and made to leave.

"Kade, what happened to Ditimer?" Raelyn asked quickly. Kade turned back, frowning. Avery paused mid-bite.

"I have neither seen nor heard what became of Ditimer after he left Malvok." Kade didn't meet Raelyn's eyes. "I sent scouts back to search for him, but I fear the worst." He sighed and met Raelyn's gaze. She searched his face. Even the light about his head and hands was dimmed to faint wisps. There was something he wasn't saying. She glanced at the amulet on his neck. It was a static circle of colored metal which matched the tree at the center.

"Finish eating," he said. "You will need your strength. Then gather your weapons." He swept from the room.

Raelyn's eyes burned from lack of sleep and her legs ached as she stood. Dizzy anxiety rambled into her mind. She took a deep breath and willed the bubbles of panic to retreat to a fearful simmer as she left for her quarters.

The stone hallway was dim and cold, and the chill penetrated Raelyn's chest. A wave of vertigo tipped the hall to one side, and she leaned against the side wall.

"Hey, Raelyn!" Joshua caught up to her in the hallway and walked beside her. "What're you thinking about Dit —" He frowned, cocking his head. "You okay?"

"I'm, uh"—Raelyn squeezed her eyes shut for a moment— "I think I need some seripyn. The last we had was, when? In the tunnel?" She swallowed and shook her head. "You were going to ask me something?"

"Yeah, I just wondered what you thought was going on with Ditimer. But maybe we should get you some tea first." Joshua glanced back in the direction of the breakfast room.

"No." She resumed her walk, trailing her hand along the wall. "I'll take some when everyone else does. I'm not sure about Ditimer." She tried to pinpoint an exact reason for her concern. But too much crowded her mind for attention. "It's likely he got caught up in the battle at Malvok and couldn't make it back." They stopped in front of Raelyn's room.

"But?"

Raelyn glanced back at the empty hallway. "But . . . something isn't right. He left so quickly. Maybe he was doing everything he could to protect us and go for help. We didn't have many options but as soon as he left, we were attacked." She shook her head. "I don't really have a reason to be suspicious."

"Maybe," Joshua responded thoughtfully. "But we should . . ."

His voice faded as Raelyn was plunged into a deep well, darkness closing in as she sank to the floor. She was back at the hospital. She leaped to her feet. It was Peter's room, the darkness chased away by a single lamp next to his bed. She took an unsteady step forward. Monitors beeped, signaling a continual countdown to his life. A flamboyant bouquet of multi-colored flowers exploded from a vase on the nightstand. A smile tugged at Raelyn's mouth. Aunt Betty.

But her affectionate amusement was doused when she looked at Peter's face. Tears filled her eyes. His ashy skin was pulled across stark eye sockets and cheekbones.

"Peter," she tried to say, but her voice caught.

A shadow, as though gathering the darkness from the room, formed in one corner. The same shadow that had threatened her dad in the kitchen.

No. It's different.

Darker, more substantive. It bubbled and crackled like frying grease. It grew, clicking and skittering, taking over the corner, climbing the walls, spreading across the ceiling, until it hung directly above Peter. It dangled from above, spitting bits of dark matter which sizzled and matted his hair.

"No!" Raelyn tried to shout and swiped at the black form. It recoiled.

She touched Peter's shoulder, but her hand passed through him. No sound, no substance. She was a spectator, not a participant.

But Peter's eyes darted behind his eyelids and the monitor beeped faster.

"Peter!" Raelyn screamed. Still nothing.

The black mass retreated, and a thin light glimmered around her brother. So faint, that if the room had not been cast in such darkness, it would have been imperceptible. The shadow had returned to the corner, spitting and fizzing. The lamp on the side table glowed brighter. A white light filled the room.

"Raelyn!" Joshua shouted, shaking her shoulders.

She wrenched away from him as she scrambled to her feet. "Peter!" She took a step in one direction, then the other, running her fingers through her hair. She had to go back. Peter had known she was there. She was sure.

"Raelyn!" Joshua stopped her pacing and held both her arms.

"I saw him — my brother!" Her heart thudded as she stared into Joshua's eyes. She swallowed hard and continued at a whisper. "He reacted. To me being there."

Joshua frowned. "You're sure?"

She nodded. "There was something else. The shadow, like before, but stronger, more purposeful." She shook her head. "I have to get to him."

Joshua shook his head. "There's nothing you can do!"

She tried to pull away from him. "You don't understand."

"Okay, okay." Joshua let her arms go. "I get it. You feel helpless. But we need you here. He needs you here."

But the fear surged ahead, rising higher, gathering strength. "I can't lose him, too! My dad is counting on me to save him. If I don't . . . I'll be the reason someone else dies."

Joshua ushered her into her room. "None of this is your fault."

"You are so wrong. This is all my fault. My responsibility." She took a great hitching breath, pressing against the coming wave of panic. "My youngest brother, Harlan, was at his first Little League game with my mom. She had cancer but wouldn't miss it, no matter how sick the chemo made her. But she got worse, and by the time the game was over, she couldn't drive them home. Dad was away for work and Peter was in Dallas getting ready for an art show. It was up to me."

Raelyn wiped her nose with her sleeve and began pacing again. The room swayed. Her head spun. She felt drunk. *Fitting.* A fierce shame flushed hot in her face. She stopped and glared at Joshua as though he were forcing the confession. But now that she had started the story, she was ready to finish it.

"I had been drinking. But I didn't want anyone to know, so I agreed to pick them up. Mom was too sick to notice, and Harlan too young to understand. I had sobered up by then, turns out not even over the limit, and I just needed to get them two miles. Two miles. Three turns. Forty miles per hour." Raelyn took a deep, shuddering sigh. The words turned her stomach. She was shaking, sweating. Joshua had gone silent.

"Peter always blamed himself. Thought he should have been there." She looked up at Joshua, hoping to see some kind of understanding for her compulsion to protect Peter at all costs.

"Raelyn." His voice was hard and stern. The soldier. About to give orders for a mission to rescue Peter. "There's nothing you can do about the shadows you see there. That's why you're here." He took a step to her. "Fear can make us forget the reason for a mission. We start to look for alternatives and quick solutions. And it always ends in disaster. Sometimes death."

Raelyn nodded, a slow realization that she had said too much twisting her stomach. She held his silent gaze, gray eyes like stone.

His jaw clenched. "Stay the course," he said, his voice as rough as gravel. He turned back to the doorway. She reached out to him, trying to form an excuse, a plea for forgiveness. But she said nothing as he left the room, leaving the door hanging open.

Raelyn sunk next to her pack, tears dripping onto the stone floor. Her hands shook as she reached inside feeling for the journal at the bottom. It was where it belonged, beneath her full canteen, pouches of food, and a Malvokian cloak. She crammed her wadded bedroll deeper, and her cheeks flushed as she wrestled her pack closed, the tsunami of panic giving way to a wave of sour anger. Jinny entered the room and the door snapped closed. Raelyn buckled her quiver of arrows to her pack and wiped at her cheeks as she stood. She shrugged into the pack before turning, keeping her eyes on the ground.

"Raelyn?" Jinny said trepidatiously.

She pretended not to hear and strode to the door.

"Raelyn." This time sharper.

"What?" Raelyn finally looked at her.

"I know something about Ditimer."

Raelyn hid her shock by glowering at her.

Jinny flinched and a blanket of guilt smothered Raelyn's anger. Jinny didn't deserve her guilt-rage.

Her shoulders fell. "Sorry. What about Ditimer?"

"Well"—Jinny picked at the hem of her tunic— "you asked Kade about him. It seemed like you thought something was wrong."

Raelyn nodded.

"When I put on the Seon. In the tunnel. Right before I saw— felt —the dokkaibi, I thought I saw . . ."

"Ditimer?" Raelyn finished.

Jinny nodded.

"You need to tell Kade." Raelyn put her hand on the door handle. He seemed to already suspect something. He would know what to do.

"Wait!" Jinny rushed to her.

"Jinny." Raelyn tried to sound reasonable, but her anger bubbled just below the surface. "He needs to know. You can't keep something like this from him —"

"I already told him."

Raelyn blinked. "What did he say?" If Jinny was telling her, it was nothing good.

"He . . . he didn't believe me."

"He said you were lying?"

"No, just that I still needed training on how to properly use the Seon. That if I saw him, he must have been trying to get back to us."

"But you think he's wrong."

"No, he's right. At least about needing more training. But I know I saw something. And it was not rescue. It was betrayal." Jinny's eyes pleaded with Raelyn to believe her.

"Okay." Raelyn stared at the floor, turning this new information over in her mind.

Jinny could be wrong.

Or Kade could be blinded.

Raelyn shook her head. "Let's just keep on high alert. If Ditimer deceived us, it doesn't change our current course."

Anger, shame, fear, all pushed and shoved for a turn at Raelyn's heart as she marched to the entrance. Joshua and Gabe were already waiting. Jinny walked up behind her, and after just a few seconds, Avery plodded into the chamber. The busy outpost had quieted, but that didn't mean danger had passed. Their horse snorted and watched them solemnly from the shadows of his stall. His dark eyes glistened.

Joshua stalked to the animal and stroked his neck.

Kade hastened into the stable, carrying his satchel and a flask. "Our scouts have gone ahead. We should —"

"Kade," Jinny spoke softly.

Kade turned his full attention to her. "Yes, my dear."

Her brow was knitted and she took a breath as if to speak, closed her mouth, then tried again. "I'm . . . I'm afraid by what I see with the Seon. I don't think I want to put it back on." Her voice was so quiet Raelyn could barely hear her. Was she also discouraged by Kade's admonishment?

"Yes, the sibukyn. Particularly horrific." Kade nodded. "But the Seon does more than help you see with your eyes, dear Chin-sun. What you saw, everyone could see eventually, yes?"

Jinny nodded.

"The Seon will allow you to see beyond sight. When mastered, you will see even beyond the Periferie. You will see the evil and the good. Because you will see with your heart."

Jinny shifted and fiddled with the corner of her tunic. "That doesn't make me feel better."

Kade smiled and looked directly into her eyes. "But the eyes of our heart see past fear. They see through the filter of love. You can overcome all fear with love."

Jinny looked even more confused and fearful.

Raelyn studied Kade, who looked over each of them. His face was troubled and tired but full of brazen and unapologetic compassion. Raelyn was transported back to her first encounter with him, in the small hut after the varga attack. This was the same display of emotion. Raw, unchecked love. Affection rained, cool and gentle, over Raelyn's anger and eased her shame. Her irritation melted away. She allowed the peace to wash away the hard edges of doubt. Blinking away tears, she took a deep breath. The sudden calm overtook her uncertainty . . . and fear.

Perfect love sees through fear.

She wanted to believe in him. Needed to. For Peter's sake. The monitor had affirmed a steady heartbeat. And the shadow had retreated. For now, he was as safe as she could hope for. She cast a quick glance at Joshua, but he was focused on Kade as he accepted the flask Kade offered him.

"The seripyn should help until we get to the Deshill Ruins and perhaps even on to Kulum. But it is many miles and you each respond differently. We will be escorted by trusty Tegerian scouts." Kade pulled his satchel across his body. It fell into the folds of his cloak. Griseld joined them and made his way to the exterior door. He pulled on a weight and the double doors opened soundlessly.

"We will pass out of Tegre and on to unprotected territory," Kade continued. "When we reach Deshill we will find our path to Shalhala."

He stepped aside and gestured for them to follow Griseld out the door. Raelyn waited until everyone had exited. She stopped in front of Kade and glanced at his amulet, glimmering on the leather cord just below his throat. The inner light was pulsing rhythmically.

"Why so little faith?" he asked, his voice quiet, but not accusatory.

"Faith? In what?" Bitterness filled her words. They passed through the doorway side-by-side.

"In your ability."

"I —" She didn't know how to respond. Her performance in the tunnel came flooding back. Her panicked confession to Joshua. She and Kade slowed, allowing the others to drift ahead.

"You said before that I needed to forgive myself." She waited for him to say something meaningless like, "It wasn't your fault," or "Bad things happen."

"There is belief by some that forgiveness is earned, yes?"

Raelyn nodded.

"But at what point is forgiveness deserved? One good deed? Twenty? One hundred?" Kade stopped and so did Raelyn. She looked into his eyes, deep pools of blue. He moved his hand to her face. Raelyn flinched as he reached her temple. He paused. She relaxed her shoulders and leaned her head into his palm, allowing him to completely cover the ragged scar that ran down the left side of her face.

"No, daughter. Forgiveness is given. As freely as the forgiver wishes. Your worth is not determined by your deeds. The good . . . nor the bad."

"If that were so"—Raelyn tried to stop the waver in her voice as she pulled away from his hand— "why was I given an empty book? I think that says something about my worth." The last statement came out rough, strained. Her face and ears burned.

"Ah, the Bokar." He nodded slowly; his patience unending. "You see an empty journal. But what belongs in a book?"

Raelyn cocked her head and peered up at him. "Pages?"

Was this a trick question?

"Aye! Blank pages. An empty canvas awaiting something new."

Raelyn scoffed. "I'm no blank canvas."

"Perhaps. But there are pages not yet written. Does the same story need to continue?"

Raelyn stared at him. Her story. The one penned in weighty strokes. A circular tale full of repeating chapters and no discernible plot. Her pack suddenly felt as though filled with bricks.

He smiled and touched her arm. "Perhaps you need a new author." Kade took a breath and increased his pace. Raelyn matched his stride.

"Our journey awaits," he said. "We travel into much that is unknown. Cosyn has not been idle. Our path will not be unhindered, but what evil we head into, I cannot foresee."

CHAPTER EIGHTEEN

The moon, a slender arc of white, hung in the east, giving off just enough light to see the wide dirt path along which Kade led them. What at first, seemed to be dancing fireflies in the tree's shadowy leaves, was revealed to be light from the leaves themselves. Griseld disappeared with the rest of the scouts into the woodland. Raelyn shivered as a chill gust of wind stirred the glittering leaves.

Avery, head bowed, trudged ten paces behind Kade. Jinny and Gabe whispered just ahead of Raelyn. Joshua lingered some distance behind.

Raelyn kept her eyes trained on Kade's silhouette. Her emotions teetered between her now-familiar anger, watchful suspicion, and a desperate desire to toss it all and dive headlong into the care and acceptance Kade offered. Thoughts of writing a new history taunted her. Could it be done? Could she take hold of this new world, this calling, and reinvent her life? Become a savior instead of a destroyer? A warrior, not a . . . drunk? Drop-out?

No. Nothing had changed. But like the torches in Tegre, a hope fluttered, feeble and dim. A flame that one quick puff of failure would extinguish. Raelyn tucked the flame away. She knew there was no point, but she wasn't ready to abandon it just yet. Instead, she focused on what was ahead. A journey to Shalhala. A place where the pages of her journal lay hidden.

The road narrowed. Scrubby patches of grass sprouted on the path, signs of less frequent travel. They met no obstacles, and the initial alertness began to wear away. Raelyn's aching feet, despite the light yet sturdy boots, became a persistent distraction. They all began to lag behind Kade, who glanced back and waited for them to catch up.

"We can rest here"—he glanced up and down the path—"briefly." He led them from the trail to a clearing with a tight grove of trees that blocked the wind, but not the cold. He allowed a small fire, around which they arranged their bedrolls. Avery settled some distance away with his back to the group and eventually everyone drifted to sleep. Just before Raelyn's eyes slipped closed, she saw Kade sitting propped against a tree. A shepherd watching his flock.

A rustle in the trees startled Raelyn awake. She waited without moving. The noise did not repeat, but she was wide awake. She looked over to find Kade in the same position and eased from her bedroll, tiptoeing to him.

"I heard something moving in the forest," she whispered.

Kade glanced to the far trees. "That would be Griseld. I am surprised he would venture so close to our position. But we are nearing the outer borders of Malvok. He is being extra watchful." Kade leaned his head back against the tree and closed his eyes.

"Kade," Raelyn said, more softly than before.

He lifted his head. "Yes?"

"I'm worried about Avery." She leaned closer, her eyes darting to Avery's sleeping form.

Kade let his head fall back against the tree but did not close his eyes. He stared at the dying fire.

"We are all in great peril but for Arkonai's protection. But what does worry offer you?" He looked at Raelyn.

She shrugged and pulled her knees into her chest. "Hard not to worry."

"Of course. But take those thoughts captive. Do not let them overtake you. Worry leads to fear. In fear, you lack love. And without love, your ability to ward off the evil is diminished."

Raelyn was in no mood for his riddles. She rested her chin on her knees and remained silent. Soon the others began to stir. The first light of dawn spread in growing shades of coral.

Kade stood and stretched. "Let us continue." He showed no signs of weariness. They nibbled a few bites of dried fruit, cheese, and crackers as they packed in their gear, hoisted their packs, and resumed their trek. The light grew and the mood relaxed. Jinny teased Gabe about his work with his 'flashlight' and they both told stories about their childhood.

"What about you, Joshua?" Gabe asked.

"Divorced. One brother I haven't seen in years. Parents died when I was young," Joshua said as though reading a report. He glanced at Gabe. "I lost the only family —" he stopped and cleared his throat but didn't finish. No one pressed.

The trees sent their shimmering leaves in a gentle cascade onto the road and the sun continued to climb into a clear blue sky, evaporating the morning chill. Ahead, a gurgle of water grew louder. The sun passed overhead until their path ended at a wide stream, the color of pale columbine in spring. It chattered happily, heedless of the hazards they faced. Stones, like polished gems, flashed multi-colored glints of light through fast-moving ripples.

Kade looked over the water. "The Bydan River. It flows into the Chamal Lake, north of Shalhala. We cross here and make for the Deshill Ruins."

They waded through the icy stream. Though never deeper than Raelyn's waist, by the time she was halfway across, her toes had gone numb. The smooth jewel-colored rocks required each step to be a precarious balance through the swift-flowing waters. Jinny and Gabe held hands for balance. Joshua stomped through the water behind Raelyn. Avery, refusing help from anyone, struggled at the rear.

The current picked up midway and Raelyn leaned into it, the water rushing around her torso. She fought for each foothold and strained against the flow — too far forward. She circled her arms to counterbalance, but it was no use. She was falling. She caught her breath, ready to plunge beneath the surface. A splash behind her and an arm gripped her waist.

"Gotcha," Joshua said in her ear and pulled her upright. She wrapped her arm around his shoulder and together they crossed to the other side.

"Thanks," Raelyn said through chattering teeth as she let go of him.

"Don't mention it," he said, shrugging his pack higher on his shoulders without looking at her and following the others up the embankment.

Raelyn looked over her shoulder. Avery, soaking wet and cursing, was nearly halfway across the river. He stopped at a high point, the water only coming to his knees. He looked upstream and then down, his chest heaving.

"Avery?" Raelyn called.

He either didn't hear or ignored her. Instead, he pulled his shield from his back. Raelyn had a mental flash of Avery using it to float down the river.

But he had other intentions.

He strapped it to his left arm and crouched. The river flowed around him. It appeared he might be taking a break, using the shield to minimize his exposure to the frigid water. Raelyn glanced up the embankment to Kade, who had his hands behind his back and a smile on his lips. She turned back in time to see an invisible dam extend from Avery's shield, blocking the river's flow a few feet ahead and behind him. He stood, remaining hunched, and took a few unsteady steps. Holding back the river, he plodded across the rocks until he was nearly to shore, his face shiny with sweat and red with effort. He grunted as a stone slid from under his foot and he fell forward. The water instantly surged around him.

Avery snapped his head up and locked eyes with Raelyn. She splashed in two steps and reached out her hand. He grasped her forearm and Raelyn pulled hard. She lost her footing in the swift flow and toppled backward but kept a grip on Avery's arm. A pair of strong hands caught her and pulled them both onto the riverbank, where they landed in a heap. Raelyn looked up into Kade's calm blue eyes and radiant face. He smiled broadly but made no comment.

"Thanks for that," Avery mumbled as he scrambled up the embankment.

Raelyn gasped for air and shook her head. "Don't mention it."

They traveled west as the sun blazed into the horizon and winked out of the sky. Raelyn hugged her waist, shivering in her wet clothes. The path disappeared in the darkness, lit only by Kade's golden light. He led with consistent haste, even when the bushes, full of sticky branches, crowded their footsteps and the trees tried to take over the path. Each of his steps was planted with purpose, commitment, even meaning. Raelyn's heart swelled with surprising affection. *Why?* Sure, he promised the only way to save Peter. And had taught them all so much. He was their protector and guide. But it was simpler than that. Without even knowing her, or maybe knowing more than she would have liked, he loved her.

Raelyn glanced at Joshua, walking behind her in cool silence. She darted around the others to walk alongside Kade, despite the narrow path. He glanced down at her and smiled.

"Kade." Raelyn dodged a fallen limb.

"Yes, daughter?"

"I was wondering about this Arkonai person you've mentioned. Is he like a prophet? Or a fallen warrior?"

"Arkonai is the Author of all that was, is, and will be."

Raelyn chuckled and shook her head, stepping around a mound of rocks. "He sounds pretty important. You didn't think an explanation might help us along the way?"

"I did." Kade smiled and gave her a sidelong glance. "However, it is best to reveal details as they are needed. Too much truth can be confusing. The temporal mind is designed to process only so much at a time."

"And now?" She'd play along. As Kade presented pieces of a puzzle, she'd work to figure out where they fitted.

"Seek and you will find," he said. "All journeys prompt a need for meaning and purpose. As you battle forces of evil to save those you love your heart is opened to receive greater truth." His deep voice was at once commanding and comforting. "Arkonai is all and in all." Kade spoke the last few words slowly.

The emphasis was not lost on Raelyn. She worked the information around her mind, struggling to connect the dots. What did it mean for her?

"Seek, Raelyn." Kade's voice was tender and forceful.

"But that's what I'm doing." She cringed. She sounded like a whiny child.

Kade smiled but offered no more explanation.

Low branches scratched Raelyn's face and shoulders and she dropped back behind Kade as thick vegetation took over the path. They waded through brambles and scrambled over boulders haloed in Kade's light. A tall column of smooth stones, much like the monument where Kade had blocked the varga, rose out of the ground directly ahead. They clambered around it to a break in the trees and Raelyn heaved a sigh of relief as they stopped to rest. Kade sat alone a few paces away staring into the forest.

Dry twigs snapped in the darkness. Something moved ahead. Kade jumped to his feet and they all moved in behind him. Raelyn strained to see what was coming. Several silhouettes, surrounded by a soft yellow glow, made their way to the clearing.

"Kade!" a voice called.

"Altizara!" Kade boomed and laughed as she, Emaline, and Tilman broke through the tree line. Only then did Emaline's sage light and Tilman's slate blue show through the darkness. "I did not expect to see you! Malvok? It stands?"

"Of course." Altizara strode to Raelyn and gave her a brisk hug. Warmth spread through Raelyn's chest and broke through the gloom, her fatigue evaporating instantly.

"A fierce battle," Altizara continued, shrugging indifferently and grinning. "But we were victorious."

Tilman grasped Joshua's forearms. His stern face was even more severe than usual. "Once the enemy became aware the temporals were no longer in the city they quickly retreated."

Kade frowned. "You are sure they knew?"

"The timing of their departure suggests they did. We were able to follow the road from the north." Emaline stood between Gabe and Jinny, her smooth, pale skin smudged with dirt. "We have prepared a camp in Deshill. But the way is . . . difficult."

"It gets worse?" Avery burst out, speaking for the first time since leaving the outpost.

Kade took a deep breath as he turned to face them. "The ruins will give us time to rest. An impassable marsh makes traveling south impossible until we reach a second outpost, Kulum. For now, rest. We will continue at daybreak."

At a sudden movement in the trees, they all went silent. Griseld ducked under the branches into the clearing and greeted the Malvok soldiers.

"You have done well, my friends," he said solemnly. "Here we must leave you. The enemy bears down on us across the lake. We will do what we can to divert them away from you. But do not tarry."

He turned to Kade and bowed slightly. "Farewell Kade. May Arkonai protect you and bless you on your journey. Farewell," he called to them as he sprang away. Kade watched him leave, his brow knitted. He had never looked so troubled.

They rested until a thin, gray light spread over the trees. Raelyn rubbed her eyes. It would be a long day.

Altizara spoke the truth. Despite the cool air, a layer of sweat covered Raelyn's face and ran down her back. They ducked under tree limbs, scrambled over mounds, and picked through thorny brush. Branches grabbed and tangled Jinny's hair. The trees grew so close that Avery's shield wedged between them and he was forced to take it off his back and carry it sideways. Gabe followed Jinny and Emaline, chattering softly, while they worked to move branches and find ways around rocky barriers. Emaline tossed her blond hair to one side as she helped Jinny over a fallen log. A fleeting memory of Lydia brought a fresh wave of sorrow.

"What is troubling you?" Altizara asked. Raelyn glanced at her trainer who had an uncanny way of reading her emotions.

Raelyn shrugged. "I still can't believe she's gone. Lydia."

"Gone, yes, but not lost."

Raelyn cocked her head. "Zara, you know how I feel about riddles."

Altizara threw her head back and laughed, heedless of the volume.

"You miss Lydia, but she is with you. Do not grieve those who pass on. It is a necessary path. One we all take." Her voice softened. "You have suffered much loss, Rae. It is natural to feel as you do. Healing will come."

They stopped to rest at midday as thick clouds moved in sinking them into an early twilight. The gusty breeze blustered into an icy wind. They each pulled a thin cloak from their packs before they continued their journey until nightfall. A misty rain sprinkled over the foliage, dampening the clearing where they set up camp.

"We will continue at first light," Kade said. But the Cord was already unpacking bedrolls and pulling blankets over their heads.

Raelyn bid Altizara good night and watched her take up sentry by a nearby tree before falling into a deep sleep.

The next day they slogged through squelching mud. Dark, churning clouds held the sun at bay and sent needling raindrops onto their heads. Joshua and Tilman marched ahead and were soon beyond sight. But Raelyn had to push her aching legs just to keep pace with Altizara. Her throat burned despite the chill. But there was no indication they would be stopping.

Finally, the rain dwindled and the clouds begrudgingly parted. A blazing sun burst through thinning trees and set the forest aflame with smoldering red and gold. A broad clearing revealed a large circular dell. A swath of dry, scrubby grass was littered with rows of toppled stone. Joshua and Tilman were already surveying the area. It was so like Durnoth, only the charred trees were missing. And, Raelyn hoped, the varga.

"This was Deshill," Kade said. "The outskirts of a grand and beautiful kingdom." His eyes nostalgically swept across the ruins.

Emaline led Jinny and Gabe to the far side of the dell next to a crumbling wall. She waved Tilman over, pointing to a pile of branches.

Raelyn hung back with Altizara. "They seem so unaffected."

"Joy can often overcome even the horrific. Especially for the young."

Raelyn nodded in the direction of Joshua and Avery. "Wish you could say the same for Avery."

Joshua marched up to Tilman, who had sparked a fire to life. Avery, now wearing a perpetual scowl, leaned against a wall, keeping his injured leg straight out in front of him.

"Everyone follows a different path, even when they are on the same road," Altizara said. "And speaking of your road"—she jogged forward to the others, raising her voice— "you left Malvok in such a hurry, we were unable to present you with your final gifts."

Altizara beckoned Jinny and Gabe to a clump of boulders. Raelyn imagined they were once cottages like the ones surrounding Malvok castle. People — temporals — had lived in peace in this strange world.

A blue twilight settled over Deshill. Fireflies mimicked the glowing stars, and a few frogs serenaded the travelers. A chill wind blew across the ruin. The dry leaves of the surrounding trees rustled, as though whispering strange secrets.

"Here, Jinny, this is for you." Altizara held up a silver chain with a large triangular medallion dangling from it.

Jinny dipped her head forward and Altizara hung it over her neck.

"Thank you," Jinny said, lifting it and turning it over.

Emaline grasped the locket and yanked, as though to pull it from the chain. Jinny gasped and stepped back.

Emaline grinned and held out a small dagger, no bigger than her hand. "A push blade." She offered it back to Jinny, who took it between her thumb and index finger, lifting it gently. A triangular blade, the color of rich amethyst, was open in the center. The handle glimmered as though forged from gems.

"Your Seon is crucial to your quest but is limited in battle. Hold it here." Emaline wrapped Jinny's fingers around the handle so that the blade jutted dangerously between her middle and ring fingers. She lifted the empty metal holder from the chain and guided Jinny's hand until the blade was secured and dangling against her torso.

"Similarly," Altizara said, "the Leohfaet is not a proper weapon in combat. Gabe!" She nodded him over.

He stepped forward and she pressed something into his palm. Gabe brought it close to his face, scrutinizing what looked like a small tube of metal.

Tilman nudged Gabe and grinned. His blue light pulsed. "I'll show you later."

Jinny pulled her blade from its sheath again, as though testing her ability, and examined it. "I'm not sure I could use this. Even if I knew how."

"Even so," Altizara said with a robust chuckle. "I bid you take it. In Alnok, the guardians exist outside the physical. You, however, do not. I pray it does not become necessary. But keep it within reach."

They opted for no fire and agreed to keep watch two at a time. Gabe and Tilman took the first shift. Raelyn, surrounded by a great group of protectors — the guardians — collapsed into a deep sleep. But after what seemed only minutes, she felt a hand on her shoulder.

"Our turn at watch," Altizara whispered.

Raelyn forced her limbs to move as they cried out objections. Shivering, she pulled her cloak tight. The half-moon, high in the velvet sky, chased away the stars and cast a blue glow on the grass and trees. The two women took up post not far from camp on an incline near the open glade. Raelyn sat on the ground and pressed her eyes with her palms.

"I'm so glad you're here, Zara," she whispered as she hugged her knees to her chest.

"We will travel with you to Kulum, but from there your path is south. We must turn back to Malvok." Altizara looked at the moon.

"What?" Raelyn gasped, louder than she had meant to. "You're not coming with us to Shalhala?" Her heart sank.

"Remember what I said about each of our paths? I must return to Malvok. We won the first battle, but there will be others." She shook her head. "Always others." Altizara peered into Raelyn's face, and she reached out for her hands.

"There is so much you do not know, Rae. So much of the Periferie you have yet to discover. You will have many join your quest, and some who turn away. Alnok may be my home, but my purpose lies well beyond."

Raelyn shook her head, refusing to be comforted. "But you came all this way. And you found us."

Altizara put her hand to Raelyn's lips. "This quest is yours. You are well equipped, Raelyn."

"Not as equipped as you think," Raelyn grumbled, her face growing hot.

"Oh?"

She shrugged. "I choked. In the tunnel. I forgot everything you taught me. I was useless."

"Our training was indeed cut short. Do not dwell on one . . ."

"Failure."

Altizara chuckled. "Missed opportunity. Your time has not yet come."

Raelyn scowled.

"Trust me, you —" Altizara stopped and sat up straight, looking into the far trees.

Kade strode swiftly past them. "Gather your things. Wake the others," he whispered as he scanned the forest. Altizara was moving before Raelyn had time to stand. Raelyn jogged to camp and shook Gabe. Joshua nudged Avery. Their quiet but frantic movements woke Jinny.

"What's going on?" Jinny said shoving her things into her pack and glancing back with wide frightened eyes.

"Shhh," Joshua said. "Not sure. Something in the woods."

Jinny looked at Raelyn, who could only shake her head and shrug. She had not heard anything. In only a few minutes, the Cord had their packs on, ready to move on Kade's signal. He stood at a distance, a dark silhouette against a gray backdrop. Then his shadow grew as he moved toward them.

He walked straight to Jinny and smiled grimly. "I need your eyes."

Jinny unhooked the Seon from her belt and followed Kade to the edge of the glade. The others followed, clustering behind her and

Kade.

She was still for a moment. "There is something . . . but very little threat."

Kade nodded. "Likely only a few scouts. But we must move on. It will take us five days to reach Kulum where we will find safety. That is if we increase our pace and are not hindered." With that, he spun around and walked past Altizara into the forest. Everyone fell into line.

CHAPTER NINETEEN

The next five days pushed Raelyn to her limits, physically and emotionally. She gasped to fill her burning lungs. Her back ached and her heart pounded. The trees thinned out and the scrubby brush gave way to low hills of hard clay. Short, gnarled trees twisted out of the baked earth. Unlike the shimmering trees in Malvok, these were dull and lifeless. The meager sun strained through high, dense clouds, but without the cover of the forest, it felt like a spotlight.

Jinny kept the Seon planted on her brow, squinting into the distance. Her fear seemed to have subsided, but whether out of a newfound bravery or frantic necessity, Raelyn couldn't tell. Jinny and Kade led the group. No one spoke, nor did they pause after many long miles.

On the third day heavy clouds gathered, and a sharp wind from the north. Kade finally called for a halt. A berm of smooth boulders was burrowed into the next hill, offering some protection from the wind and, Raelyn hoped, enemy eyes. They threw off their packs and fell to the ground exhausted. Raelyn sat cross-legged, leaning against a rock. She took several deep breaths, waiting for her heart to stop pounding.

Kade scanned the surrounding hills. "We will rest. Take some food and water. But we must continue quickly."

"Jinny, you haven't seen anything?" Gabe asked, opening his canteen.

"Seen? No. But I have felt much. A pressing in of hate. Something different from the dokkaibi of the tunnels. But just as dangerous. I do not think they are close yet," she finished, frowning.

"The second leg of our journey will prove the most urgent." Kade finally took his eyes off the horizon and surveyed his warriors, panting and sweating. "The Kulum outpost should provide protection."

"What do you mean 'should'?" Avery asked and took a deep breath, seemingly to steady his nerves as much as his breathing.

"Before the attack, we had not heard from Kulum for some time," Emaline said, handing Jinny a deep-purple apple-like fruit.

"And our scouts had not returned," Tilman added. He stood rigid with legs planted, halfway up the dune, looking west, across the plain they had just crossed.

"Most unusual." Kade gazed east. "Traveling between Malvok and Kulum may have become difficult. It may have been unsafe to send messengers." He shook his head and looked at the ground, face drawn. "There is something you must know about Kulum. You will feel very much as you did when you first entered Alnok. You must enter with caution."

Raelyn couldn't stop a guilty glance at Joshua. She had told Kade nothing of her observations back into her world.

They allowed themselves time to eat some dried meat and bread, sitting in a tight circle.

After a brief rest, they packed away their supplies.

Joshua glanced back. "Hey Gabe, what was it that Altizara gave you?"

"Oh!" Gabe dug into his pack and withdrew a short tube of gleaming blue metal. Standing between Jinny and Raelyn, he held it in his palm at arm's length and squeezed. Two poles sprang from either side. One passed within inches of Jinny's face and the other smacked Raelyn's canteen from her hand.

"Oh! Oops." He stumbled forward to retrieve the canteen and would have knocked Jinny in the head had she not dodged.

"Gabe!" she shouted, and he spun around, catching Raelyn on the arm.

"Sorry, sorry." He squeezed his hand again and the poles retracted. "Have to get used to it."

"Yeah, and fast," Raelyn said with a grin, rubbing her stinging arm.

As soon as they had stowed the last canteen they were up and going again. The packed earth loosened to sand, eventually giving way to a vast desert. Hill after hill they plodded over, pulling their feet out of the soft sand to take each step. For two days they trod the vacant landscape when the sun was highest and warming the chilly air. The nights were cold and unforgiving. They huddled around a fire, which Tilman kept stoked while Kade kept watch. But Raelyn got little sleep. She was both anxious to reach Kulum and dreading the end of this leg of the journey when she would have to say goodbye to Altizara.

On the fifth day, the clouds evaporated, and a clear blue sky opened before them. Raelyn sensed a restlessness among the soldiers. But even more so with Jinny. Kade increased their pace, but the sand was reluctant to let go of Raelyn's feet. Altizara kept her eyes laser-focused ahead, her jaw set. Jinny ran ahead several paces, climbing to the top of the next berm and looking into the eastern sky.

She stopped and spun around. "Hyram!" she yelled.

Raelyn squinted against the sun, where a black mass hung far in the distance. But it might have been nothing more than a wisp of dark clouds.

"What do we do?" Raelyn whipped her head back and forth, looking across empty desert in every direction. There was nowhere to go. No place to hide.

"Raelyn!" Altizara shouted as she and the others scrambled after Kade to join Jinny. From the top of the hill, the pale outline of a tall tower, contained within a high wall, stood in the distance.

"Hurry!" Kade shouted.

They raced across the desert and the mass in the sky moved closer. Soon there was no doubt it was a murder of the giant crows.

"The outpost is near! Retrieve your weapons!" Kade cried.

Raelyn grabbed at her bow and pulled it off her pack. She gripped it in her right hand as she pumped her arms in a sprint. Joshua drew his sword.

The dark stone tower, jutting from the top of a dune, took shape. A tall stone wall surrounded one side. Hundreds of the hyram streaked toward them, just beyond the outpost. They would never make it.

"Hurry, Raelyn!" Altizara pulled at her elbow. Somehow Raelyn pushed faster. She and Altizara pulled ahead of the others and reached the crumbling wall first.

"Here!" Altizara snatched her bow and loaded an arrow in one motion. Raelyn followed suit. The birds shrieked and dove. Altizara launched an arrow through the center, forcing them to break formation and pull off. A dozen continued on a direct path toward Altizara and Raelyn. Raelyn pulled back her bow, aimed at the leading bird, let out her breath, and fired. The arrow connected and the bird fell. Raelyn paused with a surge of wild satisfaction.

"Raelyn!" Altizara pointed to the next target.

But the lead crow, the size of a wolf, dove too fast. Its oily, frayed feathers flapped against her face. She squeezed her eyes and braced. A screech rang in her ears and ended in a surprised squawk. Raelyn opened her eyes as Joshua swung the Ruah and swiped off the bird's head. Gabe joined him, wildly swinging his new shining rod and knocking the next few birds to the ground. The others veered off and circled around

"Go!" Joshua yelled, gripping the sword in both hands, awaiting the next wave of hyram.

Raelyn followed Jinny and Emaline as they ducked through a set of charred wooden doors sagging from a gap in the wall . . .

A wave of nausea made Raelyn's knees buckle. Her vision swam. She strained to look around. The tower shifted, as though tilting out of view, and suddenly she was standing in a small park outside the hospital. On a bench a few yards away her dad and Aunt Betty sat talking.

Movement in the trees just behind them. A dark mass dispersed, scattering from the treetops. Black crows. Hyram.

"Dad!" she screamed.

He frowned and looked at her. Or through her. Aunt Betty continued her dramatic gestures as she kept talking.

"Dad!" Raelyn reached out. But they were fading. She heard shouting. Hands grasped her shoulders and forced her to sit. Something was pressed to her lips. Liquid poured into her mouth.

The tea.

Raelyn pushed her hair from her face and looked up at Altizara who held a small flask. Taking great gasps of air, her trainer patted her cheek and stood. Raelyn gazed around an open courtyard. Jinny sat closest to her, looking dazed and wary, Gabe's arm around her shoulders. Joshua lay on his side against a toppled stone wall next to Avery where Tilman crouched, inspecting his leg. Kade rushed in from the gateway, looking at each of them as though counting to see they had all made it. His golden light mingled with the rays of the setting sun behind him. Raelyn searched the sky but saw no sign of the hyram.

"Where did they go?" she croaked, struggling to her feet.

"The hyram went nowhere," Kade said, helping to steady Avery as he removed his pack.

"But —" Jinny squinted into the fading light.

"The Kulum outpost lies outside the realm of Alnok," Kade said.

"What does that mean?" Joshua asked, rubbing his face and blinking.

"Another dimension," Gabe breathed, looking at Kade with wide eyes.

Kade nodded. "Aye. This is the realm of Velare. Or rather a small opening into it. There are few such access points. Cosyn's horde are unaware of the waystations. To them, you have vanished."

"That is why we needed the seripyn, Jinny said.

Kade nodded.

"The hyram do not see the tower," Emaline said, helping Gabe out of his pack.

"Then why is it abandoned?" Avery's eyes darted to the scorched doors.

Kade and Altizara exchanged a quick glance.

"I do not know," Kade said quietly. He took a few steps toward the tower and gestured for them to follow. "We will rest tonight. By morning the hyram will have moved on."

"You're sure?" Avery asked as they picked their way through the courtyard.

"The overgrown chickens are not known for their great deductive skills," Emaline said. She and Tilman scooped up a few thick branches as they walked.

"We are hidden from enemy eyes." Kade looked up at the brooding turret. "However, we will make camp outside, should we need to escape quickly."

"We aren't safe?" Jinny said, still searching the sky as it faded to a somber twilight.

"I do not know what has become of the guards of Kulum," Kade said. "We should remain cautious."

"What do you think happened, Kade?" Emaline asked as she dropped her sticks into a pile.

Tilman knelt next to it. He swept his hand, passing blue light over it, and a blaze came to life.

Kade placed his palm on the tower and shook his head. "The hyram did not enter Velare. But something did."

"You think Cosyn has found a way in?" Tilman asked.

Kade did not answer.

Emaline and Tilman cooked a dinner of boiled rice, bread, and cheese as long shadows crept across their camp. Emaline brewed some of the tea. It was a feast. And to Raelyn's dismay, a going-away dinner.

"Why can't you come with us?" Jinny asked as the soldiers prepared to leave.

"Malvok is not safe." Emaline gave her a sad smile as she packed away some herbs into a pouch.

"Is anyplace safe?" Gabe stood and shoved his hands in his back pockets.

Tilman took a step forward, his blue light drifting around his head. "You must understand. Malvok and Shalhala, and other guardian kingdoms you do not yet know, are protectors not only of Alnok but of Earth Apparent. We cannot be so divided in our duties. The longer we are away, the greater both realms are at risk."

Jinny smiled, but a tear slipped down her cheek. "Like guardian angels."

Emaline smiled and nodded. "Something like that."

"No wings or halos, though," Tilman said gruffly.

Jinny sniffed as Emaline embraced her and walked to the broken entryway. Tilman grasped Joshua's arm and then Avery's.

Raelyn and Altizara took slow steps to the gateway.

Raelyn swallowed, holding back tears. "I doubt I'll be able to —"

Altizara stepped in front of Raelyn and grasped her shoulders. "Your ability is not rooted in what you believe, but in truth. And the truth is, you have more ability than you realize. When you no longer deny this truth, you will wield a power greater than you can imagine." She gave her a fierce hug and vanished through the gateway.

Raelyn took long, slow strides, not anxious to return to the camp, where Joshua, Gabe, and Jinny gathered around the fire. Avery was likely skulking somewhere nearby.

Altizara was gone. Lydia was gone. Harlan, her mom. The need to save Peter flashed brightly. She took two gasping breaths and her knees threatened to give. Tears leaked from her eyes. Whatever happened, she would save him. Whatever power she was supposed to have, she would find it. As she approached the flickering firelight, Kade was speaking to the others.

". . . enemy will find new ways to impede our travel." He poked the fire with a slender stick.

"I can't imagine what could be worse than what we've seen so far," Gabe said, shaking his head.

Kade's blue eyes flashed momentarily, then a hint of a sad smile crossed his lips. Raelyn wondered what he knew. Why didn't he divulge more? One word flitted across her mind: seek. Kade revealed as much as each would seek. The tea relieved some of her nerves and she decided to leave her questions for the next day.

The grim mood permeated the camp as night overtook them. But no one seemed more affected than Jinny. Raelyn found her standing just outside the circle of firelight, looking into the starry sky.

"They can't see us, Jinny," Raelyn said as she approached.

Jinny shook her head and wiped her eyes with the back of her hand. "Did you see a vision from home?" She kept her voice low. "When we entered Velare?"

"Yes. Did you?" Raelyn hadn't really thought of them as visions. For her, they were as real as looking through a window.

"Yes. It was the first time."

Raelyn nodded. "It's really hard. Seeing your loved ones like that."

Jinny sniffed. "I envied you." She turned to Raelyn. "Seeing your family. Keeping an eye on them. But" —she shook her head as fresh tears coursed down her face— "I saw my mother. In the . . . clinic. She was alone in her room. Crying and moaning. But there was something else. Tormenting her. A black smoke, as black as tar, on the ceiling. The room smelled like burning hair. Then it started to rain. Big black drops. When they landed, they evaporated. I screamed and my mother looked up. And the rain stopped. But the cloud was still there. Then I was here." She drew in a deep breath.

Raelyn touched Jinny's arm. "I think we should talk to Kade about it in the morning. Right now"—she pulled her gently toward the fire— "we should get some sleep."

It was some time before Raelyn drifted off. The last thing she saw before her eyes slipped closed was Avery's shadow, curled up, with his back to the fire.

"Raelyn!" Jinny's frantic cry jarred her from a dream where she was in her dorm room studying for an upcoming test for a class she had never attended. She struggled to understand why her roommate was so upset. Was she late for class? She lifted her head from the hard bedroll and the events of the last few days rushed at her. It was dark, the fire having burned to embers and the moon hidden on the far side of the tower.

"What? What's wrong?" Raelyn could see shadows scurrying about.

From a distance, Joshua called, "Did you see where they went?"

Gabe's fading voice answered, "His pack is gone."

"Jinny, what happened?" Raelyn jumped up from her mat.

"Avery," Jinny said. "He's gone. We think Kade left with him."

"Both of them are gone?" Raelyn's heart pounded with slow-rising anxiety, but anger stabbed through the fear.

Kade had gone with Avery. He was using them in some twisted scheme. Ditimer. Lord Talmond. Her mind reeled with conspiracy theories. She grabbed her quiver and bow and rushed to the edge of the Kulum courtyard, Jinny on her heels. Gabe stood at the wall, peering through the opening. Raelyn stumbled into Joshua as he launched back through the gateway.

"It's Kade," he said through an exhaled breath. Jinny thrust the flask into Joshua's hands, and he swayed as he took a gulp.

"What do you mean 'it's Kade'?" Raelyn asked.

Before Joshua could answer, Kade appeared in the archway that separated Alnok from Velare. As soon as Raelyn saw him, shame washed over her in an uncomfortable wave. He glanced at her, and she looked away.

Kade led them back to camp and was quiet for a moment, his hands clasped behind his back, pacing. "Avery has indeed left us."

"What? Where would he go?" Gabe's voice bordered on hysteria.

Kade raised a hand to silence him. "I believe he was lured away."

"By who?" Joshua asked, his voice low and tense.

Kade took a deep breath. "I suspect Avery has been . . . deceived. In Malvok, and again in Tegre, I think he was in communication with . . . someone." Kade's hesitation, his uncertainty unnerved Raelyn more than a flock of hyram or a pack of varga.

"If you knew —" Jinny began.

"I did not know. I had nothing but a deep and, at the time, unfounded, suspicion."

Raelyn had no words. No questions. Her thoughts spun like an out-of-control Ferris wheel. It jerked to a stop; Avery had fled. Then spun again, up and around. Another stop; Ditimer abandoned them before they were attacked. Lurching forward. She felt sick. Around and around.

"He's just . . . gone?" Raelyn heard Jinny ask. But Raelyn didn't care that Avery was gone. She didn't care that they were hiding from Cosyn's horde. Or that she was responsible for closing a portal to her world to save her brother. Right now, she only cared about what Kade didn't know. Didn't know where Avery was. Or what had happened to him. Or who might have orchestrated his disappearance. What else didn't he know?

". . . kept watch for much of the night," Kade was saying. "He was able to slip past, but he could not have gone far."

"So, we go after him?" Joshua asked, already stuffing his gear into his pack.

"How do you know?" Raelyn interjected; her voice loud but dull.

Everyone stopped what they were doing and looked at her. Kade slowly met her eyes.

Uncertainty leaked into her anger. She ignored it. "How do you know that's what happened? Or that he hasn't gotten far? How do you know anything?" Tears were flowing freely. "I, we, trusted you. We followed you. Now you're telling us there was some"— Raelyn glanced around looking for the word— "some spy? You're the one watching over Earth Apparent. Over us. And you don't know?" She was breathing hard and shaking all over. She realized she was still clenching her bow and quiver.

"No, I am not all-knowing. I am not omniscient nor omnipresent. I was appointed to this task, just as you were."

Raelyn shook her head. But her words evaporated.

"You must trust," Kade said quietly.

Raelyn glared at him. "How?" she croaked.

"Not me. Trust the one who sent me. The one who chose you."

"That's all well and good." Joshua stood and brushed past Raelyn. "But Avery is out there, and we need to go after him."

"No," Kade said simply. Joshua stopped and looked back at Kade. "Not 'we'. *I* will. The territory is perilous and unknown. And speed is needed. We cannot hope to find Avery with five of us." Kade took his satchel and pulled it over his neck.

"Listen carefully to my instructions." He looked intently at each of them. "Travel the road south, under cover of darkness. That means waiting out the day before you begin." His gaze stopped at Jinny. "Chin-sun."

Jinny looked up at him with frightened, weary eyes. Kade smiled softly and took a few steps so that he was looking down on her. He brushed a stray clump of hair from her forehead.

"You must wear the Seon at all times. I believe you are strong enough to withstand what you will see. And it is imperative you keep watch. Take this." He handed her the flask that held their supply of seripyn. Kade kissed her forehead and turned to Gabe. "Gabriel."

"Yes sir?" Gabe's voice cracked.

"You are the light of the Cord. Be a beacon for the others. Yes?" Kade gripped his shoulder firmly, stealing him with his gaze. Gabe nodded and pushed up his glasses.

Joshua had walked away, looking out in the direction Kade believed Avery had gone. Kade joined him, his back to the others. Raelyn could not hear what he said. Joshua's face was shadowed, and his expression hidden. After a moment's conversation, Kade turned and addressed all of them. Raelyn's heartbeat quickened at the clear exclusion. Maybe he was angry about her outburst.

"Gather your things." Kade passed Jinny and Gabe's packs to them. "You will wait out the day inside Kulum Tower." He gave them instructions to follow the road from the tower south to a fork. "Take the path on your right," he stressed. They would reach the Chamal Lake, north of Shalhala where they would be greeted by sentries. Kade ushered them into the dark, musty tower but touched Raelyn's elbow and motioned for her to stay.

When the others had disappeared into the gloom, Kade took both of her hands.

"Daughter, what I am about to entrust to you is both a blessing and a burden. As is often power bestowed upon someone with a high calling." Kade spoke low and watched her eyes, but she suspected he was not awaiting an answer.

His stare pierced her mind and heart, assessing her ability. *My worth.* She blinked furiously as tears stung her eyes. Lingering anger made way for uncertainty, fear, shame. Kade released her hands, reached around his neck, and untied the leather cord that held the round amulet. He placed it in his palm and showed it to her.

"This is the Durinial." His voice was deep and forceful, and his words suggested both an introduction and a warning.

"It will provide instruction and direction." He spoke swiftly.

Raelyn was mesmerized by the colors, which had again begun to undulate and spin. Pale blue, then gold, now deep emerald. The three concentric circles spun around a golden tree, its weeping branches swaying and golden leaves glittering.

"Kade, please, I —" Raelyn began, inadequacy rushing in and filling her.

He held up his hand. "It will give you warning and guidance." He paused. "In this way it provides protection. The Durinial is also a map of sorts. You will know if you are on the right path. You will feel it guiding you. It belonged to your family once." He paused once more.

"You must know, as with many of Arkonai's gifts, the enemy will emulate and mock all that is good. There is another like this. A talisman wrought in the Schade Catacombs by Cosyn himself. It allows him to gain access to the wearer of the Durinial."

"Access?" Raelyn whispered.

"Insight into your doings. Even the possibility of influence." Kade took the leather strap and quickly placed it around Raelyn's neck, tying it securely. He pulled away just enough to cradle her face between his palms. His eyes were filled with love, kindness, unending forgiveness. Her uncertainty and shame swept away like snow in a spring breeze. Her cold fear melted in the warmth of Kade's affection.

"Be on your guard. I am sorry I cannot explain more, but as time passes, Avery's danger grows."

Raelyn felt the amulet with her fingertips. It was heavy on her neck, and the metal was cold. Kade ushered her into the inner room of the tower. The others were just inside, and Raelyn wondered how much they had heard. Kade stood in the doorway, his golden light shining against the darkness.

"Farewell. You have been well trained. Make haste to Shalhala." With that, he disappeared into the night.

CHAPTER TWENTY

The shockwave of Avery's disappearance and Kade's departure was a silent roar. The after-effects of an exploded bomb. In the dark, cramped, and cold room, furnished with a small wooden table and a few chairs, they agreed to get as much sleep as possible. But the musty odor like a root cellar, the rustling and shifting of the others, and the uncertain trip ahead made sleep impossible. Raelyn propped herself against her backpack. She stared into the crumbling coals left from a small fire Joshua had made and replayed the memory of her father on the park bench over and over. If he was outside talking to Betty, Peter must be okay. She shivered.

Jinny stirred next to her and slowly sat up, pulling her cloak around her shoulders. She glanced at Raelyn. "It's no use." She shrugged and Raelyn nodded.

After a few minutes, Gabe and Joshua joined them. No one spoke as Joshua brought the fire back to life and a thin, gray light rose outside the door.

Jinny sighed. "Maybe Kade will find Avery and bring him back before we leave tonight." Her face flickered hopeful in the firelight.

Raelyn drew her legs to her chest. "Maybe."

But as the day wore on, their hope faded. They ate little and drank less, knowing they had at least a week of travel ahead of them. Joshua proved the most encouraging as they waited out the day. He showed Gabe and Jinny how to play Mancala, a Sudanese game he learned during a tour in Africa.

"How'd you have time for games out there?" Gabe asked as he and Jinny gathered forty-eight small stones at Joshua's direction.

Joshua smiled grimly. "My job doesn't always involve combat." He began scooping out a row of small divots in the dirt floor. "When we go in to protect a town or village, sometimes we have an opportunity to interact with the people." He started on a second row, then a third. "I always seemed to find the kids." He winked at Gabe, who cocked one eyebrow.

He finished three more rows. It looked like a rustic, square version of Chinese checkers. He spent a few minutes explaining the rules in which they were to move stones from the divots into the channels assigned to each of them.

Jinny took two stones from her first pit and dropped them in the second and third. Joshua nodded expectantly at Gabe, who studied the makeshift game board, frowning and moving his lips soundlessly. He adjusted his glasses and held his hand above his second pit. Jinny sighed heavily.

Gabe looked up at her. "Okay, okay." He grabbed all four stones, depositing each one in the next pit and the last one in his store. He looked back at Jinny and grinned.

Affection swelled in Raelyn's heart as she watched Joshua give tips and suggestions. Chased by killer crows, abandoned by one of their group, their leader gone; wisdom came in the form of a simple game. It was a welcome distraction and Raelyn was in no hurry to begin yet another uncertain leg of their journey.

After they had finished several rounds of their game, all of which Gabe won, a ripple of restlessness seeped into Raelyn. The light outside was fading. She began packing her gear back into her bag. The steady pressure of doubt and fear wrapped tight around her shoulders. The Durinial hung like a weight on her throat, the strand of leather, a noose. But her father's face as he looked at her from the park bench shone bright in her mind. His wide blue eyes, searching. He didn't see her, but he knew she was there. Somehow.

I don't know why I was chosen. I don't know what I'm doing. I need help. Help me understand. Guide me.

Raelyn took a deep breath, held it a moment, and slowly exhaled. Some of the fear loosened its hold.

"You okay?" Jinny asked, watching her.

"Yeah, yeah. Just don't know what to expect." She shoved the Bokar into the back of her belt and pulled her tunic over it. It seemed right, now that she was appointed leader, to have her weapon, useless as it was, close at hand. "We've seen how it goes without Kade around." She glanced at Joshua's drawn face as he closed up his pack. He had spoken only a few words to her since leaving Tegre. "But our skills have improved," she continued louder. "We have a clear road. We'll figure it out." She gave Jinny her most encouraging smile.

Joshua nodded and hoisted his pack. "Whether or no, here we go." He drew his sword and led them out the door and to the gateway.

Raelyn held her bow. Jinny pushed the Seon firmly onto her brow as she held the flask containing their remaining seripyn. They crept across the gateway with Gabe's light illuminating their path. Raelyn stepped outside the tower walls and her head exploded with pain. Jinny passed the flask around. Raelyn took a quick sip and handed it to Joshua. In a tight single-file line, they stepped out onto a wide, gritty road. The moon peeked over the horizon, sparing little light in the quiet chill of the clear night.

Raelyn glanced at the dark sky. "Gabe," she called, "we'll need you at the front."

"Right, right," Gabe muttered as he trudged by Raelyn and Joshua, swinging the Leohfaet at his side. He sighed and held it aloft, a small glimmer sputtered then brightened to a steady orange glow. The light encircled the group and illuminated a few yards ahead of them. The desert, dark and menacing, pressed in.

"The color's changed," Joshua commented.

Gabe glanced back and smiled sheepishly. "Yeah, it seems to have something to do with my state of mind. Or maybe what we need."

"Maybe both," Jinny suggested from the back of the line. "Perhaps your emotions reflect what we need."

"Never thought of it that way." Gabe gave her a lopsided grin before continuing, his steps more certain.

They kept a brisk, silent pace until the moon crested above their heads. The further they traveled the more Raelyn's anxiety grew. The oppressive darkness seemed full of hidden, watchful eyes. The silence, which should have been comforting, amplified their shuffling feet.

Raelyn looked over her shoulder. Jinny had fallen behind, glancing nervously left and right, fidgeting with the hem of her tunic. "Hey, Jinny." Raelyn dropped back. "Hey," she repeated, softer this time, wrapping her arm around Jinny's delicate shoulders. "I was thinking, maybe you should be up there with Gabe. You two make a good team."

Jinny smiled up at Raelyn and took a shaky breath. "I considered that, but I thought it might be better to be back here and keep an eye on everyone."

"I think you'll see just as well upfront." Raelyn nudged her forward.

Gabe lit the way while Jinny kept watch. Raelyn adjusted her pack but it continued to press the journal uncomfortably into her back. Raelyn took a deep breath and rolled her shoulders back, settling into a resolute march. Kade had passed his leadership to her. Made her responsible for getting them to Shalhala. A weight, having nothing to do with her pack, bore down on her shoulders. Kade believed in her. Had told her over and over she was chosen for this task. It wasn't just about Peter or her family anymore. She had three people who needed her. Who were counting on her. She gripped the straps on her pack and picked up her stride. Gabe and Jinny took her cue and increased their pace.

The night grew colder, and the moon dropped in the sky. Raelyn dug out some food as they walked, waving off suggestions for a break. They had to cover as much ground as possible. All at night.

She finished off her last drops of water. "How far do you think we've come?" she asked Joshua.

"I'd say we're less than halfway to the fork. It's hard to say in the dark, but at our pace, that'd be my best guess," he said, chewing a bite of jerky.

"We'll have to move faster if we're going to make it before dawn." Raelyn looked at Gabe and Jinny.

Gabe glanced back and shrugged. "We can try." He shook his canteen. "But we're going to have to address this water situation at some point. By the way, is anyone else surprised we haven't heard or seen anything? Not that I'm complaining," he added.

"That does not mean there are no threats," Jinny said gazing around at the dark desert. "I sense a rustling. A searching. As though strange creatures patrol, seeking us out, but pass us over."

Gabe gave her a doubtful look. "Our guardian angels?"

Joshua snorted.

Jinny shrugged. "I don't know . . . something."

Raelyn nodded. "Maybe we're being protected somehow." She cleared her throat. "I—uh, wanted to ask everyone something." She drew nearer to Jinny and Gabe, and Joshua walked a little closer. "I saw visions from home. When we passed into Velare."

Gabe interrupted, "Yeah, we all did —"

"But they saw me, too," Raelyn insisted.

"Yeah, I told you that early on," Joshua said.

Raelyn scowled and shook her head. "Not just an awareness. I have no doubt. They saw me. I shouted at my dad and he looked right at me. Has this happened to anyone else?"

"Wouldn't Kade have said something?" Gabe asked.

Raelyn sighed. "I don't think Kade always trusts what he can't see."

"What does that mean?" Joshua asked.

Jinny quickly told them about her fleeting view of Ditimer. And Kade's reaction.

"Couldn't Kade be right?" Gabe asked. "Maybe it's not what you think?"

Jinny crossed her arms and didn't answer. Raelyn couldn't blame him for doubting her. It was easier to believe Jinny was wrong than Kade. But Kade had misjudged Avery. He was not infallible.

"What about their all-powerful Arkonai?" Gabe asked. "Maybe he could just send a legion of soldiers and horses." He laughed awkwardly.

Raelyn raised an eyebrow. "Maybe they are there, but you can't see them. We're way off the map here. There's no knowing what forces are at work." Raelyn couldn't help a wry smile. She sounded like Kade.

"I'm not saying the protection isn't good," Gabe said. The Leohfaet dimmed. "I just don't always understand the point. If this realm can give invisible protection to our family, why not here? Why not close the plyes themselves?"

No one had an answer.

The half-moon left them. Raelyn pushed them faster until they were nearly at a jog. Dawn would soon approach. Kade had been explicit about traveling only at night.

For the next hour, Raelyn powered through tired legs and aching feet. A gray light crept into the sky. Rolling dunes, dark mounds against the thin light, stretched away on both sides of the road. The morning also revealed a circle of birds high in the sky. Raelyn's heart pounded as she forced her feet to move faster. But Jinny was already ahead of Gabe, nearly at a sprint.

Raelyn shot a look behind her. Joshua was squinting into the sky and had unsheathed his sword.

The birds, not much more than black dots in the sky, remained in the distance. Either they had not spotted the Cord, or they were stalking them until something else arrived.

"Jinny! What do you see?" Raelyn called.

"Only the hyram. But I think we are coming to the fork."

"You can sense that?" Gabe asked.

"No! Look!" Jinny pointed ahead.

Indeed, a part of the road broke away to their left. A clump of trees stood to their right. As they drew closer, Raelyn saw that one of the smaller dunes contained a small arched opening. The Durinial pulsed once. Raelyn startled. She wrapped her hand around the amulet. It was still, but it was signal enough that they were on the right track.

"I think this is our stop," Raelyn said through gasping breaths and rushed past Gabe and Jinny.

The opening led to a set of broken stone steps disappearing through an open door. Raelyn looked at the others before dashing through.

Joshua slammed the door behind them.

The dirt walls began to spin. Raelyn frantically searched for glimpses of Peter or her dad. Pain burst into her head and sent little stars across her vision. She squeezed her eyes shut. When she opened them, she was in a stark white hallway, with fluorescent lights above. She hurried past busy nurses in scrubs and a tired-looking couple shuffling along. Then, at the end of the hall near an open door, she saw her dad, his hands stuffed in his front pockets, listening to Dr. Brand, who was looking down at his clipboard. Raelyn moved in behind the doctor.

". . . have one last treatment to try. We will start it in the morning." Dr. Brand lowered his notes and looked at her dad. "After that, we have no options. Peter has responded to nothing . . ." A shadow moved just behind the open door. It didn't take shape, but its movement was dishearteningly familiar.

"Dad!" she yelled, but it came out barely a whisper. Her father continued staring down the doctor. The shadow rolled out from behind the door. The last time it had retreated when she called out.

"Hey!" she yelled as loudly as she could. The shadow slowed its approach, but billowed up in her direction, as though turning toward her.

"That's right!" Raelyn allowed the anger and fear to consume her. "Get back!" The mass adjusted its course away from her father but did not retreat. She shifted her attention fully onto it, staring it down, and took a step forward. It drew back, rolling in on itself. Raelyn spared another glance at her father. The doctor was in mid-sentence, but her dad looked in Raelyn's direction, his eyes searching the area where she stood.

Raelyn felt the flask pressed into her hand. She strained to see more but the scene was dissolving. She took a sip.

She was back in the dim bunker, lit by the lingering glow from Gabe's torch, now tossed on the dirt floor. The seripyn brought a calm and vigor. But it did not soothe the deep sorrow that pulled at her heart.

Jinny took the flask, her hand shaking so badly she nearly dropped it. But she knelt and helped Gabe take a sip.

"Everyone okay?" Raelyn asked.

"I don't think the hyram saw us," Joshua said, still catching his breath.

"I don't know," Gabe said, scrambling to his feet. "We could barely see them, but it's hard to imagine they didn't see us. Looks like we found another opening into Velare." He grabbed the Leohfaet and it sputtered to life.

"Right," Raelyn said, circling the small chamber, but she was not really listening.

The shadow. It had definitely reacted to her.

A table, dusty and aged, sat at the center of the room. Low wooden chairs lined the perimeter. Raelyn collapsed into one and let out a long breath.

The first part of their journey without their sage and leader was behind them. And so far, Raelyn had led them to safety. Somehow that didn't make her feel any better. The hyram had not moved on as they had hoped. Maybe Arkonai was sending celestial protection. But there was no doubt. They were being hunted.

CHAPTER TWENTY-ONE

,Kade left Raelyn, Joshua, Gabe, and Jinny to wait out the daylight and pursued Avery east across the Vastalgue Desert. The sun rose, golden and warm on his back, then faded to a pale haze as it rose into high, filmy clouds, the warmth chased away by an icy breeze. Kade took little notice of sun, cloud, cold or sand. He replayed his last conversation with Avery at Kulum and his harsh treatment of the desperate man.

Dismissive. Patronizing.

Avery's eyes flashed. "I can't stay." His body ridged, hands in tight fists, he blocked Kade in the hall of the Tegre outpost.

"I know you fear for her Avery," Kade tried to reason. "But Penelope is safer with you here. Defending her. Defending all of Earth Apparent."

"You don't understand." Avery's voice lowered to a growl. "When I couldn't pay back the loan and they took her, it wasn't just a warning." He finished through clenched teeth, but his voice belied his anger with a quiver of fear.

Kade took a step forward and pressed his palms together. "And you would have gone after her had I not offered a better way. Cosyn has targeted what you love most. But in the end, it is you he wants. He will put all his forces here. By now he likely suspects what we have planned."

They had returned to this argument throughout the training in Malvok. Avery's fear overtook his resolve each time Kade explained the risk in leaving Alnok.

"I could protect her there. From a place I know and understand. Here"—he gestured around at the stone walls— "I'm a fish out of water."

"You were chosen precisely —"

"Chosen!" Avery spat. "I make my own choices. I agreed to your bargain. Come here, save Penny. But I thought"— he faltered —"I thought you would have the money to pay the debt." His shoulders dropped.

"I never promised payment." Kade took another step. "But something more. A way to rescue and protect her. It is hard to trust what you don't understand. But I am asking you to, nonetheless."

Avery nodded and narrowed his eyes as though considering Kade's statement. "Clearly I am here for a reason," he conceded. "I have learned so much. Skills I could return to Earth with and use."

Kade was not swayed by this new approach. "There are many paths, Avery. Many that seem good but are false. Do not let fear dissolve the trust you once had in the path that led you here."

Avery had relented. But his demeanor shifted and Kade's concern turned to apprehension. Not for the quest, but for Avery.

A gust of wind blew grains of sand swirling at Kade's feet. He kicked at them without breaking stride. He could have let Avery go back with Altizara. From Kulum they could have escorted him to Malvok, and then to Ditimer.

Kade frowned as he considered his old friend. Faithful and honest, if a little impatient with the temporals. To suspect him of betrayal . . . Kade shook his head and shoved the thought aside. He would not condemn the man without cause. Jinny might simply have sensed him as he ran back for help.

Then why did I not return Avery to Malvok?

He had once believed Cosyn incapable of betrayal. Kade frowned and leaned into the wind. No. It was not like before. No matter what had become of Ditimer, Avery must come to see he was needed in Alnok. But Kade's confidence had blinded him to Avery's growing desperation. Not just for his wife, but his own festering fear rising from self-doubt. The perfect chink in Avery's armor.

Kade quickened his pace, following Avery's fading footsteps. A man desperate and deceived, lost and stubborn. He would suffer the consequences of his choice. They all would.

Kade's heart hammered against his chest, ricocheting between frustration and compassion. Another cold gust flapped Kade's cloak behind him. He squinted his eyes against the stinging sand. Though unseen, ahead lay Theurham Forest, a winding convolution of diseased trees snaking north to south, the Peostrum rising from its heart, a black tumor growing off fear and lies. Only the Schade Catacombs to the east were more formidable.

Avery would not have fled to Theurham on his own. He had help. With each step, Kade's apprehension grew. There seemed to be more hindrance than guidance. And what of Raelyn? There had been so little time to teach her and Joshua, Gabe, and Jinny. But there never had been much time. The wind seemed to blow sand across Kade's mind, clouding what he was to do. Avery, Raelyn, the Cord. How could he expect them to complete what had started so long ago?

A voice, quiet and unbidden, whispered in the wind.

Who am I?

"You are Arkonai." Warm peace, like a wave surging onto shore, overtook Kade's anxiety. It washed over the fear and uncertainty, pulling it into a massive, untouchable ocean. There it was overtaken and dissolved to nothing.

Who am I?

"You are the Author. Beginning and End. Life and Truth." Kade let each title echo through the desert.

Who am I?

"Defender. Protector. Father and Healer." Kade shouted the names and quickened his steps. The wind blew.

Kade began to sing:

"Far beyond time unknown, the Author comes to me

Lifts me up, holds me close

I soar above the storm

I am chosen, I am free."

Fine sand spun high in the distance, blotting out the sun. Kade hunched his shoulders and pulled his cloak tighter around his neck. The outcome was out of his hands. His path was to search for Avery. And like any lost sheep, he would pursue him to the ends of the universe.

The dust closed in and overtook Kade as he disappeared into the storm.

CHAPTER TWENTY-TWO

,The bunker, in better shape than Kulum, had clearly been abandoned for some time. A long wooden table and bench and a few scattered chairs were covered in a thick layer of dirt.

Jinny pulled the Seon from her head and began to pace across the sandy floor. "Did anyone see what we passed?"

Gabe dropped into a wooden chair. "I didn't see anything but the doorway." He yanked off one of his boots and poured sand out of it.

Jinny stopped pacing and looked at him. "A well!" Her eyes sparkled, like a kid on Christmas.

"We don't even know if there's water," Joshua argued.

"And if there is, if it's potable," Gabe added.

"And the hyram could be waiting for us to expose ourselves," Joshua continued.

Jinny looked at the floor. "It might be worth checking." But she was already withdrawing.

"Let's try it." Raelyn looked pointedly at Joshua. "Let's see what's here, get some rest and at dusk we check it out." Jinny gave Raelyn a grateful smile.

"All right," Joshua conceded, frowning at Raelyn and walking to the back of the bunker. "We need to be ready to make a break for it if those crows are still out there." He peeked through a small doorway and disappeared into a dark room. "Come take a look at this!" he called from inside.

Barely visible in the dim light, a wall of shelves held a collection of ceramic jars and a few cloth bags of varying sizes. Gabe set his light to the room and Joshua plucked one of the jars from the shelf. He peeled off the sealing wax, pulled out a cork, and sniffed at the contents before dipping his fingers in and pulling out what looked like a slice of a dark-green pear. He took a nibble and chewed thoughtfully.

"It's good." He shrugged and popped the rest in his mouth.

Raelyn, Gabe, and Jinny waited a moment before passing the jar around and finishing off the contents, which tasted like tart peaches. They broke into two more jars before returning to the main room. Joshua risked starting a small fire in the stove and the light brought not only warmth but comfort. Something about the steady crackle and mesmerizing flicker. They agreed to rotate one person on watch as the others slept. Raelyn took first watch and sat against the wall near the entrance where beams of light broke through the cracks in the door, creating shifting shadows and lighting the drifting particles of dust. She pulled her cloak over her, using it as a blanket against the cold and stared across the room into the firelight.

What would Peter say if he could see her? Sitting on a dirt floor, hiding from hyram on her way to shut down a portal an unknown enemy had used to curse him. He'd tell her she was crazy, foolish, smoking —

No, he would say she was brave. Because that's who Peter was. He believed in her when everyone else had given her up as a lost cause.

"Raelyn," Gabe whispered and touched her arm. "I'll take watch."

She nodded and crept closer to the fire, curling up on her side. She was asleep as soon as her head rested in the crook of her arm.

She dreamed she stood high on a sandy dune, gazing across the empty desert. A high sun blistered the back of her neck. She squinted into the distance. Dark movement. A black mass far off but advancing quickly and growing. She tried to jerk her feet from the ground, run down the dune, and find a place to hide. But her feet sank into the sand. She fell backward, her feet lodged deeper, and she was forced to watch her advancing enemy. An inky obscurity filled the landscape directly in front of her, swirling darkness, both terrifying and captivating. She struggled to climb out of the sandpit. Her heart pounded but the longer she gazed into the void the less she felt compelled to flee. The darkness shimmered, twisted, and spun. Her terror was subdued by a sudden longing to stare into the mysterious void. It was filled with secrets. Irresistible knowledge that she craved. She couldn't look away. It was beautiful.

A fierce gust of wind thrashed sand across her face, stinging her eyes and she flinched. The shadow disappeared. But it wasn't gone. Just hidden. Panic squeezed Raelyn's chest. She choked on the grit that filled her nose and throat. A final violent gust jolted her from sleep. She lay still but the wind continued to howl.

Outside a storm raged above the bunker. Wood creaked as the wind sought a way in. The Durinial, resting warm and heavy against her throat, vibrated. Though not painful, the phenomenon was disconcerting. She placed her fingertips on it and the sensation stopped. Raelyn lifted herself onto her elbow and looked around the room. She could make out dark lumps of the others' sleeping forms in the dying embers of the fire.

"You okay?" Joshua whispered from a nearby corner.

"Yeah, bad dream," Raelyn responded laying back and rubbing her dry, gritty eyes. "What time do you think it is?"

"Maybe two or three in the afternoon." Joshua's ability to estimate time was uncanny. Weariness overtook Raelyn and she rolled over, drifting into a deep and undisturbed sleep. When she woke next, the others were up, talking softly. Gabe's Leohfaet glowed steadily in one corner of the room. The wind moaned, muffled in their sunken sanctuary.

Jinny was busy wrapping her cloak around herself. "Raelyn. We are ready to check the well."

Joshua pushed his arms through his cloak, less enthusiastically, as Jinny disappeared into the back room. She returned with a handful of wooden bowls, the empty jars, and a dusty jug. She arranged everything on the table and carried the jug to the front door.

"If there is water," she said as she wiped the dust from the jug, "I will fill the containers."

"Optimistic," Joshua warned. "We may only find a well of sand."

Jinny glanced up with pursed lips and poured a small amount of seripyn from the flask into one of the jars. "We'll need this as soon as we come in." She looked up at Raelyn.

"How much of that do we have?" Raelyn picked up the jar, inspecting the caramel-colored contents.

Jinny shook her head as she walked to the door. "Very little. We might try diluting it. Even if that makes it less potent, it is better than running out." She took hold of the door handle and looked expectantly at Joshua.

He nodded, drew his sword, and turned to Gabe. "Close the door behind us." He addressed Raelyn. "Be ready for anything. If we're spotted, likely our only option is to fight our way out."

Jinny and Joshua swept out into the dwindling light, made all the darker with the flurry of silt. Gabe pressed the door closed, leaning against the incoming wind.

In what seemed only a minute or two the door banged open with a blast of sand. Jinny tumbled in, nearly dropping her jug. Gabe caught her and Raelyn put the jar to her lips. She sipped with her eyes closed.

"The storm," she said between breaths, "is in Alnok as well. As though strong enough to pass through both realms." But then she opened her eyes, and a broad smile broke across her face. She lifted the jug as though presenting an award.

"Water!" she gasped. Gabe helped her up and she began filling the jars. "I'm sure it is filled with sand, but we can strain it off," she chattered. Before either Raelyn or Gabe could comment she was back out the door and Gabe shut it behind her.

Gabe insisted on the first taste and took a small sip. He smacked his lips and grimaced.

Raelyn gasped. "Is it bad?"

He shook his head. "No, no. Just gritty."

Thirst overtook caution and Raelyn drained the second jar.

Jinny repeated the process twice more until all the jars, bowls and their canteens were filled. Soon both Jinny and Joshua were inside, breathing heavily and covered in silt, but settled after a dose of seripyn. They yanked off their cloaks and sprawled onto the bench. Jinny offered Joshua - who had not stopped to drink - a full jar.

He drained it and sighed deeply. "We should leave soon. It's nearly dark and we have a lot of ground to cover. There's no tellin' what our next stoppin' point will look like."

"What about the dust storm?" Jinny glanced at the closed door, the wind rocking it on its hinges.

Joshua shrugged. "We have to cover as much distance as possible."

In disheartened agreement, they prepared to leave. Raelyn crouched next to her pack and stowed her bedroll and some food, including a few of the pouches of dried meat from the storeroom. The black shadow from her dream loomed in her mind.

They opted to risk diluting the seripyn and filled their canteens with the remaining water. With weapons at the ready, cloaks pulled tight around their heads, and their eyes squinting from makeshift scarves, Gabe and Jinny led them from the bunker, Jinny ready with the flask. The dilution seemed to have no effect on the tea. Pulling their cloaks close, they trudged into the storm. If the moon had risen it was obscured in a thick haze of dust. The Leohfaet barely penetrated a few feet ahead. The road disappeared under the blowing sand.

They traveled as fast as they dared in a tight cluster. On several occasions, Raelyn felt the sand sink beneath her feet as they drifted off the path. She redirected Gabe back on track over and over.

Eventually, she eased ahead of Gabe and Jinny. "Maybe your focus on the Leohfaet and Seon make it hard to keep to the road."

Gabe and Jinny exchanged a confused glance but didn't argue. With no way to tell how long they had been traveling and for what seemed like hours, Raelyn led until her legs burned and her lungs were on fire. Just when it seemed the wind might relent a new gust would blow the stinging grains into Raelyn's eyes.

Jinny didn't alert them to any immediate threat, but there was no way to see if they came across a place to rest and they couldn't risk stopping without protection. With no choice but to continue their trek, Raelyn planted one foot after another on the solid path. The wind shrieked in her ears and she ground the grit between her teeth. Tears streamed down her cheeks. Every time she blinked the grains of sand ground behind her eyelids.

Just as she felt she could no longer withstand the assault, the wind abated, then disappeared entirely. At least the effects directly around them did. The sand continued to swirl and blow furiously just a few feet from them. It was as if the storm raged, but they were protected from it. Raelyn blinked and looked back at Gabe. With brow furrowed and shoulders hunched, he held the light above them, though little more than a frail flicker. An invisible barrier encompassed the four of them in a small bubble.

"Way to go, Gabe!" Joshua shouted, clapping him on the back. He grinned but remained focused. Raelyn laughed and hugged

Jinny tightly.

Joshua plowed ahead. "We should make up some time."

But that proved impossible. Even protected from the windstorm, the path continued to be covered in deep, shifting sand. Gabe could only maintain the shield for short spells as they hurried along but they made little progress when exposed to the whipping sand.

When Gabe resumed his protection after a particularly harsh march, Jinny blocked his path. "Can't we take a short break?" She wiped her eyes and looked from Gabe to Joshua.

Gabe nodded, sending sand out of his dust-covered red hair. "I can hold out for a short break."

They crouched in a tight circle in Gabe's small light bubble. The storm raged around them, flurries of sand beating against the shelter, but aside from a thin cloud of dust and a bitter cold that even the strength of the Leohfaet seemed unable to keep out, they were unaffected. They pulled their cloaks from their faces, sniffing and coughing. Raelyn passed her canteen around and Jinny shared a few bites of bread and dried fruit.

"We should keep going while it's dark," Raelyn said, putting away her canteen.

Gabe held out for longer and longer spells, and eventually the first gleam of dawn filtered through the billowing sand.

Joshua jogged up to Raelyn. "We should keep going," he said without looking at her.

Kade had told them to travel at night. Gabe could protect them from the sand, but the road continued to be buried and it was becoming harder to tell the firm path from the sinking sand. What if she lost their way and daylight exposed them to even more danger? Raelyn pressed her fingertips on the Durinial willing it to give her guidance. She had not mentioned what Kade told her about it, and it didn't seem to be doing anything anyway. But reluctance held her tongue. This was the first time Joshua had made any attempt to collaborate with her since Tegre.

Raelyn nodded. "A little further. But we still don't know what may be watching us."

Joshua glanced around them. "Okay, we'll keep an eye out for a place to stop." His words were gruff, combative.

Raelyn frowned. Would the Durinial direct her? It hung like a rock around her neck, as she continued to lead them through the storm.

CHAPTER TWENTY-THREE

On the morning of the fourth day, not long after sunrise, the wind slowed and then died altogether. Gabe lowered the Leohfaet, and they stopped for a moment, taking in their surroundings. The desert was unending. Not a tree, not even a dried shrub, broke the sand's surface. Despite their exhaustion and foreboding sense of danger, the rolling dunes had a serene beauty. A joyful morning sun stretched its rays into a pale sky and warmed their backs, oblivious to the danger it posed. Raelyn's face flushed with frustration. They were doing exactly what Kade had warned against.

"We need to keep walking," she growled.

Jinny turned in a slow circle, surveying the horizon and the sky. She faced east and gasped.

"What? What?" Gabe searched Jinny's face, which was frozen in shock, her eyes locked on the eastern horizon. Her hands hovered over the Seon as though she may rip it from her head. They all followed her gaze.

"Shadows," she whispered. "Not close but moving this way."

Raelyn tried to block the sun with her hand but wasn't surprised to see nothing.

"Can you see what they are?" Joshua asked.

"No. I feel them. The oppression. The hate. It forms a kind of image, but nothing I can describe."

"Can you tell how close?" Raelyn asked. As long as they continued southwest, they would move away from the threat.

Jinny shook her head. "No. They are far but moving fast. I can feel their urgency." She shivered and closed her eyes.

"Okay"—Joshua jumped to command— "let's move." He strode past Raelyn.

"Wait!" Jinny called. They all turned to her.

Raelyn caught Joshua's annoyed glance.

Gabe stopped any objection. "What is it, Jin?"

Instead of answering, Jinny dropped to her knees, clutching her pack. She dug around until she found what she was looking for, extracted the flask, and held it out to Gabe. "Drink," she commanded.

He took the offer without question. Each took a sip in turn. As soon as the liquid hit Raelyn's tongue, she felt the familiar warmth trickle down her throat and fill her with renewed energy.

"Great thinking, Jinny." Gabe patted her shoulder.

Even Jinny appeared calmer. She glanced back periodically, but her face was set with determination.

The day wore away, the sun climbing a hazy sky until its filtered light shone directly overhead. There was not so much as a breeze and the morning chill gave way to a radiant heat. Raelyn felt neither tired nor hungry, the elixir maintaining a steady source of sustenance. Finally, scrubby bushes and short, weathered trees began to shoot up from the desert. The sand became firmer.

"We must be getting close!" Gabe shouted.

"Shhh!" Jinny scolded angrily. "The enemy may be out of sight, but they are gaining."

"Gaining?" Joshua stopped short and turned to her. "How close?"

"I told you —"

"Yes, yes, you can't tell. But we don't know how near we are to our destination. Can you estimate?"

Jinny turned and frowned in the direction of their pursuers, then shook her head in frustration. "I don't know! Closer. Like a great wave bearing down. It's rising higher and higher. It won't overtake us yet, but it's gathering strength."

"Let's just keep going," Raelyn interceded and Joshua's face hardened. "We wouldn't even know about our danger if it weren't for Jinny and there's nothing we can do but keep moving." But the same urgency spurred Raelyn to move faster.

They increased their speed until they were at a steady jog. The sun sank to the west, bathing them in its molten glow. More and more desert plants filled the landscape, though dry and lifeless. Short hard-packed mesas replaced the vast dunes. The path widened and ahead a swath of lush trees came into view. A sprig of hope grew in Raelyn's chest. It was just as Kade had described. But the budding confidence evaporated by what she felt, more than heard.

A low whir filled the air and vibrated inside Raelyn's head, like the hum after a consistent loud noise suddenly goes silent.

Like locusts in the Egyptian plague.

The mind-numbing buzz grew. She heard Jinny cry out, but no one stopped. No need to ask Jinny what she saw. The wave. The tsunami was bearing down on them.

Raelyn stole a glance behind her. The horizon was black. Like a shadow growing out of the earth. Building, growing, rising. She caught an odd glint or flash within the black shroud before she turned back. Not lights. A reflection off weapons? If so, they were hopelessly outnumbered. No offense could be mounted to withstand the oncoming mass, no matter what it was.

Another ten minutes passed, and the weight of their assailant continued to bear down. Raelyn's chest tightened, her lungs no longer able to take in enough air. She felt as though weights were attached to her boots. Sweat dripped into her eyes, blurring her vision. She heard Jinny sobbing behind her and Gabe staggered. It was no use. There was no escape. They would have to stand and fight, to whatever end.

"We're not going to outrun them!" Raelyn yelled over the buzzing as she slowed to a stop and pulled her bow off her pack.

Joshua glanced at Raelyn, then the others and nodded as he put his hand on the hilt of the Ruah and stepped in front of them, facing the oncoming threat. Gabe retrieved his staff from his pocket. He held it at arm's length, and with a squeeze, both ends shot out. Joshua drew his sword and Jinny's knife glinted between her fingers.

Dark loping figures appeared out of a cloud of dust. The speed of their approach belied their shape and movements. First a growing shadow, then a mass of hundreds of creatures, tall and menacing. Illuminated in the setting sun, their pale, nearly naked bodies held oversized heads and long, lean limbs. Even at this distance, Raelyn could see their large dark eyes, at once intimidating and empty.

The glint Raelyn had first seen from afar revealed itself to be small disc-shaped vehicles hovering and intermingled with the army. Unlike the screeching varga and the snarling sibukyn, these new demons were strangely silent. A whispering menace. Only the vehicles gave off a reverberating buzzing that made Raelyn's head spin.

Raelyn had a mad impulse to laugh. *UFOs.* As surreal as the impression was, her gut told her the instinct held some truth.

"What the—" Gabe gasped.

"Could you block them like the sand?" Jinny asked desperately.

Gabe shook his head, his face turning red. "We need Avery's shield!"

He was right. The shield might have protected them. But Avery was gone. And Kade had followed.

So, this is how it ends. Little chance we were going to make it any further.

Raelyn's despairing thought boiled suddenly into white-hot rage. They were so close. Had come through so much. This couldn't be the end. If Raelyn didn't make it to the portal, Peter would die. She gripped her bow, glaring at the loathsome creatures about to take them over.

She yanked an arrow from her quiver. A guttural scream, raw and desperate, erupted from her throat. She pulled the bow back as far as she could and launched the arrow high into the air. And was joined by a hundred more from behind.

They all spun in unison. A battalion of warriors swept past the Cord, some running with swords, others driving simple, shining two-horse chariots. Their approach was nearly silent across the sand, but now their war-cry echoed across the plain. Unlike the Malvokian soldiers, in their mail shirts, metal helmets, and shining shields, their new defenders were wearing little more than leather sheaths across their tanned bodies, with arms and legs exposed. But the lack of armor did not lessen their threat. The creatures quailed at their approach.

Though outnumbered two to one, the warriors overran their opponents head-on with a terrible crash. Horses trampled some of the creatures, warriors on foot hewed at the gaunt, misshapen bodies. Raelyn, with heart pounding and anger surging, pulled another arrow as she bolted forward to join the fight. But after only a few steps, several chariots interceded, blocking the Cord from the enemy.

"Come!" shouted a woman with wild flowing auburn hair and a swirling orange light. She held out her hand. Raelyn spun left and then right frantically looking for the others. They continued to be swallowed by the battle. She caught a glimpse of Gabe climbing into another chariot, pulling Jinny in with him. A creature reached out, its long fingers grasping at Jinny's hair.

"Quickly!" the woman screamed, thrusting her hand at Raelyn. Out of options, Raelyn complied. She allowed the woman to pull her into the cart even as it pulled away.

"Hi-ya!" the woman shouted, whipping the reins. They were off, wide wheels lumbering west away from the desert. The sound of battle faded. Dust mingled with a swift-approaching sunset.

Raelyn gripped the sides of the chariot as it bucked across the rocky terrain; cold wind whipped her hair and froze the sweat on her face. They headed directly into the golden sunlight as it faded into the horizon. She looked behind, but the fierce fighting disappeared in the failing light, though the shouting continued to echo. The disturbing buzz grew faint, then ceased.

Raelyn stood beside the warrior, who stared stonily ahead, gripping the reins. Surely the others had got away. But the woman gave no reassurances. They didn't slow for some time, speeding on until a velvet night enveloped them and the half-moon danced in and out of high clouds. The horses' hooves pounded against the dry ground. Raelyn took a breath to ask how much further.

"We're close," the woman said.

True to her word, she soon slowed the horses to a trot and took a sharp left that pulled them onto a smooth road. A vast lake opened west of the road, reflecting the waxing moonlight. Finally, they slowed to a stop.

"We will take a moment to rest the horses," she said, now looking directly at Raelyn.

"I am Othana of Shalhala." She bowed her head slightly and jumped down from the cart.

"My name's —"

"I know who you are, Raelyn Angeline Witt, daughter of Fulton and Virginia," Othana recited formally.

Raelyn gulped, sand scratching her throat. Before she could respond, a tall, young man bounded up behind them. He jumped and hollered, sky-blue light dancing around his arms.

"This," Othana chuckled, "is Larken."

"I think the Olyaunders will think twice about mounting an attack after that," Larken said breathlessly.

"Aye," Othana responded.

Raelyn let out a breath when Joshua walked up behind Larken.

Larken glanced around. "Where's Olmund and Enloe?

"They are not behind you?" Othana scanned the desert, her eyes alert.

They heard a rush of hooves as another chariot hurtled into view.

"Othana!" a man yelled as he pulled up. He looked like a male version of Othana with a steel-gray light rising from his bare shoulders.

Gabe tumbled out of the back of the chariot. He held the Leohfaet in a limp hand and dropped to one knee. "They got her!" he moaned.

"What?" Joshua said.

"The young girl. Chin-sun," Olmund said as he strode to Othana. "They pulled her from the back of Enloe's suklo. I retrieved Gabriel and Enloe went in pursuit."

"I had her," Gabe sobbed. "I had her and then she was just gone." He looked up at Raelyn, his face dirty and tear-streaked. "I told you! If Avery could have held them off . . ."

"We have to go after her!" Raelyn said, anger again swelling in her chest as she marched to Othana.

Othana stood firm. "Where? Where will you go?" She emphasized each word. "Enloe will retrieve her or bring word. We must make for Shalhala."

This got Gabe to his feet. "No way!" he said taking a few unsteady steps toward Othana.

Olmund addressed Othana in a low voice. "The Olyaunders knew the temporals were coming."

"Of course, they knew." Othana waved her hand in dismissal.

"I'm sorry," Joshua interrupted. "But who—what, are the Olivers? Where did they take Jinny?"

Othana and Olmund exchanged a meaningful look.

"The Olyaunders. Creatures of the desert," Othana said. "Shapeshifters and rulers of mechanical sorcery."

"Deceitful and treacherous," Larken added, scowling.

"And keepers of the plye," Olmund said.

Othana nodded. "You will learn much more. We will reach the woodlands of Shalhala in one day's ride —"

"I have to agree with Gabe." Joshua stepped forward, his jaw set in solidarity. "We can't leave without Jinny."

Othana glanced to the east. "We cannot tarry. Are you injured?" She looked at them, her face impassive.

Fear and adrenaline surged through Raelyn. They could not be discussing leaving one of their own behind.

"We're fine. But there's no way we're leaving here until we have Jinny back safe." Raelyn planted her feet and crossed her arms.

Othana closed her eyes. "Very well," she conceded.

"Othana —" Olmund began.

She held up a hand. "We will rest the night and await Enloe." Othana turned to the Cord but addressed Gabe. "Under no circumstances are you to leave this area."

Olmund grunted, walked to a pair of horses and led them to the lake. Larken began unhitching the horses from his chariot.

"Larken," Othana called. "Would you please gather what wood you can find? We will make a fire."

When the fire was blazing and Joshua had filled all their canteens from the lake, they settled around the flames, staring into them. Gabe continued to sniff.

Empty shock replaced tears for Raelyn. Any minute the fourth Shalhalan warrior would appear with Jinny safely in his chariot. She would be unhurt. They would all be safe . . .

Larken tried to get them to eat, but no one wanted to think about food. Instead, Othana insisted they lie down and sleep.

"We will keep watch. You need rest. You have traveled far and we will leave early."

They finally conceded and lay their bedrolls around the fire. As Raelyn drifted off, she heard Olmund whisper.

"Othana, without Kade there is little hope their quest will succeed."

"Aye, there is little hope indeed."

CHAPTER TWENTY-FOUR

The stark tree line that bordered Theurham Forest glowered at Kade. The desert roared around him, a tumult of frenzied sand and wind that did not penetrate the forest. Only once had Kade ventured into Theurham since Cosyn drove the temporals from Alnok. When he brought the Cord from Earth Apparent through the Silom Pool. Where he could send Avery back. He took a deep breath.

One thing at a time.

Kade stepped across the forest threshold into a malignant twilight. The trees closed in around him, sealing off the sandstorm, and silence pressed against his ears. The dank carpet of fallen leaves gave under each step. Kade stood still for a moment. He needed neither torch nor lantern. His light radiated in and through him. A few steps more and the shadows gave way. A path snaked before him, winding deep into the darkness. He pressed on.

Even now, the worst of circumstances could be turned to good. Would be used for good. Kade quickened his pace and made for the center of the forest. After only a few miles the air grew thick. Something white fluttered at the edge of his vision. Creatures sent to observe, but not interfere. He was close.

Though no light penetrated Theurham, Kade guessed he had been traveling a half-day when the trees opened onto a set of steps leading to a massive circular stone dais. At the center stood a dark robed figure, his arms outstretched and with a sly smile. Kneeling beside the figure, bent forward with hands bound behind his back where his pack and shield were still strapped, and his tangled black hair obscuring his face, was Avery.

Anger swept over Kade's grief and pity. "Cosyn!" he bellowed.

"Kade." Cosyn smirked. His voice was deep and silky, his eyes, the same striking blue as Kade's. Shiny, jet-black hair spilled across his shoulders and framed his smooth, pale yet radiant face. A glowing mist-like smoke drifted from his black robes. He was both beautiful and terrible. He raised a shining silver scepter, a round talisman set in the center, in greeting.

"Welcome, brother!" Cosyn called and bowed low. Without rising, he lifted his head and winked. "I see this one was worth the rescue?"

He straightened and stepped around Avery, pulling his robes away from him as though not wanting to dirty them. He strolled to the edge of the platform, grinning down at Kade triumphantly.

"You have no claim on him." Kade kept his voice even, almost conversational.

"No? I simply offered him what he wanted." Cosyn spoke as though helping Kade to see reason. "What you refused to give him. He wished for his wife's protection. We struck a bargain. His wife's guaranteed safety in exchange for his allegiance."

Avery let out a strangled sob. A man buried in defeat and fear. Cosyn continued, ignoring the outburst.

"He came to me willingly. He is mine by right." Cosyn's face rippled. A glimpse of red eyes and sallow skin. A wide mouth filled with yellowed teeth. The image vanished. His skin impossibly smooth. His blue eyes bright and clear.

"You have no rights, Cosyn," Kade responded calmly. But the trees shook as though by a blast of wind. "You command your army of demons at Arkonai's discretion. But do not mistake that for rights. Release him."

Cosyn's eyes narrowed. He smiled, as though mustering patience, then shook his head. "After so many defeats, brother? I destroyed your precious temporals once. Yet you bring these groveling, weak, powerless beings back to Alnok." Cosyn paused as he walked back to Avery.

"For what?" he spat, turning abruptly and striking Avery's shield with his staff. Avery cried out.

"Enough!" Kade commanded.

"I will once again break the temporals. I will destroy them." Cosyn glared at Kade, his voice tight. He chuckled, thick and wet. "You once again underestimate me." He returned to the dais edge and took a step down from the platform.

Kade pressed his palms together. "I do not doubt your power. But I do know your fate."

"Do not speak to me of fate!" Cosyn slashed his scepter through the air, creating a blaze of fire that shot toward Kade, who deflected the flame with a flick of his hand.

Cosyn took another step down, the black mist trailing behind him. He smiled, showing shining white teeth, but his blue eyes had become empty black holes. He struck the scepter onto the next step, and it cracked open. A bubbling puce-colored liquid first oozed and then gushed from the opening toward Kade.

Kade took a step back. He cupped his hands and clear water filled them. He lifted them to his mouth as though to drink, but instead blew into them toward the mass. Light, a solid beam, burst from his hands and changed the substance into the same clear water, creating a trickling waterfall from the step.

Cosyn smirked as he watched the water then flicked his eyes up to look at Kade. Something disrupted the ground in a line from the dais toward Kade. He watched it approach without moving. The dirt rolled back as it wormed its way under Kade's feet. Rope shot up from the ground and wound around Kade's arms. He strained to pull his arms up and away. The rope squeezed and yanked him to his knees. He hit the ground as more rope snaked out of the dirt, winding up Kade's body and around his neck. It hung loose for a moment before it contracted. Kade couldn't speak, couldn't breathe, couldn't swallow. He tried to flex his arms and twist his head to loosen the rope. As though wicked hands in a death grip, the rope held fast. Kade looked past Cosyn to Avery, who had raised his head, watching, his mouth slack. Kade met his brown eyes, wide with panic, before closing his own.

Pinpoints of light popped behind his eyelids. His body screamed for air. Then Cosyn, Avery, the forest, all melted away. He was drifting, floating, far from Alnok. A flicker of heat, warm and calming, sputtered to life in Kade's chest. So small. So distant. He forced the last of his strength to focus on this one flame. It grew and the heat radiated into his arms and down his legs, rising in temperature and intensity. Kade, no longer aware of his body's need for oxygen, focused instead on the building inferno. The heat moved up his neck and flushed his face. He heard the ropes crackle. He could smell the burning fiber. He was back in the forest.

Kade wrenched his eyes open and locked onto Avery's. A blaze exploded from his body. The ropes burst. Kade gasped and fell onto his hands, sucking in great draughts of air. He forced himself off his knees and stood, the heat still burning through and around him.

Cosyn roared and scurried to Avery. He sliced the air behind him with his scepter and a rip appeared as though he had cut through a canvas painting. He grabbed at Avery, his fingertips finding the edge of his shield. Kade lifted both hands and directed the fire toward Cosyn. A percussion blasted the air and drove him backward. Losing his grip on Avery, Cosyn toppled through the rent in the air. Kade gave a final sweep of his arm, hurling the last of the heat into the air. As the seam closed, Kade watched Cosyn scramble to his feet. Someone stood next to him. Kade's heart pounded. It could not be. But Cosyn was gone and so was the man beside him.

"Kade," Avery choked, "I'm so sorry."

Kade rushed to him. He pulled a small dagger from his boot as he knelt and cut the leather straps that bit into Avery's wrists.

"As am I," Kade whispered to him.

Avery dropped his unbound hands and planted them in front of him. Heaving sobs shook his shoulders. Kade grasped his shoulders, helping him to stand.

Avery gripped Kade's arm and peered around him. "Where —"

"Close. We must hurry." Kade guided Avery to the top step of the dais. He pulled a vial from his robes, unstoppered it, and placed it in Avery's trembling hands.

"Drink this. We will rest for only a moment." Kade glanced behind them. "Cosyn will return with a legion of his followers. We need to be far away from Theurham Forest."

Avery sipped at the tea. He took a deep breath and let it out slowly. His shoulders sagged. "How can we win against that power? That evil?" he whispered, searching Kade's eyes.

"It is not our duty to see the war to the end. We simply fight the battles to which we are called."

A breeze rustled the leaves and Kade felt a shift in the atmosphere. A prickling like static electricity ran through the trees and across his skin. A dark, repulsive smell, like burned hair and rotten food, rose from the ground. A low moan sounded from deep in the forest as the white specters returned.

"We must go." Kade shot to his feet. Avery stood without question. He handed the vial back to Kade, his eyes darting across the dark forest. Kade strode back the way he had come without a word. He heard Avery's footsteps follow close behind. Once out of the forest, he would begin the process of teaching and restoring Avery. But for now, his sole focus was to escape. He could feel Cosyn's malevolence nearby. Another rush of apprehension filled

Kade, which he quelled with disbelief. There had to be some explanation. It was not what he thought he saw. It could not have been Ditimer standing next to Cosyn.

"Give me strength," Kade whispered.

CHAPTER TWENTY-FIVE

Like a heavy shovel being dragged over concrete, a high-pitched, metallic grating woke Raelyn just before dawn. The moon had passed on and darkness lay across the night, thick and heavy. A horse whinnied and snorted. The acrid smell of smoke filled the air as the dying embers of their fire crackled next to her.

Raelyn eased up to sitting and rubbed her eyes. The noise continued, passing north of their camp. Her skin tingled and she slid her bow closer, but her quiver of arrows was just out of reach. How fast could she retrieve one, move into position, and get a shot off? Raelyn's shoulders ached from sitting so still until the sound faded, and the first pallid light of morning crept into the sky. Voices drifted just outside camp.

"What word, Enloe?" Othana whispered in the darkness. Gabe's shadowy form shifted and stirred next to the fire.

"I pursued the enemy far into the desert. As far as I dared."

Gabe bolted from his bedroll, nearly stumbling into the dying fire as he loped toward the conversation, Raelyn and Joshua right behind him.

"You found her?" Gabe asked, nearly knocking over Larken who stood next to Othana.

"I did not," said Enloe, who towered a full foot taller than Joshua. His bald head gleamed in the growing daylight and a deep-green glow, so dark as to appear almost as shadow, emanated from his shoulders.

"So, we go after her." Gabe was already moving toward their gear.

"Nay," Othana said sharply. "Your quest indeed lies in the domain of Olyaund. But to go now would mean destruction. For you and for Chin-sun. We will not abandon her. But we must make for Shalhala immediately."

"But what if they — what if she's —" Gabe sputtered.

"We are familiar with their methods," Enloe said. "She will be kept alive. You will have a chance to save her. But we must leave now." He gestured for Othana to follow him, and they walked to a clump of trees near the lake, out of earshot.

Olmund swept his arm toward the camp. "Dawn is approaching. Load the suklos," he commanded, though not unkindly.

Larken hastened back without comment and Joshua followed. Raelyn glanced back at Othana and Enloe. Gabe remained rooted to the spot.

Raelyn tugged at his arm. "We have to trust they know what they're doing."

He let her lead him back to camp but not without a final glare in Othana's direction.

Raelyn stuffed her gear back into her rucksack. The sooner they got to Shalhala, the sooner they could return for Jinny.

Though unintelligible, Enloe and Othana's voices drifted into the camp. She glanced at Gabe and Joshua, but they were busy loading the suklos further away. Pulling at her bedroll, Raelyn edged closer to the conversation.

". . . put . . . not . . ."

Raelyn grabbed her canteen, full to the brim, and ducked away to the lake. She poured out the water, in case she was confronted about why she left camp, and crept through tall grasses, the ground turning to mud. She crouched where she could just see them through a group of reeds near the water's edge.

". . . to cover it. Once the Cord is safe we will send a unit back to glean its effectiveness," Othana said.

"We should tell them —"

"Nay. We do not yet know its uses."

Raelyn's eyes widened and her heart thumped. *Tell them what?*

But they said no more and strode back to camp. Raelyn rushed ahead of them, crouching through the grass, as the sun broke over the horizon. She got busy cramming the last of her supplies into her pack, including her empty canteen. By then Larken and Olmund were hitching the horses back to the carts.

Othana climbed into one of the suklos. "We should reach the woodlands in half a day's ride. Another full day to Shalhala."

"Are you sure we shouldn't go after Jinny now?" Raelyn said, testing the information she had just heard.

Othana cut her eyes to Raelyn. "Without a doubt." She gestured for Raelyn to climb aboard.

Joshua climbed in with Olmund and Gabe with Larken. Enloe stayed to "provide a lookout." But it could be he was guarding whatever it was they had found. Othana flicked her reins and they lurched forward, taking the lead.

They picked up speed and followed the lake's shoreline, a hundred yards to their right as the sun chased away the morning chill. The water glistened as though millions of diamonds floated just below the surface. Fleecy clouds hung in the pale sky. Lining the roadway, squatty trees sent searching roots into the water and waved small emerald leaves as they passed. Patches of low grass eventually took over the desert. The horses' steady gallop pounded along the smooth road. But the tranquility was wasted on Raelyn's heavy heart. The further they traveled the tighter the knot squeezed in Raelyn's stomach.

We're abandoning Jinny.

They continued at the same pace for most of the day until they crested a small hill. A thick forest spread out at a distance below. Othana slowed the horses to a trot. The trees twinkled with prismatic leaves of yellow, orange, green, and red, and danced in the sunlight as they welcomed the travelers into their domain. The dirt road gave way to a path of smooth, luminous stones. Raelyn glanced back. Joshua shifted his gaze to her, his furrowed brow and clenched jaw reinforcing Raelyn's guilt. Past Joshua, Gabe stared ahead with glazed eyes.

Raelyn turned to Othana. "When we get to Shalhala, how will we get Jinny back? You have a plan?"

Othana stared ahead, the reins held loosely in her hands. "Aye," she sighed. "But if we look too far into the distance we trip on stones directly in our path." She smiled wryly and glanced at Raelyn. "That is what my mother would say."

Raelyn frowned. "I don't want to see the future. I just want to know what's further up the road."

Othana chuckled. "You've clearly spent much time with Kade." Raelyn didn't respond and Othana reverted to her serious demeanor, gazing out at the road.

Raelyn noticed a deep scar running from Othana's shoulder in an arc down the side of her arm, and Raelyn instinctively touched her own scar.

"Your path leads back to the desert," Othana finally continued. "But I do not know the full journey. Shalhala is not a village of warriors like Malvok. The contingent sent to battle the Olyaunders is but a small troop meant for defense. You will find Shalhalans to be a peaceful, thoughtful people. Crafters, musicians, poets."

Raelyn tried to fit the description of the Shalahans into a strategy for battling an evil enemy. They weren't going to save the world by singing to them. The most skillfully crafted pottery would serve no use. Raelyn touched her back where the journal lay tucked beneath her tunic.

"Not all wars are fought on the battlefield," Othana said. "Shalhala uses different strategies. Not for physical harm. But just as effective."

Othana did not elaborate, and Raelyn was not satisfied. Shalhala was the place where she was to learn the purpose of the Bokar. She might finally understand what she was meant to do.

Rescue Jinny. Avenge Lydia. Save Peter.

She was counting on a purpose greater than a clumsy attempt at bowmanship.

"Kade said Shalhala had the missing pages to the Bokar. The book that's supposed to be my weapon. Is that what you mean?" Raelyn pressed.

"Aye, you will find many answers," Othana said, turning to her. "As you seek, you will find."

Raelyn's fear flashed to anger. More riddles. "I *am* seeking."

"Asking is not the same as seeking. True seeking requires an open heart. A willingness to accept the answers, even if they are not the answers you expect . . . or want."

Raelyn's hand went to the Durinial. She gripped it with a strong impulse to yank it from her neck and throw it into the trees.

"The Durinial." Othana said. Raelyn quickly dropped her hand to her side. "Do you know you would never have made it across the desert without it?"

"What do you mean?" Raelyn didn't try to hide her irritation. The amulet might as well have been a rock hung around her neck.

"There is no road past the fork where Kade left you."

"There was a road. We followed it. Gabe lit the way."

"No Raelyn. We destroyed that path long ago. To keep our people safe."

Raelyn frowned. "Then how — what —" She and Joshua had brushed the sand off the road. She hadn't imagined the path.

Othana nodded and smiled. "Seek, Raelyn. You will find your answers."

———⊰⊱———

Deep in the woods of Shalhala the sharp scent of pine mingled with the odor of wet leaves and rich soil. Moss-covered trees blocked all but scattered beams of sunlight dappling the forest floor, but gold flecks sparkled within their trunks. Evergreens rose thick and full and shining ferns hugged the road. The multi-colored leaves drifted onto the narrowing path like soft, rainbowed snow. Birds chirped as they flitted from tree to tree, heedless of the Cord's loss. Despite Raelyn's heavy heart, the forest calmed her fears and soothed the ache.

They made camp once before the trees thinned. By evening on the second day, they stood before a towering earthen cliff the color of burnished copper. The sun melted behind it, crowning it in a deep glow as they entered the gate. Throngs of people, dressed in colorful cloaks and shawls, filled an open adobe courtyard, surrounded by a high clay wall; rustic, but dignified. Some led horses carrying bulging baskets of fruits and vegetables. Young women stood by small carts filled with bread. Children ran across their path, laughing and calling out. Most of the Shalhalans they passed stopped what they were doing and bowed to Othana and the others as they passed. Raelyn couldn't tell if they were showing respect to the warriors or welcoming the newcomers. But it wasn't unlike their treatment in Malvok so Raelyn offered a tiny nod here and there just in case.

Finally, they stopped in front of a large archway that allowed passage into the cliff itself. Shaped like a Gothic cathedral, it was at least thirty feet tall and would have allowed ten horses to walk abreast. Unlike the simple clay surroundings, the arch was made up of perfectly aligned and intricately patterned stonework inlaid with colorful gems. A similar but smaller doorway opened to the left, which Othana led them through. She jumped from the chariot, gesturing for Raelyn, Joshua, and Gabe to follow with Olmund close behind. Larken stayed with the horses.

"We have food and lodging," she said as they came to a narrow stairway made up of the same lustrous pebbles as the road. It wound up and around the adobe wall. They climbed, single file, up and up, soon passing through a short, low tunnel that opened onto a small courtyard. In the fading light, lanterns glowed low and orange next to wooden doorways. A tall lamp post cast a bright swath of light. A few people, all busy at one task or another, milled about. A man sweeping in front of one of the doors looked up and waved at them.

"Chokomai!" he called. Both Othana and Olmund nodded.

"Chokomai, Lovid," Othana replied.

Lovid grinned and went back to his work. Across the courtyard, another set of steps continued their ascent. As darkness overtook the Shalhalan village, weariness seeped into Raelyn's muscles and her eyes burned. Gabe grumbled behind her. They climbed three more levels with similar courtyards.

At the top of the fourth set of stairs, Othana and Olmund entered a final courtyard and led them to a passageway, at the end of which were two wooden doors opposite one another.

Othana opened one door. "We have prepared two rooms for you to rest." Joshua and Gabe followed Olmund as he opened the other door.

Raelyn followed Othana into a massive room. Although the walls were of the same rust-colored clay as the rest of the village, they were inlaid with mosaic tiles in all manner of geometric designs and covered in colorful wall hangings. Like the tapestries in Malvok, the patterns changed and reshaped, seemingly more for the sheer beauty of it rather than to reveal messages.

The floor was made of shimmering flagstone and the domed clay ceiling rising high above was painted with a scene that also moved and changed. But the room was so dark, Raelyn couldn't discern any details, and she was too tired anyway. A pang in her temples forced her eyes shut for a moment.

Othana led her to a four-poster bed crafted from smooth trees, each post a trunk carved and honed, highlighting glints of gold. Their branches swept up and connected to create a canopy of the faceted emerald leaves, sparkling like gems. Carved trunks stood at the foot of each bed and a massive wardrobe on one wall. Raelyn swallowed hard as she looked to the second bed. The strand of urgency, pulled tight since they had left camp, threatened to snap.

She followed Othana to the back of the room on stiff, tired legs. Heavy green drapes were pulled back and revealed an expansive balcony overlooking the dark woodland. The sapphire sky stretched above the forest and held the first few stars of the night. The moon, just past full and already directly overhead, shone bright.

Gabe and Joshua walked out onto the far side of the balcony that apparently connected the two rooms.

"We will leave you to rest," Othana said. "We have provided food and drink." She gestured to a table along the balcony wall. "In the morning you will meet the elder, Olvida." Though maintaining her stoic demeanor, for the first time she sounded tired.

Gabe threw up his arms. "That's it?"

"You fear for your friend, but we have not abandoned her. On the contrary, if you stay the course and prepare for your quest, you will save her." Without another word, she turned and left.

"So now what?" Raelyn asked, her voice ragged.

"Food." Joshua nodded to the table laden with bread, meat, vegetables, and fruit.

A chill breeze rustled the trees below as they picked at the last of the vegetables. Joshua poured wine from a crystal decanter into clear delicate glasses and offered one to Raelyn. She took it and sagged in her seat.

Rather than complete thoughts, Raelyn let her mind roll through the events of the past week since Avery's disappearance. Like a slideshow, each image passed across her mind.

The dust storm. Click. The Olyaund attack. Click. The long fingers reaching into Jinny's hair.

Raelyn's face grew warm as she thought about Kade leaving them to struggle on. She frowned and took a swig of wine. Like the ale, it was effect-free.

Gabe pushed kernels of corn around this plate. "Can we trust them? You really think Jinny's okay?"

"We have no choice," Joshua said. "And we can't wait for Kade and Avery to show up."

"Assuming they will," Raelyn snapped and drained her wine.

Kade wasn't there. Avery was gone and Jinny captured. Whatever the path, this couldn't be part of it. Gabe's shocked face only increased her anger.

"If this was the right path, Avery wouldn't have left," she continued sulkily. "Kade wouldn't have deserted us. Jinny would still be with us. It's all gone wrong, and we're expected to just sit and have dinner and go to bed, while who knows what's happening —" Raelyn caught herself. Gabe's eyes were filled with tears.

She cleared her throat. "I'm going to bed." She left, still burning with anger.

She rinsed off in a tub of cool water in a connecting washroom and changed into soft pajamas from the wardrobe. She sank into a down mattress. But sleep skipped away. Raelyn rolled onto her back and opened her eyes, staring into the darkness. She put her fingertips on the Durinial. Its weight pressed on her throat.

Kade's words came to her:

"More than what you see, you will know if you are on the right path. You will feel it guiding you . . ."

Raelyn had felt no guidance. But she had found the path. Could Othana be wrong? Maybe the road wasn't actually destroyed.

She shifted onto her side and pulled the blankets around her shoulders. She squeezed her eyes shut, willing sleep to find her.

At some point, she drifted off and dreamed of the demon from Malvok. But it was Harlan, not Lydia, it attacked. Peter stood next to her.

He leaned over and whispered in her ear, "It's your fault."

CHAPTER TWENTY-SIX

Raelyn opened her eyes as the sun peered over the eastern horizon, turning the room's clay walls to a blazing copper. She pushed herself up on one elbow. The desire to bury beneath the warm blankets and pull the pillow over her head vanished as Jinny's panicked face flashed across her mind. Her shining black hair tangled in the fingers of the repulsive creature.

Raelyn slipped out of bed. In the wardrobe, she found a long-fringed leather skirt, a soft red top embroidered with turquoise stitching, and a red shawl. She changed and returned to the balcony, wrapping the shawl around her shoulders. The horizon shimmered deep gold, rising to orange, then blushed a pale pink before giving way to blue. The trees extended across the vast woodland. Beyond vision. The still morning air was icy. Puffs of her breath evaporated at every exhale. Winter seemed to be on its way. A rustle behind Raelyn made her jump and spin around.

"Sorry." Joshua, wearing a long shirt of thick, colorful fabric over light-tanned leather pants, stayed a notable distance away.

She turned back to the sunrise. "I think I may be perpetually on pins and needles."

"For now, that'll probably serve you well."

Raelyn nodded. High-alert was one thing. But the persistent knot in her stomach and tight chest wouldn't help them in whatever was coming.

She leaned over the balcony, looking at a similar balcony seven stories below and avoiding Joshua's gaze. "Hey, sorry for last night."

Joshua shrugged. "We're all wound tight."

Raelyn stole a glance at him as he squinted out at the sun.

"Kade put a lot of pressure on you to lead us." Joshua looked over and nodded at the Durinial. "I've been meaning to ask about your good-luck charm."

Raelyn touched the Durinial and let out a dry laugh. "A parting gift from Kade." She gazed across the treetops, considering how much to share. "He says it's an amulet to help guide us on the right path. Sort of a map. But I don't really understand it."

"Kade told me to trust your instincts. Is that how you found our path through the storm?"

"You mean the road we followed?"

"I don't know nothing about a road. I was just following your lead. It was all sinking under my feet."

Raelyn frowned and looked out at the now fully risen sun. Could the road have just materialized under her feet? She glanced behind Joshua as Gabe walked up, a towel thrown over his bare shoulders. His eyes were puffy and his red hair damp and disheveled. He was dressed in pale leather pants like those worn by the Shalhalans. A colorful cloak was draped over his arm.

"Good morning," Raelyn said, watching him closely.

"Morning," he mumbled. Though his face was worn with grief, Gabe's blue eyes were direct, hard, and clear. He seemed to have snapped into a sharp awareness and singular resolve.

Othana strode onto the balcony. She had traded her scant fighting garb for a soft yellow top and long pants. In the cool morning light, her chestnut-colored skin glowed and orange wisps, much like the sunrise, drifted from her dark hair and shoulders. She swept sharp blue eyes over them, but her smile was warm.

"Glad to see you all up. You slept well?" She didn't wait for an answer. "You will breakfast with Olvida. Come, I will take you to her. I bid you bring your weapons."

"Any news about Jinny?" Gabe asked.

Othana stopped and looked over her shoulder. "She is alive. And we have much to do to prepare our rescue."

That was enough to get them moving. Raelyn grabbed her bow and quiver of arrows, then dug through her pack for the Bokar. She tucked it under her shawl into the back of her belt as she sprinted down the corridor.

The activity of the night before was nothing compared to the busy morning. As they descended the stairs, they dodged people transporting heavy bolts of fabric, baskets of fruit, and buckets of water. Everyone seemed to have a job and worked with zeal. The newcomers received their share of whispers and stares, but it did not stop the clamor. As they descended the stairs, the excitement heightened. Back at the courtyard, Raelyn could hear the music of drums and flutes drifting from within the cliffside. Her world had fallen apart, and they were having a party. She inhaled, long and slow, drawing in the scent of fallen leaves on the cool autumn air. They weren't warriors, but here she would find her answers.

Othana led them through the ornate archway, across the marketplace, and back onto the main roadway. A narrower path through the kaleidoscope of trees led south. Soon individual domed structures, built from the same clay as the cliff, lined the road until they came to a large clearing with a cluster of huts. Simple gardens grew in front of a few. Just as in the cliff dwellings, Shalhalans were diligently working. They tended their gardens and navigated horse-drawn carts through the narrow roads. Under a tree, children sat on rugs as an elderly villager weaved a tall basket for them. In the distance, a pasture, dotted with sheep, stretched out beyond sight. Though not void of activity, the village was steeped in a tranquility that belied the threat lying just beyond.

They stopped in front of a dwelling, larger than the others, multi-domed with round, stained-glass windows. Smoke curled from a clay chimney. A low stone wall enclosed a garden filled with blue, pink, and yellow flowers. Othana opened the low gate and led them up a stone walkway. Without knocking, she entered the house and held the door for Joshua, Gabe, and Raelyn to follow.

As soon as Raelyn crossed the threshold, the Durinial began to hum. The vibration made her skin beneath the amulet tingle. The sensation radiated through her chest and down her arms.

A circular dwelling, with a high domed ceiling similar to her room but smaller, was encased with shelves of books. Light filtering through the windows and glowing lanterns on low tables illuminated the room with a soft, calming light. At the center a round, weighty table was set for a meal. Seated on the far side was an old woman so small she seemed to peek over the table. Her tanned face was deeply lined, and her white hair piled on her head in a bun. Her luminous blue eyes were so pale, they were nearly white. Pearly light pulsed around her head and shoulders.

Though the room was rustic, even primitive, the atmosphere held a regal dignity. This was no castle, and they were not being presented to the lord and lady of a kingdom, but the moment was no less solemn, even ceremonial.

"Chokma, kamasa Olvida," Othana said to the woman and bowed low. "I present the Cord of Earth Apparent."

Raelyn pressed her lips together. *What's left of it.* She followed Othana's example as Olvida smiled, rendering the lines around her eyes and mouth deep creases. Joshua bowed, but Gabe only twitched his head.

"Yakoke ikana," Olvida said, her voice as dry as shuffling ancient parchment. "Welcome, warriors. I am Olvida, elder of Shalhala."

Gabe stood stone still, hands clenched, leveling a stare at Olvida. His frustration was entirely justified. They were wasting time.

"How can we get Jinny back?" Gabe blurted.

Olvida nodded once to him but ignored the question. "Come." She gestured to the table, around which five chairs had been placed. "*Minti cha impa.* Let us eat. And I will share what I know."

They each chose a seat as Olvida's pale eyes followed their every move. Othana slipped out of the room through a dark doorway.

Olvida watched them silently for a few minutes as they ate. "You are weary and downtrodden and have overcome much. But do not worry. As you slept, we have not been idle."

Raelyn put down her fork, and Gabe and Joshua stopped eating.

"Only moments ago, we received word —"

Gabe shot up from his chair. "Jinny!"

Olvida smiled and nodded.

"From Enloe? You sent scouts?" Joshua asked.

Olvida nodded again. "Not only scouts." The dry raspiness left Olvida's voice. "We have a spy. And"—she pointed a gnarled finger toward the ceiling— "you fight with greater weapons. You will have victory."

Gabe frowned at Olvida. "Speaking of weapons, why is it they have spaceships and you all run around in horse-drawn buggies?"

Raelyn cringed. Gabe was afraid, and it seeped out in uncharacteristic brashness. But the anguished part of Raelyn found his question deeply satisfying. She waited for a reprimand as Olvida gave Gabe a measured stare, her head cocked to one side.

A broad grin broke across her weathered face. "You assume their method of transportation to be superior?" She nodded and looked around the table. "Aye. It may seem so. But the Periferie has a way of leveling the playing field, you might say. Here, all such conveniences are equal. What you perceive as varying degrees of advancement are simply different tools. One is not better than the other."

"Then why do you choose one way over another?" Gabe asked.

Olvida shrugged. "I like horses." She rose, using the table as leverage. "Othana!" The woman immediately appeared in the doorway.

"Othana will guide you to your mentor," Olvida explained. "You each have a particular task and your training will be most unlike what you received at Malvok. Stealth, knowledge, wisdom and discernment will be your . . . weapons." She inclined her head toward Gabe.

"We have time to learn new skills?" Joshua asked. "Even with what we've learned so far, we've got by mostly on luck."

"Ah, but luck has nothing to do with your success," Olvida countered.

"I wouldn't call it 'success'," Gabe grumbled.

"And what would you call it, child?" Olvida's tone became fierce. Her eyes flashed. Her presence filled the room, her pearly light crackling like lightning. She looked at each of them in turn. "Four temporals from Earth Apparent have learned to maneuver weapons beyond anything they've known. Traveled days without the help of a guide and have found themselves in my presence. That *is* success. And most certainly *not* the result of luck." She took a deep breath and closed her eyes for a moment. When she opened them, she addressed Gabe, her voice again quiet and raspy. "Success is not always gained in the way you expect. But do not dismiss results. Nevertheless"—she looked at each in turn—"your time grows short. The winter solstice is drawing near and soon Cosyn's assault on your loved ones will be complete."

Othana took a step toward Gabe. "Come, Gabriel. I will lead you to your Chufai, who will give you guidance for your journey to Olyaund."

As they left the room, Olvida turned to Joshua.

"You are a soldier. A protector. I would like you to train with Olmund." She beckoned him to her. Joshua cocked one eyebrow as he pushed back his chair and stood, circling the table to stand in front of her.

She smiled up at him. "You have skill with your sword, but you have not yet discovered its power. The evil you face can only be overcome by your spirit. What is here," she said, pushing against his chest, "not by your strength."

Joshua gave Raelyn a quick glance and an almost imperceptible eyeroll. Even a week ago Raelyn would have agreed the spiritual mumbo jumbo was taxing. But something was shifting. The more she examined — *seek and you will find* — the more she found Kade's, Altizara's, Olvida's teachings not only plausible but more real than anything she had encountered in Earth Apparent.

"Olmund," the old woman called. Like Othana, he appeared immediately. Joshua followed him silently and did not look back.

"Now, my child." Olvida turned her full attention to Raelyn. "Let us explore the library." Without waiting for a reply, she exited the room. Raelyn followed her outside. Olvida shuffled to an awaiting suklo.

Larken grinned down at them, loosely holding the reins.

"Chokma Kamassa, Olvida," he said as he bent down and helped her climb in. Their light combined for a moment, becoming an icy blue.

"Greetings, Larken," Olvida chuckled.

Larken held out a hand to Raelyn. When the women were settled behind him, Larken clicked his tongue and shook the reins.

Olvida patted Larken's arm. "We are in a bit of a hurry."

Larken laughed and nodded. He whipped the rains and they jolted forward. Olvida gripped the sides, grinning, as wisps of her white hair trailed from her bun.

Soon they were back inside the cliffside courtyard. Larken pulled up to the same set of stairs they had climbed to their sleeping quarters. He hopped down and helped Olvida out, then Raelyn.

"Come." Olvida made for the stairs. She took her time, placing each foot carefully on each step and balancing with her cane. Raelyn followed one step behind.

"Olvida," she said, her voice flat against the cold clay walls.

"Yes, child?" Olvida answered, continuing to climb.

"The Olyaunders . . ."

"Were Shalhalans once. Great warriors. Well trained. Loyal. Long ago, many hundreds of years, when Cosyn attacked the temporal cities, our captain, Olyaund, took a group of fighters to the Theurham Forest." Olvida grunted as she reached the first courtyard and hobbled across it. "They were never seen again. Over time others went missing. Scouts and those charged with protecting our borders." They continued through a breezeway like the one that led to their rooms. "After years uncounted, we were attacked by a strange and fearsome race. Many Shalhalans sacrificed themselves, but we prevailed. Afterward, their leader demanded a parlay. He called himself 'Radan the Overseer'. But I knew who he was. Olyaund, our lost warrior."

"But they don't look anything like the Shalhalans," Raelyn interrupted as they entered a round alcove ending in an imposing wooden door.

"Ah, but you know the enemy's greatest weapon: deception. These deceived Shalhalans rejected the image given to them by their Creator. They took a new form and chose machines over artistry. Metal over earth. War over peace."

"How did you know Radan was Olyaund?"

Olvida placed a hand on the lever and paused. She turned halfway to Raelyn and looked up into her eyes before pushing hard on the door. "A mother knows her son."

A hollow grief filled Raelyn as she followed Olvida. Even the guardians of Alnok experienced terrible heartbreak. Her sorrow was, in some measure, swept away as they entered the library. Raelyn had expected little more than a parlor of books. But three stories of towering stone shelves held rows of every color, shape, and size of book. The second landing, accessed by several winding stone staircases, overlooked the main floor by a narrow balcony that circled the perimeter. An identical third level finished in an arched ceiling swirling with rich color. The effect was dizzying and overwhelming. At the furthest end, a colorful drape fell ceiling to floor and parted over a wide opening. A large round table took center stage. Several elderly men hunched over rolls of parchment and open books. Shuffling papers whispered and echoed around the chamber.

"You have the Bokar?" Olvida asked from behind her.

Raelyn's heart gave a few thumps. The book, a source of disappointment and confusion, might finally be explained. She reached under her shawl and pulled it from her belt. She held it out for Olvida to take, but the elder smiled and led Raelyn past rows of books until they reached a back nook of the library. She went to a shelf, recessed into the wall, and pressed one of the stones. A click sounded and the shelf swung in. Olvida pushed the doorway open and disappeared inside. A lantern hanging on the wall sputtered to life, casting light onto a landing. A set of stone steps led downward.

Olvida reached up, pulled the lantern off the wall, and carefully started down the stairs. Their steps echoed and the farther they descended, the more Raelyn saw the now-familiar waves in the air. The stairs seemed to sway and swim. She ran her hand along the stone wall to steady the dizziness. By the time they reached the bottom, her head pounded, and her stomach was rolling.

Olvida's cane tapped across a room spinning too fast to see. Raelyn fell against a wall and a different room burst into her field of vision.

Peter's hospital room. The slow beeping, counting off Peter's heartbeat like a death knell. The skittering shadow filled the corner of the room, expanding and contracting as though breathing. Her dad gripped the bed rail as he stared down into Peter's slack face. She could hear his muffled sobs, as though underwater. Raelyn drew nearer. Fulton's hair hung in dirty clumps and his shoulders shook. The shadow expanded across the ceiling like before. Raelyn glared up at it.

A door opened behind her, and Dr. Brand entered the room holding a clipboard of papers and followed by a tall nurse in blue scrubs. The doctor approached Fulton and put a gentle hand on his arm. At his touch, Fulton's shoulders sagged. Not from comfort. From defeat.

The doctor held out the clipboard and Fulton looked at it, making no move to take it. He said a few dampened words. Raelyn's heart beat painfully as she stepped around the doctor, trying to see the words on the documents. But Fulton took the clipboard and held it at his side. He nodded and the doctor turned to leave.

Raelyn ran around to the other side of Peter's bed and took hold of the bed rail, facing her father. The shadow, dripping and spitting, hovered directly overhead. Raelyn looked up, drew in every ounce of air her lungs would hold, and screamed up at the shadow. "GO!!" Her eyes watered and her throat burned, but the shadow withdrew. The beeping came faster, and Raelyn glanced down at Peter. His eyes moved back and forth beneath his lids. Something clattered to the floor. Her father, his bloodshot eyes wide and chest heaving, stared down at his son. He had dropped the clipboard.

Liquid filled Raelyn's mouth. It ran down her throat as Olvida's cool, dry hands press a mug to her lips. Raelyn opened her eyes. Olvida was crouching over her on a dirt floor. A low stone ceiling swam into view. A half dozen lanterns on stone walls filled the room with cool blue light. It smelled of old leather and aged paper. Raelyn struggled to her feet.

"My brother . . ." Raelyn sobbed and gave up trying to stand. Though the seripyn sharpened her thoughts, her mind was filled with a haze of panic.

"Do you wish to save him?" Olvida's words were sharp and cut through her frenzy.

"Of course." Raelyn looked up at the old woman. Contrary to her harsh words, her glowing face shone with compassion.

"Then we must get down to business." Olvida offered her hand. Raelyn took it and Olvida pulled her from the floor with ease.

"Peter"—Raelyn pulled her hand away— "I think my dad is considering removing him from life support."

"That does not change your present course." Olvida took Raelyn's hand again and looked up at her. "Trust your path, Raelyn."

A band of panic tightened across Raelyn's chest. She shook her head and mouthed words that would not come. Tears leaked from her eyes. How could she leave Peter like that?

"Your choice was always to save him." Olvida turned Raelyn's hand over and placed the Bokar into it. "That has not changed."

Raelyn nodded and gripped the book. If closing the plye would save her brother, she'd better damn well know how to do it. She gazed around the room. The shelves lining these walls looked to be made of opaque glass. And rather than books, they held single, pale, almost luminescent pages lying edge to edge in every color. A pastel rainbow of glowing papers.

"We're in Velare," Raelyn said.

Olvida nodded.

"What do I do?" she croaked.

Olvida shuffled to a lectern near the center of the room. "Only you and I may enter this room." She waved Raelyn to her. "All of the books in the upper rooms are sacred; important and useful for instruction." Olvida pointed to one of the shelves. "However, here we have collected the Mablian pages, which hold the blessings of Arkonai. Open the Bokar and place it on the table."

Raelyn did as she was told. After having been shoved in her pack and hidden beneath her clothes through forests, across a river, and through a dust storm, the empty book should have been a tattered mess. Instead, the leather gleamed as though she had just oiled it. The engraved vine pattern was pristine, curving, and winding across the empty cover.

"Now, choose a page."

"Any page?" Raelyn looked at Olvida, surprised.

Olvida smiled and nodded. "Aye, any page."

Raelyn circled the room. The first page would be significant. No matter the outcome, it was the first step in discovering what the book meant and why it was given to her. But aside from the different colors, all the pages were blank. She focused on the Durinial but it had gone silent. She could choose a yellow one. It resembled Altizara's light. Or orange, like Othana. What color would her own light be? Raelyn walked past the pages, blue, green, purple. The purple caught her eye. She held her hand over it, imagining the purple light passing between her fingers to be her own. It looked right. With a deep breath, she plucked it from the shelf and turned it over. Nothing on either side. She held it to the light hoping for a mysterious watermark. Blank. While smooth and heavier than she would have guessed, there was no magical force or phenomenon. Her shoulders fell.

"Now, place the page in the Bokar," Olvida instructed.

Raelyn took the page to the journal as though any sudden movement may cause it to disintegrate; a tiny vibration began to pulse against her fingers where she held it. The Durinial picked up the rhythm. Together they beat in time. As Raelyn held the page above the Bokar a gleam of light flared across it. The light dwindled and fine letters in a slanted script appeared. She tilted her head, trying to read the words. There was a soft tug, as though someone was pulling at the page, urging her to release it. She let go and it settled into the binding. A hushed whisper gusted through the room. Words surfaced and settled into her mind:

You are loved.

You are light.

You are chosen.

They were the words on the page. But a voice also whispered in her ear. Speaking to her mind. And her heart. This voice. This was Arkonai. She looked at each statement, studying the words as though deciphering ancient hieroglyphics. So simple. But impossible to understand. This had nothing to do with Peter.

She kept her eyes glued to the words. "Olvida, I don't understand. How —"

"Listen, child."

Raelyn heard the words again.

Seek, Raelyn. That's what Othana had said. And Kade. These were not the answers she had expected. Or even wanted. But . . . what if they were the truth?

She let them fill her up, penetrate her heart and radiate through her body, even as she tried to deny, even debate with, this voice. Thoughts of Cosyn, plyes, home, Jinny, even Peter dissolved until they became tiny water droplets next to this vast ocean of truth: She was chosen. She was light. She was loved.

This new knowledge, this strange identity, filled her mind. It seeped into her heart. Air leaked from her lungs until she was utterly deflated. She took a great gasp of air and with it a powerful understanding surged like a current pushing electricity from the roots of her hair to her fingertips and into her gut. She not only understood but she also accepted that she was light, loved, and chosen. She felt at once invincible and entirely vulnerable. She realized she was sobbing and glanced down at the page. It was once again blank. She wiped the tears from her face and looked at Olvida.

Olvida nodded solemnly, then a great smile broke out across her face. "But just wait until you read it aloud."

CHAPTER TWENTY-SEVEN

"Hey, wait up!" Joshua called as Raelyn strolled down the stairs. The day had dwindled to an incandescent afternoon, simmering in the empty plaza. She cradled the Bokar against her chest in her folded arms and waited as he jogged to her. Though the page was again blank, Olvida had promised the writing would reappear and Raelyn would understand it in time. She smiled at Joshua, but a chill met the warmth in her chest in an uncomfortable collide. "How'd your lesson go?"

Joshua stopped and studied her face, squinting. "Your lesson must've been good."

Raelyn forced a dry chuckle. "Why?"

"I don't know." Joshua rubbed his beard looking her over. "You just look . . . rested," he finished with a shrug.

A portion of Raelyn's new found peace dissolved. "You remember the journal I was given in Malvok?" Apprehension twittered in Raelyn's stomach. The last time she had confided in Joshua, it had not gone well.

"Yeah."

"I . . . um, never showed anyone"—Raelyn's face flushed, and she looked at the ground— "but it was empty when I got it." She gave Joshua a quick glance, but he showed no reaction. "I just added the first page." She finally met his eyes. He raised his eyebrows as though anticipating more.

"Actually, the page kind of inserted itself," Raelyn mumbled and ran her hand through her hair. Now it sounded silly, not some grand revelation.

"Right," Joshua said slowly, nodding his head and narrowing his eyes as though trying to understand.

"I don't know" Irritation eroded another sliver of joy. What was the use in talking about it? "So, what about you? You seemed anxious about something."

Joshua cleared his throat. "My lesson didn't just cover sword fighting." He paused and stared into Raelyn's eyes. "Olmund went over their strategy for rescuing Jinny and closing the plye in Olyaund," he finished in one breath.

"What?" A jittery excitement, not entirely devoid of fear, pounded in Raelyn's heart.

"Actually, it was just a briefing on how to get in, where they think the plye is located, and a rough map of the city. They're leaving the strategy to me." Joshua looked at Raelyn, one eyebrow raised.

Her stomach did a slow flip.

"But you don't know anything about those creatures, the land, their weapons." Her heart sank. This was not what she had hoped. The Shalhalans went to battle for them in the desert. Why would Joshua be expected to figure out their next move? "I mean what were those vehicles they used? Like some sort of spaceship?" Now frustration evaporated the last trace of the serenity she had felt only moments ago.

"The Shalhalans seem to think I'm up for the task." Joshua stared at her as though daring her to object.

"Right." Raelyn backed down immediately. "So, do you have any ideas?" She measured her words to avoid sounding accusatory.

"Actually, I do. Enloe came back without Jinny, but he did bring something with him."

"I heard them dragging something to the camp. And Othana and Enloe talking about an Olyaund craft?" Raelyn said.

"Yeah. One of their . . . vessels . . . the metal . . ."

"Just say it. Spaceship." Now it made sense. Something they could use.

Joshua rubbed the back of his neck and shook his head. "Okay, yeah, spaceship. But I need more time to think through some of the details." He jogged back a few steps. "I'll go over the plan with you and Gabe tonight." He turned and jogged to the stairs, mounted them two at a time and disappeared, leaving Raelyn spinning in her skepticism.

"You really think that'll work?" Gabe asked, his hazel eyes unreadable in the torchlight. Gabe, Joshua, and Raelyn sat around the table on their connecting balcony. Bits of roast pork and potatoes littered their plates. The last of the daylight slipped away and the first stars winked high in the ombre sky.

"You have a better plan?" Joshua asked sharply. He had spent the last hour outlining his plan for entering Olyaund City, finding Jinny, locating the plye, and escaping back to Shalhala. At various intervals Raelyn and Gabe had both interrupted with doubts and objections. Many of their concerns centered around the disloyalty of an Olyaund defector who had passed much of the intel on to Shalhalan scouts.

Gabe shrugged. "A lot could go wrong."

Raelyn leaned close to Joshua. "We only have this spy's word that Jinny's . . . unhurt. Will the Shalhalans not help at all?"

Joshua drew a deep breath and exhaled slowly. "We'll be escorted to the edge of the forest. From there we're on our own." His eyes darted to Gabe and then Raelyn. He sat forward and splayed his fingers on the table. "There's something else," he said looking at his hands. "Starting today we have to stop drinking the seripyn."

"What?" Gabe shouted, jumping to his feet.

Joshua was already shaking his head. "I know, I know. But it doesn't work any other way. The Shalhalans have already made many unsuccessful attempts. Even joined forces with Malvok. But it seems Olyaund is impenetrable. At least for them."

"But we'll never make it that long without the tea," Gabe argued.

"Joshua," Raelyn said, keeping her voice quiet and calm. "I think I know where you're going with this. But I agree with Gabe. I can't function after just a few days without the tea. There's no way I could cross the desert, sneak into Olyaund, find Jinny and close the plye. Even fully lucid, we don't even know if the plan will work."

Joshua leveled his eyes at her. "If we can't make it work, we're dead in the water." She held his gaze, but her mind raced. Two days. That was the longest she had been able to handle without the tea in her system.

"The timing has to be perfect," Joshua continued. "We'll leave day after tomorrow. It'll take us two to get back to the main path. Olmund says it'll take us five days to cross the desert and reach Olyaund City."

"Nine days without our only means to function in this world." Gabe's voice was flat, matter of fact.

"If we don't . . ." Joshua began.

"The Olyaunders will see us coming," Gabe finished with a quiet, weary resolve.

Joshua nodded. "By day seven, Olmund says we should be faded enough to be nearly undetectable to the Olyaunders. That's the theory, anyway." Joshua leaned back as though relieved to have this complication in the open.

"Theory?" Gabe asked.

"Olmund told me about the temporals who lived here before. It was the same for them. The seripyn was supplied as a part of their food and water, a required sustenance. But early on, there were a few who bucked the system."

"And?" Raelyn pressed when he didn't continue.

Joshua locked his gaze on the table. "And they were lost. Couldn't be found."

"What makes you think that won't happen to us?" Gabe asked, barely above a whisper.

"I don't."

Raelyn leaned forward. "You're not making a very good case."

When Joshua looked up, his expression was one of hard resolve. "There are no guarantees, but they believe we should be safe for the nine days. And apparently it helps to keep yourself present here. Mentally. Resist fading into Earth Apparent. We have to be perfectly balanced. Too far one way, we'll lose you to no-man's-land. Not enough, we'll be detected by the Olyaunders."

"Is that possible?" Raelyn asked.

Joshua shrugged. "Haven't tried."

"If they can't see us, how will we see each other?" Gabe asked.

"We'll be experiencing the same reaction, so we'll see each other as normal. It's a delicate balance. We can't fade entirely, so we won't be invisible to them, but I'm told it'll be enough."

Gabe nodded, as though that made sense to him. Raelyn knew she would have to take his word for it. None of it made sense to her, but she was running out of time. Her dad had seen the spike in Peter's vitals. With that glimmer of hope, Raelyn was sure her father would keep him on life-support. And they weren't yet at the solstice, when Cosyn's tie to Earth Apparent was at its strongest.

Joshua cleared his throat and rubbed his eyes with his palms. "Nine days will push us to our limits. Maybe even past. I don't know." He dropped his hands and his shoulders sagged. "There's plenty that could go wrong. But I've gone over every alternative with Olmund. We keep coming back to this plan as the only way to get in, find Jinny, and reach the plye." He looked more drained than at any point since Raelyn had first met him at the warehouse. If she expected her dad to have hope, shouldn't she? And Joshua needed to know they trusted him.

She took a deep breath. "Okay, we stop drinking the seripyn. Starting now. In two days, we'll head for Olyaund. Let's get a good night's sleep and tomorrow we'll go over the plan again."

Gabe sighed as he stood. "Okay, but when I puke, I hope nobody's in the way." He no doubt meant it as a joke, but his worn and sorrowful face belied his words. He shoved his hands into his pockets and slumped to his room.

Raelyn sat back and looked at Joshua, but he was again staring at the table. Nothing had changed between them. Why should it? She couldn't expect Joshua to trust her, much less understand, now that he knew what she had done. But she could at least try. "Olmund must trust this spy."

Joshua shrugged. "He's been in contact with the Shalhalans for a while and apparently hasn't given them a reason not to. He supplied the Olyaund City map, and where to search for the plye. The plan hinges on his trustworthiness. If he's lying, we can only hope to make it back to Shalhala."

Weariness fell on Raelyn like she'd just pulled a lead blanket over her shoulders. She tried to reach the joy she had felt only hours before, but it was fading wisps of smoke. Joshua trusted Olmund and the spy. And in all of it, he hadn't mentioned her role. Or asked her how she would close the plye. Which was a good thing, because she had no idea.

CHAPTER TWENTY-EIGHT

As soon as the pale sunrise filtered into her room, Raelyn bolted upright in bed. She shifted her eyes from one corner to the other, squeezed them shut then opened them wide. She waited for her vision to blur, for the headache and nausea. But aside from a grogginess and an underlying thrum of fear, there were no discernible effects of her abstinence from the seripyn.

She swung her legs over the side of the bed and waited a moment more. When nothing happened, she went to the washroom and took her time splashing cold water on her face and pulling her hair back. When she returned, she found a note wedged in the door of her wardrobe.

Meet in the courtyard this afternoon. —J

She dressed in the same skirt and blouse as the day before and slipped on the soft shoes. Each time she turned, stood, or walked she waited for the familiar tea-less phenomenon. But nothing came. She tucked the Bokar, containing its single page, into the back of her skirt and left the room, hurrying down the stairs to the second landing. She crossed the small patio and made for the massive doors at the end of the hallway.

As Raelyn pushed the door open, a sudden wave of dizziness passed over her. She stopped and focused entirely on the door, half opened, in front of her. She shifted her feet, aware of the shoes pressing against the glimmering pebble floor. She took a deep breath. The chilled air held the lingering smell of burning wood. The wave passed and she was staring into the majestic library. Several men looked up from their books but went back to their reading. A tall woman glanced at Raelyn then continued her walk to one of the tables, holding a book open in one palm. Raelyn's vision held.

Encouraged, she made for the hidden door that would take her into the basement, where Olvida would be waiting. But the room was hidden in the other dimension, Velare. It was one thing not to fade in Alnok. But could she resist it when she crossed this threshold? Raelyn glanced over her shoulder then clicked the door open, slipped in and let it close behind her. The torches sputtered to life, lighting the way down the staircase. She paused, peering into the disappearing light.

So far so good.

She eased her foot onto the first step. A blast of dizziness forced her back and she tripped, landing hard on her rear. Raelyn resisted searching for visions of home. She wanted to see Peter. Confirm he was okay. But that would do no good here and now. If she could push past the fading, she could close the plye and save Peter, not just watch what was happening to him. The stairway slipped and swayed.

Raelyn squeezed her eyes shut so hard tears leaked onto her cheeks. She clenched her fists and forced herself to her feet, falling against the wall. Sweat broke out across her forehead. She took a deep breath, focusing on how the air felt filling her lungs, the cold stone, rough against her hand. As she exhaled, she opened her eyes. The stairs had steadied. Her head was clear. But she still had to make it down the steps and into the room below. Raelyn groaned with fear and frustration, but she stamped her foot back onto the first step. Her head swam for a moment, then settled. She took another step and another until she was at the base of the stairs staring into the dim room.

Olvida, tiny wisps of white light drifting from her white hair, stood at the center table, her tiny frame hunched over her cane.

"You rested well?" she asked and smiled.

Raelyn placed a tentative toe past the doorway. "I think so," she said, glancing around the room at the multi-colored pages. She took a wide step inside and the room stayed put. Raelyn sighed. "Oh, thank God."

"Aye, you are doing well." Olvida nodded approvingly. "Put all of your focus on staying in the here and now. Not only must you learn to read from the Bokar, you must do so while maintaining your presence between Earth Apparent and Alnok." She gestured for Raelyn to place the book on the table. Raelyn pulled the journal from her belt as she walked forward and set it on the table, leaving it closed.

"You have learned that power comes from the heart. In particular, the part of your heart where you feel purest love. Not twittery, flighty feelings." Olvida waved one hand. "The love that is born out of uncompromising dedication. It requires no reciprocation. Love that is unchanging, unselfish and entirely sacrificial." She pressed a shriveled hand to her chest. "Love that believes and hopes all things."

Raelyn shook her head. "I've never felt that kind of love."

"Of course, you have." Olvida let the statement hang in the air. "At least in an imperfect form. If you had not, you would not be here fighting for your brother. She grasped Raelyn's hand, her skin smooth and cool, her grip strong. "When you learn forgiveness, your love will become even more pure."

A knot lodged in Raelyn's throat. Tears blurred her vision as she looked into Olvida's pale eyes.

Olvida brought her other hand to Raelyn's and squeezed even harder. "You have long walked a path of guilt, giving rise to fear."

Raelyn swallowed. "Guilt?" Did everyone in the Periferie know what she had done? She tried to pull her hand from Olvida as shame and anger flushed her cheeks.

Olvida held tight. "Aye. You have the countenance of one looking for absolution from everyone, but never expecting it. And this produces a dangerous amount of fear. It hinders and blocks the love from which the power to close the plye will come." Olvida gave Raelyn's hand a final pat and hobbled to the Bokar. "Now, today I need you to focus on the words." She placed a hand on the book. "Let them fill you. Say them aloud with as much faith as you can muster. Even in an imperfect form, your belief will give the words power. But do not mistake the source. You are but a conduit. You are the reader, not the Author."

Raelyn frowned. Only a few words had formed before. And they could hardly be considered a powerful incantation or spell. "What if when the time comes I can't read the words?"

"Do you believe you read the words with your mind or your heart?"

She looked at the journal and then back to Olvida. "And how exactly do I read from my heart?" Raelyn hated how bitter her voice sounded. But she did not feel loving. She felt angry.

"You must first open your heart." Olvida gave her a kind smile. "And I have a feeling those are some rusted hinges."

Raelyn sighed and nodded. But she didn't make a move to pick up the book. "Olvida, what do love, faith, and forgiveness have to do with reading and saying the words?"

"Power passed through a faulty conduit is depleted, even ineffective. You must clear your heart of anything that hinders your love. And you will not feel that love until you realize you are worthy of such love."

Raelyn gave a short nod and cleared her throat. "All right." She seized the book with both hands. "Open my heart," she whispered. "Read the words."

She opened it to the single page. It stayed upright, hovering vertically for a moment and then drifted down to the right. Her fingertips tingled as she touched the page and the shimmering script rose to the surface like sunlight glistening across a peaceful lake. Raelyn watched the page fill then picked up the book. But the letters might as well have been intricate markings of some ancient, unknowable language. Foreign. Incoherent.

"The Bokar was made for you, Raelyn," Olvida said but her voice seemed to drift from a far distance on a dancing breeze. "You need only speak the words."

Raelyn concentrated on the first few markings. The Durinial pulsed and the vibration rippled into her chest, her stomach, her legs. The letters didn't change, but they became familiar somehow. As though she had read them somewhere before. Maybe a phrase, just in passing, but the message, the meaning, had lodged in her subconscious. The Durinial sent another pulse. Then again. It continued, until it thumped in time with her heart.

She knew these words.

She breathed the first one. "You." Her mouth was dry. She swallowed.

"You are chosen." Her voice cracked. Understanding spread, warm and comforting, across her body.

"You are the light . . . the darkness cannot withstand the light."

"There you are Raelyn," Olvida's far-away voice said. "The words from the Bokar will assure you victory."

"But how will I know what words will close the plye?" Raelyn asked, not taking her eyes from the page.

"Do not worry about what you will say. The Bokar will reveal the right words at the proper time."

The Bokar, *her* Bokar, would show her the words. If she read whatever was written, it would be enough to save Peter. But when the time came, would she be able to?

CHAPTER TWENTY-NINE

Raelyn, Joshua and Gabe raced from Shalhala at dawn. Raelyn rode with Othana in the lead suklo. Joshua and Gabe were on horseback and Olmund followed in a second suklo. They were wearing their Shalhalan shawls over their Malvokian clothes. Raelyn had come to consider the garb her official uniform. The protective clothing, though made of simple fabric, felt like armor. The Bokar, like a secret weapon, was tucked snugly into the back of her belt. The spy had sent word. Something had changed. Jinny was in imminent danger and they could no longer wait.

Dark trees whipped by. Raelyn squinted as the cold air stung her eyes. So far, she had withstood the fading but the impulse to surrender was coming at increased intervals. She gripped the edge of the chariot and leaned forward. Be in the here and now. The air rushed past her ears. The horses' hooves clacked and the suklo bounced against the stone pathway as the morning gave way to afternoon, the sun hiding high above the kaleidoscope forest. Raelyn focused on her physical surroundings and ran through Olvida's instructions over and over. Forgive herself. That's where it started. Or did it begin even before that? How long had she wished to be as important to her parents as her brothers? The artist and the athlete. The accident only confirmed what she had already felt for years. She lacked worth. But being chosen for this path, didn't that say something about her worth? Without having to prove anything, she had been called into Alnok to read from a book made specifically for her. Raelyn gripped the suklo harder, as this first realization, its first roots reaching out and taking hold, filled her chest with thrilling warmth. Kade had asked how much one person could do to earn forgiveness. It might never be enough. She could stop trying to earn it, and just accept it.

"Hi-ya!" Othana pushed the horses faster and the multi-colored leaves flashed by. Raelyn's back ached as they continued their frantic pace, pausing only a few times through the night, and reached the edge of the forest by dawn the next day. Othana slowed the horses to a stop as the trees thinned. The sun cast a feeble light through mounting clouds. Not only were they now out of the protection of the forest, but this also marked the end of Othana and Olmund's escort.

Joshua had already dismounted and was conferring with Olmund. Raelyn hopped down from the suklo, cinching on her backpack which was thin and light following their agreement to carry only the essentials, including a vial of seripyn each for the return trip. Othana circled the harnessed horses to face Shalhala. Gabe paced close by, staring at the ground and chewing his fingernails. Finally, Olmund clasped Joshua's arm and stalked back to his suklo as Joshua joined Raelyn.

"What was that about?" Raelyn asked, keeping her voice low. They watched Gabe walk back and forth on the roadway.

"The Olyaunders attempted to . . ."—he frowned, looking at the ground before turning his back to Gabe and meeting Raelyn's eyes —"use their own means to stop Jinny from fading."

Raelyn flitted her eyes to Gabe but his gaze remained fixed on the ground at his feet. "What does that mean?"

Joshua shook his head. "Dunno. But it's gotta be bad."

"Do we even know where she is?"

Othana joined them. "You do not. However, our spy does. He will find you and lead you to her."

"And how is he supposed to do that?" Gabe asked walking toward them, his arms at his sides and his hands clenched. He stopped, swayed for a moment and closed his eyes. When he opened them he continued advancing on Othana. "The whole point to our going instead of you is because they can't see us."

Othana faced him. "You are beginning to hover between Alnok and Earth Apparent. Less perceptible. For those unaware of your presence, you will appear as nothing more than a shift in the air, a mirage. But our spy will be watching."

"We are ready." Olmund glanced in the direction of the desert. "We must go, Othana. We put them at risk by staying here."

Othana nodded and took a step to Raelyn. "I do not know what awaits." She touched Raelyn's arm in a rare show of affection. "But rely not only on your training." She looked down at Raelyn's throat and brushed the Durinial with her fingertips. "Trust your path." She smiled grimly, then walked back to the suklos.

"Go in Arkonai's strength," Olmund called as he whipped his reins. Othana followed suit and both raced away without looking back. The Cord watched for only a moment before setting out in the opposite direction, walking side by side and leading the two horses, allowing them to recover.

"The Olyaund ship is hidden in the trees on the far side of the lake," Joshua said.

"You sure it's still there?" Gabe asked.

"It will be," Joshua said and picked up the pace.

"How is it the Olyaunders haven't missed it?" Raelyn asked, matching his stride.

"Our mole took care of that. He modified their records, marking it as damaged. At least in their reports it looks like this particular ship is just out of commission. Our timing is critical." Joshua looked at the hazy sun blocked by high, filmy clouds.

"So, you've said." Raelyn glanced at Gabe.

Gabe nodded. "We have until daybreak tomorrow, when the spy will power up the craft."

They had been over the plan a dozen times, but Joshua was clearly encouraged by the repeated instructions. "He has everything arranged. You have the key?"

Gabe pulled a quarter-sized object resembling a computer chip from his pocket and held it out to Joshua.

"Right. Once inside the city, you'll exit the ship as soon as possible. Use it to—"

Joshua grunted and doubled over. Gabe caught him before he fell forward. Joshua put his hands on his knees and took several long breaths. Raelyn and Gabe waited until he stood. "— open the south gate."

Silence fell as they retraced their steps west of the battle site. Raelyn looked across the lake near the roadway. Here, the trees were bare. Hundreds of dazzling trunks and spindly branches glimmered across the lake. A bitter wind blew across the silver water, reflecting a low, gray sky. She sighed and trudged forward.

Gabe gasped. Raelyn spun around as he sunk to his knees. She crouched and tried to help him up, but he rolled onto his side, writhing as though in excruciating pain.

"Gabe, focus!" Raelyn wiped his dusty hair from his face. "Listen to my voice!" Gabe stilled, but continued to gasp for air, his eyes squeezed shut.

Joshua knelt beside her. "Gabe?"

He finally opened his eyes and struggled to sit, and Raelyn patted his back. His hands limp on his crossed legs, he stared into the road. Raelyn glanced at Joshua.

Gabe sniffed. "We lost the appeal." His words were as dry as the sand on which he sat. "I don't know when it happened. But"—his voice cracked, and he wiped his eyes with the back of his hand —"the execution is scheduled." He looked at Raelyn and then

Joshua. "One week from today. And the shadow was there, in the courtroom. Behind the judge."

"Gabe," Raelyn whispered and stroked his arm. "It's not over yet."

"She's right." Joshua stood and held his hand out for Gabe who squinted up at him. "We've gotta job to do."

Gabe nodded as Joshua pulled him up. Joshua clapped him on the back. "Giving in to the fading only makes it worse. It'll make it harder to finish this task and save them. Okay?" He finished more gently.

Gabe nodded.

Joshua mounted his horse and Gabe scrambled up behind him. They began at a canter. But soon Joshua pushed them until they sped along the dusty road at a steady gallop. The sun sank behind them, an orange globe in a filmy sky. They stopped only once, traveling into a dark night as Gabe lit their way with the Leohfaet. Finally, they reached the same spot where they had camped with Othana and the others. They dismounted, gasping for breath and drained their canteens. Even the horses, with their apparently inexhaustible stamina, snorted and wheezed. Gabe sprawled on the road, his chest heaving.

"Let's set up camp." Joshua dropped his pack just off the road. "I'll water the horses and fill the canteens."

"You need help?" Raelyn asked as Joshua gathered the reins.

"Sure." Joshua looked at Gabe. "You good?" Gabe nodded as he unpacked his bedroll. Raelyn collected the canteens and followed Joshua though the dark as he led the horses to the lakeside. Joshua hooked the reins to each saddle and watched as the horses slurped at the water.

Raelyn pulled the lid from one of the canteens as she squatted next to the lake and dipped it below the surface. Should she say something? Whatever she said, the need to gain Joshua's acceptance was little more than a passing notion. Something nice, but no longer needed.

She sighed and stood. "Joshua, whatever you think of me —"

"Yeah, 'bout that." He was silhouetted in the fading light, gazing across the lake. He took a deep breath. "When I was a kid, five or six, my parents were killed. Head-on collision with a pick-up. The guy had a point two-five blood alcohol level."

Raelyn's stomach turned. "Joshua, I —"

Joshua held a hand up. "It was just me and my twin brother. No aunts or uncles. Nobody to take us, so we ended up in foster care. I was eventually adopted. Great family. But my brother, he was shuffled from home to home, and I just lost track of him."

Whatever Raelyn was going to say evaporated. The tender roots of forgiveness withered. She may as well have been behind the wheel.

Joshua continued. "What you told me, it brought all that back, on top of being terrified for my daughter. But here's the thing." He sighed deeply and finally looked at her, his face a dark shadow. "I get guilt. Lived with it every day since Lily went missing. It was my weekend. She was my responsibility and I"—he cleared his throat— "no matter what I think of what you did, no matter what you think of yourself, you love your family and you'd do anything for them. You got us out of the tunnel, you found the road to Shalhala. Kade trusted you to lead us."

A knot formed in Raelyn's throat, so she just nodded.

"I understand that Olvida showed you what to do?" he asked.

Raelyn blinked and pressed her lower back, where the Bokar was secured. "As much as I could understand. I just hope it's enough."

"It will be," Joshua said firmly. "It has to be. For Gabe's dad and Jinny's mom. For your brother and my little girl."

They filled the canteens, returned to the road with the horses and settled in for the remainder of the night. At the first hint of dawn, they packed quickly.

"Okay, wait here," Joshua said over his shoulder as he jogged into the trees.

Raelyn stood next to Gabe. A bird chirped nearby, and a breeze stirred the dry sand. The haze in the eastern sky grew and crept closer as a fine mist. The sun strained to burn through the thick clouds but continued to lose its battle.

Raelyn gazed into the trees. A drone, like a large swarm of bees but higher in pitch, emerged from the forest. The horses stamped and snorted but held their position. Joshua followed the levitating, silvery disc-shaped vessel, barely bigger than Joshua's pick-up out of the trees, guided it with one hand to their camp. When he removed his hand it hovered in place, but continued its disturbing hum. He gave a relieved smile and clasped his hands behind his back. The jewels embedded in the hilt of the Ruah glinted even in the misty morning. He was suddenly the soldier. Confident and commanding.

"One more time: Once Gabe is inside the ship, our spy will remotely guide it to Olyaund and through the main gate. We"— Joshua pointed to himself and Raelyn— "will travel east, leave the horses halfway, then approach the city from the south. Gabe, you'll meet us there at dawn on the fifth day; use the key to open the south gate. We follow the map from the spy to find Jinny." Joshua sighed heavily. "Then we make for the plye." He looked at Raelyn. "You'll close the plye and we'll escape back to Shalhala on foot."

Raelyn's face burned. She knew what to do. And Olvida had given her direction on how to do it. Their victory hung on her shoulders. She looked out at the desert, but it had disappeared in the encroaching mist.

"What is it with this desert?" Gabe shouted, walking a few steps into the haze. "If not a sandstorm, then fog? It doesn't make any sense! How will you and Raelyn see where to go?"

Joshua nodded. "It woulda been nice to have Jinny's Seon. But we found our way through the sandstorm. This won't be any different."

Raelyn touched the Durinial. It was cold and silent. A high-pitched hum came from the ship and an opening appeared at its base.

"That's our cue. C'mon." Joshua ducked beneath and waved Gabe over. "The spy will engage the tracking system any minute." He clasped his hands, palms up at knee level.

Gabe eyed the ship, a hint of apprehension on his face. He dropped his pack, ducked under and stepped onto Joshua's temporary foothold. Once Gabe was inside, Joshua handed his pack through the opening. Gabe's hand reached out of the darkness as though from the belly of a shining, bloated insect.

Joshua bent down and called up into the hole. "Now, remember. You need to reach the city gate before mid-day on the fifth day."

"If all goes as planned, I'll be there." Gabe's voice echoed out of the chamber as the hatch closed and the ship started forward, gliding into the fog.

Joshua stepped back to join Raelyn. The buzzing diminished and disappeared. The mist, cool and damp, encompassed them entirely. They were utterly blind.

"We'll need to ride as hard as the horses can manage if we expect to make it in time," Joshua said grimly as he handed the reins to Raelyn.

"It's not the time that has me worried," she said, heaving herself onto the horse. "It's the path."

Joshua slid into his saddle and guided the horse next to Raelyn.

He glanced at her throat. "We know to head in that direction." He pointed east to the invisible desert. "We'll start with that." He scratched his beard. "On a positive note, the mist might hide us from any scouts. Ready?" He nudged his horse forward without waiting for an answer.

CHAPTER THIRTY

Kade stood just inside the door of the Kulum outpost his arms clasped behind his back. He gazed over the courtyard, weighing his options. He and Avery had trekked from Theurham Forest across the desert without stopping. It had taken twice as long as Kade's trip to rescue him. Three days they had traveled. On the last day, Kade had very nearly carried Avery across the boundary into Velare and for the past two, Avery had slept, waking just long enough to drink some water and take bites of bread. By yesterday evening, he had begun to make his way around the bunker. As Avery's strength returned, Kade's urgency grew. They could continue on the original path to Shalhala. Or return to Malvok. But neither way seemed right.

Kade sighed. "I need a clear path," he whispered. He left the tower and crossed the courtyard, stepping into Alnok. He half-expected to be confronted by some form of Cosyn's horde, if not Cosyn himself. Instead, he was met by a thick, impenetrable mist. He chuckled.

That answers my question for today.

Kade took a step back and re-entered Alnok. He made his way back to the tower and peered through the doorway. All was dark and quiet. Kade sighed and ducked inside. After building a fire in the stove, he settled into a chair, stilled his thoughts, and watched the flames. An answer would come.

Avery shuffled into the room. "Ham, eggs, tomatoes, toast," he declared, sounding much more like himself. "And I could do with a brew." He settled into a chair at the table.

Kade smiled without looking up from the fire. "Tea I can help with." He gazed at Avery. He looked worn and battered, but not destroyed.

Kade prepared the tea and placed two mugs on either side of the wooden table. They faced each other, sipping at the steaming cups.

"We must continue, Avery," Kade said.

"I know, I know." Avery looked deep into his tea. "I've held us up. But I'm feeling stronger. Where do you suppose the others are?" He looked up, his brow knitted.

It was likely Avery was not particularly anxious to rejoin the Cord. He might have been stalling as much as recovering over the past couple of days.

"If all went as planned," Kade began slowly, "they should have reached Shalhala. From there, on to Olyaund to close the plye."

"Botched that plan, didn't I?" Avery watched Kade closely.

Kade smiled. "I am not yet convinced this was not all part of a much bigger plan." He leaned in and held Avery's gaze. "Not all diversions are bad. When corrected, even the wrong path can have a good outcome." Kade waited for another question as he watched Avery break off a piece of bread. When none came, he posed one of his own. One he had been dreading the answer to. "Avery, what caused you to leave Kulum?"

Avery was silent, chewing slowly and staring at the table. He finally met Kade's eyes.

"Right after the banquet, I went looking for a way back. I'd quit drinking the seripyn. I was at the edge of the river when he came to me."

"Cosyn?"

Avery shook his head. "Ditimer."

Kade's heart sank. He searched Avery's face, but he knew he was being truthful.

"You're not surprised," Avery said.

"Nay. I saw him as Cosyn escaped. But that was not the first warning."

"Oh?"

"Jinny. She discerned Ditimer's betrayal. And I would not believe it. Ditimer was my friend and ally."

"Ye 'ave a way of believing the best of others."

"So, it would seem. Ditimer, he offered a way back?"

"Aye. I didn't even know Cosyn was behind it. Kade, you have to understand —"

Kade held up his hand. "I do. I disregarded your requests. Dismissed your misgivings, fears, desires. I was blinded by what I felt was the only way."

Avery nodded, seemingly relieved Kade saw his predicament.

"However," Kade said, looking pointedly at Avery, who stopped in mid-nod. "Your course of action—your choice— put you, the Cord, Penelope, all in great peril. Ditimer's promise to return you to Earth Apparent came with a bargain?"

Avery looked away and wiped his face with his hand. "No, Ditimer just said it would be best if we all returned. I think he thought I might be able to convince the others. And I tried at first. But in the end, they were all so keen to stay." Avery shrugged. "I don't think he wanted anyone to be harmed or that he disagreed with the plan to close the plye. He just didn't think we were the ones to do it."

Kade nodded slowly. "A long-contested strategy."

"But then, in the tunnel," Avery continued. "Ditimer just left us. At the time, I thought maybe he had given up. But I saw him once more in Tegre. He seemed"—Avery squinted his eyes—"different. Not as sure. He said he'd come for me, and whoever wanted to leave, in Kulum. But it wasn't Ditimer who showed up in Kulum. It was Cosyn."

They were silent for a moment before Avery spoke again.

"Why do you think he came to me?" Avery asked. "Why not Josh, or Raelyn?"

Kade sat back and looked over to the fire. Cosyn would have weighed the temporals' strengths and weaknesses, removed whom he considered the strongest. Avery—shrewd, calculated, smart. He might have considered the Cord to be crippled without him. And they may very well be. "Perhaps he wished to remove the strongest member of the Cord."

Avery scowled. "Or the weakest link."

"Your resolve. Your willingness to set everything aside for your goal. These are strengths, Avery. You just used them for the wrong aim."

Avery shook his head and tossed back the remainder of his tea. After a moment's pause, he eyed Kade. "Ye really think they'll get the job done?"

"I do."

"If they can finish it without me, I could go home."

Kade searched his anxious face. Avery still did not fully grasp Cosyn's reach and power in Earth Apparent. Leaving now would not protect Avery's wife. It would likely compound his guilt. Even if the Cord closed the plye in Olyaund without Avery, there were two more. Cosyn would increase his attack on Earth Apparent even if not specifically targeting the Cord. Avery was needed in Alnok. But Kade would no longer dissuade his request.

"Aye, we can make for Herlov, and on to the Silom Pool."

Avery gave a short nod, but his expression was clouded. "When can we start?" His voice was tight with either contained excitement or apprehension. Likely both.

"I do not know, but not yet. The path will be long, and much is still unknown."

"Naturally," Avery said bitterly. He leaned forward, his hands planted on the table. "But we *will* go?"

"Aye, that is your choice."

Avery seemed satisfied and leaned back in his chair.

For the remainder of the morning, Kade answered Avery's steady stream of questions about Alnok, Cosyn, and the Periferie. With the promise of his return home, it was as though he wanted to gain as much information as possible.

"Who is Cosyn? Why does he hate us so much?"

"Cosyn was a beloved creation of Arkonai. But he was corrupted by a consuming pride. By his desire for power. But power taken, not bestowed, will always lead to corruption." Kade sighed. His heart ached over his brother's betrayal as though it had happened only moments ago.

"It was not always so," he continued softly. "Cosyn was part of the Periferie and was given great liberty. He was ranked high in the Arengast. Our order."

"Your order? You have organizations?"

Kade nodded. "The first of Arkonai's creations who ruled the Periferie."

He stood and stretched. "And now I must put all my thoughts to our next heading. We cannot stay here, but the path we take to Herlov remains uncertain."

Kade returned to the fire. He spent the rest of the day and much of the night staring into the flames as they hissed and crackled. There would be some guidance, but it was not yet revealed. Avery kept the fire burning, adding tinder from around the bunker. He slept, paced, and ate, but kept silent. Kade barely took notice of him.

Deep night set in. A wind caused the bunker to creak. The front door rattled. The fire blazed to life with a quick burst.

Kade stood. It was time. Avery was running from corner to corner as the wind raged around the tower. The bunker shuddered, as though an earthquake had struck. Kade's heart pounded and he closed his eyes as he allowed a deep peace to spread through his chest. He relaxed his shoulders. Then all was still. The fire dwindled until it was just embers. The room was doused in shadows. Kade opened his eyes. He saw their path as clearly as though he stood before it.

"Blimey!" Avery yelled, breathing hard. "What's going on?"

"We have our course," Kade said.

"To Herlov?"

"Nay, we travel to Olyaund."

CHAPTER THIRTY-ONE

The mist bore down on Raelyn and Joshua as they rode through the remainder of the day. Joshua kept an eye on the brightest point of light shifting above and then behind them, to keep them on a steady eastern course. They didn't dare travel at night, but as the faintest sheen of morning brightened the mist, they were off again. By the end of the third day, the horses began to protest.

Joshua patted his horse's flank. "I think this is where we leave them."

"You think we've come far enough?" Raelyn asked as she dismounted, cringing as the motion sent a throbbing pain from her eyes to the back of her head.

Joshua shrugged. "Hard to say. Just a feeling. We don't know how far out the Olyaunders send their scouts and they'll see the horses even if they don't see us." He pulled his pack off the saddle. "But we can afford some solid sleep. We'll continue at first light."

Raelyn tossed her bag onto the ground and slumped next to it. She leaned over her crossed legs, groaning, and pressed her hands against her forehead. "My head is killing me."

"I know." Joshua closed his eyes and pinched his brow. "Just think of something else."

"Like what, exactly?" The flash of irritation sent a fresh stab of pain through Raelyn's temples. Her stomach rolled and threatened to empty the water she had just finished. The edges of her vision were entirely blurred.

Joshua looked at Raelyn and narrowed his eyes, but his voice remained maddeningly calm. "Think about Jinny."

Raelyn's face flushed and her retort died in her throat.

He sat down next to her and gave her a tired but wry grin. "We'll get some Tylenol when we get back to Shalhala."

As night closed in around them, Raelyn curled onto her bedroll, wrapped her shawl tight around her shoulders and buried beneath her cloak. Though the cold found ways around the fabric, she dozed off. When she opened her eyes, it was light, Joshua was up, and the horses were gone. She jumped to her feet. "They left? You think they knew we were getting close?"

Joshua shoved his bedroll into his pack. "Maybe."

Raelyn felt for the Bokar, still tucked into her belt, and gazed around the mist. "They might know something we don't."

Joshua nodded. "I think this plan will soon be put to the test."

Securing their weapons and donning their packs, they continued on foot, Joshua several paces ahead of Raelyn, as the sun filtered through the low hanging mist. After only a few minutes, Raelyn felt a tug to her left. As though something prodded her north. She gripped the Durinial. Though it was still, she could not deny the urge to bear left.

"Hold up!" she called.

Joshua stopped and looked over his shoulder.

"I think it's this way," she said.

He peered through the mist. "How do you know?"

"I don't." Raelyn shifted on her feet, looked right and then left. The urgency to head north increased. She touched the Durinial. The gesture was not lost on Joshua.

"Okay." He jutted his chin to indicate Raelyn was to take the lead.

Raelyn's stomach fluttered. She didn't want the lead. But the compulsion to change their course was undeniable, like a rope gently pulling her forward. She trudged ahead and Joshua fell in behind. Her confidence built after a few steps, and she strode faster. There was no doubt. This was the way.

Miles passed and the mist thinned, bringing both relief to see their path ahead and stifling anxiety at the new exposure. Ahead was the forest and the black, ever-present cloud hovering above it. As the sun slipped behind them, dark shadows and vague shapes began to appear. Gnarled trees and large boulders took over the desert the closer they drew to the forest. As their fourth night approached, they took refuge beneath a bare, twisted tree, just broad enough for them to huddle close and eat something. They slept in shifts until a frail daylight broke, then loaded their packs without speaking.

"I think we'll know pretty soon if we're really undetectable," Joshua said as they resumed their journey.

"If not, I'm going to need a shot of the tea to bring me back," Raelyn said. "Otherwise, I won't be able to fight off an angry kitten, much less those creepy ETs."

Joshua shook his head. "Only if our cover's completely blown."

It was impossible to know if it was due to the fading, but they encountered no Olyaunders. Raelyn continued their course until they were, according to Joshua, traveling due north.

"You see that up ahead?" he whispered as the sun pulled itself overhead.

Raelyn, who had been shuffling along with her head down, looked up and focused on the pinpoint that was left of her vision. Ahead, in the distance, a stark white shape rose from the sandy desert. She stopped.

"That has to be it." Joshua put a hand above his eyes and looked at the sun. "We're close, but we need to push it to make it by midday."

The twitter of panic in Raelyn's stomach took flight into her chest as she forced her cramping legs to move. They were nearly there. She would be put to the test. She tried to recall what Olvida had told her about the Bokar and the words that had surfaced on the page. But it was as if the mist had moved into her brain. Othana's encouragement, Altizara's instructions, and Kade's teachings, were a dim wisp of memory. Even Kade's face, his fatherly gaze, was hazy and distant.

She turned her thoughts to Peter and her father. To the last time she was able to peek into her world and see them. She fought the impulse to allow the shadows to close in and fade, if only to catch a glimpse of Peter. But she was protecting them here. The irony brought her thoughts into sharper focus. She had lost her mother and Harlan when she was nearest to them. And now, from a different dimension, she had a chance to save her brother and dad.

"I am chosen. I am equipped," she whispered. For no explainable reason the fear abated. She breathed deeply and leaned into her path. A resolve began to simmer deep in her thoughts. They would succeed or they would fail. Either way, she would do what she was called to do.

The lights from the city came into view, pulsing a mystical beacon. Raelyn struggled with each step, fighting off waves of pain and vertigo and stood next to Joshua. "I hope Gabe made it."

"He made it."

She looked at him. "You sound sure."

"Even if he didn't, we continue on, right?"

"We would have to find some way in. We have no idea what to expect."

They came to a stop at the crest of a small hill and crouched behind a tree. Metallic trilling, the buzzing ships, and an underlying hum created a discordant clamor within the walls. Images of the Olyaund warriors surfaced in Raelyn's mind: dark empty eyes, long arms reaching, skittering movements. Like insects. She shuddered and a sharp pain flared behind her eyes.

Joshua crept forward but stopped short, ducked low, and held up a fist. Raelyn strained to see anything. Without changing his stance, Joshua lowered his arm and continued closer and closer. Raelyn listened for any indication of an alert. But the sun was nearly overhead. They could spare no more time. They rushed forward to the looming wall towering several stories high, trusting entirely in their fading.

A vacillating blue light spilled over the wall producing a rippling effect. Raelyn lifted her hand and touched the wall with her fingertips, mesmerized by the way it seemed to move, as though it might shudder beneath her hand. She rested her palm against the cool, smooth surface. Like pliable plastic. A membrane . . .

The place where her hand touched melted away and she was staring up into the dead eyes of an Olyaund warrior. He articulated a series of mechanical clicks, his thin mouth motionless, and ten more advanced through the opening, clicking and murmuring.

"Run!" Joshua grabbed Raelyn's hand. But her feet held as though sunk into concrete. A vise-grip of long slender fingers grabbed her shoulder, and it yanked her savagely backward off her feet. But she never hit the ground. She looked to her left. Joshua was levitating five feet above the ground. He struggled as though bound, but Raelyn could neither feel nor see restraints. She cried out but made no sound. She could make no noise at all. Raelyn's bow, her quiver of arrows, and her pack slipped off her back. Constrained and muted, they glided past the wall, and surrounded by the soldiers, they were marched into the city.

The soldiers communicated through clicks and mechanical hums. A dozen ten-foot-tall creatures, light reflecting off their large black eyes, guided their hovering prisoners through winding passageways into the city. Raelyn whipped her head from left to right, struggling against her invisible bonds. One of the soldiers carried Joshua's sword. Raelyn squirmed and could feel the Bokar still securely tucked away.

They passed white domed structures of varying sizes on either side. All made of the same membrane material. The Olyaunders stopped in front of a dome larger than the rest, an enormous structure with blue light pulsing from high, round openings. A portion of the building dissolved just as the wall had, revealing a doorway. Flanked by their captors, Raelyn and Joshua drifted through to a stark white chamber. The ceiling radiated a pale-blue light.

They floated left, then right as they snaked their way into the center of the building. Here, the creatures stopped. Raelyn felt her body float into a smaller chamber where she and Joshua were released, slamming onto their backs. Raelyn's vision went black, and she bit her tongue, tasting blood. The darkness parted, like partially drawn curtains.

Without a backward glance, the sentries exited the room and the material from the wall oozed into the opening until it was solid. Joshua, also without his pack, jumped up and bolted to the door with a guttural yell. He pounded at the wall. His shout echoed around the room.

She heard a sob and spun around. Gabe huddled in the corner of the sterile room.

Raelyn scrambled to him. "What happened?"

He looked up; his face wet with tears. "I couldn't hold on," he said, his voice ragged. "I was so close. But I had to risk it. I didn't think I could get to the south wall, and I drank my vial of seripyn. I'm so sorry," he croaked.

Gabe shook his head. "The Olyaunders brought me here as soon as the ship crossed into the city."

"They couldn't really see us, they just knew to look," Joshua said, rubbing his temples and abandoning the solid wall. "So our cover's blown. I think at this point we no longer have an advantage without the seripyn."

Raelyn shook her head. "Mine was in my pack."

Joshua reached into the side of his boot, withdrew his vial, and shook it. "Should be enough for us both. At least for now." He nearly dropped it as he handed to her.

Raelyn looked at the amber liquid in the clear glass. With shaking hands, she unstoppered it and took a sip. She handed it back to Joshua and he tossed back the rest. It was like being launched out of a dark, crowded room into one filled with light. Raelyn took a deep breath, savoring the calm and clarity.

She stood and helped Gabe to his feet. "Did you communicate with the spy?"

He wandered to the wall where the sentries had exited. "I've only seen the inside of this room. For all we know we may have been set up."

"No," Joshua said, striding back to the wall and running his hands over the surface, as though looking for a seam. "Olmund was sure the mole was trustworthy."

"Even the Shalhalans could have been deceived," Raelyn said.

"Regardless, the fact is we're stuck," Joshua said, looking around the room. "We need to find a way out."

Raelyn joined Joshua and Gabe at the wall but there was no indication of any opening.

"There has to be something —" Joshua began.

"Indeed," gurgled a voice, just outside the wall. It sounded like something was caught in its throat.

They all went silent and scrambled back as the wall drained away to what looked to be an empty hallway.

"Come," the voice said.

No one moved.

"Your opportunity narrows," it insisted.

Joshua was the first to take a few tentative steps to the open door. Raelyn and Gabe crowded behind him. Raelyn gripped the Durinial, squeezing it, willing it to direct her. Her heart pounded as she crept into the hall and saw their liberator: a thin, towering man with large brown eyes and sallow skin, resembling the Olyaunders, but more human. He was dressed in a flowing sheer cloak, sheer which seemed to mirror the walls around him. He held a slender metal spear, the top curved and razor sharp. He gestured with long fingers to follow him. The three gathered close and followed several paces back.

"I could not risk being exposed," he wheezed as he guided them down the hallway to an adjacent wall. "As soon as they discovered you had entered the city, I joined them in your capture."

He swept his hand across the wall. It drained away to reveal another opening.

He gestured for them to enter the room. "I am Olaf."

No one moved. Gabe glanced into the room, then bolted inside without a word. Raelyn shot a look at Joshua even as they raced after him. Gabe had already reached a far wall where a gleaming metal gurney held what looked like a heap of white blankets. Long black hair spilled off the edge.

"Jinny!" Raelyn rushed to the gurney.

Gabe stood over her, stroking her face. He looked up at Raelyn, tears streaming down his cheeks.

Jinny's pallid face was slack. Her eyes were closed and her lips gray. *Like Peter.* Wires coiled from under her clothes. Raelyn reached for one, meaning to snatch it away, but was nudged aside. Olaf had eased up among them.

He passed his hand over Jinny's body, just as he had to reveal the door. The wires squirmed away from her like retreating snakes. She didn't move. Gabe eased an arm under her shoulders and lifted her head from the metal cart.

"We must go." Olaf's rasping voice moved them into action.

Gabe scooped Jinny up and carried her as they once again followed Olaf out into the hall and around a corner. He opened another doorway.

This time they entered without question. Their packs and weapons lay in a pile against a far wall.

Raelyn rushed to her bag and yanked it open. She pulled out the last vial of seripyn as Gabe eased Jinny down next to her. She handed it to Gabe who tilted the vial, letting the liquid dribble into Jinny's mouth, some running down the sides of her face. Raelyn stood and retreated next to Joshua as they watched silently. No one moved, barely even breathed, as though the slightest sound would impede Jinny's recovery. Raelyn glanced up at the strange figure, the Olyaund defector, standing at the far wall. His over-large eyes gazed at Jinny. Otherwise, his face, sallow and elongated, held no emotion.

Gabe gasped and Raelyn looked back as Jinny's eyes fluttered open. She drew a harsh breath.

As she looked from Gabe to Raelyn her mouth worked to form words. "I knew you'd come," she finally croaked as her eyes settled on Gabe. He gave her another sip of the tea, which she gulped.

"Thank you," she sighed.

"Can you move?" he asked, looking over her arms and legs.

"I— I think so," Jinny said, struggling to sit up. Gabe stayed close, allowing her sit on her own for a moment. Then he grasped one of her arms and Raelyn the other as they helped her to stand. She winced but was able to shuffle a few steps. Joshua began sorting through their weapons and supplies.

"Rae," Joshua called. She looked up just in time to catch her pack and he quickly distributed the others. Gabe offered to carry Jinny's pack, but when she insisted, he helped her ease it onto her shoulders. He dug out his Leohfaet before hefting his own pack onto his back.

Joshua buckled the Ruah onto his waist as Raelyn secured her bow and quiver, still full of arrows.

Shoulders square and feet planted, Gabe looked at Olaf with bright hazel eyes. "Now what?" He held Jinny's hand. Her cheeks were pink, eyes bright and the circlet was once again on her head. She still seemed a bit unsteady but there was no time to wait for a full recovery.

Joshua pulled a crumpled piece of parchment from a side pocket of his pack. "Now, we finish the mission," he said, brandishing the paper. "This is the map of the city."

"Quickly," Olaf said in his gurgling voice as he glanced to a high round window. He took three long steps to the doorway. "I will hold them off as long as I can. Follow the map. Get to the portal." He poked his head into the hall and looked both ways, before glancing back at them.

"For the valor of Arkonai," he rasped and darted out of the room.

"Let's go," Joshua ordered as he strode to the door. They rushed in the direction Olaf had disappeared, turning the corner in time to see his reflective cloak slipping around to the next corridor. They continued until they had snaked their way back to the exit.

At the outside door, Raelyn blanched at the sun gleaming in a clear sky. The blinding light reflected off all the white domes. She watched as a loping shadow she knew to be Olaf rushed to meet other shadows and the Olyaund soldiers came into focus. One of them, taller and brandishing a shining black spear, towered at the front. His engorged head turned to look at the Cord, his shining black eyes shifting over each of them. As though analyzing them. Weighing his options. Olaf shot a look back.

"Go!" he roared and advanced on the soldiers, sweeping his spear back and forth.

The Cord tore out of the doorway and raced in the opposite direction. Raelyn glanced back in time to see Olaf overtaken and the Olyaunders surge past him in pursuit. Their long legs were moving at an impossible speed. The Cord would never outrun them. Raelyn turned and pumped her legs harder. Their clicking and buzzing grew closer.

"Here!" Joshua bellowed, glancing at the map, and banked left. Then right. The Olyaunders had gone silent, but their shadows were on Raelyn's heels.

"Straight through here!" Joshua shouted as they rounded a corner and came to a division in the road. The main road led to the right. The way to the left was barely an alley, tunneling through high white walls. Raelyn felt a jolt push her left and the Durinial burst to life, vibrating like an electric shock. Raelyn lost her footing and she skidded on the loose sand. Gabe seized her arm and steadied her as they ran.

"No! Josh! Here!" Raelyn screamed and steered Jinny, guiding her to the left and pulled Gabe with her as she made for the alley. But Joshua had already run past.

"Raelyn!" he shouted. He scrambled to return to the fork and drew his sword.

Raelyn glanced back as the Olyaunders descended on him.

She ran frantically as the alley narrowed and other soldiers advanced. Gabe and Jinny fell behind. Raelyn had no idea where she was leading them.

An explosion rent the air behind her. She glanced over her shoulder in time to see a portion of the wall crash on top of the Olyaund soldiers and Gabe swinging the Leohfaet above his head as he ran. A percussion of purple light burst from the globe and more wall disintegrated.

Ahead, a smooth, luminous outer wall loomed. Raelyn ran straight at full speed, running into the wall before she continued to her right. Gabe and Jinny rounded the corner behind her. Another pathway became visible on their right, just ahead. But they did not make it that far. Swarms of Olyaund soldiers, clicking and buzzing, spears flashing, scurried onto the road in front of them and blocked their path. The tall soldier with the black spear slunk forward, his long thin legs bending at odd angles.

"Nowhere to go," he whispered, his voice crackling and buzzing.

Raelyn looked up at the wall, pale and polished. She ran her hand across it. Cold. Impenetrable. She turned back to the Olyaunders.

"She sent you," the tallest one hissed, his face contorted in rage. Disgust. The other soldiers crept behind him as he advanced. "The old woman. No doubt hoping I might return." He made a series of popping noises that Raelyn took to be a laugh.

"Radan the Overseer," Raelyn murmured, astonished this creature could ever have been Shalhalan. "You're Olvida's son!" she shouted.

Radan blanched. He took two long strides.

Raelyn ran both hands along the wall. It had to be here. A doorway that led to the plye. A way to escape.

"Gabe! The key!" Raelyn cried. Gabe glanced at Raelyn and then the wall. He crammed his hand in his front pocket and thrust the key at Raelyn.

There were no buttons, controls, or slots. Just smooth wall in every direction. Raelyn pressed the flat metal key onto the wall. Nothing.

Gabe and Jinny moved in front of Raelyn, blocking her from the oncoming Olyaunders. She touched the Durinial, then grabbed it and ripped it from her neck. She held it in her hand and looked closely. The colors swam and swirled. Out of the corner of her eye she saw the soldiers closing the space. She squeezed the amulet and slammed the key onto the wall. The Durinial gave a jolt and a part of the wall melted away. She looked back as Jinny snapped her push dagger from its chain. Gabe nodded to Raelyn and turned toward the soldiers.

"FOR THE VALOR OF ARKONAI!" he roared.

His staff popped from his hand as he ran at the soldiers. He stabbed the Leohfaet into the air with his other hand. A flash of light shot from the torch. The soldiers let out a mechanical screech. Jinny charged after Gabe. He reached Radan, who thrust his spear into Gabe's gut. Then Raelyn was falling through the opening and it sealed behind her.

CHAPTER THIRTY-TWO

Silence pressed against Raelyn's ears. A forest of dark, towering trees crowded around her. Looming evergreens with thick, flat pine needles blocked the sky and plunged her into a shadowy gloom. The pungent smell of moist earth and decaying leaves filled the air. Her pack was gone. Her bow and quiver gone. Raelyn looked behind her. The wall had disappeared.

Another dimension? Had she been transported? The others — Gabe! She spun in a circle but there were no clues to where she was or what had happened. Or what to do next.

Raelyn gripped the Durinial in one hand and grasped at her lower back with the other. She pulled the Bokar from her belt. "Okay," she breathed. But her feet held their place. She cleared her throat. "Okay," she said louder and took a step forward as the trees kept watch.

She balanced the Durinial in her outstretched palm like a compass, then closed her hand and took a few more steps. There were footpaths leading in all directions.

Trust. Isn't that what Kade would say?

And above all, love, she thought. Or felt. Or heard. The weapons they were given, Jinny's Seon, Gabe's Leohfaet, Joshua's Ruah. Even Avery's Cieskild. They were only as powerful as those who wielded them. Or the trust with which they battled their enemy. Each of their faces swam into her mind. Training, fighting, laughing and learning. They were fighting, buying time so she could finish the quest. Kade taught them that love was the ultimate show of trust, faith, and hope. Their sacrifice. Their trust in her. That was love, wasn't it? Joshua swarmed by the Olyaunders, Radan running Gabe through with the spear. She owed it to them to finish the quest. The Cord, Kade . . . Peter.

Her throat constricted but she swallowed hard and gritted her teeth, launching into a trepid jog, dead leaves crunching beneath her feet. Left, right, back. But the trees all looked the same. Every path identical. The Durinial warmed her hand. She stopped and held it aloft, looking closely at the center tree, it's leaves glittering. Then her Bokar. Just a book, with a single page and words she hoped — *trusted* — would appear.

Raelyn turned slowly and the Durinial pulsed. She marched ahead, now with purpose. Fifty yards. A hundred. With every step her confidence grew. In the distance a point of light appeared. She quickened her pace. The pinpoint became a pale glow. The glow took shape as the trees fell away and she entered a wide clearing.

Stretched across a jagged structure of crumbling stone, at least twenty feet in diameter, an opaque membrane pulsed. It swelled rhythmically as though taking long, slow breaths. She watched it for a moment, at once mesmerized and repulsed. A thick, sweet odor, like fermented fruit, wafted from the membrane.

This had to be it. The plye.

Raelyn tucked the Durinial into her front pocket. She held the Bokar in both hands, staring at the cover. A reluctance washed over her. A new thought exploded in her mind: She could use the plye. This was a gateway home. The Olyaunders, the varga, the hyram — they all used it to cross over. If she just stepped through, she could be back in Earth Apparent. She took a step toward the portal without even thinking about it. Her lungs wouldn't fill, as though the air had suddenly thinned. Light-headed excitement took over as she imagined racing into the hospital. Telling her dad Peter would be okay —

But would he?

She shook her head violently. The plye was Cosyn's creation. She couldn't, *wouldn't*, use it. No matter how tempting. That's what it was, a temptation. Like the forbidden fruit.

And look at how it turned out for Eve.

Still, she didn't open the book. What if nothing happened? Proving her inability. She wouldn't be able to wield the weapon chosen for her. She would fail. Fail Kade. Fail Peter. Fail herself.

You have been chosen. The words drifted like a gentle breeze. Tears blurred her eyes. She wanted to throw the Bokar and run. She wanted to drop to her knees. Anything but open it. She was inadequate. Weak. Unworthy.

You have been made worthy. Again, barely a breath of wind. She glanced around. Nothing but the forest. Silence. Darkness.

Raelyn stared into the recesses of the plye. Mottled light pulsed. Shadows swirled. She looked back at the journal. Taking a deep breath and blowing it out, she opened the Bokar.

The effect was immediate. The cover hummed beneath her fingers. Lit from within, the page kindled a soft white. Raelyn wrestled away from her binding anxiety and grasped for an elusive calm, determined to take hold of it. A cool gust of wind swirled around her, ruffling the page, blowing through her hair, and lifting into the treetops. The trees stirred and hissed in response. She looked into the plye as it continued its shadow dance.

Movement on the page caught her eye. Unintelligible markings rippled onto the surface, and her heart pounded with a jittery relief. She continued to stare at the script until a familiarity seeped into her mind. Like old memories resurfacing. She lifted her eyes to see if anything was happening. Layers of shadows within the portal spun, twitched, and convulsed. A darker shape at the center pressed against the membrane. A form pushed through and took a human shape. Black, stringy hair framed a cadaverous face twisted with rage, revealing sharp yellowed teeth. Red eyes bore into her.

He was there. The enemy of her nightmares. Cosyn.

Raelyn froze. Her throat closed and she stumbled back. Cosyn stepped out of the plye and his snarl became a pearly smile. He blinked and his eyes shone a brilliant blue. Shining dark hair cascaded down his flowing black robes and a mysterious black smoke rose from his shoulders and arms. He wasn't terrible at all. Not unlike Kade, really. In fact, he was quite handsome. Raelyn lowered the Bokar.

"Not what you were expecting?" His voice was deep, calming. "So many stories told about me," he said as though hurt; grievously wronged. "I'm not the monster Kade has told you I am. He misunderstands and tells you I want to harm." His smile broadened. "In fact, I only wish to set humanity free." With these words his voice rose and he lifted a shining staff. A talisman, set in the center, beamed. The Durinial warmed in Raelyn's pocket.

Raelyn gazed at Cosyn, her whole body slack. *Yes, freedom. What was wrong with that?* The Bokar dangled at her side, thrumming against her fingers. She tried to lift her arm, but it felt weighted and tired.

"Come, let me show you." He took a step forward and held out a hand. "You could be a part of my Great Awakening. We could do it together." The last word rang with an ardent chord from his crooked, alluring smile.

Raelyn's cheeks flushed and the corners of her mouth lifted. She felt foolish and small. In his eyes she saw acceptance, adoration. A warm comfort fluttered in her stomach, as though her secret crush had finally taken notice. She longed to step forward, take his hand. To be free. Awakened. She realized her breathing had become ragged gasps. Desire filled her mind.

"Come with me," he said. His voice echoed through the forest. Enchanting. Exciting. She remained rooted, but everything in her screamed to go to him.

"I will take you to Peter," he cooed.

Peter. A chance to save him. Thoughts of entering the plye returned. It was true. She could step through. *Should* step through.

Cosyn moved to one side of the plye. The membrane melted away. A tall building shone in brilliant sunshine. The hospital. Already Raelyn's stomach clenched. The scene swept inside, into Peter's room. The lamp barely lit one corner. Her dad slept in the chair. She searched for the shadow, but it wasn't there. The scene moved closer to Peter, as though she stood right over him. His chest moved up and down as the machines breathed for him —

His eyelids fluttered. Raelyn gasped. Then they opened.

"Peter!" Raelyn shouted, and took another step forward. His eyes were dull. Not the vibrant blue she had always known. His skin was pale, almost transparent. The longer she stared, the less he looked like Peter at all. Images flooded Raelyn's mind. Kade holding her hands, calling her daughter. Walking the streets of Malvok with Joshua. Encouraging Jinny. Even fighting with Avery. Gabe, his face suspended in shock as the spear pierced his stomach.

"I am chosen," she croaked. The image in the plye dissolved and became the ghostly membrane again.

"Of course you are," Cosyn snapped. His blue eyes flickered. "I have chosen you," he continued, softer. "Just take my hand." His smile flashed.

"I am loved." Raelyn strained to say the words. She didn't know if she believed them or if she was just supposed to say them.

"Love," Cosyn spat as he dropped his arm. He narrowed his eyes. "Love is an illusion."

Raelyn forced her arm, as heavy as a concrete block, to bend and bring the Bokar to eye level. She held it with both hands, blocking Cosyn from her view. The attraction was shattered. The spell broken. Her head cleared. She scanned the page for the words.

They appeared, bold and sharp. She opened her mouth and let the words spill out.

"Many paths are laid." She understood the language, but it was not her own. Not anything she had ever heard. The words reverberated off the plye, beautiful and commanding.

Some things are lost
Some are gained
But there is no hope for peace
On the paths of deceit
Many are chosen
But not all choose
The path of love, of forgiveness
The path of truth

Cosyn's robes rustled as he paced, just steps from her. A powerful impulse overcame her resolve and Raelyn peeked over the top of the journal. Cosyn, still handsome, enticing, was nodding shrewdly.

"Yes, the path to love," he crooned. "But what is really accomplished with love? Is that why your mother and brother died?" He clicked his tongue, shaking his head as though he pitied her. "I think not."

All the air left Raelyn's lungs. Why *did* they die? It certainly wasn't for love. It wasn't even their choice. It was hers. Tears leaked from her eyes.

"Come," Cosyn said, "let me help. I can show you."

The plye burst to life. Her father, standing over Peter, sobbing. All the machines were gone and Peter lay still. Raelyn's knees nearly buckled. The words hadn't worked. Hadn't even made sense. Panic burst into her mind. She yanked the Bokar back in front of her face. But the words were blurred by her tears. She blinked. One word came into focus.

Forgiven.

"I'm forgiven," she whispered without moving the book. Did she believe that?

Cosyn chuckled. "My dear, even if that were possible, why do you need it? Let's go and explore other possibilities."

"I — am — forgiven," Raelyn repeated louder. She lowered the journal and leveled her gaze directly at Cosyn's eyes, ignoring the scenes continuing to playing out behind him. "And I choose to accept that and forgive myself." As she said it, she allowed the message to sink in. The truth seemed so simple. If she allowed Cosyn to bury her beneath guilt, anger, and injustice, she would never be free. Could never wield the Bokar. Could never close the plye.

Cosyn's face rippled, as though something beneath his flawless skin writhed, trying to break free. But in an instant he was smiling, his face placid and welcoming.

He gestured to the plye. "I can help you set it all right."

A minute ago, she had been ready to jump through the portal. But now . . . It wasn't Cosyn who would set everything right. Closing the plye would. And it was not just her life she was protecting. Not just her family's. It was the lives of everyone in the Cord.

Raelyn's heart pounded, and she took a step forward. The Durinial vibrated in her pocket. Raelyn held the Bokar open with one hand and dug the amulet out of her pocket with the other. It radiated its warmth up her arm and to her neck. It filled her chest. A blaze ignited in her mind.

Cosyn's eyes narrowed. "Stupid girl. Everyone you love will die. Their deaths will be on your shoulders."

Raelyn continued to take long steps toward Cosyn. The sickly smell of rancid fruit grew. His face distorted. His charming smile became a grimace of hate, his mouth filled with sharp yellowed teeth once more. His blue eyes darkened to crimson. Clumps of his sleek black hair evaporated into the smoke until only stringy wisps hung from his discolored scalp.

Cosyn blanched. His face continued to distort until he barely looked human.

Raelyn was at the base of the dais, just a few steps from Cosyn. She looked down at the Bokar once more. The journal she had spent so much time agonizing over. That had brought both a staggering indictment and a frail hope to what she believed about herself. A book that brought both clear conviction of her past and a balm to those wounds. It crackled as though on fire.

"You have made your choice, temporal!" Cosyn roared "Now you will die."

Raelyn ignored him. The fear, guilt, and anger drained away, and she let the words of the book fill her with love and forgiveness. She took a deep breath. "Begone," she said, and a flash of blinding light filled the forest. A jolt of energy blew Raelyn off her feet. She landed with a thud, knocking the Durinial from her hand. Strong, rough hands seized her arms and yanked her up. The smell of rotten fruit filled her nostrils.

"Now it is too late for you," Cosyn growled in her ear. Raelyn finally understood. Complete love would require her sacrifice. The prospect wasn't frightening. Not even unpleasant. Didn't her friends deserve that much? Didn't Peter? Raelyn closed her eyes and awaited death. Waited for him to tear into her throat, crush her skull, drive his spear through her chest. However, it happened, she was ready.

Instead, Cosyn let go of Raelyn's arms and shoved her away. She stumbled backward and opened her eyes. He was looking past her. For the first time, his face contorted in fear. He backed away as his eyes cut to her.

"I will come for you," he hissed, pointing a long finger at her. "This is not over."

With his scepter Cosyn slashed at the air behind him. A gap broke open like a wound. He stepped through it and the opening sealed behind him. The forest was silent once more. Stars blinked at her from the sky.

"Daughter." A whisper in the wind.

"Kade?" Raelyn spun around. White flames flickered, moving closer. As they approached, she could see someone walking in the midst of the light. A man, but not Kade. He held the hand of a child. The light surrounded him, not just from his hands and head, but all around him. It encompassed the child too.

He came close and the light dimmed.

"Well done," he said, his voice enveloping and overwhelming her. She could no longer look at him. She looked at the child instead.

"Lydia!" Raelyn cried and ran to her. Lydia met her halfway. Raelyn picked her up and spun her around.

"But how? Where?" Raelyn was laughing and crying. Lydia giggled as Raelyn gently set her down.

"Come and see," Lydia said. She grasped Raelyn's hand and pulled her to the man, skipping as she went, until they were standing right in front of him.

His face was plain. Warm brown eyes crinkled in a smile. He reached around her as though to hug her, but then fastened something around her neck. Raelyn felt the weight of the Durinial. She traced the circles with her finger.

"The plye —" Raelyn looked over her shoulder and then spun completely around. It remained luminous, pulsing. She looked back at Lydia.

The girl smiled and gestured to Raelyn. "Go on."

Raelyn walked uncertainly back to the dais. At the base of the steps, the Bokar lay closed where she had dropped it when the blast threw her back. She picked it up. It thrummed. With a deep breath she approached the plye. She opened the Bokar and held it open in one hand. She wanted only one thing. To close the place where Cosyn could reach Peter. She reached out, nearly putting her hand through the membrane and glanced at the single word glowing on the page in the book.

"Scyttan," she said softly, but everything within her was exhaled in that one word.

Close.

The blue glow winked out and the forest appeared beyond the now empty hole. The stone where the plye had been was an ancient ruin, sagging and crumbling. Raelyn turned back to Lydia and the man, who was strolling toward her as though taking a walk through the park. Lydia skipped next to him, her grin nearly taking over her face.

"Cosyn —" Raelyn rushed down the steps.

"Has escaped," he said nodding, but looked completely unconcerned.

"The others, are they okay?"

"They are continuing on the path they were called to walk."

"What do we do now?" Raelyn's voice cracked.

"Seek," he said, and the white fire rose.

"I know, I —"

"You will find . . ." The flames encompassed him, and he disappeared into them.

Lydia stood alone, smiling brightly, as though this was the most normal thing in the world.

Raelyn stuffed the book into the back of her belt. "Lydia, was that —" Distant noises, yells and screeches.

"Come." Lydia pulled at her hand and led her toward the sounds of battle.

"I'm so sorry . . ." Raelyn began.

"You still think as a temporal." Lydia lifted a tree branch and ducked under it, holding it out for Raelyn to take. They reached the Olyaund wall, milky white, formidable, and solid.

Lydia stopped and turned to her. "The words in the Bokar and their power are a part of you now." She took a step back. "You need only believe." Her voice rang out. She giggled and it became a thousand chiming bells. She skipped back into the forest and faded from view.

A crash behind the wall sent Raelyn into action. She rushed to the wall and ran her hand across its surface, not surprised when nothing happened. She walked to her right, keeping her hand on the wall. After several paces it curved around the city. She slowed and crept to the exposed south side.

Shadows moved toward, her and she backed up, holding her breath. Horses whinnied and Joshua called her name.

Raelyn rushed toward the shadows and two horses galloped into view. Jinny was riding on Raelyn's and Joshua on the other, holding on tightly to an unconscious Gabe. His body slumped over Joshua's arm.

Raelyn's heart pounded. "Is he —"

"He's lost a lot of blood," Joshua answered. "The Olyaunders are in a frenzy. We need to move," he added, glancing back.

Raelyn nodded. Jinny scooted back to let Raelyn mount her horse and then gripped her tightly.

The Cord raced away from the city of Olyaund and the now-destroyed plye.

CHAPTER THIRTY-THREE

Kade stared at the blue beam shooting into the sky from Theurham Forest. The city writhed like an agitated hornets' nest. Kade and Avery lay on their stomachs in a thicket beneath a few misshapen trees on a hill north of Olyaund. Avery still wore his pack and shield on his back.

"What does that mean Kade?" Avery whispered. "Is that good or bad?"

"That, I believe, is very, very good. But we are not here to simply witness." Kade pushed to his feet with a grunt but stayed crouched. "We must reach the south wall."

Avery let out a breath and dropped his head on his arms, giving him the look of a turtle retreating into his shell. Kade had spent most of the two-day journey to Olyaund encouraging Avery to stay the course, revealing what he could of the plan. Make for Herlov, with a detour to Olyaund. Kade's vision had clearly shown him the south wall, with Theurham on his right. A way had to be made for the Cord. Beyond that, he could only trust the rest would become clear.

"We must go." Kade watched the flashing lights and frenzied shadows within the city walls.

"Right." Avery thankfully did not argue. They made their way to the wall as the sun touched the tops of the trees, ducking behind a boulder as a group of Olyaunders skittered into the forest, followed by one of their ships. The trees seemed to welcome them.

A brief lull in the activity allowed Kade and Avery to dart across and reach the wall without altercation. Kade skirted around east, toward the main gate, with Avery right behind. Normally sentries would be posted but it seemed all forces had been pulled to other defenses. Kade and Avery stayed just out of view as Olyaunders came and went from the city gate.

"Avery," Kade whispered, still watching the soldiers. Nothing. "Avery," he whispered louder.

"What?" Avery hissed.

"Have your shield ready."

"We're going in?"

"We will continue outside the city. When we cross the entrance, you must block us from the gate. Protect us from the soldiers."

"I'm to shield us while we run?"

"Did you not accomplish this crossing the river?" Kade turned and grasped Avery's shoulders, holding him at arm's length. "This is what you were called to do." Avery searched Kade's eyes and gave a stiff nod. He slid the Cieskild over his shoulder.

They sprinted around the corner and Avery jogged between Kade and the wide opening ahead. Fifty paces. Forty. Thirty. Kade glanced at Avery who nodded and ducked his head behind the shield. They dashed across. The response was immediate. The agitated hum burst into a furious buzz. A dozen Olyaund soldiers scurried to them, ready with their spears. They clicked and murmured, and with a final screech, reached Avery.

Avery squeezed his eyes shut and hunched over. A blast from the shield threw the soldiers back. Avery opened his eyes and peered over the Cieskild. But there was no time to revel.

"You must hold them Avery. We are almost there," Kade said.

Avery did not respond but he kept his crouched position as they continued to the far side of the gate, the Olyaunders following, fighting against the barrier.

"This way!" Kade ran at full speed, trying to create some distance. The Olyaunders were emboldened as their numbers grew, hewing at the invisible blockade. Kade stopped and reached out to the wall. When his hand connected, a metallic screech entered his mind. The wall, cold and malleable, writhed beneath his touch. He walked a few feet, trailing his hand along the wall until he felt a hollowness.

"Here," Kade said, stopping and removing his hand.

"Here? Here what?" Avery panted as he scanned the wall, the Cieskild pulled tight against his shoulder. The Olyaunders closed in. "I don't see —"

Kade looked at Avery. "Hold them."

Avery cleared his throat and pulled the shield higher. The soldiers clicked and buzzed, scrambling over one another in their attepmt to get at them. Kade turned his attention to the wall. He put his hands together, as though to pray. Then he cupped them in front of his face. Golden light spun in his palms. Avery shouted, but Kade focused on the light. It spun faster. Avery shouted again.

"Kade!"

The light whirled and grew. Kade held it out, a shining, golden tornado of light.

"KADE!"

Kade directed the light at the wall, and it shot forward. It entered the wall, lighting it from the inside. The milky white shone yellow for a moment. Then it burst open, creating a crawlspace at the base.

"Now!" Kade yelled.

Avery leaned into the shield and shouted. The air in front of it erupted in a tidal wave, evaporating the closest soldiers, and launching the others thirty yards back. The rest skittered away.

Kade and Avery raced back the way they had come. As they rounded the wall and darted in front of the gate, Kade fought the impulse to run inside the city and search for Raelyn, Joshua, Jinny, and Gabe. There was no way to know their strategy, where they were. Altering his course would put them all at risk. He and Avery returned to their look out without stopping. They threw themselves at the base of the berm and waited in silence, tense and prepared in case they were followed.

After several long minutes, Avery spoke.

"Was that it?" He was still breathing hard, sprawled out on his belly, the shield tossed to one side. "We just needed to blast a hole in the wall?"

Kade turned his head to Avery. "Aye, the plye is closed. The Cord was successful."

Avery rolled his eyes and dropped his head onto his forearms. "I didn't do anything," he said, his voice muffled.

"Everything we do affects the outcome."

Avery jerked his head up, eyes wide. "So, that's it then. Penny's safe. You're sending us home?"

"Aye, if that is what you wish."

Avery peered at Kade. "Why wouldn't I wish that?"

"There are many paths to choose. But we will make for Herlov and on to the Silom Pool."

"What are we waiting for?" Avery rolled over and sat up.

Kade stood and looked down at Avery. "We are waiting for safe passage."

"Safe? Herlov isn't safe?"

"It is not Herlov. It is what lies between. To reach the kingdom of Herlov we must first pass through Theurham Forest."

Avery jumped to his feet, staying crouched. "Are you mad?" Avery hissed, clipping his words.

"There is a passage. A narrowing in the forest. It will not take more than a day to cross. But it takes us too close to Olyaund to leave just now."

Avery did not seem to hear Kade. "We barely made it out!" He began to pace "We can't go back!"

"Avery." Kade spoke as loud as he dared. "There is no other way."

Avery stopped and snapped his mouth closed. He rubbed his face, then ran his hands through his hair. "We'll be protected?"

Kade shook his head. "I can promise nothing. But"—Kade gestured to the shield, still lying on the ground— "we will have protection."

Avery's shoulders fell. "Then we'll never make it."

Kade clapped him on the back. "The first plye is closed. Already evil has been overcome."

"Then why is evil still loitering in Theurham Forest?"

"Because there is much to finish. Here and in Earth Apparent. With or without your aid." Clicking and screeching came from just over the hill. "We must find cover."

They hurried to a rocky outcrop just outside the forest while a group of Olyaunders scurried past, their buzzing, clanking, and screeching subsiding within the dark trees.

Kade and Avery waited out the night as the frenzied activity around Olyaund City wound down to an angry hum. The cool light of morning had barely tinged the sky when Kade stood. Avery, who had been dozing with his pack and shield attached to his back, snapped awake.

"Wha— What's wrong?" he said, blinking.

"It is time to begin our journey," Kade said.

Avery nodded and struggled to his feet. Kade handed him his flask. Avery took a swig without comment and inhaled deeply.

Kade glanced at him. "Better?"

Avery nodded. "Loads. This is it, then?" He put his hands on his hips and followed Kade's gaze. He gave his head a quick tilt to the left and right, cracking his neck.

"Aye." Kade spared a final glance west, toward Shalhala. He released his desire to be with the Cord and put them to the back of his mind. He could not serve his purpose if his heart was torn. His path lay east and then north to Herlov.

"For the glory of Arkonai," Kade whispered as he and Avery entered Theurham Forest.

CHAPTER THIRTY-FOUR

Golden sunlight cast long shadows across the Shalhalan village as Raelyn paced outside the healing house. For three days they had raced across the desert. On the fourth, Othana, Olmund, Larken, Enloe and a host of other Shalhalan warriors had met them and led them to the lake. It was another two days before they made it to Shalhala. They had been back for two days and Gabe had not yet regained consciousness. After a brief rest Jinny had not left his side as the healers worked to mend and treat the wound, a deep gouge that ran the length of his left side.

The Shalhalans could give no assurance as to their family's safety. All three refrained from the seripyn until they could see for themselves. This time, Raelyn didn't fade to the hospital, but to Peter's bedroom. His childhood bedroom. He was sitting up in bed, still pale and thin, but very much awake and whole. He was turning the pages of a book as sunlight slanted through the window. Raelyn sobbed and laughed as she watched him. He stopped mid-turn and looked up, meeting her eyes. Then the seripyn was trickled into her mouth and Othana was by her side, smiling.

Joshua strolled up to her and nodded his head toward the healing house. "Any news?"

"Nothing." Raelyn shook her head.

They sat down on a nearby stone bench. Joshua stared at the ground and dug his heel into the dirt.

"You ready to talk about what happened?" Joshua asked without looking up.

"Are you?" Raelyn blanched at her sharp tone. She swallowed back her sudden defensiveness. "Olvida wants us to meet her on the balcony this evening. I'm sure we'll go over everything." She wanted to share what had happened to Peter. To celebrate the victory she had thought would be impossible. But that wasn't what she was protecting. What had happened in the forest, at the plye, with Cosyn, even Lydia and the man in the white flame, revealed something. A deep change and shift in herself she didn't quite understand. Until she could explore what it all meant she felt compelled to guard the details.

"They found her," Joshua finally said, his voice strangled. He leaned forward, propped his forearms on his thighs and looked at his hands. "My Lily." He sniffed and wiped his nose with the back of his hand. "My ex had her. The whole time. Hidden in some God-forsaken shack with some of her degenerate family." He shook his head and looked over at Raelyn. "How does a mother do that?"

Raelyn put her hand on his arm. "The important thing is she's safe."

He nodded and looked back at his hands.

"I'm sorry I left you behind," she said, letting go of his arm.

He sat back and frowned. "You did the right thing."

"I should have gone back to help — "

"No, Raelyn. You did exactly what you were supposed to. I'm proud of you." He smiled. "Besides, I managed, didn't I?"

"Yeah, about that. How did you get away? You were completely outnumbered."

Joshua shook his head and chuckled. "Couldnt'a been anything I did. I swung the Ruah with everything I had. And they just fell. Even some I think the blade only came close to. Then that beam of blue light shot into the sky and held for a solid minute. The rest of 'em scattered. I followed the map until I'd just about made it back to the south wall and ran into Jinny nearly carrying Gabe. We got back to the south entry point and there was this . . . *hole* blasted out of it."

"Olaf?" Raelyn interrupted.

Joshua shook his head. "Maybe, but he could've just opened it up with his hand, right? This looked like a bomb had gone off. Anyway, with the beam gone, the Olyaunders attacked again and blocked the way out." He paused, his eyes darting as though trying to decide what to say next. He shifted to face Raelyn. "You ever notice there weren't any bushes, plants, or trees, anywhere in the city?"

Raelyn raised an eyebrow. "Must've escaped my attention." She shook her head. "I don't follow."

"Not something I woulda noticed either, 'cept for the one I did see. Right there at the south wall, next to the hole. And it . . . just burst into flames. White flames, Raelyn."

He leaned toward her, as though to emphasize the absurdity. But she immediately recalled the white flames surrounding the man in the forest.

"Missions, enemies, strategies, I get that," he continued. "Even a battle in an alternate dimension I managed to swallow."

"Joshua, is it really so strange? I mean, this place is as otherworldly as it gets."

"Yeah, and I could chalk it up to that. But it was the same tree I saw when I faded, fire an' all. I realized I'm seeing real places when I fade. Places in this dimension." He rubbed the back of his neck. "Being that connected to this realm . . ." He shook his head. "Anyway, the Olyaunders couldn't get near the flames, and we got out. The horses were waitin' for us."

Raelyn sighed and sat back. The quest was completed. She should be filled with contentment and satisfaction. But without Kade, now more than ever, she felt lost, adrift, with no direction and no guidance. All their effort had been put into getting to Olyaund and closing the plye. Then getting out of Olyaund alive. With that accomplished —

Jinny exited the house, her face red and swollen from crying. "Still no change," she said as she walked up.

Raelyn stood and put her arm around her shoulders. "So not any worse." Jinny managed a thin smile and nodded.

Raelyn stood a little straighter, the Bokar pressing reassuringly against her lower back. "I think it's about time to meet with Olvida."

"What'd you suppose we're in for?" Joshua asked as they climbed the steps.

Raelyn shook her head. "I can't even guess."

"Welcome, warriors!" Olvida said, her arms spread wide and her pearly light shining against the sapphire sky. Enloe stood to her right, stiff and stoic, his olive light barely visible in the fading light.

They had been summoned to their shared balcony and Olvida stood behind a long banquet table positioned at the center, set for a feast. Lanterns adorned every corner. Joshua walked out from his room as Raelyn and Jinny entered from theirs, though Jinny stayed at the threshold.

"Celebration is in order," Olvida announced. "But in respect for Gabe and your own grief, I felt it fitting to enjoy a more intimate gathering." She smiled, her eyes soft with compassion.

Othana slipped up next to Raelyn and gave her a rare smile, the orange light around her face dark and smoldering.

Larken appeared next to Othana nearly bouncing on the balls of his feet and grinning. "We've been looking forward to this party for a while."

Olmund strode around the table. Jinny sniffed and they all turned to her as she covered her face. It was Larken who went to her and pulled her hands so that she was looking at him. His sky-blue light seemed to surround them both.

"We are sad, yes," he said. "But Gabe is a warrior. He was successful in battle. We celebrate his victory as well." He strode to the table and pulled out the nearest chair, smiling and waving her over. Jinny wiped her eyes and joined him.

"Then let us eat," Olvida declared and waddled to the seat Olmund had pulled out for her at the head of the table.

He took the seat on her left and Othana on her right. Everyone found their places as others from the village filtered in, healers and soldiers, until the table was full.

A few musicians began to play flutes. Despite her heavy heart, Raelyn let herself relax, her thoughts drifting to Peter and Lydia, even Harlan. Larken shared stories that made them laugh and Olvida gave a boisterous toast, calling out each of the Cord in turn.

"And to Gabe!" she finished, "the light of the world, who dispelled darkness and sacrificed himself for his friends. May healing find him quickly!" They raised goblets and drank.

The night was clear and cold, and the deep sky was filled with shining stars. A sliver of moon peeked over the tops of the trees. As the evening wore on, the Shalhalans congratulated the fighting temporals once more and filtered out. Even Othana and Larken bid them goodnight and slipped away, until only Olvida and the Cord remained.

"And now," Olvida half-whispered, "we will address your path." Her mouth drew tight, and her pale eyes passed over each of them.

Raelyn held her breath. Their ship, now adrift, may get a heading. Her heart ached to be with Peter and her stomach fluttered to think of seeing her dad again. But something about the way Olvida looked around the table tempered her excitement.

"Cosyn has lost his power over your families. The plye most closely connected to you is destroyed. But, as you know, there are others."

"Olvida . . ." Joshua set down his goblet.

She put a hand up, nodding. "Another, while not linked to you specifically, is more powerful in that he has increased his access to locations over all Earth Apparent. A ply in the kingdom of Endyle allows Cosyn to send forth all manner of his abominations."

"You think we're the ones to close this one, too?" Joshua asked, as though looking for confirmation, not an argument.

Olvida finally smiled. "I have no doubt."

Raelyn leaned forward. "Olvida, what about our families?"

Olvida turned her pale eyes to Raelyn. "While no longer a target, they are a part of this larger danger, nonetheless. And Cosyn will likely turn his forces to them now that he knows your abilities."

Olvida straightened and her tone became more urgent. "Should you agree, we must make immediate arrangements."

"So soon?" Jinny looked from Olvida to Joshua and Raelyn, as though seeking a united outrage. "You're sending us, just like that?"

"Not sent," Olvida shook her head. "Called."

"What's the difference?" Jinny sighed, slumping back in her chair. Dark shadows stretched under her eyes.

"A call requires an answer," Olvida said. "You may choose to travel back to the Silom Pool and return to Earth Apparent."

"What about Gabe?" Jinny asked.

"Ah, yes. Gabe." Olvida looked around the table. "I am afraid his path ends here, at least until he recovers."

"You have a plan?" Joshua asked, raising an eyebrow.

Olvida nodded. "The village of Keala, a southern province on the borders of a vast ocean, sits near the Kaidilas Sea."

Joshua's eyes widened for a split second.

"From there you can make preparations to enter Endyle." Olvida gazed around the table. No one spoke. "Make your choice soon," Olvida continued. "The Olyaunders will not allow our victory to go unchallenged. Even now we have intercepted small bands just outside our borders." She made to stand and Joshua jumped up to help her from her seat. "You may choose a different path. Not all are bad. But only one is right."

They remained silent after Olvida left.

"We can say no," Jinny finally muttered.

"That's true." Joshua leaned back in his chair, looking out to the inky horizon.

Raelyn covered Jinny's hand with her own. "It's okay to consider not staying."

Jinny relaxed. "I finally saw my mother. She was holding onto Father's arm at the asylum. But they weren't in her room. They were walking down the hall. And I watched them walk out the door. She's home now, and I want to be, too. But there's Gabe to think of. We can't leave him."

"What about you, Joshua?" Raelyn asked.

"It kills me not to rush home to Lily." He recounted Lily's rescue to Jinny, standing up and pacing as he described the conditions in which his parents found her. "My folks have her now. But . . . she's still not safe, is she? Nobody is. So, I'm stayin'. Besides, somehow I think I'm meant to."

Raelyn stood and leaned on the balcony overlooking the library's terrace below, glowing light spilling across it from the lanterns inside. Cosyn might make Peter sick again. Or maybe he'd go after her dad. But another journey like the one they had just completed. Could she do it again?

She sighed as she turned back to face Jinny and Joshua, still sitting at the table. "I want nothing more than to be back with Peter and my dad. And I'm sure they're just as afraid for me. But this"— she gestured behind her— "this is bigger than all of that. And we're talking about the whole world." She eased into a chair opposite them. "I wish there was a way to know for sure which is the right path. But my choice is to stay."

Jinny nodded, her brow furrowed, but said nothing.

They each had their own path to walk. Even Avery, wherever he was, had to make his own choice. She had come here to save her brother, to prove to her dad she was worth something. To earn his forgiveness. But she had done something even more. She had forgiven herself. And experienced a forgiveness beyond her comprehension. Now a new path stretched out before her and she knew, despite her fear, she could walk it. She was created for this. She was chosen.

EPILOGUE

Lady Ryla looked at the cowering man, kneeling before her. After administering a savage reprimand, Lord Talmond had stormed from the room, unable to control his rage.

"Ditimer, rise," she said softly.

Ditimer stood, cutting his eyes to the doorway and back to her. "Lady Ryla, I did what we discussed," he whispered. Ryla narrowed her eyes and pursed her lips.

"But the temporals . . ." He shifted on his feet, clearly uncomfortable, uncertain of his own argument. Pathetic. "They closed the Olyaund plye. Maybe . . . maybe Kade was correct." His brown eyes pleaded with her.

"You are so quick to alter your beliefs?" Ryla would not let him escape his failure by claiming their plan was flawed.

"No," he said slowly, "but Kade found the temporals after I took them to Durnoth."

"There is no doubt Kade is resourceful." Ryla used a tone she hoped would convey reason, despite her growing irritation. "But that does not legitimize his doctrine."

"True, but what of their escape through Aldhale Tunnel?" Ditimer continued. Ryla fought the impulse to cringe at his irresolution and kept her expression neutral as he rambled. "They should have been trapped. But the sibukyn. They were in the tunnel. I could not return to retrieve them to transport them back to the Silom Pool."

"Neither Cosyn nor Kade can be underestimated. Cosyn certainly would have sent his horde in pursuit. As to their escape, Kade taught them well. It does not make the temporals the chosen vehicle to meddle in Alnok."

"Yes, but m'lady." Ditimer stepped forward.

"Ditimer," she hissed. "I brought you into my confidence so that together we could end the fallacy of Kade's precious prophecy. Do not use your ineptitude as an excuse to question the validity of our understanding." She took a sharp breath and let it out slowly. Drawing on a small reserve of patience, she slipped back into her soothing argument of reason.

"Arkonai would never choose the weak to overcome the strong. Kade was wrong. He continues to be deluded. You still agree, yes?"

Ditimer was slow to respond. "Yes, I agree. But the closing of the plye must mean something."

Ryla smiled thinly "Arkonai's ways are mysterious. Come." She glided to Ditimer. "Allow me time to listen for Arkonai's direction." She ushered him from the room.

He was gone only a few seconds before a figure emerged from a shadowed corner of the room.

"You should have struck him down where he stood," Cosyn growled.

Ryla's light dimmed, and it seemed as though icy fingers searched for a way into her chest. She straightened and forced back the cold. "He is a fool." She strode to the opposite side of the room and poured a glass of wine, keeping her back to Cosyn. "But he could still prove a useful fool." She sipped at the wine, determined to appear unafraid, forcing even breaths, willing her hands to stop shaking. She turned to him. "You might have taken Kade out of the way." She was pushing a boldness she did not feel and could prove detrimental.

Cosyn chuckled, thick and wet. "That time is coming." He was nose-to-nose with her in a second. "You, on the other hand . . ." He gripped her wrist. Ryla's essence, the light—Arkonai's light—drained from her arm.

She yanked away from him, her heart pounding. "Do not attempt your sorcery on me." She maintained eye contact, unwilling to yield.

"Sorcery is it?" Cosyn smiled, straight white teeth gleaming in the dim room. "You seem keen for me to use it for your benefit."

"And what will you do now?" Ryla held her tongue this time. Mentioning the destroyed plye would be unwise. But he seemed to read her mind.

"You suppose the closing of one point of access significant?" Cosyn strolled across the room, plucking a goblet from a table. He inspected it in a bored and distracted way. "No." His voice became low and dangerous as he glared at her. "What I have planned will put an end to this game."

"And to our agreement?" Ryla did not want to sink so low, but given their setback, she needed reassurance. His blue eyes flashed red.

"I always keep my word," Cosyn said and slipped back into the shadows.

<<<>>>

ACKNOWLEDGMENTS

Thirty-five years ago, I wrote my first short story. It's been a long and winding writing journey, complete with a few side quests, that led to this book. But the path was carefully and lovingly laid by the Creator of the universe. Along the way I was joined by so many, some leading and guiding, some coming alongside.

First, thank you to my husband Wil, who never questions my dreams, no matter how outlandish. Thank you for managing the navigation while I sail into open ocean and search mysterious coves. And, most of all, having the wisdom to know when to drop anchor.

I am supremely blessed with creative and adventurous kids. Thank you, Joshua, for your encouragement and collaboration, including naming this book! Many hugs and kisses to Jessica for your excitement and insight during our brainstorming sessions. Nearly all of your ideas were used. My sweet daughter-in-law Mariah, who's eye for design and photography made my Instagram blossom. And my niece Kadynn, who helped me imagine every creature.

Thank you to my family. My mom for grounding my life in a relationship with Jesus. My dad for memorable, practical and sometimes unexpected insights of wisdom. My sister, for hours of laughter and keeping all my secrets. My brother for modeling the perseverance I applied to my characters. My niece Ashley and nephews Brandon and Josiah for inspiring me to see the finished draft on the horizon. And my grandma who always asked if the book was finished because she always knew it would be.

Special thanks to my editor, Erin Healy whose steady guidance and talent were instrumental in bringing this story and the entire Periferie universe to life.

And many thanks to all those who, in no small way, blessed me in my journey: My best friend Barb, with whom I can always relax and let my hair down. My critique group, Karen, Michael, Nathan and Jenny, who make every story better. My church family at C3 Fort Worth, my writing community at Realm Makers and all my brothers and sisters in Christ who continually pray and cheer me on.

DEAR READER

One of the first exercises in creating a story is to imagine who might read it and for whom it will resonate. While the characters took on lives of their own and the world developed before my eyes, I never doubted who would travel with the Cord. Despite deep wounds and ongoing troubles, you understand the need to protect those you love. You persistently walk a road filled with uncertainty, not just of where the path may lead, but in your own ability, until you reached your destination. Rather than shrink, you grow and are strengthened through adversity. And you fight to overcome the enemy who wishes nothing more than to see you fail. My prayer for you is a protection from discouragement and a clear certainty as to which path to take next.

Visit me online at www.SLDooley.com and continue the journey with the Cord.